BOSTON POSH

WOL-VRIEY

BOSTON POSH

WOL-VRIEY

Boston Posh
by **Wol-vriey**

Burning Bulb Publishing
P.O. Box 4721
Bridgeport, WV 26330-4721
United States of America
www.BurningBulbPublishing.com

Cover designed by Gary Lee Vincent with the following licensed elements from Fotolia:
  - redhead woman © Maksim Šmeljov
  - dragon © molchunya
  - dragon tattoo 2 © Abrams

Second edition.

Paperback Edition ISBN: 978-0692469002

Printed in the United States of America

Library of Congress Control Number: 2013952174

ACKNOWLEDGMENTS

Firstly, I gotta say major thanks to Gary Lee Vincent and Rich Bottles Jr. at Burning Bulb, both for believing in my writing and also for doing such a great job editing/formatting it for production. Once the book leaves my hands for theirs, I KNOW it's in good hands. You guys are super-awesome.

Next, I must thank my lovely wife Victoria for putting up with me these past twenty years. (Totally love you, darling.) Now she has something else to look up to me for, other than the fact that I'm a foot taller than she. Short women rock! LOL!

And I must thank Emil Daynov and his wife Yang Yang for loaning me their names. Yang Yang's name fit perfectly for my snake goddess.

And my thanks to Lolade Akinsowon for taking the Bio photo (after much persuasion). See, it *does* look good in print.

And lastly, but most important, I have to thank everyone who's read any of my books. Whether or not you liked them. Without you guys, there's really no point writing anything. It deeply thrills my heart each time someone gets a thrill (cheap or regular) from my writing.

Peace, Everyone!
Wol-vriey.

PART 1: POSH LANE

PRELUDE: THE NEW PAST

The current state of the world was referred to as The New Past.

The dragon incinerations, the re-emergence of the dinos, the appearance of the god-like Forks, and the total demolition of national institutions were all worldwide occurrences.

China, Hong Kong, and Taiwan were dragon free, but not dino free. If anything, there were more dinosaurs in Chinese territories now than elsewhere in the world, simply because of the lack of dragons to cull their numbers.

As Xiaoping Wang, last President of the People's Republic of China, remarked: "Humanity paddles the dinosaur canoe now."

***

The biggest problem with the re-emerging dinosaurs was how much larger they were than anyone expected them to be. Like they'd been compacted/zipped for the fossil records, or . . . these new versions had been genetically re-engineered specifically to be pains in humanity's ass.

No one bothered about the herbivore dinos—the apatosauruses, brachiosaurs, and triceratops, for instance—which were the same size as previous.

The problem was the carnivores.

The New Past version of the pterodactyl—a dino bird once no larger than a stork or ostrich—was the size of a horse. Velociraptors were the size of gorillas, often bigger. Even T-Rex, which in ancient times already stood twenty feet tall, was now a larger monster. Quetzalcoatlus, the largest dinosaur 'bird,' was now the size of a de Havilland Canada Twin Otter aircraft.

And all these flesh-eating reptiles—regardless of whether their previous diet was bugs, rodents, or fish—were now ravenous for human flesh.

CHAPTER 1

Malone/Sara

The woman was a tall, bony brunette. A not-so-faded beauty wearing a queen's ransom in jewels.

Malone recognized her at once—Sara Fischer, widow of David Fischer, the breakfast cereal tycoon. David Fischer had fallen to his death from his mansion rooftop a year before.

There were rumors that Sara had pushed/tripped him.

Sara was wearing a pterodactyl-skin jacket over white silk trousers. Her makeup was as perfect as if she was attending a movie premiere.

She'd apparently come alone, which Malone thought odd. Her kind of money always had piles of hanger-ons.

Sara smiled a vulturine smile at him. "I see you recognize me."

He smiled back. "It would be hard not to."

The answer clearly pleased her, her smile broadened. He pointed to a stuffed-gorilla chair. "Please have a seat."

She did so, her eyes twinkling mischievously in their sunken sockets.

Malone suddenly realized that she was mentally undressing him. Sara Fischer was known to be sexually ravenous, out to cram into her winter years all the debauchery she'd neglected while filling her summer years with endless good works.

She reputedly told friends: "I intend fucking myself into my grave in sympathy with the fucked-up state of the world."

Malone waited till she'd made herself comfortable, pretending not to notice the amount of time she spent grinding herself into the taxidermed ape's crotch.

Then, keeping both his face and voice professionally neutral, he asked: "What can I do for you, Mrs. Fischer?"

3

Sara Fischer's calm demeanor dissolved like salt in water. "My daughter Rachel has been kidnapped, Malone. I need you to find and rescue her."

Malone smiled. "That's what I do," he said. "Find people. The more lost the better."

"Stop being cute. I'll pay you fifty thousand plus expenses to get Rachel back for me."

Malone nodded. "That'll do." He looked searchingly at Sara. "How'd she go missing?"

***

Sara Fischer relaxed back in the stuffed-gorilla armchair. It had a nice feel to it, like being in her dead husband David's arms again. David had been extremely hairy—having sex with him had felt like making love to a rug.

She looked the detective over. He was young and handsome. Nicely cut brown hair, laughing brown eyes, sensual lips. Eminently fuckable. She could already view herself wrapping her lips around his cock, stroking the tumescent organ up and down with her mouth and tongue.

"My daughter is a scientist," she explained. "An absolute workaholic. She practically never leaves the house. She's eternally slaving away in her underground laboratory. Two nights ago, she didn't show for dinner. I thought nothing about it—Rachel sometimes gets so caught up in her research that she forgets herself.

"But . . . she didn't show for breakfast yesterday either. That was unusual, so I sent a servant down to investigate and she was gone."

"She could have gone out on a date," Malone said. "Slept over at her boyfriend's place. With no telecoms anymore—"

Sara laughed. "Boyfriend? She had none."

"Girlfriend then?"

Sara rolled her eyes. "My daughter, Malone, can be accurately described as sexless. A neuter. No, don't get me wrong, she has the organs to fuck with, she's just apparently never realized what they're meant for."

Sara was amused by the look on Malone's face at her use of the word 'fuck.'

She smiled, licked her lips. *Yes, I'd like to bed this young stud—teach his penis a thing or two.* "Rachel doesn't fuck. Period. If she ever masturbated, it would never be for pleasure. It would be to calculate the average time it took her to reach orgasm, and divide that figure by the number of strokes on her clitoris that created the effect. Then she'd use the results as data for some perpetual motion machine."

Sara smirked. "That's the kind of mind my daughter has."

"She sounds quite the committed scientist."

Sara batted her eyelashes at Malone. "You have no idea."

Malone nodded. The sex vibe coming from Sara Fischer was messing with his head. The woman was at least sixty. Well preserved for sure, definitely still pretty, sexy even, but . . .

"Was there any sign of a struggle?" he asked. "Any broken doors? Smashed furniture?"

She shook her head. "No signs of a fight."

"So why'd you think she was kidnapped?"

Sara opened her purse and pulled out the ransom note. "This."

He took it from her, read out the cursive scrawl:

'It'll cost you five million dollars in cash if you ever want to see Rachel alive again. Bring the money to Hailey's Toy Factory tomorrow night at 10 p.m. Fucking come alone, rich bitch, or you'll get your nerdy kid back in bits.'

The note was signed: 'Frank.'

Malone looked at Sara. "Who is Frank?"

"Your guess is as bad as mine."

He nodded. "Now, Mrs. Fischer, what I'd suggest—"

"Call me Sara, please. Everyone does."

Malone nodded. "Okay . . . Sara."

She smiled. "What were you going to suggest?"

"That our smartest approach is to pay the ransom."

Sara Fischer's face wrinkled in disgust. "Oh fucking no. Don't get me wrong—money isn't the object here. But if I pay, there's no guarantee that I'll ever see Rachel again. You know how punks like this are—He'll likely rape and kill her, then feed her body to a dino."

Malone nodded. "True. But remember, we don't really know who's got her. 'Frank' is likely a pseudonym."

He waved the ransom note. "All we really have are these directions. So I suggest we go along with them. I'll take the money to the drop-off point, retrieve Rachel for you, then follow him afterwards and get your cash back."

Sara still didn't like it. "This is one of those times I wish there was still a police force," she said testily. "This nonsense would never occur if we still had patrols up in North End."

Malone agreed. He gave a mental shrug. It wasn't his fault that the dragons and dinos had eaten up all the cops, along with four-fifths of Boston's population.

"Okay," Sara said. "So I give you five million bucks. What happens if Rachel isn't there—the bastard takes the money, and asks you to pick her up elsewhere?"

Malone nodded. It was a good question—he'd been jumped before, had the scars from the double-cross. "I've thought of that. He *won't* get away. I intend bugging the case containing the money. That way it doesn't matter if Rachel's there or not, I'll be able to track him to his hideout."

Sara nodded in turn. "Those who recommended you to me weren't wrong about you."

Relieved to have a workable plan, Sara relaxed, shifted back down into seduction mode. She pouted her lips at Malone, penetrating them with her tongue. He couldn't miss the point of that.

She made herself comfortable in the gorilla chair again, stroking its taxidermed left hand.

Malone smiled nicely back at Sara. It disturbed him how alluring he found her, this geriatric seductress. He realized that if he wasn't careful, he'd shortly be laying Sara Fischer backward on his office table, ripping off her pants, and fucking her super-hard.

To forestall that, he asked: "How soon can you have the money ready?"

Sara sighed, both from having her sexual game thwarted, but more from the mundanity of the question. "The money's outside in the car. I had a sneaking suspicion you'd want it anyway."

Malone gaped at her. "You left five million dollars outside in your car?"

She shrugged. "There's more where it came from. Loads more."

That *really* impressed Malone.

CHAPTER 2

Malone

Malone's office was a bungalow. This seemed logical to him: bungalows were excluded from the beetle/skyscraper circle of death and rebirth—they were never laid by beetles, never became beetles, were never randomly attacked by dragons.

And they didn't go on unscheduled hikes like Condos.

Besides, a neighbor-less single-story building made Malone feel more secure. It was like sitting in a bar watching the door with his back against a wall.

***

Malone was tall and thin. Most times he wore black.

He was neither particularly athletic nor exceptionally brave. He'd become a private invest-igator simply because, after the world went up in smoke, there were no other jobs and he needed to earn a living.

Realizing there were now an unlimited number of people with something or someone to find, Malone opened an office as 'BUD MALONE: PRIVATE INVESTIGATOR.' He'd immediately been swamped with work.

What had *really* attracted his clients, however, was the smaller text at the bottom of his signboard:

'Our Motto: No case too difficult or dangerous!'

These were VERY dangerous and difficult times.

Malone had often regretted writing that small print in the eighteen months since starting his agency.

CHAPTER 3

Malone

Through a quiet night, Malone drove crosstown to Hailey's Toy Factory for the drop off.

The ransom money was in a large briefcase beside him. Five million dollars in the newly reissued thousand dollar bills.

Malone whistled, imagining what *he* could do with five thousand Grover Clevelands if he didn't have to kidnap a heiress to earn them.

***

Hailey's Toy Factory was located at the far end of Commercial Street, right by Lewis Wharf on the North End waterfront.

The dragons reigned supreme over Boston's Inner Harbor. No one went out that way anymore. Even the Chinese seldom ventured that far.

The east limit of Boston's anti-dragon Grid was the John Fitzgerald Surface Road. Going beyond there was suicidal. The dinosaur concentration towards the wharfs was even higher than the dragon con-centration.

In North End, the grid cut out long before it got to the Fischer Mansion on Wiget Street, as the Surface Road turned northwest, becoming North Washington Street and crossing the water into Charlestown to link up with the I-93 to New Hampshire.

***

Most North End residents lived in private mansions. Like Sara Fischer, most were wealthy enough to afford electronic dragon-repulsor technology on both their homes and cars.

Living outside The Grid was less risky for the rich, as after a while the dragons had learned to avoid the tell-tale metal spikes that warned a house had electrical shielding.

But repulsors only protected what they were attached to. Mansion *grounds* were just as susceptible to attack as the rest of the world. Many had become dino nesting/breeding sites.

The rich only ventured out warily, if at all. And when they did—just like the poor—they watched the skies and the world around them for snapping reptile jaws, and ripping claws.

Malone wasn't surprised then that Sara Fischer had preferred to be chauffeured crosstown to Joy Street in Beacon Hill, west Boston, to hire him, rather than make the *much* shorter trip to the wharf to pay her daughter's ransom herself.

Most of her trip to his place was under The Grid. All her trip to Commercial Street would be out in the open. Even with the amount of protective technology she had mounted on her limo, it would be foolish to risk it.

Malone admitted 'Frank' was smart. The wharf area was a great place for a kidnapper to hide out, assuming of course he didn't become dragon/dino food.

***

Malone drove with his lights off. No fucking way was he attracting dino attention to himself.

He watched the sky cautiously. The night's silence wasn't a guarantee of safety.

The shithead pterodactyls in particular had become more cunning of recent—like being oversized wasn't enough bother.

In stark contrast to the early days of the dino reappearance when they attacked humans openly, now the dino-birds *stalked* their human prey. They perched motionless, flesh gargoyles atop buildings, then dropped silently and glided towards their intended victims.

And sometimes the fuckers hunted in packs. Armored as his silver Ford Mustang was, Malone wouldn't trust it against a horde of jaws.

The fucking raptors were even more cunning than the 'dactyls.

(Malone had heard tales of raptors nesting in freshly-laid skyscrapers, waiting for occupants to move in.

In the current age of nightmares become waking reality, it was one of the ultimate horrors for a family to wake at night to the sound of reptile knuckles insistently tapping their door, expecting to be let in to eat them.)

So Malone drove carefully through the burnt rubble that now composed most of east Boston, Massachusetts.

Several times he saw distant reflective flickers that fractured moonlight into the colors of the rainbow, turning the air surrounding them into a kaleidoscope. Dragons.

Malone was relieved that the reptiles were far away. One didn't fuck with dragons. The sort of weaponry required to deal with them wouldn't even mount on his car.

Malone sensed more than saw the destruction around him.

It's strange, he thought, *how the entire country simply burnt to ash. Even in their wildest, most paranoid imaginings, no defense strategist could EVER have predicted that the USA, the greatest country Earth has ever seen, would crumble to dragons and dinosaurs . . . and Forks?*

No one understood how everything had gone up in flame. Like Malone, everyone had just woken up one morning to discover that they now lived in a version of Hell. In a totally fucked-up world.

CHAPTER 4

Malone

Malone pulled into the parking lot of Hailey's Toy Factory and parked.

The lot was a large concrete expanse filled with burnt cars.

Great place for a meeting, he thought with grudging respect. *Frank's a smart bastard. These wrecks everywhere mean I can't keep an eye out for accomplices.*

He honked his horn, flashed his lights twice. A replying flash of light came from the dark doorway of the factory building directly in front of him.

Malone got out of his car and raised the case with the money in it overhead.

The light flashed again.

I guess that means bring it over.

Walking briskly, he headed for the light in the factory door.

He heard footsteps behind him.

"Stop," a male voice said.

Malone froze. "Frank?"

A laugh. "Dumb question. Do you have an appointment with someone else here?"

He was jabbed in the back with something hard. "Okay, turn around."

He turned around.

Frank was tall, about Malone's height. In the moonlight, Malone made out that he had blond hair. His face was however hidden by a fright mask designed like a skull.

How fucking appropriate, Malone thought.

Frank was pointing a blaster at Malone. The gun was big and ugly. Malone recognized it as a military model. One blast from that fucker and anyone seeing his remains would think a dragon had fucked him up.

"I told Mrs. Fischer to come *herself*," Frank said in a soft, cultured voice. "Or did she have a sex-change overnight?"

"She didn't have the balls to come," Malone said. "You know how that can be a problem."

Frank laughed." I like your sense of humor," he said. "Who the fuck are you?"

"Bud Malone. I work for Mrs. Fischer. Security."

Frank's behavior bothered Malone. He showed no traces of the nervousness normally associated with kidnappers. But his voice wasn't entirely level.

That marked him out as a sociopath. Malone hoped Rachel Fischer was still alive.

Malone held up the briefcase. "Here's your five million dollars, Frank. Now, can I have Rachel Fischer back?"

Frank shrugged. "She's a big girl. Tell her ma she'll be back home tomorrow night."

"Uh uh. Not good enough. I was asked to bring her back *with me*."

Frank waved his gun at Malone. "Don't be a dickhead. Just deliver the message."

Malone raised his hands. "Okay, I'll tell the old girl."

"Good," Frank said. "Now put the briefcase down and back off."

Malone did so. The flashlight from the doorway behind him flickered on and off, a warning to not try any heroics.

Frank picked up the briefcase. "Okay, messenger boy, your business here is done. Go back to your car and get lost."

Malone walked back to his Mustang and drove out of the factory premises.

He didn't get lost. He sped down the street, turned into Christopher Columbus Plaza, and parked.

Then he activated the tracker for the bug he'd planted in the money case and watched the signal.

The tracker was good for ten miles and overlaid position data over a map of Boston.

The indicator—a red dot—moved in a zig-zag. Malone smirked; Frank was clearly trying to lose any tails. *Keep trying, dumbass.*

North Commercial Wharf . . . Atlantic Avenue . . . Richmond Street (Malone heard the car zoom past him). . . Arch Way . . . Cross Street.

Reaching Cross Street, the red dot's progress stabilized into a straight line.

Malone set off after the kidnappers, driving with his lights off.

In the middle of Cross Street, the indicator froze and kept blinking.

Malone smiled. He reached in his glove compartment and pulled out his gun. A weapon as big as Frank's.

Time to retrieve Rachel Fischer and her mother's money.

**

The house the tracker singled out was by the old post office at the Hanover Street intersection.

It was a mutant. This happened occasionally—a beetle laid a corrupted skyscraper. This one was squat and lopsided, with monster spidery legs sticking out between its floors.

Just looking at the building gave Malone the creeps. *Yes, this is the sort of place I expect a kidnapper to reside in.*

Dim light shone through a broken ground-floor window.

No sign of Frank's car. That meant nothing. Good criminals didn't leave markers. Malone had left his own car in a parking lot two streets back.

He dashed to the house's front door, ducking between its dangling legs. The legs stank like nests of cockroaches.

The front door opened easily. Light shone from an ajar door on Malone's right. He padded across the turd-tapestried living room and kicked the door open.

"Okay, Frank, the games—"

He shut up. There was no one in the room. Just the briefcase the money had been in. A glowing flashlight stuck into a side compartment illumined the room. Shards of glass stuck in the case meant it had been thrown through the broken window.

Malone checked the briefcase. It was empty.

He cursed silently. *Shit!* Sara Fischer would be pissed about this.

Then he heard the snuffling sound behind him.

Malone spun around firing.

He got off a shot which hit the fractured window, before the raptor's jaws clamped shut over the muzzle of his gun.

Fuck! he thought, staring momentarily past the lizard's head at the charred window frame.

The raptor held Malone's gun in a vise-like grip. It wrenched its head left and right, seeking to yank it from his grasp. It made no attempt to attack Malone, just kept its teeth clamped on the weapon.

The raptor was huge, almost Malone's height. A miniature T-Rex—green scaly skin and a body built for the kill. It pushed against him with its tiny upper limbs, trying to make him to release the gun.

Malone winced. This was the problem with the fucking raptors—they had delusions of intelligence, were continually learning from their mistakes.

This one clearly knew that guns were dangerous and wanted to disarm Malone.

Looks like I'll have to do this the hard way.

Unable to free his blaster, Malone let the raptor have it. He reached down for his knife instead. Then he quickly cut the flashlight off the money case.

The raptor was reared up, fighting with its prize. It tried biting into the gun, but the metal defeated its jaws. Malone heard the distinct crack of two of its teeth breaking. He expected the raptor to spit the weapon away in disgust.

He was disappointed. With a massive gulp, the raptor swallowed Malone's gun whole.

Malone was surprised. He'd never seen this sort of dino behavior before.

He grimly conceded the raptor's action made sense. It wasn't smart enough to consider the weapon a separate entity from Malone. It likely thought guns were simply dangerous human symbiotes.

The dino finished gulping down the gun. It burped, then looked at Malone, its eyes windows to a primal hunger.

The reptile's nostrils flared with its breathing. Its tongue floated between its teeth. It crouched in the room's dim lighting, limbs tensed to leap. It was confident that its hunger would soon be assuaged, but wary of the knife its prey clutched.

Malone played the flashlight into its eyes, disorienting it.

He groaned. Behind it, another raptor shambled into the doorway. This one was larger than the first. It stood and regarded Malone, eyes glittering like diamonds made of urine.

Malone looked at his knife, then at the two reptiles that intended eating him.

I'm really going to have to do this the hard way, he thought.

"Bring it on, shithead," he spat at the raptor. "What the fuck are you waiting for?"

Like it had been awaiting the invitation, the lead raptor leapt at Malone.

He waited till it was too close to change direction then jammed the flashlight crosswise into its mouth. He forced the flashlight deep into the angle of the jaw, so it snagged on the raptor's molars, wedging its jaws open, so it couldn't bite.

Confused, the raptor staggered back. Malone rushed after it, pushing it into the doorway to prevent the other dinosaur from entering the room. He held it tight there, embracing it like they were dance partners.

Then, while the raptor scrabbled at the flashlight in its mouth with its tiny upper feet, Malone gutted it with his knife.

A long scream exited the dino's throat as he worked, cutting a deep rive in the soft belly below its ribs. Its intestines spilled out into his hands, hot like they'd been cooking inside it.

Bracing a shoulder against it so he could free his other hand, Malone quickly felt upward for the raptor's stomach. He slit the sac open and reached inside it for his gun. He winced as the raptor's digestive juices scalded his hand.

Malone freed his gun and quickly wiped it off on his shirt.

The raptor had meanwhile managed to work one end of the flashlight free and was trying to swallow it. It was in horrendous pain.

The one behind it, sensing something was wrong, was trying to push it out of the way.

Malone stepped away from the raptor. Guts hanging out of its belly, it staggered to one side, screaming in pain. The flashlight beam danced over Malone and the walls.

Immediately the doorway was clear, the second raptor charged Malone.

He was prepared for it.

He hit it point blank with a single blast between the eyes.

There was the quiet 'whoosh' of controlled cold-fusion, then the now headless reptile tottered on its feet in front of Malone. No blood spurted from its truncated neck—the blast had cauterized the wound it had made.

The dino's brains were splattered all over its companion, which had now succeeded in swallowing the flashlight and was bent over wondering why its guts were hanging down to the floor and why light was shining out of its belly.

Bloodlust got the better of its good sense.

Malone grimaced when the raptor picked its intestines up off the floor and began eating them. The flashlight's lamp was now poking out of its ripped stomach, throwing red-streaked beams around the room.

The raptor ripped apart its guts and swallowed them. It screeched piteously with each burst of pain it caused itself.

"Damn," Malone said disgustedly, "and I thought you fuckers were smart."

He blew its head off with a blast of gunfire. It collapsed on top of the other carcass.

Malone regarded both dead dinosaurs for a few moments. Then he picked up the empty money case and left the house.

He was disgusted with himself over this fuckup. Worse still, he doubted Rachel Fischer would turn up at home tomorrow night like Frank had said.

CHAPTER 5

Sara

Sara Fischer waited for Malone in her armored limo, in the John Fitzgerald Expressway tunnel entrance by Haymarket Square.

The profusion of repulsor rods coating the car made it look like a metal porcupine.

The rendezvous point was quite safe. It was close enough to The Grid for dragons not to bother it, while dinos didn't like being underground.

Sara had vetoed Malone's suggestion that he simply bring Rachel home.

"I relish any chance to leave the mansion," she'd said. "There's almost nowhere to go nowadays."

***

Now, Malone parked and walked over to the limo.

The black chauffeur opened the rear door and he got in.

"I see things didn't go according to plan," Sara said simply.

Malone looked pained. He explained.

"No bother about the money," Sara replied with a smug look when he was done. "It was mostly counterfeit."

Malone gaped at her. "Di . . . did you just say *counterfeit*?"

She nodded back, amused at his confusion. "I expected this to happen—that you'd lose my cash. So I had a banker friend find me a stash of funny money."

Malone winced. Sara continued:

"Frank will think the money's real. There's about fifty thousand in real notes that we used to pad both sides of each bundle so they'll pass an inspection."

Sara was very pleased she'd thought of this. No way was she parting with that much cash. Her daughter's life was important, but so was her money. She'd be no one without money. *No one.* And if some kidnapping son-of-a-bitch thought he was getting the dough she'd fucked her dead husband David for forty years for, he was more stupid than the dinos.

"You should have told me about this," Malone said.

Sara giggled. "Why? So you could tell me it wouldn't work?"

"You hired me to get your daughter back. I assumed you meant *alive.*"

That shook Sara a little. "He said he'll deliver her tomorrow night, didn't he?"

Malone nodded. "For five million dollars, yes. But now he hasn't gotten it . . ." He let the words fall into emptiness.

"Stop being negative. He can't discover the trick by then."

Malone got out of the back of Sara's limousine, then leaned in through the window. "You're forgetting how confident I was that my tracker would work. He found that out, didn't he?"

Sara's worry reflected on her face. "But . . ."

"I think this Frank fellow is very smart. And remember too that he isn't working alone. We're dealing with at least two kidnappers, maybe more. Associations lend to the chance of someone having useful random knowledge."

"You're scaring me, Malone."

He frowned. "I'm just being realistic. Okay, we'll wait till tomorrow night. Maybe the kidnappers won't notice that the money's fake, and they'll deliver Rachel as planned. If she isn't home by then, I'll start looking for her."

Sara nodded. "You do that."

She watched Malone walk to his car with major misgivings. Her simple plan to protect her money had seemed so smart, but now it looked like it might possibly get her daughter killed.

***

Riding home in her armored limo, Sarah let her worries come to the fore. She wept, dabbing her tears dry with a silk handkerchief.

Rachel was all she had in the world. She didn't want to be left all alone.

Shit, David wasn't even dead eight months yet.

CHAPTER 6

David

David Fischer liked to pretend that he was an ape.

The current state of affairs made such pretense viable. The once perfectly manicured mansion grounds were now overgrown, bearing more resemblance to prehistoric jungle than anything else.

Aiding the illusion was the fact that David Fischer was an extremely hairy man; squat and powerfully built too. Apelike.

He was sixty-four. His wife Sara was sixty-three.

"It's as if the dinosaurs brought the Mesozoic Era back with them," he'd once told Sara, while she was fellating him.

Sara, her mouth full of penis, had been unable to reply. She'd simply grunted and redoubled her efforts to make him cum.

(Sara prided herself on her blowjob technique. It angered her immensely, when like now, her husband's thoughts wavered from the pleasure she was giving him.)

She wet a finger by sticking in her pussy, and slid it up his backside, pushing it in deep and massaging his prostate. With her other hand she tapped his testes gently.

David groaned and spurted in her mouth. Afterwards he ate her out in return.

"You were thinking of the fucking dinosaurs again," she chided him afterwards, her pride in her sexual prowess still wounded.

He grinned and stroked her hair. "I'm sorry dear. I can't help it. Something about the modern world—The New Past— brings out the caveman in me. It's like I'm . . . no . . . like *we're all* regressing back to the Stone Age."

He raised an arm and gestured expansively at their bedroom window, now protected by an iron grill specially tempered to resist pterodactyl attacks.

Outside the night was black as coal, the moon unable to dispel the darkness. Sara, following her husband's finger, felt a cold chill.

"Are we really reverting, dear?" She didn't believe it, but wasn't certain what she believed. Two years ago the world was normal, and now . . .

Her chill deepened. She snuggled close to David, seeking refuge in the familiar, in the certainty of sensation. "Make love to me darling, I'm cold."

He did, rolling her onto her belly, and inserting himself from behind. Her pussy was still slick with his saliva and he slid into her easily. Sara relaxed and moaned beneath him.

Sex never changes, she thought as she savored the deepness of the penetration, the feel of his hairy chest pressed on her back. *As long as a fuck still gets you off, nothing is really bad.*

David however, didn't share her thoughts. Even as he thrust and ground on her buttocks, his mind was really outside. He fantasized that he was a gorilla, swinging from tree to tree in the Neo-Jurassic jungle the City of Boston had become.

***

One night a week later, after making love to Sara, David Fischer had slung a rope with a grappling hook across his shoulders and walked off naked into the bushes surrounding the mansion.

His intention was simple—to free the ape-man in himself.

David wasn't stupid. Around his waist he wore a military-grade issue in a holster, in case of dino trouble.

He figured he cut an iconic figure—primitively dashing—as he stalked across the grass to the nearest oak.

This oak had a ladder that led up to the tree house Rachel had 'played' in as a child. David had never gotten his head around the fact that even at the age of eight, his only child's idea of play was to sit down reading books about the solar system and mechanics.

"I want to make robots," she kept saying.

It had gotten worst when she'd reached puberty. He'd never been certain if Rachel was taking refuge in her books as a refuge from boys or not. But then she'd shown no interest in girls either.

After a while David Fischer had stopped worrying about Rachel's apparent sexlessness. In a way, he was even pleased. She differed from her mother for whom the social life was life itself.

Having two such women under the same roof would have been too much for his peace-loving soul to cope with.

***

David reached the tree ladder and began climbing. Some of the metal struts were shaky, and at sixty-four he wasn't as nimble as he used to be, but he managed to reach the tree house without difficulty.

He sat on its front porch, looking across the overgrown mansion grounds. He thought he saw movement in the grass. He wondered what creatures might lurk there.

He thrilled with the danger and speculation. Maybe even saber-toothed tigers might return again.

Damn, he thought, wincing, *what the hell is wrong with me? Saber-toothed tigers? As if the world isn't screwed up enough already.*

He pulled his mind away from the grass. What he'd come out here to do was more important. He needed to know if it felt like he'd imagined it would.

He stood up on the tree house porch and unslung the rope from around his shoulder.

Weighing the grappling hook in his hand, he surveyed the closest trees, finally settling on one with a branch projecting a good way out from its parent bough.

He swung the grappling hook at this. It caught on the second try, looping around the branch and embedding its barbs in the bark.

After a few tugs to ensure it was firm, David Fischer gripped the rope and launched himself into the air, swinging for the tree.

Me, David; you, Sara, he thought happily as he flew through the air. *Yes, this is right. I feel great. Wooooo! I'll bring Sara out—*

His thoughts were abruptly truncated when the dragon ate him.

The dragon's glittering body flashed over the Fischer Mansion like a bolt of transparent lightning.

Its massive jaws clamped down over David Fischer, truncating him from the thighs upward. His severed legs fell to the ground. The rest of him was in the dragon.

It flew away with a bloody smile, chewing on this unexpected morsel it had found.

David Fischer didn't die immediately. While in agony, being masticated by the horrendous jagged jaws, bleeding to death, and also asphyxiating from oxygen lack, he experienced a kind of glorious exaltation—an understanding of what caveman death had been like.

***

The servants found their master's legs the next morning. They identified them by their hairiness.

***

"We *can't* say he was eaten," Sara had told her daughter while weeping profusely. "That'll make us a laughing stock. It's one fucking thing being a widow, totally another having everyone thinking your dad was a kook. Whatever will the Rothschilds, for instance, say?"

"What *do* we say killed him then?" Rachel asked.

She was even more distraught than her mother, totally unsettled since hearing the news. She however agreed with Sara as to the need to maintain appearances for status' sake.

Sara dabbed at her tears. "He fell. From the roof, while taking the night air. A portion of the banister came loose and he plummeted to his death."

"Rachel nodded. Then she burst into tears herself. "Yes, mother, he did fall, didn't he?" She stopped crying for a moment. Her face was already growing puffy. "Only I don't know, mother; what on earth was he doing outside swinging in the trees? Father has never struck me as that kind of person."

***

Sara had mourned her husband, whom she loved deeply. She was technically still mourning him.

His death however had one unexpected effect on her. She became slutty—determined to fuck her way into the grave.

It was odd, but whenever she thought of her dead husband, she never saw his face. The image that reared up before her eyes was of his cock, his rampant erection about to penetrate her, to escort her to erotic bliss.

With him dead now, it became her mission in life to sample every penis she could. Her aim was to return to that sexual place David had always taken her to.

CHAPTER 7

Posh

Posh Lane was twenty-four. She was gorgeous and shapely, with shimmering auburn hair.

Now, naked except for a blue bathrobe, Posh stood outside Mr. Reuben's bedroom door.

She knocked twice. There was no answer, so she let herself in.

Mr. Reuben was in bed, naked and feigning sleep. He lay on his back, hand draped over his crotch to cover his erection.

"Mr. Reuben, Mr. Reuben," Posh whispered, "Wake up, sir. It's time for breakfast."

Mr. Reuben opened his eyes and regarded her. He was a distinguished gent in his fifties with silver-grey hair, bushy eyebrows and sideburns, and a mustache.

"Is that you, Genevieve?"

"Yes, sir." She raised the bottle of olive oil she was holding. "It's time for your breakfast, sir." She smiled. "I'm sure you're hungry after the night's rest."

Mr. Reuben nodded. "Yes, I'm ravenous." He looked at her reproving. "But, Genevieve, you've left the tray of food downstairs again."

Posh giggled fruitily. "Oh no, I haven't, Mr. Reuben. I've a surprise for you today."

She quickly undid her bathrobe. "See, doesn't it look delicious?"

Mr. Reuben gasped at the sight of the MASSIVE cucumber that poked from her crotch in its special strap-on harness like a farm-grown erection.

She tapped it, causing it to bob up and down. "Here's your breakfast, sir. Is it big enough?"

Mr. Reuben nodded. His erection throbbed in his crotch. Sweat had begun beading on his forehead.

He sat up and licked his lips. "It looks scrumptious, Genevieve, and I'm really hungry. Bring it to me! Let me eat it!"

"And how will you eat it, sir?"

He looked shocked by the question. "With my mouth, of course. How *else?*"

Posh gripped the cucumber like the fake penis it was. She shook it menacingly at Mr. Reuben. "Oh, so you want to chew on my cucumber?"

"Yes, yes."

She scowled in mock anger. "Oh, not today. You're a greedy fucking pig, Mr. Reuben, and I'm going to fuck you as punishment." She jerked her hand on the vegetable dildo. "Oh yes. It's your tight little butthole that I'm feeding this breakfast to. It doesn't eat cucumber regularly enough."

Her expression turned serious. "Now lie back down and lift your legs up to your chest."

Mr. Reuben looked horrified. "Oh please, Genevieve." He gaped at the cucumber. "It's so *massive*, my butthole can't stand it!"

"Do it," Posh said testily. "Assume the position at once or I'll get an even bigger one."

Mr. Reuben hastily complied, lying on his back, raising his legs to his chest and clasping his thighs tight. "Please, Genevieve, forgive me—my anus isn't hungry."

"Shut up," Posh said, with conviction now. She'd moved from mere play acting into actually becoming the dominatrix maidservant whose role Mr. Reuben was paying her to play. Her clitoris was burning like it was on fire, her pussy felt like one of Hell's fiery pits—she was that aroused.

She smiled at Mr. Reuben's genteel face with its gunmetal hair. He was clearly as aroused as she was now. The veins on his cock visibly twitched. He looked into her eyes in an agony of anticipation.

Posh quickly lubricated the cucumber with the olive oil. She squirted some more into her palm and greased Mr. Reuben's anus, sliding two fingers into the tight hole and finger-fucking him with them, while jerking him off slowly.

"Have you changed your mind?" she asked throatily, fighting to keep her own excitement from her voice, to still sound severe. "Is your butthole hungry now?"

"Yes!" Mr. Reuben gasped.

"Are you absolutely certain?" Posh stopped fondling and finger-fucking him. "Now that I think about it, you may be right. This breakfast might be too big for you—"

"No, It is just the right size," Mr. Reuben interrupted her in a hoarse voice. "PUT IT IN RIGHT NOW!" He reached between his legs, took the cucumber in both hands and guided its oily length into his anus.

The massive vegetable went in smoothly, deep to about three quarters of its ten-inch length. Mr. Reuben lay back and gasped like he was in heaven.

(When she'd originally taken on this job, Posh had been afraid that the cucumber might break inside Mr. Reuben's ass, leaving them with the problem of extracting it. But no, she later discovered that the strap-on was very cunningly designed. Each cu-cumber was anchored to the harness by a plastic corkscrew that penetrated its entire length. Even if it broke it would hold together.)

Posh began fucking Mr. Reuben hard in the ass, trying to keep the strokes slow and firm like he liked it. It was hard going—her burgeoning excitement made her want to fuck him like a rapist, till she saw blood pour from his asshole.

She managed to keep herself focused, however, jerking him off in time to her strokes into his ass. She watched the expression on his face change, going from the merely pleasurable, to the outrageously tantalized, then finally, just before his orgasm, to a rictus like he was in exquisite pain.

While she did him, he caressed her breasts, fondling and squeezing them. At one point he pinched her right nipple so hard she bit her lip from the pain. But it was good pain—it helped her keep her mind on fucking him at a measured tempo, not the butt-rape her own pleasure was inclining her toward.

And while his pleasure increased, so did hers. The inside of the harness rubbed against her clitoris, lifting her high on wings of sensation. She'd cum herself any moment now, possibly before him even.

"Oh, yessssss!" Mr. Reuben gasped as his cum squirted. It arched through the air and splattered his chin and chest.

"Oh, shit!" Posh gasped. She came and came.

Mr. Reuben lay back happily. Posh fucked his ass hard while her orgasm ran its course. Then she collapsed on him and gripped him hard.

"Oh, Genevieve," Mr. Reuben groaned. "I do believe today's is the best breakfast I've had in a looonng time."

"Me too, Mr. Reuben," Posh said with deep satiated sincerity. "Me too."

**

Afterwards, they had the cucumber for breakfast. Posh first scrubbed it clean and peeled the rind off, then she cubed the white flesh and mixed it up with eggs and other veggies in a salad.

After this, Mr. Reuben paid her. Eight hundred dollars. "So I'll see you on Friday, Genevieve."

She smiled and bent to kiss him. "Of course, sir. Assuming the dinos don't eat me before then."

He laughed. It was a popular saying in modern Boston.

Posh got dressed in her own clothes and left Mr. Reuben's apartment. He lived on the third floor of the skyscraper.

Herbie would be waiting downstairs for her. While descending the steps, she smiled. Her shared orgasm with Mr. Reuben had left her feeling nice and tingly.

She felt really positive about today.

That was until she got in the car with Herbie.

**

Posh gaped at Herb. She felt like killing her pimp.

"Beth Riggs asked for a special session? And you fucking accepted? Are you nuts? You *know* that woman is crazy."

Herbie *knew*. He grinned guiltily.

Herbie Stanton was thin and weasel-faced with dark hair and eyes. He looked naturally untrustworthy.

"Take it easy, Posh," he said. "I'll be there. She won't do anything stupid."

Not do anything stupid? Nothing stupid? The words revolved around in Posh's head like the solar system. *Beth Riggs not do anything stupid?*

She regarded Herbie with tired brown eyes. *Herb, you idiot, how the fucking hell can't you see that that crazy bitch is going to kill me one of those days?*

Herbie patted her hand soothingly. "We can't turn Beth down, baby. She pays real good money. And since today's a special request, she's offered us a bonus."

Posh considered. Herbie was making a valid point here. One never turned down good money. Money was everything.

"Okay, let's go," she said coldly. "Just make sure you've got my back in case she gets funny."

CHAPTER 8

Malone

Malone drove through Chinatown.

Like he'd suspected would be the case, Rachel Fischer hadn't come home last night. That meant the clock was ticking—time fast running out for his client's daughter.

With no idea where to find 'Frank,' Malone had decided to seek help . . . of the supernatural sort.

***

Chinatown Park thronged with prostitutes of all races and ages and sexes. The mob of women, men, and hybrid sex workers thronged the chessboard by the paifang gate with disregard for any danger.

There was no dragon danger here.

All the prostitutes plied their trade in Chinatown for the same reason that the Boston Grid ended at Essex Street, Chinatown's northern border: China-town's immunity from dragons.

Dragons *never* attacked Chinese people.

***

The Boston Dragon grid—or just The Grid—had been the ambitious undertaking of the Boston City Council in the days before the sheer overwhelming immensity of the changes to the world had dawned on anyone.

The Grid extended outward in a rough hexagon from Boston City Hall.

(Its northern limit was the curve/angle formed by New Chardon Street and the John F. Fitzgerald Sur-face Road. Its east boundary was the same Surface Road descending to Purchase

Street. South, it ended at Essex Street, right at the boundary of Chinatown. West, it terminated in a zig-zag line formed by Tremont, Park, and Bowdoin Streets.)

The idea behind its construction was a simple one: build a dragon-proof protective shield over Boston's lower levels.

The only construction material capable of withstanding the dragons was wiven, a metaloplastic stronger than tempered steel. And most important—utterly fireproof. Building a meltable shield would be pointless.

The work had initially proceeded fast, with everyone understanding the need for speed. Like a spreading cobweb, the wiven shield had expanded across the city, shutting off the streets and roads from the transparent fire breathing reptiles that were Earth's new reality.

Then construction had halted.

There'd been a pay/union dispute, and all the Chinese workers (whom no one realized were the reason the dragons hadn't been attacking the construction companies), had gone on strike.

Calling their bluff, work had gone on. Less workers meant more pay for everyone.

Work had continued until the next day.

Unknown to the workers, a herd of dragons were nesting in the New England Aquarium. The dragons flew inland that morning while the crew were setting up the grid suspension pillars and fried and ate everyone. Similar dragon ravages decimated the other construction crews.

That was the end of building The Grid.

The Grid was a strange construct. At a height of sixteen feet above the ground, it covered everything, like central Boston was sheltered underneath an endless bus stop, or was part of the world's most extensive subway station.

The Grid protected Boston's lowest two storeys. Just about everyone higher up than that lived in skyscrapers, the insect-buildings possessing in-built defenses against dragon attack.

CHAPTER 9

Malone

Ma Cure — real name Lin Yi-Chun — lived in a solitary three-tiered pagoda in the middle of China-town Park.

The building had previously been a temple, then a theater for classical drama. Now with most of the actors/actresses eaten by dinos (against whom the Chinese weren't immune), Ma and her daughter Jade had taken the building over.

Ma was a well-respected elder in the community. No one contested her ownership of the old pagoda.

***

Malone parked his Mustang outside the mob of prostitutes and walked to Ma's place.

Whilst crossing Chinatown Park, he was again struck by the oddity of such dragon-free airspace existing in Boston.

"Dragons remember ancient kinship," Ma Cure reminded Malone when he saw her. "Dragon, legend creature we Chinese give life. Always thankful for this."

Malone nodded. It was as valid/invalid an explan-ation as any he'd heard.

And no less odd than the woman explaining it to him.

Ma Cure was a wizened old head transplanted onto a nine-year-old female body. Her hair was straggly and as white as a bleached sheet.

Ma's old head and young body were held together not by surgery, but by a thin wrap of yellow paper with Chinese script written on it.

"Old Country magic," she'd told Malone more than once. "Flesh lock strong than steel."

(This was one thing about Ma Cure: Her English was horrible. "Too old learn American," she often said proudly. "Me old-school Guangzhou woman. Leave Jade learn. She young—throat talk good American.")

"You're saying that you can live forever like this? Just keep switching bodies?"

Ma Cure nodded. "Unless grow bored, of course." She'd laughed and stroked her thin hair with child-fingers.

Then her expression turned girlish, coquettish. She pointed from her top-floor window at the milling prostitutes on the heaven-earth chessboard near the paifang gate, then she tapped her crotch meaningfully. "Need new body, Malone. Much sexy men downstairs. Little girl pussy useless."

They'd both laughed.

Now Malone told Ma: "I need to consult Yang Yang."

Ma regarded Malone with aged eyes. "Shit serious, huh?"

He nodded back. "A kidnapping. The victim's time is running out like it's in the Olympics."

Ma nodded. She liked Malone. He'd once helped her out of a problem that had threatened her with great loss of face. Now she always did what she could to help him.

"Yang Yang always need blood," Ma said.

"I know." Malone extended his right arm.

Ma Cure cut Malone's arm with a crystal lancet. She collected the dribbling blood into a large crystal cup. When the bowl was full, she placed it aside and bound up Malone's wound.

"Jade!" she called.

Jade Cure appeared at the inner door. She was tall and graceful, with twinkling eyes and perfect lips. Attractive, but reserved-looking; beautiful when she smiled.

Jade smiled on seeing Malone, then turned to her mother.

"You called, Ma?"

"Yes." She nodded at Malone. "Malone need help. Bring frozen goddess."

Jade nodded and left.

***

Yang Yang was a four feet high white stone carving. A lifelike representation of a naked serpentine mermaid—beautiful Asian woman to the waist, snake coils from there down. The snake coils coiled in a spreading cone, forming the base the statue rested on.

With the statue's size, it should have been impossible for Jade Cure to carry. But it was hollow.

Jade placed the Snake Lady statue in front of her mother, then sat in the lotus position on the floor beside her. She pulled a little scroll from her pocket. She unrolled this in her lap, and then watched Malone, wondering what had brought him here.

Malone's attention was focused on the Snake Lady statue. Ma Cure said Yang Yang was a goddess frozen as punishment for challenging the Eight Immortals to a duel.

"We begin?" Ma asked, her old voice ethereal.

Malone nodded.

Jade began reading from the scroll. An ancient Chinese spell that seemed to turn the room yellow. Ma stood and tilted the transparent bowl of Malone's blood to Yang Yang's mouth. The Snake Lady's white lips stained red, like she'd just lipsticked them.

Jade kept reading. Yang Yang opened her eyes. She smiled, then opened her mouth and drank from the bowl of blood. Her body unfroze to the waist. She took the bowl from Ma with both hands. Ma stood back and watched her drain it.

Yang Yang handed the empty bowl back to Ma, then she turned to Malone.

He felt a cold shiver as her eyes met his. She was truly beautiful, but there was no humanity whatever in her gaze. There was however knowledge. The knowledge Malone needed. Unimaginable wisdom.

Jade was still reading from the scroll, her voice now a low background mumble as she repeated the spell to keep the goddess animate.

The Snake Lady smiled coyly at Malone, then addressed him in Chinese. Her voice was pleasant, guttural but seductive.

Ma translated. "She say: Blood always delicious, Malone. Tight ass fantastic also; accept sacrifice. What want know?"

Malone winced at Yang Yang's reference to his backside. Sex was an ongoing issue between them. He explained about the missing Rachel Fischer.

Ma translated this to Yang Yang.

Yang Yang shut her white eyes for a moment, then opened them again and addressed Ma.

"Stolen girl alive," Ma said. "Goddess ask: You want send you fight kidnapper?"

Malone thought quickly. This was unexpected. None of his previous consultations with Yang Yang had had to do with kidnappings—he'd had no need of translocation before.

He was suspicious of being thrown into the ether, with no control over where he'd wind up. *I can ask for directions, then drive over. But that will waste time, and time is something Rachel Fischer doesn't have. Still, I've got my gun.*

He looked to Ma Cure for advice. She and her daughter both nodded, Jade's lips moving silently in her chanting.

Malone looked back at the Snake Lady. "Yes, send me there. But not into a trap."

Yang Yang smiled at Malone, the expression on her beautiful face so cold it chilled him. She winked at him.

She said some more to Ma. "Is done. But warning: Is danger, unexpected danger."

"Can you be more specific?"

He never got an answer. With no sense of motion or changing locations, he suddenly found himself back in the parking lot outside Hailey's Toy Factory.

Why am I not fucking surprised about this? he thought, looking at the open doorway from which Frank's accomplice had signaled him with a flashlight two nights ago.

He climbed into the rear of a burnt-out bus to think out his attack strategy.

CHAPTER 10

Posh, Herbie & Beth

Beth Riggs was a tall blonde with piercing amber eyes. Her nose was slightly crooked and her jaw a little square. She looked powerful—almost masculinely muscular.

Now in her late thirties, she'd been a prison warden before the world burnt to ash.

Beth was currently naked, seated on a sofa with blue plastic upholstery. She, Posh, and Herbie were in her living room, its beige carpet covered with a plastic drop cloth.

Beth ran her palms slowly down over her toned belly to her crotch, then back up to her breasts.

Her breasts were big, with tiny nipples. Her pubic mound was shaven. Her clitoris peeked out between the folds of her cunt wings like a little fingertip.

Beth looked Posh over, her eyes severe like Posh was a prisoner under inspection.

Posh looked back at her timidly, like she knew Beth liked. Her submissiveness wasn't just an act—Beth scared her no end. She was glad Herbie was always present when they fucked.

"Take your clothes off," Beth ordered. "You too, Herbie."

Posh hastily did so. Beth's voice always felt to her like a whip. Unlike fucking nice old Mr. Reuben with his cucumbers, she dreaded these sex sessions.

Herbie stripped off too. His cock was short and thin, his body skinny like he didn't eat enough. He also had the beginning of a paunch.

Beth watched them undress. She *loved* seeing Herbie nude. For a man, he looked incredibly weak—she could flatten him with a single punch. And she knew he fucking knew it.

"Bring the toys," she ordered Herbie once both her visitors were naked. Herbie rushed to comply. Beth spread her legs wide

36

and pushed her crotch out so her cunt was splayed over the sofa edge. She crooked a finger at Posh.

Posh knelt between her spread legs and began eating her.

Herbie returned with Beth's 'toys'—a chopping board, a cleaver, and a bucket full of live chickens that clucked nervously and rolled their eyes in confused anticipation.

Beth took the cleaver from Herbie. He carefully laid the chopping board over Posh's back and head.

"Yes, Posh," Beth said. "Keep up a good tempo on my clitoris. Move your tongue faster, honey . . . like that."

On that note, she pulled out a chicken from the bucket, placed it belly-down on the board on Posh's back and hacked into it with the cleaver.

Her first chop broke the fowl's back. Blood spurted between its feathers. It squawked and thrashed, seeking an impossible freedom.

Beth laughed.

"Herbie," she said. "What the fuck are you waiting for?"

Herbie gulped. He hated these sessions as much as Posh did. But the money, the money . . .

"Wank for me!" Beth commanded harshly.

Herbie focused his eyes on Beth's breasts, which were almost perfect. By imagining there was no dying chicken below them, he willed his penis to full erection.

He began stroking himself.

"*Slower,*" Beth ordered. "Wank *slower.* Remember, *you* don't cum until I tell you to."

Beth hacked into the chicken again, shattering both its wings. Blood fountained up from its body now, squirting to its heartbeat. The bird squawked continuously, its tongue poking from its beak like it was having trouble breathing.

Its blood dribbled off the board onto Posh.

Beth, her face now set in a grimace, attacked the chicken with the cleaver, hacking it into a mass of little pieces.

She was lost deep in sexual pleasure. Her hand moved in a blur, smashing the blade through the bird into the board beneath. She was oblivious to Posh's shudders as the bird disintegrated above her.

Damn, Posh can eat pussy. Beth felt each tongue stroke tingle up into her nipples.

She groaned at Herbie, who was jerking off slowly, a look of pained concentration on his face.

"Does it disgust you, Herbie? That you're getting off on watching me fuck up dead meat?"

Herbie grunted. He was excited now despite himself. He slid his hand slowly over his erection, careful not to push himself over the edge. *It's bad business to cum before Beth wants me to. She might hold back our fucking bonus.*

And all the while, Beth's hand kept chopping up the chicken into an indistinguishable mess of bone, brains, meat, and blood . . . the ever-dripping blood.

***

Posh shuddered as the chopping board pounded on her. Thunk . . . thunk . . . thunk.

Shit, this bitch is fucking crazy. Okay, so what else is new? She wondered how in the world Beth Riggs or *anyone* got into cunnilingus while killing birds.

The chicken blood poured over her. Warm like skin lotion, it spilled over her back.

Shit.

Posh ate Beth's cunt mechanically. She was not aroused in the least. She licked Beth's clitoris and tongued her pee-hole and vagina.

"Give my asshole some tongue too!" Beth ordered in a drawn-out gasp.

Posh complied, sticking her tongue into Beth's tight, pouty anus.

***

Beth finished chopping up the dead chicken. Using the cleaver like a spatula, she swiped its remains off the chopping board to splatter the drop cloth.

She replaced it with another live fowl.

Before hacking into this one, she smiled at Herbie. "Almost time for you to cum, Herbie."

He nodded, his expression feverish. It was taking Herbie all his concentration not to ejaculate.

Beth hacked this chicken's head clean off with her first chop. She raised the bird, pointing its severed neck at her breasts in turn, squirting its blood on them while its feet kicked spastically. The blood splashed her chest, then dribbled down into her crotch.

She felt her orgasm near now, extremely close.

***

Posh tasted the first dribbles of chicken blood as it ran into Beth's cunt.

Thank heavens, she thought. *She'll soon be done.*

The blood's metal taste disgusted her, but she kept her tongue moving over Beth's clitoris.

The sooner this is over, the better, she thought glumly. *So she pays a bundle, but . . .*

She felt the tell-tale thud of Beth splatting the chicken back onto the chopping board. She tensed, expecting the maniacal thudding to resume. It didn't come. Instead, she heard the sluice of the blood-slickened blade, and the gentle press of the board on her shoulders and head.

She realized that Beth was skinning the bird.

Posh knew what was happening—Beth had done this before.

She turned to looked at Herbie. His face was white with disgust. She laughed in her mind. *So you wanted to watch me, did you? Let's see how you like this, you greedy son-of-a-bitch.*

Pleased that Herbie would be sharing in today's humiliation, Posh resumed licking Beth's bloody vagina.

Now she did so with gusto, finger-fucking her to bring her off.

***

Like Posh, Herbie knew what to expect when he saw Beth skinning the dead chicken. Beth looked up once and smiled at him, licking her lips.

Her breathing's coming faster and faster, he thought desperately. *She'll surely cum any second now, before she . . .*

But no. Beth finished skinning the chicken and handed its bloody skin to Herb. "Put this on, handsome."

Herbie took the skin from her with trepidation. Beth had skinned the fowl expertly. All its feathers were still intact.

Herbie slid the empty skin over his head like a hat. As he knew Beth would insist, he packed his hair up beneath the feather 'hat's' rims.

That done he quickly resumed masturbating. If he lost his erection now, he'd never regain it—this shit was too fucked up. He knew what Posh would say about that: "This was your fucking idea."

Herbie wondered how he could really be so greedy, out to make every single buck, no matter how dangerous. *No,* he thought again, *I'm not greedy, I'm just realistic about how important money is.*

Beth—breathing in short gasps now—was working inside the skinned bird's body with a knife.

Herbie watched her with dread anticipation. He kept jerking off, just enough to remain hard. He was no longer in danger of ejaculating—his orgasm had fled back into his testicles.

Beth looked up at him. She handed him the dead chicken. "Here's your wife, birdman, all prepped for your wedding night." Her voice was a strangled croak. "Go on, hurry up, I want to see this!"

She pulled another live bird from the bucket and began maniacally hacking into it.

Herbie stared at the chicken. Beth hadn't gutted it. She'd simply widened its cloaca, expertly sculpting it into a white meat vagina replica, complete with a flap of upturned flesh that looked like a clitoris.

"Hurry up!" Beth gasped.

Gripping the skinned chicken by both wings, Herbie inserted his penis into its new 'vagina' and began fucking it.

***

A fresh wave of bird blood splashed Posh. The chopping board began slipping across her back. She grabbed it with a hand, steadying it. Beth was fucked-up enough to use her back as a chopping board and not notice. She paused in her tonguing Beth's clitoris, rubbing it with her fingers instead, and watched Herb's torment.

"Don't be selfish with the chicken, Herb," Beth gasped, "Make *love* to it. Give it *pleasure*."

Posh grinned. Herbie looked like he wanted to cry as he screwed the headless, skinless bird.

Men are incredible, she thought, amazed that Herbie could actually maintain an erection.

Her enjoyment of his debasement was also getting her excited. Watching his cock disappear into and reappear from the chicken's ripped hole was turning her on too.

Maybe today is a good day after all, she thought, as Herbie began grunting from the tight bird pussy, fighting not to cum before their employer did. He looked utterly ridiculous in his chicken-skin hat—a king wearing a crown of bloody feathers.

She returned her full attention to Beth's bloody cunt, slipping a hand between her own legs while she licked the other woman to orgasm.

Above her another chicken disintegrated under Beth's assault.

***

Beth came. She dropped the cleaver. She grabbed handfuls of shredded chicken meat and smeared the white pulp across her breasts.

"Sheeeeiiiiiitt!" she gasped. Her legs tensed hard around Posh's head. Her ass clenched like she'd shit herself from the pleasure. Her pussy felt like a white-hot furnace, feeding fire through the rest of her body.

She squeezed her breasts through the gore, bucked her hips into Posh's face. She rode Posh's lips and tongue like her mouth was a horse.

Finally, her pleasure subsided. She lay back trembling.

Between her legs, Posh was still licking her like a dog, like she'd taught her too. *Oh yes, girl. I trained you well.*

Beth crooked a finger at Herbie, who was still fucking the chicken, a look of desperation on his face. "Okay, baby, cum for me now."

Herbie walked over to her, his hips pumping.

Beth pushed Posh and her chopping board away.

Posh sat down on the floor, an amused smile on her face. She kept rubbing her clitoris.

Good bitch, Beth thought on seeing Posh was masturbating.

"Sit in my lap," she commanded Herbie.

He did so, facing away from her.

Beth now took over control of the chicken from Herbie. She reached around him with both hands, gripped it by its wings, and rammed it up and down on his erection.

Up and down, faster and faster. Harder and harder and harder and HARDER.

"You're just a stupid cock, nothing more," she laughed, as his breathing became ragged. Herbie leaned back on her, flattening her breasts on her ribcage, and gasped.

***

Herbie gritted his teeth and came, spurting into the chicken's guts.

He hated it. Hated how horribly fantastic screwing the bird felt. How incredible this orgasm felt.

His semen spurted from him. It felt to him like someone was pulling a long spaghetti strand out of his balls.

Herbie's eyes rolled back in his head. He went limp on Beth. He was relieved that she didn't immediately push him off her. Her breasts were soft pillows cushioning his fall from grace.

Thank God, he thought. *This is over.*

Only it wasn't.

***

Watching Herbie cum pushed Posh into her own orgasm. While her sensations flooded her, she kept her eyes on his ass, on his pumping groin as he spurted his seed into the bird, imagining it was her pussy he was flooding with it.

Her sex spasm ended. She relaxed, watched Beth and Herbie.

Herbie looked murdered. He lay draped over Beth like a starfish. The chicken in his crotch looked like a bald head.

Beth's eyes were flickering with cold amusement. And there was something else in them . . . a deadly intent.

Posh was suddenly very scared. *Oh fucking no!*

It happened incredibly fast.

Before Herbie realized what was happening, Beth had extricated herself from under him and pushed him down on the sofa. Next she yanked the chicken off his limp member. Then she picked up her cleaver again.

***

Herbie watched Beth with disinterest. What the fuck now? She's going to chop it up again?

He was horrified when she put the cleaver blade to his neck. "Sit up," she ordered.

Herbie sat up. Behind Beth, he saw Posh sitting bolt upright, terrified at what Beth might do.

Herbie was terrified too.

"Just one more thing, Herbie," Beth said, raising the chicken ass-first to his lips, her face glazed with manic excitement. "Your darling wife demands that you drink the signs of your love for her from her cup."

She tilted the chicken's 'vagina' towards his lips.

Herbie struggled, shook his head, lips sealed tight.

"Drink or die," Beth said. "I'll count to five, then I'll slit your throat. One, two three . . ."

Lips twisted with disgust and revulsion, Herbie opened his mouth and drank his cum out of the chicken's guts.

***

Posh was initially about to grab the chopping board and smash Beth over the head with it. She relaxed when she saw Beth was only making Herbie drink his cum.

Ewww, that's gross! she thought in amusement, watching the blood-pinkened liquid stream out of the chicken's backside into his mouth.

***

Herbie got all the cum in without vomiting.

"Swallow it all," Beth said with a cold smile. Amber eyes glittering, she pressed the bloodstained blade into his throat.

Herbie swallowed, gulped the cum down.

"Don't you dare puke it back up."

Beth waited to ensure that he'd be unable to puke it back up, then left him alone. Herbie instantly got to his feet and staggered away to pick up his clothes.

Beth replaced him on the sofa. She picked up her purse, took out money to pay the pair. She felt wonderful. It had been a fantastic sex session.

She wondered what Herbie was all worked up about—you'd think he'd swallowed a lemon. She giggled. *A little cum never hurt anyone, Herbie. I've guzzled lots in my time.*

***

Downstairs in Herbie's pimpmobile—a sky-blue Lincoln Continental with the number 'L3t5 4k'—an uneasy silence reigned.

Posh thought what she'd witnessed hilarious.

She faked a solemn frown however—Herbie was clearly MAD.

Herbie hadn't protested to Beth afterwards. Posh hadn't expected him too. Herbie was weak and spineless. In a fight he'd be no match for Beth, and he knew it. She'd wipe the floor with his ass.

So Herbie simmered in his anger, raged impotently.

Posh was totally unsympathetic. *So now you know how she makes me feel,* she thought.

Other thoughts of hers:

Wow, Herbie, I never knew you grew up on a farm! So what did the hen's guts feel like, baby? How do birds compare to girls? Was she tight enough for you? Was the drink a Bloody Mary?

She thought these, but didn't dare say them. Herbie looked so fucking mad—he'd beat the living crap out of her.

She didn't even dare warn him that there was still a patch of semen smeared over his chin. It would dry up later and flake and look odd. Then Herbie was certain to blame her for not pointing it out.

"She gave us a fucking HUGE bonus," she said finally, getting the money out of her purse. She spread the money before him. "Two thousand dollars for an hour's work ain't bad."

Herbie had been so traumatized upstairs that he'd shambled out of the apartment, leaving Posh to collect their payment.

Seeing the money now, his eyes brightened for a moment, then they dulled again.

"We're not visiting her *ever* again," he said.

Posh looked at him, saw that he meant it. His eyes were cold as ice.

"You were right: that bitch *is* crazy."

Posh was suddenly really pissed off. She couldn't resist saying:

"So now the shoe's on the other foot, eh? Your pride's more important than mine?"

To her surprise, Herbie didn't slap her or anything. He just started up the car and drove them away from there.

***

Posh was wrong. It wasn't pride/humiliation motivating Herbie, but that Beth had held a *cleaver* to his throat to ensure he complied.

Looking into her eyes then, Herbie had been utterly certain Beth would have slit his throat without a second's hesitation if he'd refused her order to drink the cum.

Posh was right—Beth Riggs *would* kill someone one of these days. Best it wasn't either of them.

CHAPTER 11

Malone

A long white truck covered with repulsor spikes pulled into the toy factory parking lot.

From his place of concealment, Malone watched it back up to the warehouse door.

The driver and his assistant, two Asian men in work overalls, disembarked and began offloading long brown boxes that resembled coffins. Once they'd gotten two down they reloaded them onto hand trucks and pushed them into the warehouse.

Malone frowned. This was getting odder. He was confident, however, that he'd not walked into a trap. The Snake Lady never lied.

The two men kept offloading the brown boxes. Malone counted thirty in all.

Once they were done, the pair got back into their truck and drove off.

Malone studied the men's faces as the truck pulled out of the lot again: Their short black hair, their oblique eyes, their inscrutable expressions. Neither man struck him as a criminal. The pair were sharing a joke like regular workmen.

He was intrigued. They didn't look Chinese, like Ma Cure and Jade, but still seemed a familiar Asian subset. But definitely not Japanese.

He refocused on the task ahead.

Malone had gleaned one important piece of information from watching the delivery men:

No one had come out of the warehouse to either assist them in offloading their odd cargo, or to supervise them.

That meant there were very few people in the warehouse, possibly only Frank and the captive Rachel Fischer.

Malone primed his gun. Full charge, set to burn.

Time to kick ass, he thought. *And this time I'm certain there aren't any dinosaurs waiting.*

He loped across the concrete to peer in through the factory door.

***

The warehouse interior was a long room with two stories of prefabricated cabins at both ends.

It was dark, packed with overlapping shadows, squares of light filtered in through high windows, their beams universes of dust motes.

Malone smiled grimly—light glimmered in a single cabin window to his right. *Gotcha, Frank.*

The boxes the workmen had brought were stacked in the middle of the warehouse.

This clearly wasn't their first such delivery.

Malone estimated that there were at least two hundred, maybe more, of the coffin-shaped containers piled in the building's middle space. He wondered what the hell was going on. Was Frank dealing arms? Or drugs?

His curiosity of the boxes contents would have to wait however. Freeing Rachel Fischer was his priority here.

Keeping close to the walls, in the consuming shadows, Malone padded across the warehouse toward the lit cabin.

***

Malone peeped in the lit cabin's window.

It wasn't the office he'd expected. It was a laboratory. Amidst banks of chemical and electrical equipment, a human figure lay on a metal table, draped over with a green plastic sheet.

Malone winced. *The son-of-a-bitch hasn't already killed her, has he?*

There was no one in the lab. Malone opened the door and slipped inside.

He uncovered the body on the table. "Miss Fischer, are you al—"

He stopped speaking. He gaped instead at the robot he'd just unveiled.

The robot was totally white and shiny—a new machine. Human in size and proportion. Its limbs, however, were thinner than a person's, and it had only four digits on each hand.

Its face was a smooth expanse—a single T-shaped hole its only feature. Set in each end of the T's crosspiece was a red eye.

The robot's braincase was open. Its plastic brain was hooked up via a profusion of wires to a switchboard that in turn connected to a computer. The computer monitor was a mass of endlessly scrolling code.

Malone considered the setup—someone was clearly re-programming the robot. *But what the hell for? It's brand new.*

Then he was struck by another thought. He looked around the office for the robot's packing crate. He located it—partially open in a corner and spilling Styrofoam.

He frowned. The robot's packing case was a duplicate of the coffin shaped boxes outside in the warehouse.

'Product of New Korea' read the thin white lettering on its side.

Malone grunted. Yeah, the workmen making the delivery had been Korean. That's why he'd been unable to place them in the racial grid.

(With overland/oversea/air traffic now rendered impossible by the dragon presence, what little international freighting still existed was conducted by submarine. The Koreans controlled most of the shipping from Asia. Using converted military subs, they freighted people, produce, and weapons around the world.)

Malone looked at the white robot again. The wires flowing from its open head to the switchboard filled him with apprehension. Frank being a kidnapper was one thing. His messing about with humanoid machines was totally another.

And what does the shithead need so many of them for?

He pulled his mind back from this new puzzle to what he was here for.

"This shit isn't helping me none," he said out loud. "Where the hell is Rachel Fischer?"

Then a narcotic haze descended over him and he passed out cold.

He crashed unconscious to the floor.

CHAPTER 12

Posh

Next morning.

Herbie pushed Posh's bedroom door open.

She groaned on seeing his weasel smile. That meant he had work for her.

"Wakey, wakey, baby," Herbie sang.

"Fuck off, Herbie. I'm bushed."

He sat on the edge of the bed and ran a hand through her auburn hair. "Can't. Your gorgeous ass is required uptown."

She knocked the hand away. "Shit, Herbie, have a fuckin' heart. I'm not yet recovered from yesterday."

Herbie looked pained. "This is a big payer, baby."

"Herbie, we made lots of money yesterday. Give me a fucking break, and by that I mean a vacation."

He gave her his weasel smile again. "We didn't make this kind of money yesterday. This guy is loaded. He's the heir to some soda pop fortune. He's offering four thousand up front, another thousand if you get him off real good."

Posh instantly smelt a rat. She sat up, pulling the duvet over her breasts to keep them warm. "What's the fucking catch, Herbie? We both know no one throws that sort of money at you for nothing. He want me to fuck a corpse?"

Herbie shook his head hurriedly. "No, nothing like that. The guy's a war veteran, got invalided in the Syrian war. He picked up a skin condition. Looks like shit now, can't get a girl except he pays."

Posh looked at him aghast. "Did you just say *skin disease*? Are you out of your friggin' mind?"

Herbie shook his head quickly. "Not *disease* a . . . . condition. Nothing contagious. He got hit by some experimental weapon that has his skin falling off in patches. It's like skin cancer, only it doesn't kill you."

"I'm not doing it," Posh said. "I'll have nightmares forever."

"It's not that obvious," Herbie said quickly. "You won't even notice. On the plus side, he's very good-looking too."

She pouted at him. "Forget it. There's only so much shit I can stand in one lifetime. What if he wants a blowjob?"

Herbie looked pained again. Posh tensed herself in case he tried to hit her, to force her. She'd rake his face so bad he'd look like a tiger pelt.

Then her good sense kicked in again. She winced. No, she wouldn't fucking scar Herbie. She didn't dare. Herbie's younger brother, Bulldog, a real ugly son-of-a-cunt, would beat the living shit out of her.

Bulldog, who was soft in the head, was unwaveringly loyal to Herbie. He'd have absolutely no compulsions over breaking all Posh's limbs.

So, no, she wouldn't mess with Herbie like that. She could however hold out for better treatment.

Herbie looked exasperated. "Look," he said, "If this guy likes you, you get *all* his business. Even if you only screw him four times a month, that's twenty grand."

"Nope."

Posh watched his face drop as he saw this incredible earner evaporate. She wondered if he would hit her.

She preempted the possibility. "I'll do it on one condition," she said angrily.

Herbie instantly looked relieved. "What's that?"

"You say this guy is loaded, right?"

Herbie nodded.

Posh nodded. "If I convince him to keep me as his steady, I get to pick and choose who I do from now on."

She saw him weighing it in his mind. She pressed her point:

"Look, I'll fuck him so good, he'll be begging me to come back. Besides, if he's as rich as you say, I won't really have to bang too many other people, will I?"

She saw that Herbie got her point. What he didn't get, was that she'd figured out that if this guy was that rich, he might be her ticket to making a break with Herbie — her chance to escape her dead-end hooker's life.

"It's a deal," Herbie said. "Get this fish hooked and you screw only who you want. I'll get another girl to take up the slack."

Posh nodded. She got out of bed and went to have a bath.

***

Herbie dropped Posh off at a large house on New Sudsbury, just off the city center.

The house sported banks of electronic metal repulsors to ensure hungry reptiles never troubled it.

That simple fact assured Posh that her new client had MONEY.

***

Just like Herbie had promised, Oswald Watkins *was* handsome. He was polite and instantly made Posh feel at ease.

They had drinks, then retired to the bedroom.

They stripped off. Oswald's body was covered with swollen shit-colored patches. Even his erection.

Shit, Posh thought, *I hope Herbie wasn't bullshitting that this guy isn't infectious.*

"Herbie said you were in the war," Posh said, pointing to his mottled skin. Do they hurt?"

He gripped the edge of one of the brown patches and peeled it off, wincing as it separated from his skin. It left a moist pink skinless patch that looked like gingiva. "Yeah, they hurt like shit. And also, every now and again I have an allergic reaction to some chemical they produce that almost kills me."

Posh felt for him. He was so nice, and yet . . .

Oswald dropped the skin patch in a bedside bin, then turned back to her. He smiled, reached out hands for her. "Come, let's fuck. It's been ages since I've had a woman as beautiful as you in bed."

Flattered by the compliment, Posh climbed into bed with him.

***

Once they were both in bed, Oswald's behavior changed.

Posh realized she was in trouble when she saw the way his eyes were gleaming. Oswald looked like Herbie's retard brother Bulldog when he was about to fuck someone up.

Shit, she thought with dread, *I'm fucking going to regret this.*

Her fears became reality.

Like a scene from a horror flick, Oswald Watkins ripped a long sliver of skin off his right arm, from shoulder to wrist. It looked like his arm was a banana he was peeling.

Posh gaped at the revealed bleeding flesh.

Fuck! I'm getting out of here right now!

She moved to leap off the bed. Before she could reach safety, however, Oswald had looped the bleeding skin strip around her neck twice and was choking her with it.

He spun her around to face him. He spat in her face—

"Arab slut!"

—then slapped her hard. Posh felt her brain explode inside her head. She collapsed back on the bed stunned.

What the hell?

She watched in dull horror and disbelief as Oswald tore a long strip of skin from his chest, digging fingers into skin that ripped like pink Plasticine. He peeled the strip from his left collarbone down to his belly. His exposed flesh glistened like a bloody mouth.

After twisting the length of skin into a cord, Oswald rolled Posh over on her belly then bound her wrists behind her back with it.

He resumed choking her with the skin looped around her neck.

"Camel-fucking bitch," he growled, his voice guttural like he was demon-possessed. "You will tell me what I want to know. Or else . . ." He pulled the ropes tight, ". . . or else I will kill you now."

Posh began gasping for air. With her wrists tied, all she could do was flail about desperately, trying to buck him off.

Oswald halted her resistance with a clout to the back of her head that left her feeling paralyzed.

"Terrorist desert whore!" He cranked her bound arms up till she screamed in pain.

"Please, please let me go! I'll do anything."

Oswald relaxed the pressure. "Good. You are cooperative. Now you will answer my questions. Okay, bitch?"

Posh nodded. "Yes!" Tears were in her eyes now. Her head felt like her brain was made of cotton.

"Now tell me, you clitless cunt," Oswald said in a cold deadly voice, "Where did you hide the Sunburn antidote?"

"I don't know—"

Oswald clouted her again. "*You know*, Habibi. Sunburn is the drug that makes soldiers' skin fall off in patches. Where have your terrorists hidden the cure?"

It hit Posh then like a rain of bricks. *Oh, God, no! He's having a wartime regression, and I'm in it!*

She began praying for Herbie to miraculously turn up here, else she was fucking dead.

Behind her, Oswald laughed. "You still refuse to talk? I will convince you I am serious."

Keeping a firm grip on the skin cord around Posh's neck, he turned her over so she faced him. She now lay on her bound hands, which was painfully uncomfortable.

Posh was horrified. Oswald now looked like a nightmare. His eyes bugged out of his face like they'd been inflated. His lips were curled back in an insane snarl. Worst of all, the skin of his face, neck, and shoulders was now cracked and dribbling blood. He looked covered in bleached alligator skin.

Posh fought back her desire to puke.

Her disgust incensed Oswald. "So you approve of what your fellow terrorists have done to me?"

"It wasn't . . . I didn't—"

He slapped her again. "You will *pay* for this!"

He folded Posh's legs up onto her chest, spat on his cock and inserted himself forcefully into her anus.

***

Posh hardly noticed that he was fucking her ass. She was a prostitute—her anus was used to being used. (She was even grateful for the familiar sensation of a penis in her ass. It was the only normal thing about this nightmare.)

What she found scary was that he kept choking her while fucking her.

She blacked out twice. Each time, on seeing she was unconscious, Oswald would stop choking her, and slap her awake again.

Posh would resurface from negation back into her unending nightmare of Oswald still pounding HARD into her anus, his face a mad grimace, his eyes ghastly white expanses with tiny black central dots, his mind clearly far-off in the Syrian trenches again.

"Please . . . Please . . . !" she moaned. Copious spit dribbled from both corners of her mouth. Crushed under her, both her arms now felt dead, beyond pain, like frostbitten appendages.

In response, Oswald tightened the noose around her throat and fucked her HARDER, making her knees dig painfully into her breasts.

"Slut! Septic cunt!" Spitting in her face. "Tell me the cure!"

Once he bit her nose.

Finally, while yanking the cord around Posh's neck so tight she felt her head would pop off her shoulders, Oswald came.

He froze atop her, orgasming in a long shudder that looked agonizingly painful. Posh, her brain close to shutdown from oxygen deprivation, almost felt sorry for him.

He ejaculated an immense amount inside her. His cum spurted hot like liquid hatred.

Then Oswald went limp and collapsed on top of her.

Then he began crying. "Oh, mummy, I'm so sorry, so, so sorry. I didn't mean to come home like this."

He rolled off Posh.

Posh lay beside him, gasping desperately for breath. She was scared to move in case he assaulted her again.

Between her legs Oswald's semen seeped out of her ass and stained the bedclothes.

***

Oswald's sobs ceased.

He sat up, looked down at Posh.

She stared at him in scared apprehension, but no, his face was once again normal. Serene and calm, human, not the monster who'd just been killing her.

He smiled at Posh. "Did I hurt you?"

She shook her head, as terrified by how horrible he looked as she was horrified by the terrible swiftness of the change in him. "I'm used to rough sex, but you didn't warn me."

He grinned. "My mistake. I can't cum except I fantasize that I'm raping one of those Syrian cunts."

Oswald's eyes glazed over. For a moment his demons possessed him again. He indicated his nightmare face and body.

"It was a *woman* that did this to me. She was lying in a doorway, holding what I thought was a baby. I thought she was wounded . . . ordered my unit to hold their fire, ran over to pull her out. Next thing I know, I get a faceful of—"

"Untie me, please," Posh interrupted him. Though she felt back in control of the situation now she knew Oswald hadn't been planning on killing her, she was worried by the crazed look that had momentarily reentered his eye.

Oswald snapped back to the present. "Yes, of course."

He quickly rolled her over and undid the skin tied around her wrists.

With almost no sensation in her arms at all, Posh pushed herself up on her hands. Oswald unwrapped the noose around her neck.

Posh looked down at herself.

Oh, shit. Her thighs were covered with blood. It looked like she was menstruating. Thin translucent slivers ran between the red, but the semen was in the minority.

Posh immediately lost all sympathy for Oswald. *You veteran asshole, you've ripped up my asshole, you—*

Her thoughts froze. Other than for the familiar soreness normally associated with unlubricated sodomy, she felt normal. So where had the deluge of blood come from?

Oswald turned round from retrieving his wallet from his bedside table. "Here's six thousand dollars, you get a two thousand bo . . . what's the matter?"

She pointed to his crotch. "Your cock, it's skinless."

He laughed. "Oh, that. I must have left its skin in your rectum. Happens occasionally." He grinned at her worried look. "Don't worry about it. It'll be the first thing out next time you poop."

Posh's eyes widened in disbelief. She gaped at his skinless penis. It looked like an overfed earthworm.

Worse even was the fact that Oswald didn't seem bothered.

Left it up my rectum. She was once again horrified. *Shit it out? Are you fuckin kidding me? Asshole, your cockskin is up my asshole!*

Face rigidly calm, Posh took the money Oswald held out to her. She was now desperate to be as far away from him as was humanly possible. Another planet wasn't enough separation.

She got off the bed and began pulling on her clothes, not caring that his blood was messing up her pants.

Oswald lay back in bed, watching her dress. "I like you, Posh," he said. "You've got class. I think I'd like you to be my regular woman. Maybe twice a week."

Posh smiled tightly. "I'd *love* that, honey." In her mind she was thinking, *You must be fucking crazy!*

***

"How'd it go?" Herbie asked when he picked her up.

"That guy is fucked up. A freak!"

"Yes, yes," Herbie said disinterestedly. "But did you fuck him okay—is he pleased with you? That's what matters. Does he want to see you again? Did he give you a bonus?"

She glared at him. "Money, that's all you fucking care about." *Shit, Herbie, you're such a turd, can't you even see the mess my pants are in?*

Herbie's eyes narrowed. "Don't tell me you fucked this up for us. Remember our deal: If you don't become his steady, you keep screwing anyone I find for you."

It was too much. Posh lost it.

She slapped Herbie. So hard that his head rolled on his shoulders. She slapped him again. His eyes rolled in his head.

The Lincoln swerved across the road, almost hitting an oncoming truck.

"Watch where you're fucking going, dickhead!" the female trucker shrilled at them.

Herbie quickly parked. He grabbed Posh's hands as she was about to hit him again. He glared at her, his face already bruising.

"What the hell is wrong with you? I just asked a question."

Posh freed her hands. She threw the six thousand dollars Oswald had paid her at Herbie. "Here's the fucking money. And yes, he *does* want to see me again—with his skinless cock."

Herbie gaped at her. "Skinless?"

Posh didn't reply. She burst out crying.

"I'm sorry," Herbie said worriedly. "I honestly didn't know."

"Just get me out of here," Posh said coldly. "And I promise that if you *ever* mention Oswald Watkins to me again, I'll murder you."

Herbie mused on that. He figured Posh was just upset. She'd calm down after a bit. He put the car in gear and drove off again, thinking of the six grand they'd just made.

And the guy wants to see you again? Shit, girl, we're fucking made, can't you see that?

Suddenly, Herbie saw a pterodactyl swoop down through a hole in The Grid and disappear behind a skyscraper. It was followed by another. He instantly forgot about money, began thinking about getting them both home alive.

The dino birds reappeared in the sky. Both had writhing, screaming people in their jaws trailing liquid crimson streamers.

Herbie only stopped shivering with fear when the pterodactyls were well out of sight.

Beside him, Posh was oblivious to the dinosaur threat. She was angrily brooding—in a hurry to shit Oswald's crap out.

CHAPTER 13

Malone

Malone woke up to the certainty that he was in a fix.

Oops, he thought.

He was in a blue room—not the lab with the robot. This one was large and well lit.

Naked from the waist up, he was strapped down on a metal table.

His belly was cut open and there was a man fiddling in his innards, adjusting something.

With each adjustment odd sensations flooded Malone. Though he clearly felt that his body had been sliced open between his ribcage and groin, he felt no pain. He felt only lightheaded, as if the drug that had knocked him out now floated around his mind in clouds, seeking an exit.

"Hey!" he said. "What the hell are you doing to me?"

The man turned to face him. "You're awake."

Malone instantly recognized his voice. "Frank."

Frank nodded. He straightened up, smiled down at Malone predatorily.

Frank was tall but stooped. He was handsome, with straw-colored hair and pale blue eyes.

With Frank out of the way, Malone could now see the machine sticking out of his abdomen. It was square in shape and covered in blood. An equally crimson power cable ran from it to a wall socket. The table Malone lay on was covered with his blood.

"What the hell is this thing?"

"You'll find out." Frank's voice was even, his facial expression mild, but his eyes. . .

Frank's blue eyes chilled Malone. They glittered with madness.

Malone shuddered. He suspected Frank's insanity was the logical sort. He seemed the sort of monster who'd fit in normally

58

in society, giving the illusion of being an everyday Joe whilst meanwhile committing the most horrendous atrocities. The neighborhood serial killer who was also a devoted husband and father.

"Where's Rachel Fischer?" Malone asked, dreading the reply.

Frank laughed. "She's okay. Don't worry your head about her."

He pulled up a chair, sat beside Malone.

Malone didn't get it. "Have you sent her back to her mother?"

Frank sniggered. "Did you expect me to?" He laughed out loud. "That was a neat trick, making Mrs. Fischer pay us fake bills. Thankfully my partner's smart."

"It was—" Malone shut up. Frank would never believe it was Sara's idea. " —a gamble."

"A gamble that didn't pay off," a woman's voice said from behind Malone. "We needed that money. You're going to pay for sticking your nose in where it didn't belong."

The speaker walked into view. "Sorry I'm late, Frankie. There was a dragon attack over on Fleet Street, I had to hide in Sumner Tunnel for two hours."

She turned to face Malone. "I assume you're here to rescue me, right?"

Malone groaned.

Frank laughed at Malone's surprise. "I told you she was okay, didn't I?"

Rachel Fischer was a younger version of her mother. Pretty, with an overly large mouth. Skinny, but heavy-breasted.

Unlike her mother, who made a point of dressing provocatively, Rachel was conservatively clad. She wore a grey trouser suit and cream blouse, and a cream scarf knotted under her chin.

In addition, she wore no makeup or jewelry.

She removed her scarf. Her brown hair was cut short and boyish.

Malone was surprised by how sterile Rachel Fischer looked. She gave him the same vibe one got from a hospital corridor as one smelt the disinfectant. Though she was undeniably good-looking, Malone found it impossible to imagine sex with her. What had her mother called her? Yes, a *neuter*. It was an apposite/accurate description.

Malone slowly came to terms with the fact that the woman he'd been sent to rescue had faked her own kidnapping.

What was it Yang Yang said? Ah yes, 'Danger—unexpected danger.' So fucking true. So now here I am, strapped down on a metal table, with my belly slit open; which can't be good.

He was particularly wary of the way Frank kept darting 'interested' looks at his guts.

Malone frowned at Rachel. "Your mother's very worried—"

"My mother is an outdated cunt," she snapped back. Her grey eyes smoldered. "A cunt too concerned with sex to realize that the times have changed. In this screwy age I'd have at least expected her to put her sex drive on hold."

She smiled, an expression that seemed forced upon her face. "I, however, have changed with the times, embraced them even. I've sublimated my sex drive—"

"According to your mother you *don't have* a sex drive."

She scowled. "Frank has opened my eyes to—"

"Okay, so you don't wish to be rescued," Malone interrupted again, "Can I leave now?"

"Surely not before dinner!?" Frank remarked testily. He looked inquisitively at Rachel.

She smiled her grim smile at him. "Of course not before dinner."

"Okay," Malone said. "I'll stay for dinner, but can I leave afterward?"

"Definitely not," Rachel retorted. She looked to Frank for approval. He nodded back.

Malone caught the exchange. "Okay, so you two are lovers."

"No," Rachel said coldly. "We're *not* lovers, we're just *work* partners." Malone thought he saw Frank wince when she said this, but he couldn't be certain.

"Sex disgusts me," Rachel continued. "It's nothing but the brutal animalistic fulfillment of violent instinctive drives. Science is my lover."

"Science is a whore," Frank said. "She fucks everyone is sight."

Rachel looked at him sharply. Then she smiled her creepy smile again. "I'll not dispute that. If science seems a whore, it's because most of those screwing her are men, who rape knowledge for their personal exaltation."

"You think women make better scientists?" Frank asked in something like exasperation.

"I sense disagreement in the ranks," Malone said.

"Yes," Rachel said.

Malone smiled. "So there is disagreement."

Rachel spun around and glowered at him. "I wasn't answering *you*. I was replying Frankie here, with his sexist view of intelligent women."

"I have nothing against intelligent women!" Frank thundered. He calmed himself. "My simple point, which I keep making to you, Rachel, is that most intelligent women *don't want to be* research scientists. Your sex is addicted to money. Making the world a better place doesn't pay as much as modeling, or being Mrs. Millionaire, or—"

Malone burst out laughing.

Rachel rounded on him, her eyes daggers. "Were you about saying something?"

Malone shook his head. "I can't think of what to say. While on the surface Frank's comments sound misogynistic, on a deeper level—"

Rachel silenced him with a wagging finger.

Malone shut up. She looked mad enough to kill him.

He suddenly realized why he was making such blithe conversation with his captors despite his dire straits—he'd been drugged.

That struck him as extremely funny. Frank and Rachel also struck him as insanely funny; they were an insanely funny insane pair.

Wow, he thought, *that's a good one.*

He burst out laughing: "Ha ha ha ha ha!"

Rachel misinterpreted his mirth to be mockery of her.

She smiled tightly back at him. "Oh, so you think women with brains are funny, eh? Just wait a bit; I'll show you what funny is."

"No, Rachel, he doesn't find female scientists funny," Frank said tiredly. "You, for instance, are definitely no comedienne." He smiled nervously. "Now please can we eat our fucking dinner?"

"Yes, Malone said. "I'm hungry too."

Rachel smiled evilly at Malone, "But of course, let's have dinner."

Malone wondered what she was suddenly so happy about.

***

He found out.

Rachel and Frank were cannibals.

"What the hell is that thing?" Malone asked as Rachel bent over it. Frank had meanwhile ambled out of Malone's view.

"It's a sectional microwave oven," Rachel replied.

"Microwave . . . ?" The horrible implications of what she'd said punched through his drug daze. Malone forced his head up and looked at the machine.

Still angry at him, Rachel held it up for his horrified inspection.

The machine's lowest portion was a series of transparent overlapping concave plates. These were currently clamped over the innermost lobe of Malone's liver.

Malone watched the clamped part of the organ turn dark-brown as it cooked.

"Fucking shit!" he shrieked, straining against his bonds. "Let me go, you psychopaths."

Frank's voice floated over. "Is he done yet?"

"Two more minutes." She smiled at Malone. "We're not eating all of you right now. Like I said—this microwave is *sectional*. It grills you in bits." She glorified in his horror. "My design," she added proudly.

"Fucking let me go!" Malone yelled, extremely alarmed now.

"Fat chance of that happening," Frank said, returning then. He was carrying a tray with plates, a bottle of white wine and goblets.

He set them down on his chair, then glanced into the microwave, licking his lips. "Surely it's ready now."

"Be patient, Frankie!" Rachel snapped. "You know I can't stand rare food."

Malone began bucking his midriff, attempting to dislodge the microwave. "Fucking let me go, you creeps!"

"And I," Frank retorted to Rachel with a pointed stare, "utterly cannot stand *noise* during dinner."

Rachel nodded. "Me neither. I'll take care of it." She gestured to Frank. "Watch the timer." She disappeared from Malone's view for a moment.

"I'm going to fucking kill both of you for this!" Malone screamed.

"We'll kill you first," Rachel said, reappearing. "You can't live without a liver. And we're eating *all* of yours."

She jabbed Malone in the neck with a hypo.

He instantly felt his aggravation dissolved in the drug dissolving in his bloodstream.

Suddenly everything seemed funny again.

The timer sounded. Rachel disconnected the microwave from Malone's belly, then raised his liver out of his body by placing a plastic stand under it.

Malone thought his liver looked funny, like a map of Australia, with the cooked part the province of New South Wales.

Rachel and Frank sat down beside Malone. Frank poured glasses of wine. The pair picked up forks and knives and tucked in.

"How'd you two become cannibals?" Malone asked, watching Rachel chew part of him.

"The food of the gods," Frank said. "You talk too much. Please be quiet."

Rachel swallowed. Malone watched the muscles of her throat move, ferrying his masticated meat to her stomach. "Human liver is packed full of nutrients," she said. "It's perfect for consumption in these dinosaur days."

"Why not just eat dino liver?"

Frank replied: "Stupid question. Have you ever tried killing one?"

Malone smirked. "I killed the ones you set up to kill me two nights ago. Nasty trick, that."

Frank shrugged. "You should have taken the hint and left us alone."

"How'd you find us anyway?" Rachel asked.

"A snake told me."

"You're just dumb," Rachel said. "You should have let mother pay the ransom. It's *my* money, anyway."

Malone was intrigued. "Then why steal it?"

"Because," Frank muttered around a mouthful of liver, "her father died without leaving a will, so his money all went to her mother." He swallowed, washed the meat down with a sip of wine.

Rachel spat. "He actually *did* make a will, but dragons torched his lawyer's office—"

"—With old Rosenberg in it," Frank added.

"—So everything went to mother. Which is fine, really, as we get along and she gives me all the money I need—"

"So *why?*"

Rachel looked pained. "Mother wants me to meet *men*, have a social life, get married, raise a family. I want *none* of that."

She said this last with emphatic fierceness. Now Malone was certain: Frank *had* winced. *Oh ho,* he realized, *Frank's in love with her.* He laughed inwardly, *and Miss Ice Princess Nerd here clearly isn't reciprocating his emotions.*

"Okay," Malone said. "But how come you need five million dollars to remain single?"

Rachel glowered at him. "Stop making smart cracks at my expense." She calmed herself, forking a chunk of Malone's liver into her mouth and chewing savagely on it. "I need the money for my . . ." she gestured to Frank, ". . . our research."

"What research?"

"Robots."

The coin dropped. Malone was so surprised, he forgot that Rachel Fischer and Frank were currently eating him. The humorous overtones haunting him dissolved.

"I saw the robots downstairs, and the one in the lab with its brain exposed. What the hell do you want with so many of them?"

Neither of his captors immediately replied. By now the cooked sector of Malone's liver was all gone. Frank poured two more glasses of wine, handed one to Rachel.

They sipped and regarded Malone.

"I'm waiting," Malone said. "What do you need two hundred New Korean robots for?"

Frank gave Rachel a questioning look.

She shrugged back. "Tell him. He won't *liver* long enough to tell anyone."

Malone winced at the pun. The pair laughed.

Frank smiled at Malone. She's right—you won't *liver* long enough to rat on us."

"Okay, so you're going to kill me. What's the big secret?"

"Simple," Frank replied. "We intend on taking over the country. The robots are our prospective army of conquest."

Malone was stunned. Had he not been im-mobilized, one could have knocked him down with a feather.

"Conquest?"

Rachel nodded. "That's what I needed money for—to buy more robots. And mother wouldn't give it to me. So Frankie came up with the kidnap idea."

CHAPTER 14

Posh

Posh waited impatiently till evening for her next shit. Then she did it, not in the toilet, but on a spread of old newspaper.

Once it was all out, she poked it with a coat hanger, separating the stinky chunks, till she found what she was after.

Ewwww, she thought.

Oswald Watkins' cockskin really was in her shit. It looked like a flesh condom, some poop had even gotten inside it.

Posh raised the cockskin on the hanger and stared at it for a long time.

And the freak wants me to come be his old lady, she thought. *And Herbie—my greedy bastard pimp—wants me to go back there.*

A vision of Oswald Watkin's skinned penis flashed before her eyes. She gagged, then puked on her excrement.

Posh packed puke and excrement up in a plastic bag, then threw the bag out of her window into the window of the almost full-grown skyscraper-beetle next door.

She sat on her bed to think.

She quickly made up her mind. *I'm done with Herbie for good. All he ever thinks about is payday, not the crap I have to go through to make his money. Thank heavens, Oswald's skin problem wasn't contagious. I'm quitting now, before Herbie puts me into a scene where I catch something dangerous.*

There was a problem however—Bulldog, Herbie's Neanderthal brother.

Posh knew that if she just upped and walked away from Herbie, Bulldog would simply come kicking down whoever's door she hid behind. He'd beat the shit out of that person and yank her back here.

And, oh fucking no, I'm not coming back here. When I'm gone, I'm gone for good.

She realized she needed to think her 'escape Herbie' plan through properly.

It had to be foolproof.

Thirty minutes of thinking brought Posh no solution. She decided to visit a bar for liquid inspiration.

She grabbed her purse and set off for Winthrop Square.

***

Jade Cure was sipping a Martini in Tony Motta's bar when Posh walked in. The pair knew each other from high school. They weren't friends, but most of their friends were dead anyway. Acquaintances were the new friends.

Their eyes met. Jade waved Posh over.

They kissed cheeks.

"What'll you have?" Jade asked.

Posh eyed her Martini. "Same as you."

Jade signaled over a waiter and placed the order.

"Been ages," she said after.

"Yeah," Posh replied. Though pleased to see Jade, the weight of her current worries dulled her enthusiasm.

Jade heard the stress in her voice. "You alright?"

Posh forced a smile. "More or less. Life is shit anyway, right?"

Jade raised an eyebrow. "Shit? Girl, I heard you'd moved up in the world."

"I'm about moving down and out," Posh said.

Her drink came then. Both young women were silent as Posh paid the waiter.

Posh decided to tell Jade her problem. "I'm in big trouble," she said miserably.

"What *sort* of trouble?" Jade asked Posh.

"I need to quit my pimp. But if I do, then his asshole brother is going to kill me."

Jade was shocked. "Girl, that's fucked up."

Posh nodded. She explained her plight in detail.

***

"I know someone who can help you," Jade said when she was done. Around them, bar chatter ebbed and waned.

Posh stared gloomily into her drink. "Forget it, the guy would just get killed. Even bulldogs are scared of Bulldog. Herbie's a spineless punk—even I can kick his ass—but Bulldog . . ."

"Trust me," Jade said. "This guy, Malone, will eat your bulldog for lunch."

Posh looked up from her glass. "For real? I mean Bulldog's a fucking monster."

Jade laughed. "So what's new?" She indicated Posh's glass: "Want another?"

Posh searched the Chinese girl's face for sign she was joking. But no, Jade seemed serious. Posh dared to believe she could swing her escape.

She waved away Jade's suggestion of a drink. "Not yet. Let me hear about this Malone. He sounds too good to be true. What is he? Ex-SWAT, ex-Marine?"

Jade shook her head. "Neither; that's the odd thing. He's a shamus, but Ma says he only took that up when life burnt down and he needed a job. Used to be a pencil pusher. From what Ma told me, he set up his detective agency because people kept saying they needed someone to locate their missing people."

Posh nodded. "Okay, so the guy's a badass—tough as rocks."

Jade shook her head emphatically. "Nope, he's smarter than he's tough. He's fast, but brains are his main advantage. Now, to your problem. Ma says—"

"How's your mum know so much about this guy anyway? They lovers?"

Jade winced. "I forget that you're a hooker. Sex is the only thing on your sleazy mind. Posh, my mother is two hundred years old. Malone is thirty-six . . . I think."

Posh was shocked. "Two hundred?"

Jade made a face. "Look, you want to hear about this or not? I remember you saying just now that your ass is on its way to getting killed."

Posh raised her hands in apology. "Sorry, I got carried away."

Jade finished her drink. "Now, how I know Malone *can* help you is this story my mother told me about what he did for *her* . . .

Uncle Lee's Golem: Part 1

"Do you know what a golem is?"

Posh wrinkled her nose and brow a bit. "That's like robots, right?"

Jade nodded. "Yeah, only they're made of meat. They're supernatural shit, magic."

Posh remembered that Jade's mother was some sort of Chinese witch. "Okay, I get you. You're saying your Ma made one of these golems?"

Jade shook her head. "No, not her. It was her brother, my Uncle Cheung Lee, who did." She laughed and signaled the waiter over again. "Look, let's have some more drinks."

When the waiter had departed with their orders, Jade continued. "Now you need to understand something." She peered intently at Posh, her slanted eyes mere slits. "Haven't you ever wondered why dragons never trouble Chinatown?"

Posh *still* wondered about that. "I always assumed they didn't like the taste of Asian meat."

Jade smirked. "You're close. But they eat the Japanese and Koreans don't they? But not us. It's because they're allergic to us. No, not in the usual sense, they won't drop dead after eating us, but, legend says that long ago in our history when both races were few in number, Chinese and dragon folk made a pact to help and protect each other."

Posh shook her head. "But that's ridiculous."

Jade smiled superiorly. "Not if you're Chinese. The point I'm making is they don't attack us; *not even if they're dead.*"

Posh gaped at the last statement.

The waiter placed fresh Martinis before them.

Posh took a sip of hers, then asked the obvious question: "How the hell can a dragon attack you if it's *dead*?"

"I'm coming to that," Jade said. "It's easy. They can be made into golems." She shrugged. "You reshape dead dragon meat into human shape and animate it with magic. The problem with that is—the golem, being made from dragon meat, won't attack a Chinese."

Posh nodded. "Okay, I've got that, but I'm still confused."

"You won't be much longer. That's just background. Remember I mentioned that my uncle Cheung Lee made a golem?"

"Yeah?"

"Okay, time to tell you *why* he made it." She looked around the bar, regarded the asses of a pair of guys shooting pool for a moment.

She turned her attention back to Posh. "We've a magical heirloom in our family. It's a frozen goddess—a half woman, half snake statue."

"Magical?" Posh was growing skeptical with all this talk of the supernatural.

Jade nodded. "Oh yeah, it's magical all right. You wouldn't believe the stuff it does. The problem is, everyone in our family wants it. My Ma has it by right, being the eldest, but that doesn't stop her sisters and brothers scheming to steal it away from her."

She laughed. "Ma's always been a step ahead of them though. That was, until Uncle Lee came up with his idea of making a golem."

Posh thought a bit. "I don't see how that would be difficult to deal with. You just said the monster wouldn't attack anyone Chinese."

Jade laughed out loud, causing some bar patrons to glance their way. "Oh, but he didn't make it of dragon meat," she said, flicking her hair away from her face. "He made it from *dinosaur* meat."

She laughed again at Posh's surprise. "That's right. Uncle Lee camouflaged the golem so it looked like it was made of dragon meat, but it wasn't. I was out when it attacked our home. According to Ma, she kept invoking the old human/dragon truce spells, but none of them worked. The meat machine knocked her aside, picked up the statue and made off with it."

"Wow."

"'Wow' is right. Ma said she chased after it with another family heirloom 'The Dead God's Sword,' which cuts through just about anything. No matter how hard she slashed the golem however, the sword made no impression on it. It just knocked her down again, this time knocking her out cold. She woke with a banging headache."

Jade stopped talking on catching the eye of one of the pool players. Handsome, blond hair, with a short mustache. He grinned back at her, then surreptitiously tapped his partner's ass and winked.

Jade immediately got the point. "Wow," she groaned. "What a waste of dick."

"Huh?"

She remembered she was talking to Posh. "Oh nothing, just thinking aloud, about Richard, a guy I once knew who was playing on the wrong football team."

Posh looked confused.

Jade smiled. "Now where was I? Okay, Now Ma knew immediately that Uncle Lee had stolen the statue. She confronted him and he didn't deny it. She even saw the golem there."

She sipped her drink. "Ma's a small woman, but a hardheaded one. She raised a fuss. Uncle Lee had the golem remove her from the premises. It didn't harm her,—apparently he'd told it not to, he was her brother after all—just lifted her up like a kid and dropped outside the gate in front of passersby. Ma was so mad and embarrassed, she burst into tears."

Posh giggled. "I'd be mad and embarrassed too."

Jade nodded. "Now, Ma doesn't want to give up, but she's got no choice—she has no idea how to build her own golem from dinosaur meat, see? Then someone recommended Malone to her."

She paused. "Go on," Posh prompted.

"Ma says she was unimpressed when she met Malone, but his office had a sign outside saying it would take on any job, no matter how weird. So she told him her problem. He told her not to worry and asked her where Uncle Lee's place was. She takes him there, he goes inside. There's the sound of loud crashing and banging, and ten minutes later Malone comes out with the Snake Lady statue."

"Wow!" Posh was impressed. "How the fuck did he do that?"

"How else? He fought the golem and defeated it. When people entered the house later, they found bits of the creature everywhere."

Jade's face became solemn. "Unfortunately, Uncle Lee died during the battle too—the golem turned on him before it expired."

She smiled coldly. "Now to the point of my tale. After that, news got around, not just in Chinatown, but the rest of Boston as well—you don't mess with Malone." She stared pointedly at Posh: "You get my point here?"

Posh nodded. "I think so."

Jade pushed her point. "You hook your ass up with Malone, neither your pimp nor his doggy brother gonna DARE bother your ass ever after."

"Hmmm," Posh said. "The question is, *how?*"

Jade looked at her in surprise. "Girl, you're a hooker, aren't you? How *fucking* else?"

Posh rolled her eyes. "You know where I can find him now?"

"Come home with me. Ma will have his address. He was at our place yesterday. Some rich heiress kidnapping case he's working on. He should be back home by now."

Posh nodded. They got up.

"Hold on a minute," Jade said.

Posh waited while Jade sashayed over to the bar and chatted up the bartender, a handsome dark Brazilian.

She came back beaming. "Romantic life's looking up," she said. "Got a date with Mario at eight to-morrow night!"

They left the bar together and headed for China-town Park.

***

Posh pulled up at Malone's house at a quarter to midnight.

In addition to taking Herbie's pimpmobile, she'd also taken three-quarters of the money he kept in his shoebox 'safe.' *She'd* earned it after all. She'd drop the car off later somewhere where he'd find it easy.

All her belongings were in the trunk. There wasn't much: Some clothes and shoes, cosmetics, and a photo album.

Leaving had been easy. It was Friday night—Herbie was out partying with friends. She'd had excused herself from the revelry, claiming period cramps.

Posh sat in the darkened Lincoln for a long time, gazing at the bungalow with its faded 'BUD MALONE: PRIVATE INVESTIGATOR' sign.

So this is the place. It struck her as odd that her potential savior would reside in such a nondescript, inconsequential building.

While driving over, she'd changed her mind on one detail: She wasn't going to try and seduce Malone into helping her. Oh, no. If this guy was as badass as Jade said, he was certain to have loads of women.

An offer of one more pussy would make very little difference.

Posh planned to *hire* Malone. This was part of the reason she'd taken the money. Her story would be simple: She was being targeted by a serial killer called 'The Bulldog' and needed his protection.

(Simple lies were the most effective.)

Posh was conscious of the fact that she was vulnerable out here in the open. Joy Street was a mile west of The Grid. It wasn't wise sitting in a car with hungry dinos on the prowl. And Herbie could never afford repulsors.

Damn, he hadn't even *bought* the fucking car—he'd stolen the Lincoln out of a dealer's display window. It had been the only vehicle in the showroom not burnt up.

True, it was pretty. Security, however, it wasn't. A raptor would open this pimpmobile up like it was a sardine can.

She got out of the car.

"Well this is it," she said, "I'm in, sink or swim."

She was immensely angered when she rang the doorbell several times and got no answer.

He isn't home? Okay, now this isn't going according to plan.

She looked back to the street, at the car she'd assumed was Malone's ride. She winced on realizing that its tires were all deflated.

Malone not being immediately available was the one thing Posh hadn't calculated. Jade had said he should be back home now hadn't she? *Shee-it!*

She considered her dilemma. *I can still make it back to Herbie's before he notices I'm gone. Fuck that! I'm not going back.* She glanced again at the unwelcoming front door. *I've come too far to turn back.*

I've burnt my bridges.

She waited an hour, growing increasingly worried by the crystal rainbow flashes—like celestial chandeliers hung from the moon—that indicated dragons in the distant night sky.

Don't you dare fly this way, she thought nervously, *I'm not fucking Chinese.*

Also, every moment she waited increased the danger of dinos discovering her.

In the end, Posh broke into the house. When Malone didn't show by 2a.m., she forced the kitchen window open and humped her luggage in through it. She climbed in herself, put the lights on and dragged her stuff through the house to his bedroom.

He'll meet me here when he gets home, she decided. *If anything, it'll strengthen my story.*

She flopped down on his bed. *Hey, Malone, say hi to your new permanent housemate.* She sniffed the pillows, savoring their manly musk. *Okay, and where the fuck are you anyway?*

CHAPTER 15

Malone: Next Evening

"You know it can't work, don't you?"

"It will. Don't you dare doubt it."

Malone was talking to Rachel Fischer, who was holding a bedpan under his buttocks so he could shit.

Ordinarily, the situation would have caused him extreme embarrassment. Now, however, no. Combined with the drugs in his system, Rachel Fischer had so much of the antiseptic quality of the nurse about her that Malone felt he was in hospital.

Staring at her face, he wondered how it was possible for a pretty woman to be so sexless. *I mean, even nuns look desirable.*

But no, Rachel Fischer somehow negated sexuality.

Malone finished his poop. Rachel wiped his backside and pointed to his penis. Do you need to urinate?"

He nodded.

She took hold of his penis, directing it into the pan. Again with total disregard that she was holding his most prized possession.

He looked into the red crater of his belly, at his truncated liver. Yes, this antiseptic woman and her partner really were eating him. Their sectional microwave lay on the table beside him. Its transparent plates looked like huge housefly wings.

He'd now discovered that the procedure of cooking his liver was more complicated than simply just connecting the microwave oven to it. To ensure he didn't bleed to death, Rachel had first painstakingly severed and clamped/stitched up the blood vessels supplying the lobes they'd eaten.

Malone winced. *Yeah, they're keeping me alive so they can kill me. And I'm tied down here and helpless.*

And horribly, the idea struck him as hilarious. He'd however now begun fighting the dangerous impulse to laugh at the danger he was in. He had to find a way to escape these two sickos.

He finished peeing. Rachel put the bedpan on the floor

"This is Frank's idea, isn't it? He's got you thinking—"

Rachel snorted. "Aha, male chauvinism strikes again! It's my idea, you fool; I sold it to Frank as a way of ensuring our liver supply never runs out."

"It's an impossible dream."

She stood back from him, hands defiantly on hips. "Not with enough robots, it isn't. They're not scared of tackling the dragons and dinos. Once the fear element is removed from the equation, the rest is easy. Everything's already so messed up, any sort of authority will be welcomed."

Malone realized she was right. With enough robots, she could take over the country. But her and Psycho Frank as US presidents? And both already with a liver-consumption agenda?

"I still say it won't work," he said.

She smirked. "You know you're lying."

She ran fingers through her cropped brown hair, her grey eyes losing focus with her reflection. "All that previously stood in our way was making the robots more intelligent than they leave the factory in New Korea. The machines we're buying are household and medical models—the New Koreans won't sell military robots to anyone except governments. So I've been reprogramming them, giving them battle incentive, weapons-handling skills, and knowledge of tactics."

She smiled proudly. "The machines come with loads of fail safes built in to prevent them harming their owners. But I got rid of those. You wouldn't believe how much re-coding that took."

Seeing Rachel's satisfied smile, Malone was convinced she and Frank would succeed in their plan of conquest.

"Where's Frank?" he asked.

"Out looking for someone else to kidnap."

Malone flinched.

Rachel shrugged. "Your fault."

Malone nodded. "Actually it's your loving mama's fault."

"Huh?"

"Sorry, just thinking aloud. Hold on a moment. You two have obviously been planning this for a while. How many robots you got?"

Rachel frowned. "Still thinking of escaping and warning everyone, are you?" She smiled. "No reason not to tell you—you aren't leaving here alive."

"Spare me the reminder. So, how many?"

She frowned again. "Not enough. I've three hundred robots programmed, and six hundred more in the warehouse. I need two thousand more."

"So why this kidnapping spree? Why not just rob a bank? You've got the soldiers for it."

She shook her head. "Uh uh, I see what you're trying to make us . . . me . . . do. You're smart, Malone, I'll give you that, but I'm smarter, *much* smarter—"

"I wasn't saying that you—"

"—You're trying to make us show our hand, right? Get into a bank shootout between robots and guards? Sure, we'll get away with the money, but the word will then be out about the robots. Our Korean shippers won't supply us any more machines once they know we're using them for criminal activities, and also human authorities will be alert to their existence."

She smiled coldly at Malone. "Sorry, buddy, but I saw that one coming."

Malone was stumped. He'd not considered those consequences. Rachel Fischer clearly thought like a chess player—several moves ahead of the opposition.

"It just seemed a more hassle-free way to make a dishonest dollar," he said.

"Sure," Rachel said. "Sure."

Frank returned then.

"Hey," he called from the lab doorway, "What's for dinner, honey?"

"Male chauvinist pig," Rachel mouthed at Malone. "Shithead believes a woman's place is in the kitchen."

She then turned and smiled sweetly at her partner. "Well I got some liver for you, Frankie, if you want it?"

She turned her face away from the kiss he tried planting on it. Frank's face clouded over, then he smiled and peeked into Malone's gaping belly. "But of course. Let's have some liver."

"Just a minute then, we don't want to eat with Malone's poop around, do we?"

Frank noted the bedpan for the first time. He wrinkled his nose in disgust. "Oh no, we don't."

When Rachel had left with the bedpan, Malone said conspiratorially to Frank: "You know, you'd get a lot further with Miss Frigid there if you just ignore her."

Frank gaped at Malone. "Huh?"

Malone nodded. "True. Girls like Rachel, their biggest fear is being alone in the world. She's been pampered and fawned on all her life, so now she feels she's too good for anyone. Once you stop minding her, however, she'll start inventing lots of little ways to make you notice her again."

Frank sniffed. He made no reply, just pointedly stared at Malone's liver. When, after a while he sniffed louder, Malone realized he was crying.

CHAPTER 16

Malone

The next morning, Rachel Fischer was visibly pissed off. Her normally strained expression was even more so. Her generous mouth was compressed like an oversized raisin. If Malone didn't know her better, he'd have thought her sexually frustrated.

"What's the matter?" he asked. "Something about last night's dinner didn't agree with you?"

Rachel glowered at him. She considered the scalpel in her hand for a long time before replying. Malone began worrying that she might stab him with it to let off tension.

"It's that jerk Frankie," she finally said. "He's refusing to talk to me."

Malone hid a smile. So Frank had taken his advice. "What happened?" he asked.

"Nothing. It's just everything he's been doing this morning. It's like I'm not even there."

"Guy's having a bad day. Happens sometimes."

"She looked at him curiously, like she'd not considered that possibility. "You think so?"

"Either that or he's fallen in love and the lady isn't requiting his romantic advances."

Rachel spat. On Malone's exposed guts. "It has to be that. Typical male behavior."

"Don't spit inside me please." It hurt Malone to even look inside himself. His liver was three-quarters gone now. He had no idea if he was particularly delicious, or if they'd both just been extra-hungry last night, but they'd eaten twice as much of him as they'd set out to, while all the while Frank kept lamenting on the shortage of abductable heiresses.

Malone had heard that given enough time, a liver would regenerate itself. But not from scratch. And tonight was D-Day as far as his liver was concerned. He had to escape inside today or he was fucked up the ass with a baseball bat. That and dead.

Rachel spat inside Malone again.

"You're acting like you're knocked up," Malone said spitefully. "What's so odd about Frank getting a girl? Are you jealous?"

Rachel was pole axed by the suggestion. "Me? Why the hell would I be jealous?"

"Dunno, maybe you have feelings for him too?"

She laughed. "Feelings? I deal in the beauty of logic, Malone, mathematics is my . . . did you say 'too'?"

Malone nodded.

Rachel was disgusted. Phlegm pooled in her mouth. She spat inside Malone again. "How *dare* you imply that Frank is in love with *me*?"

Malone said. "Because the psycho *is* in love with you."

That pulled Rachel up cold. "Love? You're *serious*?"

Malone nodded. "He worships the very liver you eat together."

Rachel turned six shades of pale. Her breathing became irregular. Her breasts rose and fell rapidly.

She scowled at Malone. "Frankie doesn't love *me*. He loves a *concept*, an idea called a 'wife.' Frankie just wants a piece of property to claim ownership to. He wants to *marry* me . . . keep me pregnant and barefoot. But I'm wise to him."

But her words were unsure. Her protest wasn't angry, it was confused and scared. Terrified. Like she'd just run into the lair of all the horrors she'd fled from all her life.

Rachel Fischer was facing a crisis of similar magnitude to that of the atheist who awoke one morning to the undeniable knowledge that *he* was God in the flesh.

Her tortured emotions swirled around her face, rippling her skin like worms writhing beneath it.

"No!" she moaned. "No!"

Malone pitied her.

"Rachel, it isn't wrong to have sex and get married, you know. It didn't hurt your parents none."

She glared at him but didn't reply.

Malone prayed she wouldn't start crying like Frank had yesternight. Even doped, it was pathetic to be comforting people busy killing you.

He replaced this minor worry with a MAJOR one. Rachel had just picked up a circular saw. She switched it on.

"What do you plan on doing with that?" he asked.

She frowned. "It's for removing your brain tomorrow during your autopsy."

She spoke calmly now, coldly enunciating her words precisely and without emotion. There was no longer any sign of the flustered woman of mere seconds ago. She was now clearly in perfect control of herself again. A sexless machine.

Malone was scared by the suddenness of the change in her.

She's as bad as Frank, he realized. *As fucked in the head as he is, but in a different way. Nobody should be able to turn their feelings off like she's just done. It's a good thing she doesn't like bedroom athletics—she and Frank must never soil the world with any offspring.*

***

Rachel Fischer *was* still flustered by Malone's comment.

She hid it well, however, exerting iron self-control born of years of practice at repressing her feelings.

Science was all important.

A momentary vision of herself in a lip-lock with Frank, then of the pair of them in bed, their bodies joined like dogs, sliding over each other . . . *Fucking.* And then that horrible messy disentanglement—semen like baby puke pouring from her ugly, disgusting, animal hole . . . the sloppy, grotesque, cunt . . .

Disgust flooded Rachel. The vomit rushed up her throat.

She controlled herself from puking into Malone. Frank would be incensed if she flavored their dinner.

"I'll be back," she spat at Malone. Then she ran off to the toilet to vomit.

In her physical distress, Rachel forgot a scalpel inside Malone's belly.

***

The possibility of escape cut into Malone's drug-addled mind.

By straining against the restraining cord till his wrist skin chafed off, he got fingertips to the scalpel.

The rest was easy. He reversed his grip on the surgical knife and cut the hand free. Working quickly, he freed his other wrist. Then, still viewing his current dire situation as the funniest practical joke ever played, he waited for Rachel's return.

***

Rachel returned. She held a syringe over Malone.

"What's that?" he asked. He'd re-draped the cord over his wrist so he appeared still bound. The scalpel was covered by his palm.

She frowned down at him. "More happy serum to shut you up. You talk too much—gives me a headache."

She bent over to jab him with the hypo.

Malone grabbed her hair with his left hand and pulled her across his body. While Rachel floundered off balance in confusion, he pricked her in the throat with the scalpel.

"Don't resist, or I'll kill you."

In response, Rachel stabbed him in the side with the hypo and depressed the plunger. She twisted her head in his grip to stare at him. Her eyes were cold and relentless, merciless as a car crash.

"You aren't screwing up our plans, Malone."

He winced as he felt the drug force itself into him.

He realized he had to stop Rachel before she pumped him full of the happy serum, and danger once again seemed hilarious to him.

That meant killing her.

That decision taken, he acted fast. Yanking her head down into his open belly, Malone coldly slit Rachel's throat, slicing it deep and across in a swift motion.

There was the momentary futile resistance of meat meeting surgical steel, then Rachel's neck yawned open wide as a raptor's jaws. The floodgates of her lifeblood broke and blood spurted everywhere.

She instantly let go the syringe. The ingress of liquid into Malone's side stopped abruptly.

Malone quickly dropped the scalpel. He pulled the hypo of his chest, and flung it away.

Then with both hands, he held Rachel's head down amidst his guts, both smothering her with his intestines and drowning her in her own blood.

She thrashed furiously, arms beating against him, fighting to break free. She glugged and spluttered. Blood and guts muffled her attempted screams. Malone imagined he felt her biting him in her desperate attempt to not die. His abdomen filled with blood that overflowed—Rachel's crimson effluent spilling over onto table and floor.

She forced her head out of the blood once, to stare at him.

Her face was a liquid Venetian mask, her eyes crimson lakes, sightless red pools that somehow still reflected her stupefaction.

She stopped fighting. Malone let go of her body. It slumped.

Rachel's head slurped out of his body, the sound like a dog lapping, like a penis 'sucking' out of a vagina.

She crumpled dead onto the slickly red floor.

Malone collapsed back, breathing heavily.

He now realized that Rachel had lied about the syringe's contents—it wasn't the happy serum. This—whatever it was—was designed to incapacitate him.

He felt strange—distant from himself. Weak in a way that transcended his flesh.

The adrenalin rush from his struggle with Rachel was however countering the drug's attempts to cloud his thinking. He fought to clear his mind further.

He glanced at the fallen syringe—still half-full of yellow liquid. He was relieved Rachel hadn't pumped him with the full dose of whatever that was. Half was bad enough.

He finally looked at Rachel, lying on the floor with the huge red gash in her neck.

Malone hated having to kill her, but it was either his life or hers. And he still wasn't out of the woods yet.

There was still Frank, Rachel's besotted partner to contend with.

Frank was out now, once again seeking a kidnappable heiress.

Malone needed to be well away from here before Frank got back. He was in no condition to single-handedly take on Rachel's co-psychopath.

Ha ha, he thought, *I don't have the stomach . . . no, the liver, for conflict at the moment.*

Try as he might, he couldn't find the joke funny.

Okay, time to go, he thought.

He sat up and cut his feet free, then swung them down onto the floor. He took care not to slip on the blood sloshing out of him like water from an overfilled bathtub.

He had no idea where either his clothes or shoes were.

Fuck 'em, he thought. *My underpants will do. They're original Yves St. Laurent's. I'll never have a better chance to show 'em off.*

He however found a blaster on a side table.

Gun in hand, Malone paused at the lab door and looked back over the room. Rachel lay like a broken red doll, which his addled mind found interesting.

He remembered something.

"Her mother asked me to bring her back," he said aloud. "But that's impossible—she's dead weight, and I can hardly carry myself."

He decided on a compromise.

Vaguely aware that he was thinking odd and behaving irrationally, Malone nonetheless knelt in the blood pool surrounding Rachel, and used her circular saw to cut off her head.

While dividing flesh from flesh, his thoughts whirred in his head, as blurred as the tool he wielded. His brain seemed itself to be spinning, twisting his perception as it rotated.

Confusion threatened to overwhelm him at any second. His resistance to it pushed him to the limits of his sanity, then temporarily beyond it.

For those moments, the spinning metal saw became his truth, his reality the bits of spine and flesh it splattered his already messy body with.

He took it all in his stride, in this strange place he existed now, his zone of not-quite-insanity.

Rachel's head separated from her body.

Malone stood, sawn-off-head in hand, staring down at the rest of her.

"Your mum will have to make do with getting just this much of you back," he told Rachel's head. "Frank can have the rest."

He mused a while, then added: "He's certain to eat your liver in mourning. But he *loves* you, so maybe—if you're lucky—he'll screw your corpse too. Sex after death is better than none at all."

He had a brief moment of perfect mental clarity.

I'm thinking consolidated nonsense, he thought.

Then the drug haze refilled his brain and nonsense made sense again.

Carrying his gory trophy by its hair, Malone turned and stumbled out of the lab.

***

Emerging, he discovered he'd been incarcerated in one of the warehouse's upper cabins. Leaving a trail of bloody footprints, he tramped down the metal staircase to the ground level.

Downstairs, another delivery of robots was in progress, with the same pair of Korean delivery men rolling coffin-shaped boxes across the warehouse on hand trucks.

Both men pulled up dead in their tracks when they sighted Malone shuffling towards them.

Malone held up Rachel's head so they could see it. He waved his gun at them.

The Koreans gaped at him. One of them pointed to his ripped-open abdomen, from which blood still dribbled down into his crotch. "You need a doctor, man."

"Just don't fuck with me," Malone retorted and walked past them.

***

It was about noon.

Malone trudged down Commercial Street, across John Fitzgerald Expressway, and under The Grid. Once under dragon-proof cover again, he set off south.

He was headed for Chinatown Park, to Ma Cure's place. Ma would be able to fix him up.

With luck, and assuming he didn't keel over from pure exhaustion, or run mad from the chemicals fighting to subdue his will, he'd get to Ma's pagoda by nightfall.

His mind was fuzzy, he didn't trust himself to not crash a car if he hotwired one—assuming he could find one that worked.

Naked except for his briefs, carrying Rachel Fischer's severed head in plain view, belly yawning open, and so smeared in blood that he looked painted red, Malone shambled through the city.

The few people he encountered got out of his way in a hurry. The few of those that he knew added this current incident to his legend.

***

The blood on Malone attracted a single incident of dino attention.

It happened in Faneuil Hall Marketplace—an area with a profusion of skyscrapers and condos. The buildings had been laid through The Grid, shattering the wiven shield in places, creating too many haphazard spaces for the grid-repair crews to effectively patch.

Past the North Market, a solitary pterodactyl launched itself from atop Quincy Market and swooped at Malone, thinking he was easy pickings.

Malone fried the dino-bird with a blaster bolt.

He ducked. Its burning body flew over him to crash into the road behind.

He looked back disinterestedly. The pterodactyl lay on its back, kicking and flapping in agony as it burnt. Several mangy dogs already waited impatiently for it to finish roasting so they could tuck in.

"Stupid bird." Malone turned away again.

He lifted Rachel's head and smiled at it. "I wonder what your super-hot mama's getting up to now?" he said.

CHAPTER 17

Sara

The humming came again. This was what Sara Fischer *really* disliked about the Forks—their humming. Most of the time it was subliminal and she could ignore it, but at times like now, when they were feeding? It rose to a crescendo, an orchestra of tuning forks. An irritating atonal wall of sound.

(Though honestly, Sara couldn't really call it *atonal*—Forks never hummed in dissonance, it was more a barrage of irreconcilable pleasances.)

And over the humming was the sound of an animal in incredible pain.

Sara grimaced. She'd been napping, but the noise had woken her and would make further sleep impossible.

She got out of bed and walked over to her window to watch the Forks feed.

A solitary terrified tyrannosaur was their lunch. The hapless reptile stood paralyzed by both fear and the Fork's mental powers while they ate it.

***

Forks were just that. Human-sized kitchen cutlery now blessed/cursed with semi-divine powers. The other name for them was 'kitchen gods.'

Like ordinary cutlery, Forks came in different compositions, depending on social status. Their aristocracy were gold. Most others were silverware. Then there were the tin and plastic servant categories.

Their normal position was prong-upward, with their 'handle' end floating a foot above the floor.

They had no hands or feet or facial/speech organs—their voices resonated from them like sound through water.

While male Forks were totally featureless, female Forks had breasts like human females. These hung in relatively human position, two thirds of the way up their bodies, just below the base of their prongs.

Forks fed by inverting themselves onto meat—'pronging' it— and then absorbing it into themselves. They were indiscriminate eaters, feeding even on human flesh if there was nothing else available, and not being too particular if the provider was dead or still alive and unwilling to donate him/herself.

As far as anyone could determine, Forks were indestructible, which, taken with their omnivorousness, made them extremely dangerous. Though they rarely attacked humans unprovoked, everyone generally kept their distance from them.

Most people—Sara included—regarded Forks with concealed disgust.

Forks were generally considered the de-facto rulers of Earth, if only because there was no other species—definitely not man or the dinos, or even the dreaded dragons—capable of mounting any sort of challenge to their powers, such as they'd so far chosen to exhibit.

***

Poised like they were being held by giant hands, the Forks on Sara's lawn stabbed themselves into the tyrannosaur and dissolved its flesh away, absorbing it as they sank deeper into its body.

Sara counted sixteen Forks pronging the hapless dino.

The creature was mostly a mass of huge craters now.

It shrieked loudly. It realized that it was dying, and also that nothing it could do would alter that fact.

Sara shuddered. *It looks like someone's taking scoops out of it with a monster spoon.*

The pronging process was doubly horrible because there was no bleeding—the Forks instantly absorbed all the blood their victim produced.

***

The tyrannosaur gave a piteous shriek and died. Its corpse remained standing, held upright by Fork psychokinesis.

A gold Fork tunneled all the way through its body, leaving a circular tunnel with shreds of meat dangling from its ceiling.

Sara was revolted and horrified. She turned away.

What scared Sara wasn't the Forks feeding. No, it was the morbid parable that the animal they were eating represented.

T-Rex—the tyrant lizard—was the alpha dino, the creature everyone feared.

Shit, even the fucking dragons treated it with respect. It was a creature that asked no quarter, gave no quarter. Was believed incapable of fear.

If T-Rex, however, shrieked like a whipped puppy from dread of the kitchen gods, what hope did humanity have?

She shut her drapes on the feeding scene, forced her mind onto other thoughts.

How was Malone doing with rescuing Rachel?

There was a knock on the bedroom door.

"Yes?"

"It's Jeff."

Sara immediately brightened up. The one good thing that had happened with the kitchen gods arriving at her house was that they'd brought US President Jefferson Lincoln with them.

The knock came again. "Sara, are you in there?"

She quickly checked herself in her wall mirror. She looked okay. Jeff wouldn't notice anyway.

Her heart beating like a schoolgirl on her first date, Sara let Jeff Lincoln in.

***

Jefferson Meredith Lincoln III was tall and beefy. He was handsome, with bright blue eyes and a face that had aged well. He was sixty-four years old, Sara's age, and both his hair and mustache were now greyer than their original black.

Jefferson Lincoln, 48th President of the United States of America, was currently a prisoner of the Forks.

Two nights ago, when Sara had arrived home from her abortive attempt to ransom Rachel, she'd found a contingent of Forks waiting in her living room.

Sara had accepted their presence in her home with equanimity. She couldn't exactly shoo them away. They were simply a fact of modern life.

Sara had been shocked to see Jeff with the Forks. He'd been just as surprised to see her.

The pair had rushed at each other and embraced.

"The President mentioned that he knew you," Lord Tav said, while they kissed and wept. "We thought you might like to get reacquainted."

Later, Lord Tav and Lady Yaz—the Fork heads—had told Sara in private *why* they'd brought the ex-president to her. "He is incredibly depressed. Please try to cheer him up. We'll be *very* grateful if you do."

As Jeff had explained it to Sara. "I'm their symbol that they're running things now."

He'd shrugged. "It's a challenge too. Like, if *they're* not in charge, whoever *is* should come rescue me."

CHAPTER 18

Jeff

Forty years ago, Jefferson Lincoln and Sara Goldman had been college sweethearts.

Both political science majors, they'd planned to get married after graduation.

But then, Jeff, who'd graduated first, had joined the army and had been shipped to a base in Okinawa, Japan. Sara, still with two years of school to go, hadn't been able to follow him.

Those two years had been long enough for her to meet and marry David Fischer.

Jeff had taken Sara's dumping him badly. After two suicide attempts (which his parents hushed up), he received a honorable discharge from the army.

Jeff was however still emotionally traumatized.

His parents immediately rushed into looking for a woman to replace Sara in his affections. They hosted an endless series of parties, inviting all their friends' daughters.

They were relieved when their son fell for Stacy Levin, daughter of Senior Senator from Michigan Martin Levin.

Immediately after the wedding, Senator Levin hired Jeff as his re-election campaign manager.

Jeff, reinvigorated by his new wife, put all his energy into the election fight. His father-in-law was re-elected by a landslide.

When Senator Levin returned to Washington, he took Jeff with him.

That was Jeff's start in politics.

By putting one careful foot after another, thirty-four years later Jeff was sworn in as president of the USA.

Washington Burning. July31st, 2026 AD

Jeff had lost his entire family in the attacks that had destroyed civilization.

He still had nightmares in which he saw his daughter Chelsea (who'd been visiting Washington then), reaching out a bloody hand towards him, her body crushed under a collapsed East Wing wall. "Dad, promise me you'll look after Derek and Jason for me."

Jeff, his world reeling around him, had promised.

Then a dragon had smashed through the adjacent wall. Jeff's bodyguards had rushed him out of the room just as falling masonry totally obliterated his daughter from view.

Jeff had never found his grandchildren.

Seared into his mind was his vision—as the helicopter conveyed him and his wife, First Lady Stacy Lincoln, to safety—of the White House imploding in on itself as a horde of fiberglass reptiles bathed it in flame and rammed their bulks against its stone.

What remained there now looked like Stonehenge.

***

They'd flown to Joint Base Andrews, Maryland, through a world gone mad. The sky was filled with living, solid rainbows spurting fire and eating roast corpses. Down in the streets, extinct reptiles smashed into houses and pulled out people for food.

And those starship-sized black things overhead; were they really beetles?

Jeff's plan was to get airborne in Air Force One, establish communications with military bases around the country, and mount a counterattack against the reptile invasion.

They met Andrews Air Force base demolished on their arrival. Everywhere lay the half-eaten corpses of pilots and ground crew, strewn between dead dinosaurs and the wreckage of F-16 fighter jets and choppers destroyed before takeoff.

Attacked by a spinosaurus, a taxiing C12 Huron had veered off the runway and crashed into the first of three parked Stratotankers. Both dinosaur and refueling aircraft had erupted into a humongous blaze that engulfed the base's administrative buildings. The raging inferno turned nighttime to day, leaping be-tween buildings like it was alive.

Allosaurs and raptors stalked the carnage like marines seeking enemy troops. Most had blood-dripping human parts in their mouths.

Jeff surveyed the destruction in disbelief. To their right as they landed was an upside-down Bell Twin Huey helicopter. Balanced on its propeller, it looked like a one-legged metal chicken. Black smoke streamed from its inverted underbelly.

The Huey's dead crew hung out of its sides. Two still-living passengers screamed as a mob of raptors ripped them apart.

Heart in mouth, Jeff's eyes scanned the base for the pair of presidential jets.

He saw them—neither would ever fly again.

One Air Force One lay on its back, wheels up in the air. The rear half of its fuselage was a melted silver puddle. The second Boeing VC-25 was burning fiercely. It exploded as the choppers landed.

Whilst refueling, they were attacked by tyrannosaurs.

Six of their eight choppers were destroyed.

Jeff's and one other helicopter—that ferrying Secretary of State Isabel Harris—had managed to take off.

The sky around them as they fled the airbase was full of pterodactyls.

With ravenous pterodactyls hot in pursuit, they headed south, to Langley Air Base in Hampton, Virginia.

"It's like a dinosaur version of Armageddon," Stacy whispered in horror, as their pilot swooped the helicopter between the pursuing, harrying swarms of reptile birds, "Where did they all come from?"

Tears filled her green eyes, eyes evocative of the skin color of the reptiles milling around them. Her previously impeccable mascara was dissolved into black streaks on her cheeks. Her silver hair was a total mess.

Jeff was extremely worried about his wife. She had a weak heart, had just recently had open heart surgery. This was stress she didn't need.

Thirty miles south of D.C., flying over Gilbert Run Regional Park, both helicopters were finally caught in a pterodactyl ambush.

Isabel Harris's chopper plummeted like a bomb when several dino-birds got wedged into the propeller assemblage and jammed it.

As her helicopter fell, Jeff saw Isabel staring up at him, her disbelief paralyzing her ability to scream. Then the helicopter was obliterated from view by the sheer number of reptiles dive-bombing after it.

The pterodactyls had forgotten Jeff's helicopter once they'd disabled Isabel's.

The reptile birds had however already damaged the presidential chopper. Fuel was spurting from bite punctures in the fuel tanks.

"We have to land in these woods, sir!" the pilot yelled. "We risk an explosion if we keep flying!"

"Take us down!" Jeff yelled back.

The pilot landed the whirlybird safely and they disembarked.

In addition to Jeff, Stacy, and the pilot, two others had made it alive out of Washington. These were Jeff's head of security Mike Morris, and a bodyguard.

The five survivors had tramped through the park till they'd found an old log cabin where they spent the night.

***

The next morning, Jeff and Stacy had been woken by the sound of gunfire.

Stacy stared wide-eyed at Jeff. "What the hell?"

He leapt up and rushed to the window. Their cabin was surrounded by dinos. T-Rex's, giganotosaurs, raptors, and even species that Jeff had never associated with violence—triceratops, hadrosaurs, brachiosaurs, stegosaurs—all stared pointedly at the cabin. Further back he saw dragons.

"Jeff, What are those glittering things?" Stacy asked.

Jeff looked around, startled. He'd not heard her get out of bed. "What things?"

"The shining ones between the dinosaurs." Her hand gripped his arm, fingers clenched tight with fear.

Jeff now focused his attention on what he'd initially mistaken for particularly brilliant rays of sunlight penetrating the tree cover.

With the sun reflecting off them, they were difficult to see clearly.

"They look like giant forks, dear."

That had been Jeff's first sighting of the kitchen gods. He'd gripped Stacy tight, wondrous of the monster gold and silver cutlery levitating between the besieging dinosaur horde.

As if sensing their intended prey was awake, a loud thumping now began overhead, the tramping of pterodactyl feet and pecking of beaks, trying to rip a way through the ceiling.

The gunfire from the front of the house ceased.

The bedroom burst open. Mike Morris rushed in, blood streaming down his face.

"Sir, you've got to—"

Mike Morris was yanked back by two raptors. Jeff and Stacy watched horrified while the dinos jerked Mike this way and that, finally literally dividing the spoils by yanking him apart down the middle in an explosion of lungs and guts.

Stacy gave a sudden start beside Jeff. He turned as she went limp and crashed to the floor, pulling him down after her.

He didn't need a doctor to tell him she was having a heart attack. She was clawing at her chest with stiffened fingers, her face set in a grimace. Her green eyes were murky pools housing demons of dread.

"I can't breathe!"

"Dammit, Stacy don't die on me," Jeff pleaded.

She went limp, her hands falling to her sides.

Her lasts words were: "I hope it's true what they say about Heaven, darling. I've been good, haven't I?"

She died, green eyes staring at him.

Jeff stared back at her corpse in horror. He closed her eyes.

Now he had nothing left, not his family, not his country. Not even his belief in the overcoming power of right remained.

Everything he'd spent his life building, everything he'd given his life for, the country he'd both served and overseen, was being demolished before his very eyes, with no explanation of why.

Jeff was beyond traumatized. Losing Stacy was the last stray.

He stood up, no longer scared. If he died now, he'd be with Stacy, wherever she was. Her last words haunted him.

He turned around to find the room full, not of hungry ravening dinosaurs, but of the giant gold and silver cutlery.

"What do you want?" Jeff said.

A gold fork floated toward him. "I am Lord Tav," it said. "Head of the Forks. It is sad that your marriage partner is dead."

"You killed her!" Jeff screamed. He rushed at the Fork.

He found himself suddenly floating in the air, immobile.

"We regret it," Lord Tav said. "We are unable to raise the dead, otherwise we'd have done so. Still, we are not ones to waste food."

Jeff had watched in disbelief as Lord Tav had inverted himself in mid-air, then stabbed himself into Stacy's torso.

With a loud crackling and the smell of ozone, the First Lady's corpse disintegrated into a hill of shredded meat, one that was instantly sucked into Lord Tav's body.

The Fork righted himself again.

"You ate my wife," Jeff gasped in disbelief, tears rolling down his cheeks.

"It is a great honor for royalty to eat royalty. Or would you prefer we left her for the servants—or even the dinosaurs outside?"

Jeff had no reply to that. But, *honor?* What *honor?* Lord God Almighty, Stacy had looked like hamburger patty. . .

"You will come with us," the Fork leader told the weeping erstwhile president of the USA, "we have much to talk about."

The Forks floated out of the room, levitating Jeff after them.

CHAPTER 19

Sara

Now, two years later, in Sara Fischer's bedroom, Jeff burst into tears again from his horrible memories.

Sara cradled him to her ample bosom, and rocked him.

She ran her hands soothingly through his hair, wrinkling her nose in disgust as she inhaled his scotch stink.

This was her problem with Jeff now—he was a drunk. From the stoic leader she'd known (and guiltily admired), he'd degenerated into a bum.

Sara wasn't judging Jeff. She was still herself in free-fall fucking over David's death. And Jeff had lost so much more. He'd not just lost his family—he'd lost an entire country.

As if reading her thoughts, Jeff looked up at her then, his booze-reddened eyes tortured.

"You know what bothers me the most about the present mess, Sara?"

Without waiting for her reply, he continued: "It's that I'll never be sure that this mess isn't my fault—a direct result of some agency taking a Hollywood flick too seriously and messing with research better left alone."

Sara said nothing. She often had the same suspicion.

"I feel utterly impotent. The American people put their fate in me and I completely failed them."

Sara disagreed with this last. "It wasn't your fault. You did the best you could, Jeff."

He gazed into her eyes, looking for relief. "Do you really think so?"

She nodded.

"Oh, I really love you, Sara." He sank back down to his pillow on her breasts.

"I love you too, Jeff," Sara mouthed into his hair as she resumed stroking it. And she meant it. Since he'd resurfaced two days ago, it had been like they were twenty again, and she was falling in love all over again.

And I'd love you even more if you'd suck on my nipples, darling, she thought dizzily.

But Jeff didn't. Sara grimaced in frustration. Jeff wasn't impotent, just drunk all the time—too drunk to fuck her.

She was tired of using her vibrators. She wanted to feel his lips bruising hers, his hands roughly handling her breasts, his body crushing hers into the bedding, his manhood piercing her deep, deep, deep, then lifting her to the heights of ecstasy.

But sex wasn't happening while Mr. President was a wino.

Oh no, Sara thought, *I have to wean him off the booze somehow, and fast, before my desire burns me up.*

She wanted to fuck him, fuck him, fuck him. Now, now, now, al-fucking-ready.

She wanted, no . . . needed . . . sex. *Hard* fucking.

But despite her fizz of sexual frustration, Sara was being extra-cautious here. With Jeff around, she was keeping her cunt in her pants. She wasn't about to ruin their rekindled relationship by getting it on with anyone else.

And it wasn't just romance guiding her actions. She was being pragmatic also.

Jeff was a very sensitive sort. She'd already broken his heart once. She wouldn't take a chance on doing it again.

Last time he'd tried to kill himself. Bearing in mind his current mental state, this time he might try to kill her instead.

CHAPTER 20

Sookie

Sookie Ling drove her car fast along Myrtle Street. This far outside the Boston Grid, only a Chinese madam like herself would dare deliver call girls to clients.

Sookie took full advantage of her dragon immunity. No point not making a buck whenever you could.

Not that she was taking anything for granted. This far outside the Boston Grid there was the constant danger of dino attacks. Sookie felt relatively safe, however. Her pink Porsche 911 Turbo was fitted with the best electronic repulsors. And in case a T-Rex showed, she had her energy rifle to give it something to bite on.

She'd just dropped off two girls, Cinnamon Xu and Devi, for Mr. Clinton on Irving Street, and was on her way back down to Chinatown.

Mr. Clinton was rich and appreciated classy cunt. Sookie supplied the classiest cunt in Boston.

***

Sookie Ling's real name was Soong Ching-Ling. She'd however 'Americanized' it shortly after her arrival from China. For two reasons:

Firstly, it was hard for Americans to pronounce smoothly, and secondly (and much more important), Sookie didn't think it was right for a prostitute/brothel owner to share the same name with the 'Mother of China.'

Sookie was patriotic like that.

Sookie Ling was forty-nine. She was still good-looking, but had begun filling out with middle-age spread.

Must schedule lipo, she thought while making a turn. *Fat madam bad for flesh-selling bizness.*

Sookie had cute almond eyes under heavy eyelids. She had plump lips and long, long, black hair. A hooked nose. She always wore her nails 'dragon lady' long—it impressed the clients.

Like Ma Cure, Sookie was a recent immigrant from the Old Country. She had a *thick* accent—you had to listen good to understand her.

Also, like Ma, Sookie's 'American' wasn't the best in the world. In fact, it was worse than Ma's.

Sookie always wore dark shades. This was because she was addicted to dragonreich.

***

The drug dragonreich—named after Joseph Reich, the rock musician who discovered it—was simply dragon semen dried into powder. It was more potent than cocaine, and users reported enhanced clarity of their senses.

The downside of using 'reich,' was its side effects.

These differed according to user.

Using the drug had turned Sookie's eyes into featureless, permanently green ovals, without iris or pupils.

In addition, she now had furry three-inch-long tentacles ringing her anus.

All Sookie's girls who did reich also had body mutations.

Amy Wang had feathered ears. Then there was Tai-Ching Fang, who'd started going transparent. And Lily Wu, who was sprouting copper wires from her thighs.

And Sookie's Swiss friend Markus Fleiss, who began dripping vegetable oil the moment he snorted reich.

Weird shit like that.

The other downside of constant reich use was that it killed one's sex life. Murdered it dead as a hooker with a slit throat. It wiped out libido from existence like a divine eraser.

In this regard it was worse than heroin.

Sookie hadn't been fucked for two years now. And hadn't noticed. Occasionally, while peeing, she found herself—like a six year old—wondering what her vagina was meant for.

The drug even had *physical* sexual side effects.

Janet Hong was one of Sookie's sexiest girls. Her current 36D breasts were dino-fat implants. When she'd begun using reich, she totally lost all her breast fat—her breasts had shriveled to nothingness. She'd also lost all her pubic hair.

Booty Hustler, one of Sookie's black studs, had suffered a reduction in erected cock size, from seven to three inches.

Carmen Eliza and Rosa Rios, Argentinian lesbian friends of Sookie's, had both lost both nipples.

Joseph Reich theorized that using dragonreich imparted some of a dragon's amplified senses to the user.

Sookie didn't know about that. She did know however, that the rush Reich gave was second to none.

She wasn't giving up that high for nothing. With the country fucked-up, one needed all the alternate pleasure one could get. And with no cocaine making it up to Boston anymore, dragonreich was the perfect substitute.

***

Sookie turned off Myrtle, onto Joy Street. She slowed as she approached Malone's office.

Malone had once helped her rescue her kidnapped nephew, Gorgeous Wong.

Sookie laughed at a memory.

Delighted over his recovering Gorgeous from her abductors, Sookie had invited Malone over to her brothel for a celebration party.

There—just for the hell of it—she'd spiked his drink with reich. Whereupon Malone immediately began speaking fluent Mandarin. What Sookie found funniest was that Malone hadn't realized what was going on. Sookie still hadn't told him.

She now noticed Herbie's pimpmobile parked outside Malone's place.

Sookie giggled on seeing the Lincoln's 'L3t5 4k' number plate. Its audacity always amused her. *Ah, Herbie. Fuck all he know.*

Sookie considered. Herbie good friend. Have four hours must kill before pick girls up again. I chew fat with Herbie, catch old times with Malone.

She parked and rang Malone's buzzer.

Sookie raised an eyebrow when Posh answered. Posh looked disheveled, unmade-up, had apparently slept here. So Malone too fuck call girls, now? Wonderful. I have soft Asian cunt for him that kung fu him out of socks. He think he fight Jet Li in the bed.

Then, she noted the fear that flashed across Posh's face on sighting her, then the girl's quick look up and down street as if to ensure that she was alone.

What she fear of? Sookie wondered. She know me Herbie friend.

She smiled at Posh. This girl cutest American pussy—money mint. Nice breasts, long legs, tightest ass, lips men want around hard prick.

Sookie would have stolen Posh from Herbie if she wasn't scared shitless of Bulldog.

Hmmm, she look terrible worried. Something not right.

"Hello, Posh," she said. "Is Herbie and Malone here?"

Posh yawned affectedly. "No, Sookie. Malone's out on a case, be back by evening. Herbie's . . . I've no fucking idea where he is."

Sookie was taken aback. "You is leaving Herbie?"

Posh had now recovered her composure.

She smirked at Sookie's surprise. "Oh, you haven't heard? I'm with Malone now. We're getting married."

"Malone not marry prostitute," Sookie retorted. "Have high hero standards. Only fuck you to purify blood."

Purify the blood? Posh laughed. Yeah, Sookie you really are old school. "Okay, so it's not love, but it's not bad."

She stepped back from the door, "Sorry, I forgot my manners. Please come in."

Sookie shook her head. "I heading back to Chinatown before. Only stop because think Herbie with Malone." She smiled. "I go look for Herbie now."

She smiled coolly at the look of fear that momentarily rushed into Posh's eyes. Ah, you runaway. This good gossip.

Sookie left.

***

Before driving off, Sookie snorted some reich. Her eyes flashed lime green behind her shades as the drug kicked in.

Her heavy lips creased into an evil smile. She laughed. *I not try imagine look on Herbie face when I tell cash chicken Posh have flown coop.*

CHAPTER 21

Herbie

Herbie gaped at Sookie. "Malone? Posh is with Malone?"

She nodded, then turned and stared out of Herbie's window at the skyscraper next door.

The building's walls were already totally chitinized—glittering obsidian black surfaces. Outside, downstairs, she'd seen that it was practically a beetle now—its wings were fully formed, the most telling sign.

"I don't believe you," Herbie said.

Sookie shrugged. "Not need believe me. Biggest evidence. Lincoln pimp-car outside Malone's house, Posh pussy inside. What else proof need? Herself claiming they lovers."

(She returned her attention to the building outside. Wouldn't be long now before it uprooted itself and flew away. Dangerous for Herbie to be living so close to it. But Herbie was like lots of people she knew—they didn't move house until it was practically in the air.)

Herbie felt like he'd been blackjacked. This was utterly inconceivable. Posh had deserted him for good? He'd thought she'd just left for some days, to drive home her point about not going back to Oswald or that kooky Beth Riggs, but to run away, and to . . . *Malone?*

Damn, Herbie wasn't fucking with Malone. That was a simple way to an early grave.

Sookie watched him pityingly. "Always tell you, just one girl not good for pimp," she said, trying hard not to gloat over his misfortune. "Old Chinese proverb say: Pimp like horse breeder—need stable."

She stared intently at Herbie. She knew her featureless lime eyes were unsettling him. *Ah no,* she thought, *maybe was better not tell—look like he commit suicide. Good thinking bring solution with me.*

"I see like this," Sookie said. "You need girl suck cock, fuck on behalf till get Posh moneymaker back, correct?"

Herbie nodded grimly.

Sookie smiled tightly. "Have solution outside. Lend you my niece Gorgeous."

Herbie groaned. "Not *Gorgeous*, Sookie." Gorgeous was anything but.

"Looks not everything, Herbie. Gorgeous wonder-ful at eating penis. Also know 'dragon grip pussy clench' technique."

Sookie went to the door and indicated to Gorgeous to enter.

***

Gorgeous Wong wasn't ugly—just plain. Her eyes were pretty, but her lips were thin, neutralizing their effect. In addition, her nose was just a little too flat, making her face seem spread out.

She was also skinny, with breasts the size of golf balls, and had almost no buttocks at all.

Her nickname 'Gorgeous' was a translation of her birth name, Mei. Her parents had hoped the name would bring her the fortune her looks clearly wouldn't.

Gorgeous made absolutely no money whatever for Sookie—no one ever hired her.

And despite her modest, virginal demeanor, Gorgeous Wong was a bundle of trouble. Particularly, she was always getting into fights.

Sookie mentally rolled her eyes at the memory of when she'd gone missing.

Investigating her kidnapping, Malone discovered that Gorgeous hadn't been abducted by triads who wanted to force her aunt to pay protection money, nor even by rapists.

No, Gorgeous had been kidnapped simply to teach her a lesson.

A gang of Chinese boys—fellow kung fu students whom she was always fighting with and beating up—had gassed Gorgeous and locked her (along with enough food and drink for three months) in an empty shipping container in Foster's Wharf. They'd warned her not to make any noise and alert dinos to her presence and that they'd let her out when she'd learnt some manners.

Sookie still regretted Malone freeing her niece from confinement before she'd learn her lesson. *What fucking use is hooker who beating up men?*

But . . . Gorgeous was family and couldn't be fired. So Sookie was grateful for this opportunity to offload her somewhere.

***

Herbie nodded at the thin Chinese girl in her neat white kung fu getup.

Gorgeous Wong bowed. "I'm honored to serve you, Mr. Herbie."

Unlike her aunt, Gorgeous had been born in the USA. She spoke impeccable unaccented English.

Herbie forced a smile. He pointed to a chair.

He scrutinized Gorgeous while she demurely stared at the floor. She sat prim and proper, hands crossed in her lap, her knees and heels together.

Shit, Herbie thought. *She looks like a secretary, not a hooker.*

Sighing, he turned to Sookie. "Thanks, Sookie, you're a real friend. What'cha call that special technique of hers again?"

Sookie rose to leave. Her one-color green eyes and heavy lips made her look vampiric in the shaded light. "'Dragon grip pussy clench,'" she said, putting her dark shades back on. "It excruciating tight wonderful vagina pleasure for gentleman customer. When cum, not know if he live or die."

She waved and left.

Herbie sat morosely, by stages growing depressed. Occasionally he stared at Gorgeous who smiled brightly back. Seeing her just increased his dejection at Posh deserting him. *Shit! No way is Miss Homely here going to make me any money.*

"Look," he told her after a bit, "make yourself at home. I'm off to see my brother."

Gorgeous nodded. "Is there anything you want me to do before you get back, Mr. Herbie?" Gorgeous wanted to please. She didn't get along with her aunt and was delighted to be away from her.

Herbie thought, then frowned. "Yes, there is. Try not to run away too."

CHAPTER 22

Blondie & Stacy

Sugar Ray's Bar was situated at the Bedford Street/Kingston Street intersection, tucked just inside The Grid's south end. From its front entrance one could see, eighty yards away, the final steel pillars that propped up Boston's wiven shield, and down beyond that, Chinatown.

The bar owner, Sugar Ray Badass, was a huge bald negro who'd once almost been world heavyweight boxing champion.

He was a calm man, silently powerful behind a ready smile. His reputation was more than enough to keep the peace in his establishment.

No one messed up in Sugar Ray's.

***

Drinks in hand, the two women sat at a shadowed table in Sugar Ray's.

Both women's eyes surveyed the men walking into the bar.

Several patrons had already made eyes at the watching pair, but been pointedly ignored.

"Damn carpet lickers," the last muttered under his breath.

"No one yet, Blondie," Stacy said. "This place is the pits."

Stacy was a redhead. She was short and pretty, but thin-lipped and looked unpleasant.

Her companion checked her watch, then laughed. "You're so fucking impatient," she said. "Give it time, baby. It's still midafternoon. Lots of time for someone cute to show up.

Blondie was middle-aged and beautiful, full-lipped, and generously endowed breast-wise. Her satiny yellow curls flowed to below her shoulders. Unlike Stacy, she was gregarious, and had a warm smile. There was steel concealed in her smile, but it wasn't obvious.

The bar door swung open. A fat dark-haired guy made his way over to the bar, plumped his ass down on a stool.

Blondie watched him with anger. "Shit!" she swore, "another fucking unsuitable. The guy looks like a dressed-up pig." Her scowl deepened. "Where the hell are all the cuties?"

The door swung open again.

Stacy's eyes brightened. "Him, let's do him!" she whispered excitedly.

Blondie looked up from her glass of wine. She regarded both new entrants with mixed interest. "Which one? Bulldog-face, or hangdog-expression?"

"Hangdog. Isn't he cute? So, so cute?"

Blondie regarded Herbie Stanton with interest, as he and his brother made their way to a table and signaled a black waitress.

"Yeah, *he is* rather handsome," she said, "in a spineless, weasely kind of way. He needs to lighten up though—he looks like he just lost his job."

"Or his *wife*," Stacy said. "Oh, Blondie, I'd so love to comfort him." She stared pleadingly at Blondie, fluttering her eyelashes little-girl-style. "Let's do him, pleeeaaaseee!"

Blondie laughed. "Okay. It's impossible to refuse you anything you've set your mind on anyway. So Hangdog here's a definite prospect." She reached over and squeezed Stacy's hand. "But simmer down, girl. There's sure to be lots of other men, real hunks, coming through the door shortly."

Stacy shook her head. "Not for me." Elbows on table, chin in palms, she gazed dreamily at the oblivious Herbie Stanton. "I think I've fallen in love."

***

Across from the two women, Herbie was suffering a major crisis.

"She just fucking up and left, Bully. All the thanks I get for picking her ass off the street and keeping a roof over her head."

Bulldog ran a finger through his thick brown hair. Like his name suggested he was ugly as a pile of fresh shit.

He also had a huge dent in the left side of head where he'd been hit with a lead pipe and left for dead a year ago.

The dent had scrambled Bulldog's brains. He'd been unable to reason clearly since then. Except to poop and pee, Bulldog now counted on Herbie to do most of his thinking for him.

"Yeah, Herb," he said. "I mean that's ingratitude for ya. You even kept her ass full of all kinds of dicks—ensured she made full use of her woman's right to get fucked regularly."

Herbie glared at his younger brother. Despite its benefits, Bulldog's dimwittedness was often irritating. "Don't fucking make jokes about this."

Bulldog look surprised. He raised both hands in apology.

"Sorry, Herb. But I ain't joking. Ain't that what those women's groups used to complain about? A woman's right to fuck and make babies?"

Herbie smiled for the first time since discovering Posh had run away.

"It's campaign, Bully, not complain—"

"Seems the same to me, campaigning is complaining isn't it?"

"—And it was for their right to abort babies, not to fuck and make 'em."

Bulldog scratched his wrinkled forehead. He took a sip of his beer. "Still seems one and the same complaint to me. I mean if they don't have a right to fuck and make babies, there's no babies to abort, right?"

Herbie winced. Bulldog's logic was too illogical for Herbie. It gave him a headache.

"You're right, Bully," he said tiredly. "But that's neither here nor there—it doesn't help me in the least to get my runaway slut back, does it?"

The booze was getting into him now, turning his depression into anger.

"Way I see it," Bulldog said. "You say you know where she is, right? I say we head over there now, I'll bust the sumbitch's head in and take Posh back. Your hooker's your property, Herb. That's stealing! And besides, Posh even took your fucking car! We can't stand for that! Imagine it—your *property* stealing your *property*!"

"Lower your voice," Herbie whispered. "We're in a bar, for God's sake."

Posh stealing his prized Lincoln irked Herbie greatly. *Now that's a pimpmobile! Old fucking gold—not like all these modern Japanese fiberglass cars! And Posh had run off with it.*

Looking over Bulldog's shoulder, Herbie now noticed the blonde and redhead seated opposite them. The redhead looked away when he looked their way, like she'd been staring at him.

He looked both women over, while they affected not to notice his staring.

Both were pretty, but the oldish blonde was more his style, with that flowing hair, luscious lips and those breasts . . . Wow! Herbie could just imagine what her nipples would feel like between his lips.

He remembered he was talking to his brother, pulled his eyes down from Blondie's breasts. "It's not that simple, Bully. We can't just break in and take her."

Bulldog looked confused. "This is the part I don't get, Herb— *why* isn't it simple? And *why* won't you tell me who's got her?" His face tightened with anger. "Just tell me the bastard's name and I'll bash his head in."

Herbie smiled. *Not this time you won't.* Finding out that Posh had fled to Malone had complicated issues greatly.

Herbie wasn't about taking on Malone without a guaranteed edge. Possibly not at all. The guy's reputation was practically superhuman badass.

Herbie also knew Bulldog was scared shitless of Malone. If his brother got even the slightest whiff that Malone was involved in Posh's disappearance, he'd be out the back door faster than Herbie could flush a turd.

"Have you heard the expression 'patience is golden,' Bully?"

Bulldog polished off his beer then nodded.

Herbie's eyes thinned to pissed-off slits. "This guy who's got Posh is too fucking tough to tackle at the moment. So we wait, bide our time—"

"Yeah, but who the fucking hell is it?"

"Don't worry 'bout it!" Herbie snapped in a harsh whisper. "Just do what I tell you, like you always do. The one thing I ain't having is you rushing off hotheaded and screwing this up for me, okay?"

Bulldog nodded. "Sorry, Herb. I didn't mean—"

Herbie jabbed a finger at him. "It's okay—don't sweat it. Just wait till I tell you we're good to go on this one. No one fucking cheats me and gets away with it." He glared at Bulldog. "You know that, don't you?"

Bulldog gulped nervously. "Sure, Herb. No one messes with you, 'cos I got your back."

Herbie smiled now. "Yeah, no one messes with *us*. We're getting that bitch Posh back. How fucking dare she run out on us?"

Bulldog called for fresh beers.

Herbie now turned his attention back to the women opposite. Neither turned away this time. The pruny redhead gave him the eye. The blonde smiled coolly. Herbie wondered if they were hookers. He eyed the blonde's breasts again. *Oh, mama!*

The black waitress delivered their beers.

Herbie paid, then, pointing with his chin, said: "Serve a bottle of red wine to those pretty ladies over there. Tell them it's from me and my brother."

"Who's that for?" Bulldog asked, after the waitress had left.

"Look over your shoulder, Bully," Herbie said. "I see there two possible replacements for our runaway Posh."

Bulldog looked, then turned back and nodded. "Wow, Herbie they'se pretty. Real pretty."

Herbie waited till his order of wine was delivered to Blondie and Stacy. Both women waved at him, all smiles now.

"Our gift has been accepted," he told Bulldog, getting to his feet. "Come on, let's go and introduce ourselves to our new girlfriends."

CHAPTER 23

Posh

Oh my God, no!

Posh gaped at her reflection in shocked horror.

With Malone not returning, and herself unable to go anywhere till he did show, she'd slept till now, late afternoon.

A feverish feeling (which she'd put down to strenuous over-fucking) had encouraged her to sleep her fatigue off. She'd only woken up now to get a drink of water and take a pee.

And then she'd looked in the bathroom mirror.

Now naked in front of the mirror, she stood frozen in shock.

Fear flooded her. There was no doubt about it at all.

Her body was covered with the same shit-colored swellings that Oswald Watkins had.

"I've picked up his fucking war infection!" she whispered to herself. "The sick bastard fucking lied to me! He lied to me! He is contagious!"

Posh stood motionless before the mirror for an eternity before daring to touch herself.

The bumps didn't hurt, no. They were soft to the touch, however, like they were full of pus.

And they're all over me—my face, my breasts, belly, my legs—everywhere. Posh was as disgusted as she was scared. *Shit, there's even one covering my right nipple.*

And this change clearly happened overnight. When Sookie called yesterday she never said I looked odd.

Terrified as to what the result would be, Posh pinched the crusty edge of a tan protuberance on the outside of her left breast. She pulled it up. With the barest sensation of pain, the entire 'bruise' separated from her body in a six-inch-long strip of skin that ripped down across her rib cage.

Posh stared at it aghast. The strip of removed skin was half an inch thick. She clearly made out the separations between the skin itself and the connective tissue and fatty layers beneath it.

She turned her attention to the wound.

Where she'd removed the skin from was a trough of wet red flesh. White rib peeked through muscle that seemed no longer firmly attached to its bone supports.

Pink serum began trickling from the excavation. It ran down over her belly.

Posh fought down her urge to scream; to scream and keep on screaming till she lost her mind.

I'm fucked up, she realized with brutal conviction. *Totally screwed for good.*

She finally pulled herself away from the mirror. Carrying the sliver of removed skin like a gory prize, she returned to Malone's bedroom, and began dressing.

While she dressed, Posh's thoughts were black, like nightfall condensed into her head.

Herbie, she thought. *That bastard has fucking ruined me with his greed. But, oh, oh no. I'm not about going down alone.*

Posh was now too enraged/depressed to feel fear. Her single thought was to kill Herbie Stanton for what he'd done to her.

Fully dressed, she smiled coldly. Then she went to the wardrobe and got out a gun—Malone's backup blaster—she'd noticed lying in back of it when hanging up her clothes.

She checked that the weapon had a full charge, then put it in her coat pocket.

Posh left the house and got into Herbie's pimpmobile.

She drove off, looking for him so she could kill him.

CHAPTER 24

Herbie, Stacy, Blondie, & Bulldog

"Haven't seen you ladies in here before," Herbie said.

Blondie shrugged. "We're new in town."

"From Chicago," Stacy added.

Herbie raised an eyebrow. "What's it like over there?"

Stacy put down her empty wine glass. She wrinkled her nose in disgust. "Utterly terrible. Like you wouldn't believe."

Blondie scowled. "We've now got Nodrix."

Bulldog leaned forward, ugly face perplexed. "What's those?"

"Area 51 stuff. Aliens that the Lincoln administration caught and locked away. The dinos broke into Area 51, ate everyone and the aliens escaped. Now they fly around zapping people as revenge. The Vodiods that escaped from Guantanamo Bay are even worse."

"Shit," Bulldog said. "That's fucking terrible."

"No, bro," Herbie said, "that's worse than terrible."

He signaled Sugar Ray to send over another bottle of wine. The hulking negro barman grinned white teeth and nodded.

"You'd have thought," Herbie continued, "that making dragons and these Jurassic Park reptiles would be enough shit to shovel on the American people, but no—administrative assholes gotta add aliens to the mix."

"I'd like to get my hands around that cad Jeff Lincoln's neck and break it," Bulldog said with deep feeling.

Blondie shuddered. The cretin looked mean and strong enough to do it too. "The dragons aren't the government's fault," she said.

Herbie scowled. "Then *who's* to blame?"

(Herbie had been out to the Boston harbor only once since the New Past began.

Even without the accompanying danger, that once was enough.

The sight of the monstrous thunder lizards wading offshore, with massive Ichthyosaurs swimming between them like reptile dolphins had unnerved him.

There'd been HUGE beetles in the sky, the sheer massiveness of the creatures defying conception. Herbie had watched one of them lay a skyscraper on India Wharf, then he'd split.

Washington has to be responsible for this mess, he'd thought, shifting gears whilst driving off.)

"Shit like this doesn't just happen," Herbie said.

"This shit did," Blondie retorted with a creamy smile. "Deal with it, man." She decided she liked Herbie. Nice face with sexy lips; hopefully a nice tight backside too.

She could do without his brother though, with that apish frame, that face like dog shit someone had stepped in, those tiny piggy eyes under brows a Neanderthal would be embarrassed of, that nose belonging to a boxer with no defensive skills, and those lips spread so flat over his gappy uneven teeth that they looked like pancakes.

Then there was the HUGE dent in the side of his head, deep enough for her to stick her fist into.

He looked strong as a bull, but brains clearly weren't his strong point.

Blondie was relieved that Bulldog—what a fuckingly apt name—didn't drool when he spoke.

Beside her, Stacy was fucking *delighted* with Herbie.

"So tell me, Herbie," she said, letting her fingers play on his wrist, "what business do you do?"

Herbie laughed. "I'm a contractor."

"He deals in pretty women," Bulldog interjected.

Herbie winced. This was why he preferred not taking Bulldog places with him. The lout was trying to fuck up this pussy recruitment drive. And this was classy cunt here, not some strung-out junkie trash who'd fuck even a pig for her next fix.

Herbie was super impressed with these ladies. Even Stacy—the shrewish redhead—had it going on when she smiled. Nice teeth, nice lips.

Blondie and Stacy looked at each other and smiled.

Then they both looked enquiring back at Herbie.

"You're a *pimp*?" Stacy asked teasingly.

Herbie forced a laugh. He poured more wine into both women's glasses. He had no idea why they suddenly seemed very pleased.

He shrugged mentally. It made things easier that they weren't prudes.

"I prefer to think of it as providing a quality specialized sexual supply service for the discerning purveyor of perverted pleasure," he replied.

Blondie and Stacy gaped, trying to work out what he meant.

"What he means," Bulldog explained helpfully, "is that he does girls for people who like kinky sex."

Herbie shot him an angry glare. Then he shrugged self-depreciatingly. "I handle only the business of gentlemen . . . and ladies . . . of the highest class."

"He means only the stinking rich get to do his girls," Bulldog finished.

Herbie simmered. Stacy took his hand in both hers.

"That's great," she said, staring deeply into Herbie's eyes now with undisguised lust. "You're just the sort of person we're looking for."

That floored Herbie. "You ladies *want me* to represent you? You're hookers?"

Blondie grinned. "Need you ask? We've hooked you, haven't we?"

The quartet all laughed.

Oh, yes, Herbie thought. *Now to the nitty gritty. Time to discuss terms. Mustn't be too stingy. These girls are major class ass. Maybe—*

He stopped thinking. Gorgeous Wong had just entered the bar.

The Chinese girl looked around, searching for Herbie. He signaled her. She rushed over to his side, face even more serious than normal

Shit, Herbie thought, *something's wrong.*

Gorgeous bowed to Blondie and Stacy. "Good evening, pretty ladies." She turned back to Herbie. "I've been searching bar after bar for you, sir. Posh is at your skyscraper."

Herbie was stunned. "Posh?"

"She's asking after you. She seems very angry."

Bulldog smirked at Herbie. "Maybe that other guy ain't as good as you in bed."

Herbie groaned. *Bulldog, for heaven's sake, shut your yap.*

Gorgeous left. Herbie watched her go. He saw she was waiting for him outside the bar.

The girl's smart, he thought. *Okay, so she got no looks, but she's got brains. Maybe I'll just make her my secretary.*

He turned back to Blondie and Stacy. "Sorry, ladies. I've urgent business to attend to. You're not in a hurry to leave, are you?"

Both shook their heads. "Who's Posh?" Stacy asked with a hint of jealousy.

"She's—" Bulldog began.

Herbie silenced him with an angry glare.

"She's a chick who ran away with my money," he lied smoothly. "I guess she's back to pay her debt." He smiled at them both. "Don't worry, this won't take long. I'll be back before you even notice I'm gone."

He and Bulldog made their way across to the bar door.

***

"I don't like this," Stacy told Blondie. "They might not come back."

"Doesn't matter," Blondie said. "I'll tag him."

She cupped her hand over her nose and sneezed into it. She winked at Stacy, then picked the little transparent fly she'd sneezed up out of her palm.

"Follow Herbie," she mouthed at it.

She flung it towards the bar door.

The fly zipped across the bar and out the door. It settled unseen on Herbie's hair, then dissolved into it.

Herbie, Bulldog, and Gorgeous set off to the left.

Blondie gave Stacy a satisfied smirk. "Doesn't matter where lover-man goes now, we'll find him easy."

"Do you believe his story about the girl owing him money?"

Blondie shook her head. "He was lying. He most likely owes *her* money."

She put a hand on Stacy's thigh, massaged her muscles. "Now relax, baby. Night's still young. You never know, someone *much* cuter than Herbie might come through the doors."

Stacy scowled. "I *utterly* doubt that."

CHAPTER 25

Malone

Malone trudged down Milk Street, then onto Devonshire.

Devonshire Street continued uninterrupted south to Lincoln, then on to Chinatown Park.

Good, Malone thought in groggy relief. *No need to think no more. My legs will take me to Ma Cure.* He was barely aware of what lay ahead or around him.

Malone's current problem was how to not die of exhaustion before he made it to Chinatown.

Ironically, it was the last drug Rachel Fischer had injected him with that kept him going. In the same way it numbed his mind, so it numbed his body—he couldn't feel the pain he was in. He felt like an automaton, like he was one of Rachel's robots.

Occasionally, it stabbed through his mind that even now, Frank could be driving around looking for him, desperate for revenge.

Malone scoffed at the thought. *Nah, he's likely making sweet love to Rachel's corpse.*

Blaster in right hand, severed head in the other, Malone shambled down Devonshire Street.

Closer, closer to help.

CHAPTER 26

Herbie

Herbie, Bulldog, and Gorgeous hurried up Devon-shire.

Then they noticed the bloodied man walking zombie-slow down toward them.

From a distance, they had no idea who it was.

Just seeing him, however,—bloodstained, abdomen gaping like Callahan Tunnel entrance, huge blaster in one hand, Rachel Fischer's head in the other—was enough of a caution.

The trio ducked into a doorway to let him pass.

"Shit, man," Herbie said. "Just let this son-of-a-bitch go his merry way. I ain't messing with no serial killers."

Herbie was unnerved by the approaching figure. The female head he gripped had its eyes open. The dead blood-obscured orbs seemed to be looking into his.

Gorgeous' plain face wrinkled in disgust. "This is a very sick man," she said. "Where is he taking—"

Then she gasped and squeezed Herbie's hand. "That's Malone!"

Herbie tensed like he'd just felt a bug walking in his ear. "For real?"

Herbie had only ever seen Malone once, and that was ages ago. He squinted at the bloody man, racking his mind for a facial match. It was no use. Malone's face was too covered in blood for Herbie to identify even if he could remember him.

Herbie looked at Bulldog. "This him?"

Bulldog was as confused as his brother. "Can't be sure. Too much mess."

Malone shambled past them.

Herbie stared moodily after the departing man.

He turned to Gorgeous. "How the hell can you be so sure it's him?"

She blushed. After he rescued me from my kidnappers, Aunt Sookie ordered me to give him a taste of my 'dragon grip pussy clench' technique."

"So you screwed him. How does that help?"

She blushed deeper. "Malone has a scar on his left thigh, just under his balls. I saw it just now."

"Sure?"

"Yes. It's unmissable. When I sucked his—"

Bulldog cuffed her. "We don't need to hear that part, you dumb slit."

"Ouch."

Neither Bulldog nor Gorgeous noticed that Herbie was now grinning as he watched Malone shuffling away from them.

Gorgeous stepped away from Bulldog to prevent him hitting her again. Her expression became concerned. "We must help him, Mr. Herbie. He needs—"

"I'll get him to a doctor," Herbie interrupted smoothly. "Bully, you two go and intercept Posh. Just keep her waiting till I get back."

Bulldog was skeptical, though obviously relieved to not be accompanying Herbie. "You sure 'bout this? He looks psycho."

"Malone isn't a psychopath," Gorgeous interjected from a safe distance. "Unlike you, he's a gentleman."

Bulldog turned menacingly to her. "Shut your trap before I break all your teeth."

Gorgeous glowered back, then assumed a kung fu stance. "Try it, monkey."

"That's it," Bulldog growled. "You're dead meat, you ugly Chink whore."

"Shit-filled asshole!"

Bulldog balled his fists. "Damn, you—!" He shut up because Gorgeous had lifted her left leg and placed her sole flat on his face. She held the ballerina-like pose, hands chop-ready.

Her eyes were frigid. "I dare you to fuck with me."

Bulldog staggered back. Gorgeous held the martial arts pose, her foot in the air like a 1970s movie poster.

"You . . . you . . ." Bulldog sputtered. He regarded Gorgeous warily, prepared to circle around her.

"Stop it, both of you," Herbie snapped.

Both stared sullenly back at him. Gorgeous slowly lowered her outstretched leg. She and Bulldog both lowered their hands, relaxed their fighting stances.

Herbie was impressed with Gorgeous. No women he knew dared talk back to Bully. And to actually pick a fight?

He doubted that her kung fu was any good, though. It hadn't prevented her getting abducted, had it? Still the chick had spunk.

He stole a quick glance down-street to ensure that Malone was still in view, then turned back to his companions.

"Now listen," he said sternly, "don't you dare start fighting."

"I'm not your brother's punching bag," Gorgeous said. "Warn him. If he touches me again, I'll break his arm."

She looked intently at Herbie. "I'm not going with Bulldog, Mr. Herbie. I'll come with you to help Malone."

Oh, no. Herbie thought. *You're not coming with me. I'm going to kill this Malone bastard and I don't need any fucking witnesses.*

(The IDEA had struck Herbie suddenly, hard as a bullet to the brain. He realized he'd never have another opportunity like this—Malone gutted like a pig and clearly half-blind.

Bulldog would never agree to help—he regarded Malone with semi-divine awe.

And Gorgeous? His secretary-slut sounded besotted with the private dick, like she wanted to 'dragon pussy clench' him again.

So he'd do this alone, using his pocketknife. He'd head after Malone, knock him off, then meet up with the others to knock some sense into his thieving whore Posh.)

Herbie looked pointedly at Gorgeous. "Malone is carrying a woman's head. He obviously killed her. So you *can't* come with me. He clearly doesn't like chicks at the moment. Maybe his wife left him."

"He's not married!"

Herbie winced. "Just git, or I'll return you to your aunt!"

The threat worked. Gorgeous instantly turned pale, then she turned away, glaring angrily.

"Now, you get," Herbie addressed Bulldog in a rush. "And *don't* you *dare* fucking rough her up. Just both of you go and get Posh. Kapish?"

"Yeah, sure." Then he looked all embarrassed like he had a question.

"Yes, *what is it?*" Herbie was growing exasperated by these seemingly endless delays. Malone was still in sight, but any moment now, he could turn onto a side street and Herbie would lose him.

Then Herbie also remembered the two superfine ladies he'd left at Sugar Ray's Bar. He winced, this mustn't take forever. He didn't want to miss that svelte pair.

(Herbie had decided to take Sookie's advice. With Blondie, Stacy, and Posh, he had the beginnings of a high class slut stable. His re-acquiring Posh, however, depended on his killing Malone, which Bulldog seemed intent on scuppering.)

Bulldog grinned. "This 'dragon grip clench pussy' technique of hers sounds interesting. Er . . . is it okay if I try it later?"

Herbie rolled his eyes. "Of course, of course, you can screw her."

"No, he *cannot* 'screw her,' Mr. Herbie," Gorgeous said with a sweet, geisha-like smile.

She leered at Bulldog, then tapped her crotch. "Hidden in here is a great Chinese sexual delicacy. Unfortunately, you won't ever taste it."

Bulldog glowered. "You little . . .I'll . . ."

"And if you dare to rape me, I'll dragon clench your cock so tight it will come out looking like a pencil. You won't even be able to pee through it."

Bulldog's ugly face turned red. "You wouldn't dare!"

Gorgeous smiled with Buddha-like serenity. "I won't? Just you try and fuck me without my permission."

Herbie couldn't stand their bickering anymore.

"Just fucking get lost, both of you!" he yelled. "Go on, fuck off!"

Without waiting to see if they'd heeded his in-struction, he set off at a run after Malone, now visible only as a distant red speck.

Shit, he thought, *what sort of dolts do I have to work with?*

CHAPTER 27

Sugar Ray

Sugar Ray Badass hated dragons.

Two years ago, Sugar Ray had been the number one contender for Vlad 'The Punch Impaler' Utkin's undisputed world heavyweight crown.

Vladimir Utkin was a Russian giant, six-feet-eight in his socks. Ugly motherfucker, with a broken nose, two cauliflower ears, and flat lips. But he'd been champ for ten years now, and showed no sign of slowing down his unprecedented domination of world boxing.

No one could fucking beat the guy. He'd won all the heavyweight belts: IBF, WBF, WBC, WBO, IBA— the list just went on.

An even bigger problem was, that, with no surprises left, no one watched heavyweight boxing anymore. Box office receipts for fights were at an all-time low.

It got so bad that the boxing promoters and federations held an emergency meeting, where they decided to ask Vlad to relinquish his title—in exchange for ten percent of all heavyweight title purses for the next ten years.

The deal would have made 'The Punch Impaler' close to two hundred million dollars. But Vlad turned it down. He intended, he said, to reach his goal of a hundred title defenses of his heavyweight crown, after which he'd retire undefeated.

The federations pleaded and pleaded. Vlad refused to heed them.

So the Cold War resumed. East versus West, with gloves on.

Every boxing trainer in America began looking for that magic fighter who'd take 'that arrogant Ruskie who refuses to worship the Almighty Dollar' down.

Enter Sugar Ray Badass.

The young black kid was tall—six-feet-four inches. Nowhere near Vlad's six-eight, but Sugar Ray was lightning fast. He was the fastest thing anyone had seen in a ring since Muhammad Ali or Manny Pacquiao. And he could hit like Mike Tyson.

He was handsome too, though everyone knew his cover boy looks were finished once he fought 'that damn re-communist.'

After Sugar Ray brutally punched his way into the number one contender's spot, the big fight was set up.

***

Madison Square Garden. July 31st, 2026, 1.45 a.m. Vlad 'The Punch Impaler' Utkin vs. Sugar Ray Badass, for the Undisputed World Heavyweight Belt. 15 Rounds of boxing. Midway through the eighth round.

Sugar Ray had been in fights before, but nothing like this one. He was taking the beating of his motherfucking life.

Nothing but sheer willpower was keeping him in the match. Vlad kept coming at him, kept coming. Sugar Ray weaved, ducked and feinted, and even got in a few good punches of his own, but all in all, he was getting his ass whipped.

He'd been okay in the first few rounds, but since then it had been all Vlad. *Dammit, man. No wonder they call this guy 'The Impaler,' it feels like each punch he's hitting me with is going right through my body.*

Vlad was roughed up too, with a black eye and his flat nose already flatter, but Sugar Ray was a total mess. His right eye was almost fully closed and the left wasn't much better. Blood was dripping down his face on to his chest from his broken nose and split lips.

He wasn't going to be no cover boy after this beat-down that was for sure.

The referee had come over to Sugar Ray's corner during the break.

"Look guys," he said wearily. "This kid can't keep taking this sort of punishment for the next seven rounds. He'll have permanent brain damage. You guys either throw in the towel, or I'm stopping the fight."

Freddy Crucial, Ray's trainer, had nodded. He'd looked down sadly at Sugar Ray. "Sorry, kid, the man's right. You're getting murdered in there."

"I'm still good to go," Sugar Ray insisted.

"You got heart, kid, but—"

"I'll fucking win this fight!"

The ref smiled down at him. "You ever watch 'The Champ,' son? What use is winning if you're dead? See that Russian there, he don't give a shit about you. He'll kill you then go out clubbing."

Sugar Ray laughed. "Just give me one more round." He gazed at both men with fervent bloody eyes. "Just *one more* round."

Freddy looked at the referee.

The ref was obviously conflicted, then he nodded. He too wanted to see the Russian dominance end. And even though this kid looked like he'd nothing left in the tank, he'd seen miracles happen in the ring before.

He sighed. "Okay, kid, you got one more round. After that I'm declaring a TKO."

Sugar Ray laughed. "Just watch me."

***

The fight resumed. Vlad came out with guns blazing. The long delay in Sugar Ray's corner had him thinking his opponent was total walking wounded now.

Ray ducked the haymaker that Vlad threw and went into a clinch with him.

Vlad didn't like that. "Stop bleeding on me, you pig!" he growled.

He pushed Sugar Ray off of him, then waded towards him flinging punches, any of which—if it landed—would have sent Ray to the emergency room.

Ray kept dancing back, dancing back—remembering Ali in the glory days. He leaned back on the ropes, took some body shots like he'd seen Ali do against Foreman in the 'Rumble in the Jungle.'

His head cleared a little, he focused his attention.

There were only thirty seconds left in this fucking round—he trusted the ref to keep his word not to stop the fight, not to pull the plug prematurely.

Ray needed an opening to throw just one punch. He saw Vlad's face ahead of him, ugly as shit.

I mean, I don't understand why the guy looks so bad—I've seen his younger brother and sister, both are good-looking.

Then Vlad made his single mistake of the entire match. Sugar Ray was languishing on the rope looking paralyzed. The ref was nervously counting down the clock, praying this kid's concussion wouldn't leave him a vegetable for life.

Confident of his victory, Vlad let his guard down. He dropped both arms to his sides and danced like Ali used to do.

In a flash, Sugar Ray lunged off the ropes and hit him. Caught him flush on the jaw. Hit him with all the strength he could muster in his ravaged frame.

Sugar Ray distinctly felt Vlad's jaw break under the impact of the punch.

The Russian giant stood, gaping like he'd been sledgehammered. He staggered forward towards Sugar Ray.

Sugar Ray hit him again—this time with an upper cut delivered from the waist. "Here's one for the road, sucker."

Vlad toppled over backwards. He hit the floor like a crashing WWII bomber.

Madison Square Garden erupted in noise. The commentators were going wild. The judges threw their scorecards away.

The Russian dominance was over.

The ref gaped at Sugar Ray in astonishment. "He's out cold, kid."

Sugar Ray smirked. "Count to six hundred if you want, old man. That sucker ain't waking up before morning."

The ref didn't bother counting. He waved both hands, calling the fight.

Pandemonium ensured. Freddie Crucial and Ray's corner rushed into the ring and carried him on their shoulders.

"You fucking did it, son, Freddy wept. "I didn't think—"

Ray didn't hear the rest of what he said. The screaming in the arena had just taken on a new, scared, tone. He looked up and realized why.

The arena roof was on fire.

His first thought was: *Damn, the Russians sure are pissed that I beat their guy.* He smirked. *Just for this stunt, there ain't gone be no rematch.*

Then the roof burnt away and the transparent dragons flew in and began eating everyone.

All Sugar Ray remembered after that was the wild race to escape alive.

A dragon ate Freddie Crucial. Old Freddie had a limp and couldn't run. On reaching the entrance to the tunnel leading to his dressing room, Sugar Ray realized that Freddie wasn't behind him anymore.

He turned back in time to see Freddie bitten in two by teeth like arm-length shards of shimmering glass.

He turned around and ran and ran and ran and ran.

***

Sugar Ray winced now in his reminiscing like he always did. He utterly hated dragons.

Shit, man. How is it that a brother can't get ahead no matter what the hell he do? First it was slavery and the white man; now the fucking dragons? Why couldn't the dragons simply wait one hour—no fifteen fucking minutes—so I could have been officially crowned world heavyweight champ? Just fifteen minutes?

No it isn't even the dragons. This is a DIVINE conspiracy against me, a black man simply trying to get along in this hard cold world.

Wow, he thought, *God must REALLY hate me.*

Sugar Ray popped out of his daze.

Posh was pointing a gun at him.

"Where the hell is Herbie?" she asked angrily. "I heard he was in here."

Sugar Ray scowled back at her. "Look, girl, you know I don't take no gunplay in my bar. Put the damn gun down before I take it from you and whip yo ass with it."

Posh retreated back four steps. "Oh, yeah? Whip this, asshole!"

She shot holes on either side of Sugar Ray's head. Bottles shattered, glass sprayed everywhere. A shard cut Sugar Ray above the left ear.

Sugar Ray turned and gaped at his shot-up booze display. Then he turned back to gape at Posh.

"What the hell is *wrong* with you, girl?"

Posh pointed the gun at him again. "Next time I'm shooting *you*. Now, where the fuck is Herbie?"

"I don't know! He was here, then he left. I ain't his goddamn babysitter." Blood was dribbling down his face, messing up his white shirt.

Sugar Ray was seriously thinking of jumping Posh and spanking her ass here in front of everyone. *Teach the stupid girl a lesson. No one comes into my bar and starts shooting.*

What stopped him from taking her on was the don't-give-a-fuck look in her eyes. He'd seen that look many times before—in the eyes of old winos with nothing to live for, and junkies who didn't care no more if they lived or died.

Besides, there was something wrong with Posh's face. She looked like she had clumps of excrement on it. Her hands too. *Oh, no. No way am I touching a prostitute covered in shit.*

"Look, girl," he said calmly. "I honestly don't know where Herbie is. Now please don't shoot up my bar."

Posh ignored him. She spun around to face the bar patrons. Everyone looked back, scared as startled rabbits.

"Okay," she said. "Everyone here knows Herbie Stanton. Where the hell did he go?"

The young man seated next to Blondie and Stacy raised his hand. "He went looking for *you*."

Posh pointed her gun at him. "Do I look stupid? If he's looking for me, why am I here looking for him?"

"It's true," the young man said. He pointed to Blondie and Stacy. "Herbie and Bulldog were talking to these two women when a Chinese girl came in and said you were over at his place. So they left to find you."

Posh mulled on that. She scowled at Blondie and Stacy. "That true?"

Blondie smiled coldly back. "If you're Posh, it is."

Posh glared pointedly at Stacy, who finally nodded. "Yeah. Out the door, he went left."

Posh appraised both women with a hooker's eye. "So I'm gone two days and Herbie's already scouting fresh meat." She smirked. "I'm not jealous—I wish you girls all the fuck in the world."

She turned to leave.

"Hold on a moment," Blondie said.

Posh turned back. "What?"

"What do you want with Herbie?"

Posh laughed acidly. "What does it *look like* I want with him? I intend killing the son-of-a-bitch."

She left the bar.

Behind her, everyone resumed their drinking activities.

CHAPTER 28

Blondie & Stacy

Once Posh had driven off, Blondie and Stacy left the bar too. Both women strode down the street and into a dark alley.

"Oh, Blondie. I hope we're in time," Stacy said, worry etched all over her face.

"It's okay, we will be. I *sensed* that Herbie got diverted from his journey home. That's why I corroborated that guy's story."

Stacy grinned. "Can't wait to fuck him silly."

"Me too."

"Let's do this, Blondie."

Both women concentrated intensely. Their eyes locked in distant focus. Their faces turned to masks of strain. Their breathing quickened with their mental effort, their breasts rising and falling rapidly.

Then feathered wings sprouted out of their backs. Large vanilla-pink bird wings that grew and grew.

A passerby the alley now would have noticed the bulge in each woman's crotch revealed along with her wings.

Stacy and Blondie were trangels—transsexual angels.

When their wings were full grown, they took to the air. Wings flapping, they flew at speed under The Grid's ceiling.

After a while, Blondie pointed to her left. "He's over that way."

Both trangels turned and zoomed in that direction.

CHAPTER 29

Herbie

Herbie slowed to a walk. He was fifty yards behind Malone, who he'd now determined to be headed for Chinatown.

Now that he was close to carrying out his plan, Herbie was nervous. He'd never killed anyone before and the Dutch courage he'd been feeding off was running low.

He felt the knife in his pocket. One slice across Malone's throat was all it would take. (He gulped, remembering what it had felt like when Beth had held her knife to *his* neck.)

He'd sidle up to Malone like he intended to help him, then . . .

Malone reached the end of Devonshire. He turned left along Summer Street.

Herbie rushed after him to keep him in view, then stopped dead.

Up ahead—like they were tailing Malone—a procession of Forks floated into view, traveling right to left along Summer Street.

Worried that Malone was getting further away, Herbie ducked into a doorway. No point pissing off the kitchen gods. Or even being noticed by them.

Herbie impatiently watched the mob of giant gold, silver, and plastic cutlery float across.

But no matter, he thought, *I'll get Malone for sure before he reaches Chinatown.*

Then he noticed something odd. Above the Forks, outside/above the Grid, flew a herd of dragons in file formation. The dragons were flying without flapping their wings. Which meant the Forks were levitating them also.

The dragons and Forks passed. Pondering the relationship between the two species, Herbie prepared to continue after Malone, who was now out of sight.

Then he heard the sound of rustling wings overhead.

Herbie instantly forgot Malone. Panic filled him. *Shit. A dragon's made it through The Grid!*

He turned. His panic turned immediately to surprise.

"What . . .?"

Blondie and Stacy landed in front of Herbie. Both flapped their wings twice to clear them of dust, then folded them neatly—like birds would—on their backs.

"You're . . . You're . . ."

Blondie decided to help him out. "We're trangels."

"Tra . . . tra . . .transsexual angels?"

Stacy grinned sweetly. "We're here for you—to take you back to Traven with us."

Herbie overcame his initial surprise. The import of both women's words sank in. "Traven—Transsexual Heaven? But I'm neither married nor a philanderer. Nor am I *dead*." His brow wrinkled. "Aren't those the conditions?"

Blondie giggled. "Don't believe everything you hear, Herbie." She sobered. "Actually, yes, *those are* the conditions. But we're here illegally. Our worman died . . ."

"Worman?"

"Our wife," Blondie said. "She died, and we need a replacement. The council prescribes six months mourning . . ."

"Much too long!" Stacy yelped. Her wings beat furiously behind her, spraying the ground with pink feathers.

"I agree with my co-husband," Blondie said. "Six months is too long. So we came to Boston to find . . . you."

"Oh, how I love you, Herbie," Stacy gasped.

She unzipped her pants, then reached in and pulled out her cock.

Herbie gaped at how hard it was. It looked like a tiny pink cannon with a mushroom head.

Next, Stacy got a tube of red lipstick from her purse. She smeared lipstick all over her penis-head till it looked like a set of lips.

She pumped her hips at Herbie. "Come on, darling," she said playfully. "Kiss, kiss, kiss my cock-lips."

Herbie was horrified. He looked between both women after Malone, now once again a distant pinprick.

Why the hell did I send Bulldog away? He'd be able to handle this pair of demented sluts for sure. Shit, I stupidly sent away Gorgeous also—she'd kung fu these girls to bits.

He remembered the knife in his pocket.

About reaching for it, Blondie gripped his hand and placed it over her groin. Herbie felt her erection through her pants, throbbing like a motorcycle engine. "See, I love you too."

"But . . . But . . ." Herbie was now utterly terrified. He fought to free his hand from Blondie's and get out his pocket knife. Her grip was iron however, crushing his fingers against the undesired penis.

Blondie pulled him close to her, forced his head down onto her breasts. "You wanted to suck on these, didn't you?"

"No, no, no!" Herbie shrieked. The body scent coming off Blondie's immense breasts swirled in his head like pot. It made him weak, sapped his will.

"Yes, yes," Stacy moaned in pleasure, stepping up close to the entwined couple and humping her lipsticked member HARD against Herbie's trouser rear. "Oh fucking yeeessss!"

Herbie had no time to even be disgusted that Stacy was ejaculating against his buttocks. He'd realized that Boston was fading away around him. Devonshire Street seemed like it was being wiped from existence.

"Oh, you're such a dirty girl, Stacy. Tell me: Is he good?"

"Fantastic! The best ever! And he still has his *clothes* on!"

"Help me, somebody!" Herbie screamed. "Malone! Help me, Malone! Help!!!"

But there was no street anymore.

Just Herbie and the two trangels who'd abducted him.

✳✳✳

Herbie looked around and gaped in horror.

They were in midair now. Blondie and Stacy were airlifting him towards the biggest skyscraper-beetle he'd ever seen. The building-insect was so HUGE it hurt his mind to conceive the size of it.

"Welcome to Traven, darling," Stacy said. She leaned to kiss Herbie's cheek. "It's your new home. Trust me, you're going to fucking love it here."

"Forever and ever," Blondie added, rubbing her breasts against Herbie's face.

Herbie made no reply. He lacked words to express the extent of his dread now. Unable to look down at the impossible drop if the trangels let go of him. He instead focused his attention solidly ahead, on the immense monolithic mass he was being relentlessly borne toward.

Traven—Transsexual Heaven.

CHAPTER 30

Posh

On leaving Sugar Ray's bar, Posh had driven back the way she'd come, via Chauncy and Arch Streets. That meant going right. She couldn't head left, like Herbie had, because the upper half of Otis—across Summer Street—was blocked off by a skyscraper planted in the middle of the road.

Then, on reaching the Franklin Street junction, she'd remembered that Herbie wouldn't be driving—she had his car—and she'd be ahead of him. She'd also realized that Herbie would have avoided the Otis Street blockage by crossing to Devonshire Street, which also led home.

So now she doubled back down Devonshire to find him.

***

She noticed a couple jogging toward her and slowed. Is that you, jerk? Start saying your last fucking prayers.

Fear gripped her when she saw it wasn't Herbie approaching, but Bulldog. She'd recognize that squat cretin's build anywhere.

In the headlights, she saw Bulldog's eyes widen with recognition of Herbie's pimpmobile. Posh winced. No way anyone could miss its 'L3t5 4k' plate number. She also recognized Bulldog's companion as Sookie Ling's niece.

The pair ran toward her.

At first, Posh's fear threatened to overwhelm her. She felt like putting the Lincoln in reverse and hauling ass out of there.

Then she thought: *What the hell?*

She drove on. She swerved to the other side of the road from Bulldog and Gorgeous and pulled up opposite them. Then she pointed her blaster out through the car window.

"Hey, you two!"

Bulldog smiled nastily. "We's just coming to find your ass." He started across the cracked tarmac toward Posh. "So you wanna run away from Herbie, huh?"

Posh shot the ground in front of him.

Bulldog halted. He gaped at the new two-feet-deep pothole at his feet. It smoldered with bubbling tar.

"Just stay back, asshole" Posh said. "I got no time for your shit. Next time that'll be your legs. Now, where the hell is Herbie?"

For a moment Bulldog looked like he'd call her bluff. Posh tensed to shoot the asinine motherfucker.

Then he just looked at her odd. *Dammit,* Posh thought. *That's the same way Sugar Ray was staring at me—like I'm leprous.*

"What the hell is wrong with your face?" Bulldog asked. "It's all brown and swollen."

"You look like you're falling apart," Gorgeous added, walking closer. "Like your face wants off your head."

Posh groaned. *I don't need this crap. I feel worse than I look.* But she wasn't letting that on.

"Just tell me where the hell Herbie is, or I'll shoot both of you."

Once again Bulldog looked conflicted over whether to rush her or not. Then Gorgeous squeezed his bicep and whispered something into his ear.

(From being initially disgusted with Bulldog, Gorgeous now found herself immensely turned on by him. Not by either his looks or character, but by his primal brutishness, a physicality the likes of which she'd rarely encountered.

He literally reminded her of the mythical creatures Ox-Head and Horse-Face—the Guardians of the Underworld—all strength and no sense.

As they'd jogged up together, she'd grown wetter and wetter between the legs. Now her nipples felt tingly, they pressed hard against her bra. She imagined Bulldog's flat lips bruising them, suckling on them, his rough calloused hands sliding over her hips, squeezing her ass hard . . .)

Bulldog looked at her. "Dragon grip pussy clench? For real?"

Gorgeous nodded, her face flushed.

Bulldog grinned broadly.

"What the fuck was that?" Posh said. "You two better not be planning—"

"We wouldn't *dare* attack you," Gorgeous interrupted. "You look contagious."

"Yeah, Bulldog said. "Like shit come to life." He smiled lewdly. "And besides, we're in a hurry to go screw."

Gorgeous pointed. "Just keep going down the road. Herbie went to help out Malone."

Posh felt a chill. "Malone?"

Gorgeous nodded. "He's injured. Someone cut him up bad. Herbie's getting him some help."

Posh gaped at them, then still wordless, she gunned up the car and sped off.

Fuck! she was thinking. *You two dumb horny rabbits*! *Herbie isn't going to help Malone, he wants to kill him!*

CHAPTER 31

Malone

Five minutes after Herbie's disappearance, Malone's body finally gave out on him. It quit on the willpower that had forced it across the city.

He collapsed to the ground, rolled over onto his back, and lay staring through The Grid at the evening sky overhead.

Looks like I'm dino dinner tonight, he thought.

Posh drove up a minute later.

She leapt out of the car and ran to Malone's side. She gaped at his mutilated body and the female head he clutched in his hand.

Malone opened his eyes wearily. "Who're you? My guardian angel?"

Posh nodded. "Sort of. I'm your new girlfriend."

Malone smiled. "Close enough." He saw she was looking around. "You expecting anyone?"

"My pimp."

Malone grinned. "Knew you were too good to be true. You're a *paid* girlfriend?"

"I'm retired." She tried hauling him up. "Help me out here, will ya? You weigh a ton."

"It's kind of hard," Malone said. With a huge effort he made it to his feet. He stumbled across to the car. Posh opened the rear door. Malone sprawled across the seat on his back. He folded his legs in so she could shut the door.

Posh was disgusted with the way he was holding Rachel Fischer's head to his chest.

"Can't you let go of that head?" she grunted.

"Uh, uh. You've no idea of the hell I went through to get it. It's worth fifty thousand dollars."

Posh didn't argue. Malone *looked like* he'd been through hell. Once again she looked around for Herbie. *Where the hell has the shithead gotten to? I'm still gonna fucking kill you, Herbie. Then I'll die myself. But at least I'll die satisfied that I took you with me.*

She got in the car.

"Where were you headed?" she asked Malone.

"Take me to Chinatown Park—Ma Cure's place. You know there? The old pagoda theatre?"

"I know it," Posh said.

Then she saw that Malone was staring intently at her. "*What?*"

"You're pretty. At least you used to be before you caught your skin disease somewhere. That stinks. I knew a guy with the same problem once. Oswald Watkins—a Syrian war vet. Has to be dead by now—he was always suicidal as a lemming."

Posh couldn't reply. Knuckles white on the steering, she drove on, forcing back the tears threatening to spurt from her eyes.

CHAPTER 32

Malone, Posh, Jade, Ma

"You look like—" Jade began.

"Don't you say it!" Posh snapped. "Just help me get Malone up to Ma."

Jade nodded. They woman-handled Malone into the house and dragged him to the top floor.

"I don't get it," Jade said. "What's with the head?"

"It's the woman I went to rescue," Malone said.

Jade stared into Rachel's dead staring eyes. "Yeah, you rescued her all right."

Malone smiled. "Not my fault. Honest. She was a total fucking prude. She didn't want to come, so I forced her."

Posh winced at the pun.

Jade grimaced too. "He's doped out of his fucking mind. Let's put him down and I'll fetch Ma.

***

Two hours later, Malone was almost himself again.

Ma Cure had first anesthetized Malone with acu-puncture needles. Then she and Jade had washed all the blood off him—both inside and out.

Ma then trimmed off the destroyed parts of Malone's liver, coated the rest with a healing salve, and stitched his belly back together.

Finally, she'd given Malone several potions to drink—Chinese herbal infusions that both wiped all the drugs out his system, and filled him with strength.

He sat now in a corner, drinking hot soup. Between sips, he filled Ma, Jade, and Posh in on what had happened at Frank and Rachel's wharf hideout.

"Yang Yang could have fucking warned me," he said angrily. "I almost lost my life back there."

"She not tell you as fun," Ma said, her withered face creased in a smile.

"Fun? That's sick," Posh said. "He's right—he could have been killed."

Ma shook her head, swiveling it inside the paper loop that secured it to her nine-year-old neck more firmly than a spine. "No, not sick at all. Yang Yang, goddess. Divine idea of fun different from mortal." She thought a moment. "Most likely she see in future that you survive anyway. Remember she like you—for when you rescue her from brother Cheung Lee."

Posh scowled.

She looked at Malone. "They actually *ate* you?"

Malone nodded. He turned to look at Rachel's head, now also washed and wrapped in transparent plastic. "Likely you're right that she knew I'd survive," he told Ma. "It still hurt though."

Ma grinned broadly, revealing all ten teeth in her mouth. "Painful experience part of human growth."

Malone nodded. His mind went back to the day he'd faced Uncle Lee's golem.

Uncle Lee's Golem Part 2

Arms crossed and hidden in the sleeves of a long red robe, Uncle Lee stood by an interior rose garden.

He regarded Malone coldly.

Uncle Lee was as old as Ma. Wiry and withered, with long white hair and white mustaches that hung well below his chin.

But his ancientness only applied to his head. Like Ma's, his body was young—broad-shouldered and muscular.

Like Ma also, he had a single paper loop wrapped around his neck.

Back then—just like with Ma—Malone had no idea that Uncle Lee's body and head each came from a different source.

"What want here, young man?" Uncle Lee asked Malone. His voice was ghostly.

Malone smiled. "Your sister asked me to collect a statue of hers."

Uncle Lee raised both eyebrows, then smiled dismissively. "Yang Yang is family heirloom. Ma, me, family. No business of yours. Leave now."

Malone shook his head. "Ma Cure paid me—that *makes* her business my business. Hand the statue over."

"Leave or I throw out."

Malone smirked. He pulled out his gun. "Not without your sister's property. Fucking hand it over."

Uncle Lee smiled. "Ah, you one of *stupid* American. I think most of you extinct now, but I wrong. Okay, follow, I give heirloom."

He turned and led the way.

Malone followed him through a door, wondering where the Golem Ma Cure had warned him about was.

They entered an inner hall.

Uncle Lee pointed. "There is goddess. Take if can."

Malone regarded the four-feet-tall half-woman half-snake statue. Beside it stood the golem.

Malone winced.

The golem was seven feet tall. Its head was a single chunk of seeping flesh. No eyes, nose, or mouth, just raw bleeding meat, cut straight from an animal.

Its body was similar—chunks of meat and bone assembled into human form. A flesh patchwork cobbled together by magic.

Dinosaur teeth stuck out of its body at random. Here and there Malone saw patches of scaly dino skin, some of which folded inside the creature.

The only properly positioned parts in the monster's composition were the raptor claws that formed both its 'hands.'

The meat sentinel stood motionless beside Yang Yang.

Malone shrugged off his fear of it. *It's meat. Meat will fry.* Gun held at the ready, he stepped towards the Snake Lady statue.

The golem came alive immediately. It stepped in front of the statue.

"If leave now, you still live," Uncle Lee said. "Attack golem, die."

Malone turned to look at him.

Uncle Lee sat cross-legged on the floor, holding a piece of raw meat. Malone grimaced in disgust. The piece of meat was carved in shape of a large doll.

"Aren't you a little too old for toys?" he asked.

Uncle Lee laughed. "Like say, you fool. Stupid kill you." He began chanting slowly to the doll.

Malone ignored him. He turned back to face the meat creature guarding the statue he was after. It hadn't altered its position.

Malone took a step toward it. It took a step toward him. He stepped right, it moved block him off. He went left, it did the same.

This is bullshit, he thought. He shot it.

The blast—at full power—should have reduced the golem to ash. But it did nothing. The meat creature was totally undamaged.

While Malone came to terms with this, it grabbed him and flung him across the room.

He crashed into some crockery. He got up painfully, holstered his gun, and headed for the golem, which was also heading for him.

They met in the middle of the hall. The golem swiped at Malone with its claws. He ducked its talons and caught its wrists. They grappled like that, his hands sinking into its wet flesh. Meat juice squished out around his fingers as he wrestled it.

He was quickly overpowered. The creature was too big, too strong. It bent Malone backward, then freed its left arm from his grip and raked it down his chest, shredding his jacket.

Malone yelped from the pain of his skin and muscle ripping open.

Behind him, Uncle Lee's chanting grew louder.

Malone flung a punch at the golem's featureless face. His hand left a dent in the wet meat, but the monster was unfazed.

(The golem's total silence during their struggle made concrete Malone's understanding that he battled something undead.)

It ripped him with its claws again, slashing across his right shoulder.

Malone kicked against it, freeing himself.

He leapt back, then stood panting, gripping his shoulder. Blood dribbled between his fingers. Blood similarly poured down his chest, which felt on fire.

This fucking thing will kill me, he realized. *It has to have a weakness, but what the hell is it?*

Uncle Lee's voice grew yet louder still behind him, building to a crescendo that Malone knew presaged evil for him.

He turned to look at the old man.

Uncle Lee still sat cross-legged on the floor. He held his meat puppet overhead. His eyes were fixed on it in religious reverence. His lips curved in an evil smile as he chanted.

Malone heard the golem moving behind him.

He spun around as it launched a chair at him.

He ducked, but not fast enough.

The chair hit Malone a hard blow on the left side of his chest, before spinning away and crashing into a display of ceremonial plates.

The plates blew apart.

Malone went down to one knee, then leapt up again.

He winced in pain. His side fucking hurt—he suspected he'd broken at least two ribs.

The golem next bent over a locked eight-feet-long, four-feet-high oak cabinet. It wrenched the massive piece of furniture off the ground.

Malone groaned on seeing how effortlessly it lifted the cabinet.

Its contents rattled ominously.

It's powered by magic, he thought. *Voodoo shi—"*

Understanding hit Malone then. *Voodoo. The golem is being controlled by that fucking doll Uncle Lee is holding.*

He jerked out his blaster again.

Oak cabinet held overhead, the golem turned toward Malone.

Malone spun toward Uncle Lee and shot at the meat puppet he held aloft. Then he spun back to face the golem.

Behind Malone, Uncle Lee stared in disbelief at the empty space above his head where his hands and the meat puppet had been seconds earlier. Malone had incinerated them. Lips still moving in his incantation, Uncle Lee gaped at his charred wrist stumps.

Powered by Uncle Lee's last command before the meat puppet was destroyed, the golem flung the huge cabinet at Malone.

Malone leapt out of the way. The cabinet sailed past him and crashed down on Uncle Lee.

Next, the golem slowly fell apart into chunks of raw meat.

Malone rushed over to help Uncle Lee. Except for a single kicking leg, the ancient Chinese elder was invisible beneath the heavy oak furniture. A flood of blood pumped from under the cabinet edge.

Uncle Lee's leg kicked twice more and stopped.

Malone winced. He turned away. Gripping his aching side, he walked past the still disintegrating meat monster. He picked up the Snake Lady statue, which was lighter than it looked, and left.

***

Back to Now again

Malone stared at the Dead God's Sword hanging on the wall opposite him. The weapon was long and curved, with a handle of delicately worked white jade. While bandaging his wounds back then, Ma Cure had said it would cut through anything, metal, concrete—whatever. Just not through Uncle Lee's dino-meat android.

Now her aged voice broke into his thoughts.

"Yang Yang still want gratitude fuck you," she told him. "She old school goddess—always have wet pussy for hero who save her."

Malone sipped his soup and blushed.

"Stop teasing him, Ma," Jade said. "And why're you calling the goddess old school? *You're* old school."

Ma laughed. "True, but her school much ancient than mine." Her eyes twinkled at Malone. "What say? You try divine sex?"

Malone laughed "How? She's a snake, Ma."

Ma smiled serenely. "Snake fuck well. She know many tricks that—"

"Yeow!" Posh yelped then. "Yeoooooowwwwww!"

The other three turned to look at her. Then they gaped.

Posh's skin was falling off her face. Strip after strip peeled off and slithered down onto her neck. She picked a strip off her chest and stared at it in incomprehension.

"Yeooowww!" she screamed again, when, like the petals of an opening flower, all her remaining facial skin flopped off, leaving her face a raw bleeding mess. Next, her entire scalp broke apart—skin and hair popped off her head like it was being yanked off, leaving her skull exposed.

Jade winced at the sight. Her stomach churned.

Malone dropped his bowl of soup. "This is fucking bad," he said softly. "Trust me, Ma—I've seen it happen before."

Mewling like a cat, Posh now toppled over onto the floor. She lay twitching, while all the skin on her arms peeled off. Her clothes stained red as the rest of her skin peeled off under them.

Malone and Jade rushed to her side. Ma joined them.

Posh twitched and gaped, mumbling incoherencies, in too much agony to think straight.

Ma bent over Posh and studied her now totally raw body, then turned to Malone.

"Not know disease," she said. "We consult goddess. She for sure know what do."

Malone nodded, he glanced down once at the mess Posh had become, then bared his arm. "Bleed me."

Ma nodded to Jade. Jade rushed in to fetch Yang Yang.

Ma smiled at Malone. "You very good man."

He made a face. "She brought me here. I'd be worse than shit if I let her die."

* * *

Yang Yang—her lips painted with his blood—smiled at Malone. Her mouth looked like a rose garland slung between her white cheeks.

Malone chilled at the amorality in her eyes—their reptile suggestion that she knew neither right nor wrong.

Yang Yang said something in her heavy accented Chinese.

"She want know how rescue go," Ma translated. Beside her, Jade sat cross-legged, chanting to keep the goddess animated.

(This was something that Malone had wondered about more than once: If he said yes to the goddess' request that he sleep with her, would Jade need to be in the room also, chanting so the deity could fuck?)

Malone winced at the 'rescue' question.

Yang Yang laughed, then said some more.

"She say know you survive," Ma said. "Only liver die."

Posh, lying beside the goddess, groaned.

Fearing infection, none of them had dared to touch her. Instead, they'd formed their summoning circle around her. The floor around Posh was stained with her blood and body fluids.

"She's dying, Ma," Malone whispered. "Ask her quick."

Yang Yang said something before Ma could ask. Then she took a deep sip of Malone's blood from her bowl. Her perfect body swayed on its serpent coils.

"Say, still cute, tight buttocks—good hero quality."

Malone gasped in exasperation. His eyes pleaded with Ma.

She nodded. She bowed to Yang Yang, explained in Chinese what they wanted.

The Snake Lady replied. Ma looked at her confused. Even Jade looked up from her chanting, perplexed.

Ma questioned her again.

The goddess nodded, her beautiful face serious. She spoke emphatically now, gesturing with a delicate white hand at a bottle in a cabinet, pausing occasionally to sip blood.

Ma turned back to Malone. "Goddess say dragon sperm cure."

Now Malone was confused. "Dragonreich?"

Yang Yang finished up her bowl of blood and froze again into immobility.

Ma nodded. "Powerful secret ancient remedy. Not modern drug abusers think."

"Only problem is," Jade added, her pretty face serious, "she warns of great danger if we use it. She says it's better we let Posh die."

Malone stared at the once-again motionless white sculpture. "And of course—she didn't say *what* the danger was."

Jade nodded, then shrugged.

"Can't she just fucking speak *plainly?*"

"She goddess," Ma reminded him. "Immortal enjoy puzzling mortal."

Malone grunted. He pointed to the twitching woman on the floor. "I honestly can't think of any danger worse than this mess she's in." He looked from Jade to Ma. "I say we do it."

"No good," Ma said. "Better let her die. Goddess never wrong."

"Let's do it, Ma," Jade said. "She's a *friend* of mine."

Ma nodded. "Okay, do, but not blame me if skinless girl explode, infect all with falling-off skin."

CHAPTER 33

Malone, Posh, Jade, Ma

Jade got the bottle of dragonreich down from the cabinet shelf.

She tipped six tablespoon's measure of the powder into a large soup ladle, then dissolved it in water.

Using the legs of a stool, Malone rolled Posh over on her back. Then he wedged a handful of chopsticks between her skinless lips and forced her mouth open.

Jade dangled the ladle over Posh's lips and dripped the milky liquid between them.

Posh moaned as the liquid filled her throat. From out of her cocoon of pain, her eyes gaped sightlessly at the ceiling.

"Don't spit it out," Jade said. "It'll cure you."

Posh managed to nod. Malone heaved a sigh of relief when she swallowed and kept swallowing.

"That's the dose the goddess advised," Jade said when the ladle was empty. "Now we wait."

***

The shed strips of Posh's skin lay about her like flayed snakes. Her raw face was a portrait of Hell's torment.

They waited.

It happened slowly, from the inside out. White substance filled out Posh's flesh. It looked like putty, like wet plaster. It built up on her like it was being poured into a mold.

The white substance became new skin over Posh's face and arms. She grew hair out of her scalp again.

On her back, eyes shut, she breathed gently, a sculpture in white clay.

"Except that she's all white, she looks normal enough," Jade said. "I wonder what the danger—"

"She's not done yet," Malone whispered.

Jade saw what he meant. Posh's body was now swelling. It burst through her clothes, spraying skin strips everywhere.

"This very not good," Ma said.

"She's growing a tail," Jade said.

"And teeth and claws," Malone said.

Posh, eyes still shut, grew larger and larger. Her skin visibly altered into glazed ceramic. Patterned with roses.

"She becoming dragon," Ma said.

Malone considered. Yes, a ceramic/clay dragon.

Large white reptilian wings grew out of Posh's back.

Malone looked questioningly at Jade.

"No," Ma interjected into the loaded silence, "she not overdose. Goddess say one ladle."

Posh stopped growing. She sat up on her haunches like a dog would. She looked around. Her eyes were snake yellow; her teeth transparent nails; her tongue hung out of her mouth like a dog's.

Her wings flapped slowly behind her.

She looked from one to the next of them. Like she was making up her mind about something.

Then she bent and picked up her shed-skin-snakes and ate them.

"This, danger goddess warn of," Ma said calmly.

Malone turned to look at Ma. Aged face serene, she nodded back. "Yes. Much best kill her before. Now she attack."

The white ceramic dragon wolfed down all her erstwhile skin.

Then she looked at Malone. Her gaze caressed his face, inquiringly.

Malone sighed. "She remembers me," he told Ma. "We'll be . . . oh no!"

He'd noticed that Posh was inhaling air, her body visibly swelling.

The woman-dragon swung her head toward Jade.

Malone was a second faster. He dove at Jade, barreling into her before the blast of fire hit her. Incandescence streamed over them both. They crashed to the floor together.

Ma screamed. Malone looked over at her.

Damn! he thought. Immense clawed feet clinking as she walked, wings gently beating, Posh was advancing on Ma, herding her into a corner.

Ma looked at Malone in confusion. "Immunity spells not work! She not Chinese dragon!"

This was the second time Malone had ever seen Ma Cure flustered. The only other time was during the golem incident. This was more serious than he'd thought.

"We've got to help Ma," he told Jade over his shoulder.

She didn't reply.

Malone looked back. He winced. The fall had knocked Jade out. A thin line of blood ran from the forehead cut where her head had struck a table leg.

Malone leapt to his feet.

Smoke billowing from her snout, Posh was now snapping at Ma, while Ma fended her off with a stool.

Then Posh swiped the stool out of Ma's hands, grabbed her with sharp white claws.

Ma gaped at Malone from around the woman-dragon. "Do something! There is . . . arggghhh!"

Posh had bitten into Ma, bending her head so she chomped down on Ma's body.

Malone ran across the room. He remembered Posh had a gun in her handbag.

He got the blaster out and spun around.

Carrying Ma in her mouth, Posh was attempting to climb out of the window. She was having difficulty, however,—Ma's head and legs wouldn't go through the window the way Posh held her clamped in her jaws.

Malone sighted on Posh's wings, then hit her with a long pulse of fire.

The flame glittered like glazing on her porcelain pinions. It zipped like lightning around her painted ceramic body, then faded harmlessly away.

Posh ignored it. She continued trying to force Ma's head and legs out of the window. Blood overflowed her jaws from the myriad punctures her jagged teeth had made in Ma's torso.

Malone was very worried. He knew Ma's head wouldn't die if her borrowed body did, but if Posh bit into her *head* . . .

Malone shot the woman-dragon again. Again, no effect. He stared at the gun in disbelief, then looked at Ma helplessly.

"Fire not kill dragon!" Ma shrieked, flopping like a toy in Posh's mouth. "She child of fire! Use Dead God sword!"

Posh jerked Ma back then and rammed her entire body against the window frame. The whack knocked Ma out cold. It also broke Ma's right thigh. Blood flooded the window ledge.

Malone rushed and got down the Dead God's sword from its wall hanger. He rushed back at Posh-dragon.

Encouraged by her success in breaking Ma's right leg, Posh was now backing off for another charge at the window frame.

Sword raised overhead, Malone stopped his charge and quietly waited for her to reach him.

Posh backed up closer to him. Her flower-patterned tail swayed beside Malone like a gator's. Her huge white wings looked like unfurling sails.

Malone brought the sword down. But not on the ceramic dragon woman.

He realized he *couldn't* kill Posh—it would be a hell of an asshole way to repay the woman who'd saved him from certain death.

Instead, he chopped through Ma's chest.

The Dead God's Sword separated flesh from flesh like it was slicing paper. Ma's head and shoulders dropped to the floor as Posh rushed at the window again.

This time she had no trouble getting through. A moment later the woman-dragon was airborne with her grisly burden, then a mere speck in the night sky.

Malone walked over and picked up Ma's remains.

"Thanks for saving Ma," Jade said softly.

Malone looked over at her. She was just getting up, holding her head and scowling.

She winced. "Thanks also for giving me the world's biggest headache."

Malone smiled. "You're welcome." He held up Ma's remains. "What now?"

Jade walked over and took the grisly burden from him. She chanted in Chinese a bit. Ma's neck and shoulders fell out of the paper loop that connected it to her head.

She walked over to the cabinet that had held the bottle of dragonreich. She cleared a space on a shelf and placed Ma's head on it.

Then she turned and grinned at Malone.

"She'll keep till I find her a new body. She won't be awake of course, but . . ." She shrugged. "Better than being dead."

She looked pointedly at Malone. "What are you going to do about Posh? She's EXTREMELY dangerous now." She winced. "You really should have killed her. Now she's likely to go around eating people."

Malone sighed. Jade was right. "I'll keep an eye out for her. Hopefully she'll just join the other dragons, or break herself to bits on a rock when landing." He frowned grimly. "If she makes a nuisance of herself, I'll hunt her down."

Jade shook her head at him. "You'd *better*."

Wow, Malone thought, *what the hell was I thinking? That chick is likely to start eating her way through half of Boston.* He remembered Ma's perplexed look. *Damn! Even the Chinese aren't safe from her!*

***

"That sure is one sharp sword," Malone said while Jade hung the Dead God's Sword back on the wall.

"It's from the Old Country. It once belonged to Emperor Taizong of the Tang Dynasty. Before succeeding to the throne, he was a great soldier and adventurer. The legend is, he found the sword in the Tianshan Mountains, in a cave filled with beings not entirely human. They were all dead, but perfectly preserved. One of the corpses spoke to him in his mind and told him to take the sword."

Malone nodded. "Lots of strange things in the Old Country."

"Much stranger things here," Jade said. "I never ever saw anyone become a dragon before. And she's made of porcelain, like a china plate." She grinned. "That still makes her Chinese, I guess."

***

154

Jade found Malone an old black kung fu suit to wear. It had white knot-buttons and drawstring pants. She also found him a pair of slip-ons.

"Nice fit," he said, buttoning up the jacket.

"They used to be Uncle Cheung Lee's. He once had a body about your size."

Malone smiled tightly.

He picked up Rachel's head and headed for the door.

"Today's a day for headless women," Jade quipped.

Malone grinned wearily back at her. Now that the day's rollercoaster of excitement and its corresponding adrenalin rush was done, all he wanted to do was sleep forever.

"You sure you won't just crash here tonight?" Jade asked. "You look almost as shit as Posh did before we supposedly *cured* her."

Malone shook his head. He tapped the plastic-wrapped head under his arm. "Her mum lives in North End. Easier to reach from my place if I wake up late."

He hugged Jade.

Leaving, he paused at the door. "Just in case I forget to mention it later: When you get Ma her new body, make it an adult one. You know how she's always complaining about not being able to have sex."

Jade laughed. "Yeah, Ma *would* like that."

CHAPTER 34

Malone

Malone's car was still where he'd left it when he'd come to consult Yang Yang over Rachel's disappearance. He ignored the shocked looks of those prostitutes out daring the night's cold, threw Rachel's head onto the front passenger seat, then got in.

Jade had packed him some medicines to accelerate his healing. While driving back to Beacon Hill, he chewed on one of these—a ball of brown gummy substance that stank like unwashed armpit and tasted like peppermint.

'Horse medicine balls,' Jade had called them. Malone now almost believed she'd meant that literally.

This time of night most of Boston's streets were deserted.

Once out of Chinatown, Malone drove under The Grid for as long as possible. Looking east, he saw distant sparkles of moonlight diffracted through dragons' fiberglass bodies.

No point making a snack of oneself.

Leaving The Grid at Derne Street junction, Malone momentarily drove through a patch of darkness—a beetle obscuring the moon with its immense bulk.

He ignored it. Beetles were safe, so long as they didn't take a shit on you. Then the sheer immensity of their bowel evacuation overwhelmed any attempt to evade it. Like being buried underground.

Malone had seen that happen once. A parked school bus drenched in a mountain of white poop that had drowned the kids inside before they could be rescued.

He kicked the unpleasant memory from his mind.

He looked at Rachel Fischer's head and smiled. America was safe from her proposed war of conquest, at least. There was no way Frank could take over the entire dragon-fucked US of A. with only three hundred battle-ready robots.

***

Home again.

Malone turned onto Joy Street and rolled home. He parked the car outside his bungalow with great relief.

He got the key from the glove compartment and let himself in.

The first things he noticed once he put the light on were the bloody bones strewn everywhere in his office.

Malone immediately got out his gun. *Shit! there's a fucking dino in my house. This is what I get for not living under The Grid.*

Tense—tiredness once again forgotten—he quick-ly scanned the carnage.

In addition to the bones, there were lengths of intestine draped over his stuffed gorilla chairs. Then he realized that the hill of ash in the middle of the carpet had previously been his office table. And saw that the wall behind it had a burnt patch on it.

That meant dragon.

But in a house? In my house?

Then it hit Malone. In dismay, he smacked his forehead. *Oh, good heavens, no! She didn't come back here, did she?* But Posh *had* called herself his new girlfriend.

He forcibly calmed himself. He walked to the office's inner door and listened. No sound of tramping, clinking feet.

He felt relief. Maybe she'd left.

To make certain, he walked quickly through the bungalow, checking each room.

He pushed open the bedroom door and found she hadn't left.

Posh lay naked and asleep in Malone's bed. Her body was fully back to normal now. Her skin was pink and pure again.

Her breasts rose and fell with her unlabored breathing.

Malone smiled when he saw her face. *Yeah, she is great-looking. Nice breasts too.*

He held back from smoothing her tousled auburn hair.

He sat beside her on the bed, entranced by how cute, how innocent she looked in sleep. Posh dozed on, oblivious to his presence.

Malone thought.

The bones scattered all over his office told a different story about this lovely woman in his bed.

Two hours ago, she was a dragon, spitting fire and attacking people.

Malone now realized his huge dilemma. *She looks fine now—cured. But . . . the goddess said GREAT danger. but, maybe she just meant Ma.*

But does one incident count as GREAT? But I can't just kill her, and I can't kick her out, either. But she said she's a hooker . . . okay, used to be—she's retired. But she mentioned a pimp. What about him? Sheeeit! This is fucking complicated. Okay, so she stays. At least this way I'll be able to keep an eye on her. And kill her if she attacks anyone else.

Even thinking this last however was hard for him. Deadly or not, Malone suspected killing Posh would prove EXTREMELY hard for him to do.

Yeah, you are my new girlfriend, he thought, realizing he was already falling for Posh.

CHAPTER 35

Sara & Jeff

There was a dragon on Sara Fischer's front lawn. It was there courtesy of the Forks, and although it wasn't harming anyone, it was making everyone in the Fischer Mansion nervous.

Sara—who never drank before lunch—had already had four whiskies today, and it wasn't yet eleven. Just the sight of the HUGE creature with its see-through body like solid water was unnerving.

The Forks were out there with the dragon. They weren't 'pronging' it. This part bothered/scared Sara. The Forks were *talking* to the dragon.

Standing by her living room window, she could clearly hear their modulated hums as they spoke; then in the pauses between these, the beast's own replies.

Its answering growls were indecipherable as language, but were clearly meant to be interpreted as such.

Sara could cope with the Forks humming, but this dragon was taking liberty for license.

This fucking beast has to go, she thought angrily.

"Come away from the window, Sara," Jeff slurred drunkenly. "You're just agitating yourself."

The erstwhile US president was the person least bothered by the dragon's presence outside.

Leaving the drapes open, Sara went to sit beside him.

Jeff took her hand and patted it. "You know, I see it clearly now. Earth is Hell now. The dragons are God's fire; but solid and alive—not the lake of brimstone we've always believed in."

Sara snorted. "If we're in Hell, where's Satan?"

"In New York." His booze-gaze cleared for a moment. "I'm serious, Sara. The Devil does live in New York City now. I met him once."

Sara shuddered; Jeff looked serious—like he was telling the truth.

More depressing truth Sara didn't need, however, particularly not something as scary as this. So she changed the topic.

"I'm worried about Rachel." In addition, she felt horny, the result of both her unaccustomed morning alcohol binge and her boiling-over sexual frustration. *Dammit, Jeff! Get a hard-on and plow me, will you?*

Jeff took a sip of scotch. "Don't worry," he said. "The private eye'll find her. They always do."

"I'm worried about him finding her *alive*."

He looked into her eyes. "It'll be okay, you'll see."

In that moment, Sara loved Jeff fervently.

Jeff looked down at his glass of brandy like he'd just remembered it. He downed the remainder in a single gulp.

He staggered to his feet, pulled Sara up after him. "I'm sleepy—let's go to bed."

She smiled, feeling oddly happy. Yes, even snuggling would be nice.

Outside, the humming stopped. Sara looked out through the window. The dragon was airborne and disappearing fast—a sparkling streak heading out towards the harbor.

She sighed her relief.

***

Malone arrived at noon.

The Forks immediately made themselves scarce like they always did whenever Sara had visitors.

Sara was glad Malone didn't see them—*how could I ever explain their presence here?*

Jeff was still sleeping when Sara made her way downstairs to receive Malone.

All the warmth she felt from cuddling nicely with him disappeared immediately when Malone unwrapped the paper parcel he'd brought with him.

His explanation made it even worse. No way was it possible that her own daughter Rachel had . . . But . . .

She grimaced in disgust when he revealed the jagged line of stitches down his belly and explained their significance.

She nodded glumly, when he was done explaining. "I'm sorry, Malone, but I'm in no condition to talk money now. I'll have it delivered to you later."

He nodded, rose to leave. "No problem. I understand."

Malone left.

Sara sat rigid in his wake. She heard the voice of the maid letting Malone out, heard the click of the front door shutting behind him. Her eyes were riveted on the head laid on the table in front of her.

She broke down and began crying.

Still weeping profusely, she made her way back upstairs.

***

Mary Eloise Baker, the maid who'd let Malone out, came in to tidy up the living room.

She caught one look of Rachel's head, shrieked, and fainted.

***

Jeff gaped at Sara. "She *what?*"

Sara nodded, sniffling, dabbing her eyes with a tissue. She caught a glimpse of herself in mirror. *Damn, I look a total mess.*

She wondered how she could be thinking of her looks at a time like this. *I'm sixty-four dammit, not some teen on a date.*

Jeff put his arms around her. Sara forced herself against him as tightly as if she wanted their bodies to fuse into one. The gravity of what Rachel's death meant horrified her. She couldn't hold back her tears. They flowed like the proverbial river.

"I'm all alone in the world now, Jeff. All alone."

"No, you're not," Jeff asserted. "I'm here with you, and I'll never leave your side again. We'll be together, till death do us part."

His words were exactly what Sara needed to hear. Her depression melted off her shoulders like snow in sunshine. She smiled. Unconsciously, she routed her pain over Rachel's passing into Jeff's promise.

She looked up into his eyes.

"Oh, Jeff, I really love you."

He smiled. "I love you too."

"You're really serious about not leaving me?"

He laughed. "I should ask you that question. As I remember it—you dumped me, not the other way around."

Sara laughed. She did feel much better. She realized however that she needed to keep this happy feeling going, else the sheer horror of Rachel's decapitated head downstairs would send her into a total out-of-control emotional downward spiral. Love, love, love. This love could heal her, but she had to work on it, build it up.

"So promise me you'll not jilt me this time," Jeff said.

"There's no chance of that happening," Sara said.

Jeff nodded. "You're right," he said soberly. "David's dead."

Sara hit him playfully. "Don't tell me you're still upset over that. If I'd known you were going to be Mr. President someday, I'd never have left you for him. Look how I missed out on being First Lady."

They both laughed.

Then Jeff kissed Sara. She responded eagerly. Her body, her pussy was aflame with desire for him. Her soul burnt with passion.

She pushed him back onto the bed and lay on top of him. She kissed him furiously, tears of joy falling from her eyes into his.

All the while she squashed her body against his, so that he'd be in no doubt what she wanted—if he could give it to her.

Then with a thrill she felt him harden in his trousers. His cock pulsed greedily against her thighs.

Jeff freed his lips from hers. "I do believe little Mr. President down there wants to make a State of the Union address to you."

Sara giggled. "Let him out. I'm desperate to hear how things are heating up down south."

She suddenly felt evil. "Go on," she added, "free the poor frustrated slave like your namesake did. Let your negro have white pussy to eat without fear of being lynched."

Jeff burst into laughter. "Damn, Sara. That's the most politically incorrect thing I've ever heard in my thirty-seven years in politics."

She grinned. "All's fair in love and war."

She quickly unzipped him and released his erection. *Yes,* she thought, *finally.*

She lowered her lips to it, not minding that it stank a little. She slurped it up greedily, running her lips rapidly up and down over its unwashed length.

Jeff pulled her off his member. "That's even better than I remember."

"Jeff, you *can't* remember; last time I gave you head was forty years ago."

He shrugged. "I'm mixing it up. First Lady gave first-class head too. Reason I married her."

He pulled her up to him and undid her blouse, then slipped his roughened hands under her bra, freeing her breasts. Sara ditched both items of clothing.

Jeff gaped at her massive breasts, their skin taut as opposed the sag that dominated most of her flesh. Delicate veins marbled each curved white expanse. "These are much larger than I remember them. Did they grow up over the years?"

She giggled throatily. "Of course not, silly. They're dinosaur fat implants. But you're sucking them anyway." She bent over his face.

Jeff took her massive left nipple into his mouth and vacuumed it. It throbbed between his lips. Sara groaned with the pleasure.

His unkempt beard prickled her breast. The contrast of this rough sensation made the feel of his suckling lips all the more exquisite.

Her pussy clenched with each caress of his lips.

Jeff pushed her away. "Fuck! I can't wait any longer."

Me neither, Sara thought.

He quickly stripped naked. Like Sara's, his skin sagged on his body, and he had a little paunch.

Jeff rolled Sara over on her back and spread her legs. He spit on his penis, and placed its swollen head between her engorged labia.

Sara gasped—a sharp intake of breath that felt like she was choking—when he entered her. The feeling hung between pleasure and pain—she had no idea which it was.

The strangling feeling dissolved into familiar pleasure as Jeff slid to the depths of her.

We're just two old people who've found love again in our twilight years, she thought happily,

Her eyes rolled up in their sockets as he thrust into her. The sexual pleasure galloped through her like a field of racehorses.

Hard and fast, harder and faster.

Images of dead Rachel threatened to douse her passion. Sara wasn't having it. She pulled Jeff's body down on hers. She locked her lips to his, digging her tongue deep into his mouth. She held him tight to her, gripping his neck with her hands. She wrapped her legs around his buttocks and locked her ankles.

She disentangled her lips from Jeff's and looked deep into his eyes, saw that his passion was as fierce and intense as hers. His eyes were wide and staring, his lips curled down in a scowl, his overall expression a strangled grimace.

Damn, Sara thought, *he looks like he's having a fucking heart attack. Guess he's got a lot of frustration to work off.*

Jeff was still fucking her however. Long, HARD strokes of cock that danced between pain and pleasure. *Wow,* she thought, *this is the real meaning of 'ass-whupping.'*

Jeff's breathing became labored.

Sara willed herself to meet his orgasm with her own. She let go his neck, and reaching down between her legs, rubbed her clitoris so her pleasure peaked as his did.

Jeff came. "Yessssss!" he growled like a bear as he spurted into Sara.

Sara came also, pumping her bony crotch up against him. The pleasure was so intense she screamed. "Oh, my God, yess!!"

She spiraled upward in ecstasy forever.

Jeff went limp on her and rolled off. Sara descended in stages from her fucked-out bliss.

"Oh, Jeff," she gushed, when she could finally speak. "That was incredible."

He didn't reply. Sara turned to look at him and saw he was staring up at the ceiling with a fixed expression—a broad grin like he was the happiest man alive. She looked at his chest; he wasn't breathing.

Alarmed, she grabbed his wrist, felt for his pulse. There was none. Jeff was dead.

Dammmit, Jeff. You were having a heart attack?

Sara stared at his corpse in utter disbelief. Then, like a band of al-Qaeda suicide bombers, despair rushed at her from all sides. Despair that threatened to fracture her mind.

Sara lay beside Jefferson Lincoln, holding his arm and weeping copiously. She held tightly onto the memory of his love for her, of the beautiful lovemaking they'd just shared, the knowledge that he'd died *happy*, in *her* arms.

It was all that kept her from cracking up.

Slowly, Sara came to terms with losing him.

She shut his staring eyes, kissed him on the lips one final time, then got up, and got dressed.

She had to inform the Forks that their favorite captive was dead.

Sara was remarkably calm now. Everything bad that could happen to her anymore had all happened in the space of one morning.

She parted the bedroom drapes. *What the hell is that white stuff raining down? Looks like popcorn.*

CHAPTER 36

Sara

When Sara got downstairs, there were still no Forks in the house.

She roused the fainted maid in the living room.

Mary Eloise Baker woke up. Then she sighted Rachel's head and almost fainted again. Then she recognized Sara through her terror and her sense of duty won out over her emotions.

At her mistress' request, she staggered outside, then back in again to confirm that yes, *it was* indeed raining popcorn. She held out a handful so Sara could see.

Sara nodded. "It's a fucked-up day all around. Jeff's dead, Mary."

The maid gasped. "Mr. President?" Her eyes misted. "But how? He looked fine this morning."

"Heart attack."

"Now listen," she told Mary. "The Forks left when Malone delivered . . ." she pointed to Rachel's head, which was now stinking. ". . . and they aren't back yet. I want to bury Jeff before they return. Otherwise they might eat him like they did all the senators they caught."

(Sara recalled very well her conversation with Lord Tav and Lady Yaz about the legislators.

"We assumed that ingesting your leaders would help us understand humans better," Lord Tav had said.

The Fork sighed. "Unfortunately we were wrong. No matter how many senators or congressmen we ate, we learnt nothing we didn't already know."

"We did however learn that human politicians generally have no idea what they're doing," Lady Yaz added helpfully. "If you knew what we do about their motives for aspiring to office, you'd be thanking us for ridding you of them.")

Mary nodded. "What should I do, madam?"

"Call all the servants away from their duties. Smith used to be a military chaplain. Tell him he's conducting the service."

Mary nodded and hurried off with great urgency.

**

Jefferson Lincoln was buried out on the front lawn of the Fischer Mansion.

A guard of liveried male servants carried his body—wrapped in a US flag and laid out on a long silver dinner tray—out to the grave in military fashion.

Dressed in their Sunday best, the rest of the house staff stood around the grave, their faces draped in sorrow.

Two servants stood sentry a distance from the funeral party, concealed beneath trees, watching sky and ground for dinos.

It was still raining popcorn. A light patter of it that floored the grave like tiling.

Old Smith, the butler, a small, portly man with heavy muttonchops, officiated, using Sara's ancient wedding Bible.

"Dearly beloved, we now commit this departed one into the bosom of our—"

The mourners all gasped as the Forks materialized amidst them.

Lord Tav and Lady Yaz, the golden leaders of this Fork grouping, were surrounded by several plastic and tin Forks—lower officials and servants.

Lord Tav and Lady Yaz levitated out over Jeff's still-empty grave.

"We were delayed," Lord Tav said. "Now we sense that President Lincoln is dead. As your conquerors, it is our privilege to prong him. You will therefore hand over his corpse."

There was a collective gasp of horror from the assembled mourners. Then an angry grumbling.

Sara immediately stepped in front of Jeff's star-spangled corpse.

"Oh no, you're *not* eating him," she growled at the Forks. "No one *eats* a US president. You should know that."

An assenting murmur went around the servants.

"It is our right," Lady Yaz said. "Do not be impertinent, Sara."

"If you insist on eating Jeff," Sara retorted. "I'll stop cooperating with you immediately."

(This was a gamble/bluff on her part. Other than their request that she babysit Jeff for them, they'd not asked anything else from her. Okay, except for somewhere to park their fucking fiberglass dragon.)

The Forks hummed between themselves for a long minute.

"Okay, we will not prong him. You may bury *most* of him."

Sara scowled. "*Most* of him?"

"Yes. *Most.* We need . . ."

Two white beams pulsed out of Lady Yaz's breast-tips. Both rays of light curved around Sara's body to rest on Jeff's corpse behind her.

Sara turned and watched.

The tips of the beams of light formed into two knives that cut a hole through the stars and stripes wrapping Jeff. Then they cut deeper—into Jeff's body.

Next, both knives became hands that pulled the edges of both wrapping and body apart and delved inside him.

Then, one hand, one knife, holding and cutting.

Then two hands again, emerging with something big and brown, which they left lying on the corpse.

Both light beams blinked out.

"What is that?" Smith the butler dared ask. He looked set to faint from horror.

"Yes, *what?*" Sara seconded in a strained voice.

"His liver," came the reply. "You may bury the rest of him. We however exert our right to keep *this*."

Sara gaped at the chunk of meat lying on the flag-wrapped body.

"Jefferson Lincoln's liver," Lord Tav continued, "is crystal-clear, irrefutable proof of Fork greatness, and how pathetic you humans are in comparison to us."

Sara stared at the brown mass with its pale splotches and truncated blood vessels. *Damn,* she thought, *it's wobbling like its alive.* She choked back her urge to upchuck all over it.

She was relieved that the Forks hadn't said they wanted Jeff's head, but still . . .

"What the hell do you want with his *liver?* I mean, how can this disgusting thing possibly show how fantastic you are?"

Lady Yaz—her gold body glittering—replied to Sara. "It is symbolic. This American president was previously the most powerful man on the planet. But he died a weakling, his body ruined by the ravages of alcohol addiction—at death, he was a glorified wino. And why? Because he could not handle what we Forks had done to his kingdom."

Sara didn't get it. She said so.

Lord Tav laughed. "But surely, this is obvious. The human liver is the organ that most directly suffers the effect of alcohol abuse. Simple ownership of Jefferson Lincoln's mortally messed-up organ therefore suffices as incontrovertible evidence—"

"Of your greatness," Sara finished glumly. She brushed popcorn out of her hair. The white stuff was everywhere now. Sara wanted the forks to get lost before Jeff's grave filled up with it. This funeral was absurdist enough already.

"Exactly," Lady Yaz said, pleased. "You too see it now. It's very obvious."

Tree shadows now dappled both Fork's bodies. A breeze blowing from the trees chilled the humans assembled around the grave.

Lady Yaz turned to the Fork entourage. "Take the president's liver away and give it a drink," she ordered. She and Lord Tav laughed loudly.

Four plastic Forks instantly floated forward. They levitated Jeff's gently twitching organ into the air and floated it away into the house.

Sara was horrified as she watched them go. "Why give it a drink? It's just a dead organ."

"It is still *alive* and addicted to alcohol. We want it to be a happy captive."

Jeff's liver was 'still alive?' Sara decided that when the shit hit your fan too often, you either threw your fan away or allied yourself with those pooping on it.

She smiled tightly at the Forks. "Okay, now you've got what you came for. Please leave us to bury the last President of the USA with some dignity. Jeff was a great man—whatever you Forks think."

"But of course," Lord Tav said. "He *was* a great man. That is the whole point of this."

The Forks faded from view. Jefferson Lincoln's funeral continued under the popcorn rain.

CHAPTER 37

Malone & Posh

Two days later, Malone drove over to Hailey's Toy Factory again.

This time he was armed to the teeth. His trunk was loaded with all the military firepower he'd been able to scavenge and borrow— six blasters, three energy rifles, a machine gun, grenades, and a bazooka.

Frank wanted a fight? Malone planned on giving him one.

Malone was under no illusions about the magnitude of the task he'd taken on. Though he'd seen none activated during his captivity, he expected to have to contend with Rachel Fischer's robots.

There was, however, the slight chance that only Rachel could switch her machines on.

Slight, but unlikely. Sure, Frank was crazy, but he wasn't a lunk.

Posh rode beside Malone in in the car.

"I really wish you stayed at home," he told her. "I foresee this getting quite messy. I don't want you getting hurt."

"Don't worry. I'll stay in the car, be your getaway driver, just in case things don't work out."

He couldn't argue with that.

Posh looked him over with concern. "I'd still have preferred you waiting till you're healed better."

He scowled. "I already told you—I'm too pissed-off to wait. More important—Frank will still be mourning Rachel now. He should be too mentally tattered to resist capture. I'm counting on the element of surprise."

He considered. "I'm also hoping I can retrieve Rachel's body for her mother to bury."

Malone drove past the Old State House. The entirety of the redbrick building above The Grid was invisible beneath layers of pterodactyl excrement. Some of the dino poop had streamed through the space between dragon-shield and building, coating its walls like dripping wax.

"No idea why they like pooping on it so much," Malone said. "I liked seeing the old lion and unicorn."

Posh smiled. "I guess they have to go to the toilet somewhere. And it does looks like a mountaintop now."

***

Since transforming back to a human again, Posh was happy.

Topping her list of pleasures was the fact that Malone had accepted her. He'd not questioned her story about Herbie, or even seemed to care about her profession.

But then Sookie had suggested he wasn't overly prudish.

And with the turn of events after her rescuing him, Posh felt they'd both accepted to stay together.

She was falling deep in love with Malone. And she had a strong intuition they'd be very good for each other.

There *was* however the slight matter that they'd not made love yet.

Posh didn't feel horny in the least. She suspected this had to do with the dragonreich she'd ingested. Or maybe, it was fallout from her fucked-up experiences of the past week—it was hard to think of intimacy with anyone after Oswald Watkins.

Lust or not, however, Posh knew it was imperative she and Malone get it on as soon as possible. That would set the seal on their relationship.

However, Malone's stitched-up torso meant she couldn't force the issue. She'd look really silly if he couldn't get it up because of the pain he was in.

***

Malone had told Posh what had happened after she became a dragon. She had a snapshot sequence memory of events—of herself ripping Ma Cure apart—and departing with the old woman's body.

Of eating it.

She was horrified by the memories, but unable to relate them to herself now she was herself again. They seemed the actions of another.

Posh was intensely relieved that Ma was 'okay'—that Malone had saved the old woman's head.

***

The one thing Posh hadn't mentioned to Malone was her new hunger for the drug dragonreich. Whilst becoming a dragon, she'd experienced a rush like never before. Every fiber of her being craved that sublime feeling again.

***

"Oh, no," Malone groaned, sighting the black blob in the sky over their destination. "You've got to be shitting me."

Posh patted his arm. "What's wrong, baby?"

He pointed to the monster beetle floating up overhead on the right, laying a skyscraper. "That's where we're currently headed. I think it just flattened the factory."

Posh grinned. "Great. Eliminates the need for you fighting then. I no longer need to worry about you getting shot to bits."

A scowl on his face, Malone drove the rest of the way in silence.

The Toy Factory was already half-submerged under a mountain of cement when they arrived at it.

They parked a safe distance away and watched. Both were entranced—building birth was an arresting sight.

***

Like concrete shit, the building slowly extruded itself from the floating monster insect's birth-hole.

The beetle took a long time giving birth. The skyscraper was very large—Malone estimated it might easily be fifty stories high.

Rivers of liquid cement mix dripped from it. These coated the factory afresh—now completely drowning it—before flooding its parking lot, and running out into the street.

Finally, however, the building was totally extruded.

Now began the tricky part, when the beetle—manipulating the new skyscraper with feet and jaws—slowly lowered it to ground, centering it in the pool of cement slime that had accompanied the building out of it.

It placed the skyscraper directly atop Frank's robot storage warehouse.

Malone imagined the shattering iron girders in the building's skeleton as it crumpled and was forced deep underground by the building being planted in its place. He also imagined Frank's broken and pulped body inside the warehouse.

Then the new building stood tall in its new domain. A residence on its path to becoming its own insect

The beetle hovered awhile longer over its odd child, an asteroid-sized black insect flapping wings the size of jumbo jets, its train-legs twitching beneath it. Its yawning birth-hole poured a final river of cement down over the skyscraper.

Then it flew off.

***

Watching the beetle depart, Malone fought off the sense of overawe which always consumed him when he watched building-birth.

"Quite a spectacle," he said.

Posh nodded, snuggling up close to him. "You don't sound happy though."

"It's inconclusive as shit. I'd love to believe that that shithead Frank was inside and just got crushed to death—but there's no way we'll ever know for sure now."

Malone sounded so cheated at being deprived of his revenge that Posh felt she had to cheer him up.

She turned his face to hers and kissed him.

He initially resisted her lips. "You don't have to," he said.

"I want to," she replied.

And that was that. Their kisses became more fiercer, till they tumbled together into the rear of the car and ripped each other's clothes off.

Posh gasped, her eyes widening in pleasure when Malone penetrated her. She still didn't feel aroused, but oh, the satisfaction of being with him! Finally she felt she belonged somewhere, with someone.

She relaxed with satisfaction, accepting his thrusts into her body with a gladness, a love for this man she'd just met that transcended passion.

And in response, passion flowed from her love. Her body lit on fire, her loins and lust burning hotter and hotter, till it felt like she was a torch.

She lifted her head off the car-seat and kissed Malone hard, sucking his tongue deep into her mouth.

Malone fondled her breasts, then gripped them hard. "I love you, Posh," he gasped as he spurted his cum deep into her.

"I love you too, baby," Posh replied, rising to meet his orgasm with hers.

Then they hugged each other tight, staring deep into one another's eyes to preserve this moment in their hearts.

CHAPTER 38

Smith

It was two in the morning.

Old Smith, Sara's butler, made his way through Rachel Fischer's basement laboratory.

The room was dark except for the single lamp at its far end illuminating the table on which rested both Rachel's head and President Jefferson Lincoln's liver.

Smith greatly disliked coming down here. Normally he let his mistress handle her own business. Tonight, however, he'd had no choice. Sara Fischer had accompanied the Forks somewhere and he had to 'feed' the president's liver its booze.

There was a carton of Jack Daniels under the table. All Smith had to do was pour it and leave.

Smith considered even this little task too much work.

Smith was supposed to have done this at nine p.m., but he'd fallen asleep. Being conscientious, he'd decided better late than never, hence his coming downstairs this late.

Best I get this over with as fast as possible, he thought. In addition to the sheer morbid absurdity of the task, he'd of recent begun suspecting that Jefferson Lincoln's liver was developing intelligence.

Absurd? Maybe. Stupid? Very likely. But whatever anyone says I can't shake off the thought that that chunk of meat is trying to talk to me.

He hastened past tables of scientific equipment of different kinds, all dusty now since their owner's demise.

His view of his destination was blocked by several large screens. Rachel had initially used the screens to partition her lab. Sara had now arranged them all in the corner housing Rachel's head to give her privacy when down here.

Dammit, Smith thought, *she's turned this place into a shrine to her dead daughter and boyfriend.*

For Smith, an ex-army chaplain, the concept was too morbid. The dead should be permitted to rest in peace.

He'd more than once asked Sara to bury Rachel.

"Forget it!" she'd snap each time. "Back to work, you! The pantry's that way!"

***

Smith reached the closest screen and walked around it.

He pulled up sharply.

There was a man seated there, holding the specimen jar containing Rachel's head.

Frank wasn't startled like Smith was; he'd heard him approaching.

Smith regained his poise. He coldly regarded the thin young man with distaste. To Smith, who'd served in the trenches in the Syrian War, Frank looked weak.

Weak, yes; harmless, no.

Smith found the young man's gaze disturbing. His sky-blue eyes were unbalanced, like he was surfing sanity's edge.

Smith felt chilled. His years as a chaplain had made him a good judge of people. This young man was dangerous. No doubt about it.

"What are you doing here?" he asked gruffly. "How did you get in?"

Frank frowned. "I'm here for two reasons.

"Firstly . . . ," he tapped the specimen jar, "The rest of Miss Fischer is over in my freezer. I want to bury her as a complete woman."

Smith now realized who the man talking to him was—the psycho who'd kidnapped and murdered Rachel.

(To maintain family appearances, Sara hadn't let on to anyone that Rachel had actually colluded with her 'abductor.')

Smith began looking around him for a weapon.

"You said *two* things," he said to distract Frank. "What's the second?"

Frank smiled. "I got ahead of myself. There's actually *three* things." He swiveled on his chair to the table and hefted up Jefferson Lincoln's liver. "Whose liver is this? This is literally most cirrhotic specimen I've ever seen."

Smith went with the flow. "You're a doctor?"

"A hepatologist—liver specialist." Cold eyes stabbed into Smith's. "Whose liver is it?"

"Jefferson Lincoln." Smith saw no harm in telling Frank this— he'd spotted a crowbar just outside the screen on his right. One tap on the noggin with that and sicko here would be out for the count.

Frank gaped. "The president?"

Smith nodded. He cautiously edged closer to the crowbar. He had no idea if Frank was armed or not.

Frank moped. "But he never looked like a drinking sort of man. Dear God, just look at the state of this thing—like the current state of the nation." He lifted the organ to his nose and sniffed it. "Smells absolutely awful."

About to bend down, Smith saw that Frank was almost crying. "Such a shame. It would have been an absolute honor too to eat the First Liver. But now? The fucking thing is totally inedible—has to be poisonous even."

Eat Jefferson's liver? Kid, you really are a sick fuck.

Smith bent quickly, grabbed the crowbar, and lunged at Frank with it.

Then he felt an incredible pain in his arm and the crowbar wrenched out of his hand. Or maybe the order of events was reversed—Smith wasn't sure.

After the sharp burst of pain, Smith looked at his arm. It was broken. The front half of his forearm hung off the rest at an angle.

Frank laughed. "You should have stuck to talking, old man. Glory days have passed you by."

Smith stared mutely as the white robot stepped into view. It was human-sized and human shaped, with a 'T' slot in its face in which two red lights blinked.

Frank considered Smith's agonized face impassively. "You honestly didn't think I came here all alone did you?"

Smith looked back. He gasped. Behind the robot that had disarmed him stood a second one of exactly the same design. He made out the inscription 'Product of New Korea' on the robot's side.

The fight drained out of Smith.

"Lay him on a table," Frank said.

"Wha . . . ?"

Both robots grabbed Smith and lifted him off his feet. They carried him out of the screened enclosure.

The robot carrying Smith's upper body, swiped a hand across a lab table, knocking an array of test tubes and an electron microscope to the floor. Metal clanged. Glass smashed.

The robots arranged Smith on the cleared table. He squealed when his broken arm thumped its metal edge.

Both robots stepped back from the table and froze into immobility.

Smith made no attempt to flee or scream for help. For one thing, this was a basement and the door was closed. No one would hear him. But second, and more important, was the white robots' pose. Motionless as they were, their only sign of life the red dots blinking in their faces, they gave off an air of subliminal menace that petrified Smith.

Frank walked out from behind the screens. He was carrying Jefferson Lincoln's liver, now flopping like a landed fish. He stared down at Smith. His blue eyes gleamed like he was dying of fever.

"Don't kill me, kid. Please. I got no fight with you."

Frank smiled. "Let's talk. Tell me what I want to know and I won't kill you. Understand?"

For emphasis he tapped Smith's broken arm.

Smith howled. The pain felt like his arm was being broken all over again. He nodded quickly. "Yes, yes!"

"Good," Frank said. "Now . . ." He stroked Jefferson Lincoln's liver like it was a baby. The liver calmed. ". . . Tell me everything you know about this organ."

Smith hastily explained all about the late president's death and burial.

***

Frank listened in silence. Only an imperceptible widening of his eyes betrayed his surprise on hearing of the Forks' involvement.

This is very interesting, he thought. It would also explain why the organ he carried was still alive and seemed aware of its surroundings.

"That's all I know," Smith said finally.

"There are bottles of booze in the enclosure. What are *they* for?"

Smith explained.

Frank nodded. *This is even stranger than I thought. This liver leaves here with me in any event, along with Rachel's head. The Forks, eh?*

"Where is Mrs. Fischer now? I want to talk to her."

"She's gone off somewhere with the Forks. I've no idea where."

Frank frowned. A setback. He'd intended asking Sara where Malone lived.

He scowled. If Malone thought he'd gotten away with murdering Rachel, he was an idiot. He still had hell to pay, but with Sara Fischer away today, Frank's revenge would be delayed.

He smiled at Smith. "You will deliver a message to Mrs. Fischer for me when she returns, old man."

Smith nodded. "Whatever you say."

Frank nodded back. "You'll not need to remember it. I'll write it out for you."

Smith nodded.

Frank dropped the president's liver on an adjacent table, then returned.

Smith shivered when he saw Frank was now holding a switchblade.

Shit! He made to rise.

Frank gestured to the robots. "Hold him down."

The white machines grabbed Smith's arms and legs.

Frank flicked the switchblade open.

"Hey wait! What are you doing? You said you wouldn't kill me!"

"Don't be a dick," Frank said angrily. "I'm *not* about to kill you. I just missed dinner earlier and intend making up for that oversight. Ordinarily, I'd eat that liver over there. But it's clearly poisonous now, so some of yours will have to suffice."

Smith gaped at Frank. "What? Eat my liver?" He fought to rise, but the quartet of metal hands held him firmly in place. He gaped at Frank. "Are you fucking nuts?"

Frank smiled coolly. "Quite a few people think so."

Ignoring his pleas—and later, screams—Frank unbuttoned Smith's shirt and began cutting.

PART 2: PORCELAIN

INTERLUDE: THE ODS

Since the day of President Lincoln Jefferson's death, the world had become a much stranger place.

In retrospect, the popcorn rain over the last US president's funeral had been a prophecy of the future.

***

The new changes to Boston reality were both drastic and subtle.

In addition to obvious oddities like it now raining cornflakes and popcorn, there was the constant suggestion that Boston—nay, the entire USA—was now overlaid by other dimensions, places no sane person would rightly wish to visit.

Places accessible via the Otherworld Doors,—ODs—the wormholes through space-time.

The ODs were upright shimmering 'spaces' that could occur *anywhere*—in the middle of the street, in the middle of the air, in the middle of a kitchen or living room or toilet. There was no rhythm or rhyme to their placement.

Some ODs only teleported the user across Boston. Some seemed to teleport the user across the universe. Yet others appeared to teleport those entering to realms that seemed versions of Heaven and Hell.

Many different versions of Heaven and Hell.

On the ODs initial appearance, many had attempted entering the worlds they were granted access to.

A few of these adventurers had returned with unbelievable stories to tell. A few had returned mauled/maimed by creatures they could find no words to describe.

Most hadn't returned at all.

So now the ODs were left alone, with only the intrepid, the extremely/congenitally foolish, or the desperate venturing into them.

Thankfully—from a Bostonian point of view—there were few Otherworld Doors in and around the 'livable' parts of the city. The Grid itself, Chinatown, South Boston and the Charles River Basin out east were mostly free of the shimmering distortions that announced a passage to another realm.

The area north of the city—all through Cambridge and across the harbor to Logan International Airport in East Boston—was riddled with these wormholes through space-time.

Logan Airport was particularly plagued with ODs. It was as if someone had earmarked it as a transit portal.

If anyone other than the dragons and dinos had ventured out to Boston's erstwhile international transit point, they'd have been amazed by the profusion of upright mirror-surfaces dotted all over the place. Some of the portals were tiny. Others were LARGE.

The dragons NEVER went near the portals. The dinos, lacking in brains, frequently did, and generally never returned.

Most people believed the Forks were responsible for the ODs. Only the kitchen gods were powerful enough to open these portals to anywhere and hold them open.

The idea that the Forks had opened the ODs greatly worried everyone.

If it was true, the kitchen gods must have opened the wormholes for a reason—most likely to let something through them to Earth.

Why this possibility worried everyone was because some of the ODs were ridiculously huge. Big enough to pass an aircraft carrier or oil tanker through. Big enough for an Amphicoelias Fragillimus—the largest dinosaur that ever lived—to walk through with ease.

But Amphicoelieas Fragillimus was vegetarian.

Everyone prayed that whatever the Forks planned on bringing through the Otherworld Doors didn't have sharp teeth.

CHAPTER 39

Malone: Three months later.

Malone sat in Ma's house, facing Jade Cure and Yang Yang. Ma's head still resided in the cabinet, next to the bottle of dragonreich that had 'cured' Posh.

Malone's arm ached from where Jade had just bled him.

Jade chanted; the snake goddess came alive.

Yang Yang raised the bowl of Malone's blood to her lips and took a long sip. Then she looked at Malone and spat the blood in his face.

She sat back on her white tail coils, scowling at him, her slanted eyes dark moods in her flawless white face.

Jade gaped at Malone's bloody face, then at the animated statuette. She broke off her chanting: "I don't understand. This has never happened before."

She turned to the stone goddess and unleashed a long stream of angry Chinese. Yang Yang smirked. She jabbed a finger at Malone, then calmly replied Jade.

Jade looked at her, growing perplexed, she turned to Malone.

"She's extremely angry with you."

He nodded.

"She's asking why you're here bothering her again, when you don't love her."

He wiped blood out of his eyes.

"Yeah," he said dryly, "I suspected it might be that. Tell her I'm sorry. And that I really need her help."

Jade relayed his words to the snake goddess, who shook her head. "No help."

Jade chanted some more, while Yang Yang alternately drank Malone's blood and glared knives at him. Then she smiled a bloody smile and spoke to Jade.

"She's wondering how your blood tastes so sweet, when you're such a ugly, horrible person . . ."

Malone winced.

". . . And that she's drinking it because, well, one never wastes good blood no matter how nasty a person its provider is, even a heartless troll like you."

Malone stared at the Snake Lady. She nodded back scowling, and said more:

". . . A heartless person who toys with her fragile emotions, breaking her stone heart, while she pines for you in her frozen state . . ."

Malone was shocked now. Yang Yang was weeping, red tears which he suspected were his blood that she'd just drank.

". . . And that she knows you're only here now because of her rival, the dragon woman Posh, and no, she of course will not help you cure her rival. Why should she? What woman would be so stupid?"

Malone gaped at Yang Yang. She was weeping profusely now, blood tears running down her cheeks and dripping off her chin into the bowl of blood, amazingly to refill it. She drank deeply from the bowl:

"No, she won't help you. She wants you to feel her pain each time the dragon woman eats some—"

Jade broke off, gaped at Malone. "She's been eating people? How many?"

"Too many."

Jade nodded, her eyes were cold. "You promised that you'd kill her. But no—"

The goddess was speaking again. Her pose was defiant and proud, her beautiful face a model of regal haughtiness. Her back was arched, pointing her flawless breasts at Malone. Drops of red polka dotted their upper halves. Her breasts heaved with the contempt of her words.

Jade lost her anger on hearing what the goddess said. It was all she could do not to laugh out loud.

The weeping goddess finished speaking. Next she drank up her bowl of Malone's blood, promptly spewed it all in his face again, then froze into rigid immobility.

"Well you've really got her riled up," Jade said.

"Don't I fucking know it." Malone wiped his face off again. He was a mess now, red-splattered everywhere.

Yang Yang wasn't in much better condition. Jade wiped her besmirched front down with a rag.

"You know," Jade said as she worked, "It'd be better if you just slept with her. That'll put you *permanently* in her good books."

Malone's skin crawled with revulsion at her suggestion. The very thought felt like cockroaches trampling him. Only over his corpse was that happening.

"What was the last thing she said? That made you laugh?"

Jade laughed louder than before. Her slanted eyes thinned to slits in her mirth.

Jade calmed down and grinned.

"She said that she doesn't understand why you're so choosy— always rejecting her advances. She asked what the difference was between you fucking *her*—a snake woman—and fucking that 'stupid dragon woman' you have at home?"

Malone had no answer to that.

***

Malone pointed to Ma's head in the cabinet. Cobwebs linked her white hair to the dusty varnish.

Ma's eyes were shut, her expression solemn, like she was in meditation. The Chinese script on the strip of paper ringing her neck flickered occasionally.

"What are you going to do about Ma?" Malone asked. "You can't leave her up there forever."

Jade shrugged. "She's been on the shelf for longer periods. Nothing I can do, until the right body turns up."

"*What is* the right body anyway?"

Jade grimaced. "There's the rub. It can't be an actual corpse. It has to be someone dying, but who won't survive it. In the past three months I've been offered three kid bodies . . ."

"Ma'll be mad if you use those."

Jade nodded. ". . . Two young men's bodies, and one old woman's."

"Why didn't you use the old woman's?"

"Ma would have hated it. The old girl had arthritis so bad, her fingers were permanently hooked into claws." She smiled. "Though I did consider using one of the young men. It would have been priceless—seeing the expression on Ma's face when she wakes up to find she has a penis."

Malone smiled. He couldn't imagine it either.

"Look," Jade said. "Forget Ma—a nice female body will turn up soon enough." She stared him dead in the eye. "What I want to know is: What do you intend to do about Miss Dragon, who—according to the goddess—you're busy happily screwing?"

Malone stared glumly at the floor.

"Okay," Jade said, "let's start again. How many people has Posh eaten to date?"

"Six."

She stared at him, slack-jawed. "Why the hell haven't you offed her then? Is reptile pussy that great? And if it is, what's your beef with screwing the Snake Lady?"

She groaned. "Shit, you men are really something, you know that?"

Malone shook his head.

"It's not like that, and not that simple," he explained wearily. "Posh is in human form most of the time. But she's addicted to reich now—it's a craving with her. She only becomes a dragon when she's high on the drug. That's when the murderous impulse comes. At those times she doesn't even recognize me." He winced. "Shit. You should see her afterwards, Jade. She's the sweetest girl in the world. She really fights her craving . . ."

"But the drug is stronger than she is," Jade finished unsympathetically. "That's a con; all junkies say that to excuse the criminal shit they do for their next fix."

Malone nodded. It was a fair—though unequal—comparison. "So what's to do?"

Jade's eyes were merciless. Her epicanthic folds looked like meat scimitars. "Kill Posh. Before she murders some other innocents."

"I can't. I love her."

Jade shrugged. "Okay, I'll concede that to you. Love's a good reason not to kill a killer." She pointed to Yang Yang. "Only other option is to fuck the goddess. Then, ask her to fix Posh for you, for good."

"She's likely to advise me on how to kill her instead."

Jade shook her head. "You don't understand women. The goddess has nothing against Posh. She's however angry that you're rejecting her when she clearly feels for you, and has *openly expressed* those feelings to you—it's embarrassing to be publicly rejected. Yang Yang doesn't want you to leave your girlfriend. She knows that won't work—she's divine and a statue after all. All she wants is for you to make her feel special, to let her know that she has a special place in your heart . . ."

Jade couldn't help grin, ". . . by your filling up that special *place* in her tail."

"You make it sound so simple. *All* I have to do is make love to her?"

And tell her how incredible she is compared to other women you've slept with. Flatter her vanity."

Malone nodded. "Considering the alternative, I should be able to do that."

He had another question, though. "One more thing. She needs blood to activate her during lovemaking, doesn't she? Where does that come from?"

"That's easy. I'll make a cut in your shoulder that she can suck blood from while you get it on."

The blasé way Jade said it chilled Malone.

She looked at the white statue, then back at him, her expression dark as storm clouds.

"I won't lie to you—loving her is dangerous. If you don't make her orgasm quick enough, she could bleed you to death."

Malone nodded.

"I'll do anything to cure Posh," he said. "The deaths are weighing badly on my conscience. I've already moved us west towards the river, into an old funeral home, so I can use their incinerator."

Jade whistled. "Wow, that's what I call long-term commitment!" She stared at him in grudging admiration. "How long were you planning on cleaning up after her?"

Malone winced. "Not that long. But I got tired of coming home to find bones strewn everywhere. Sooner or later a client is bound to see them and think me a cannibal."

Jade nodded.

"Okay," Malone said, running a hand through his hair, "let's do this." He grimaced at the half-woman half-snake statue, the gorgeous white stone upper body over the repulsive reptile coils, at the flawless Chinese face, that face so incomparably beautiful, yet so forbidding ugly in its amorality.

"No," Jade warned. "You two screw tomorrow, not today. If we unfreeze her again now, she's very likely to turn you down out of sheer spite, just to make you suffer." She smiled. "Come back tomorrow afternoon. I'll calm her down before then."

Malone nodded. He got up to leave.

"You're forgetting something," Jade said.

"Huh?"

She wagged the crystal summoning bowl at him. "I need to bleed you to wake her up to plead on your behalf."

Malone groaned. "Aw, shucks! Can't you just feed her chicken blood?"

Jade eyed him coolly. "Dude, how angry exactly do you want the goddess to be with you? She utterly ABHORS non-human blood. Feeding her chicken blood is the ultimate insult. Do that and you'll be number one human asshole on her divine shit-list. That isn't a preeminence you want—trust me. Currently, your only crime is that you won't fuck her. Insult her divinity however . . ."

"I get the point," Malone snapped. He bared his arm for Jade to jab the crystal lancet into.

He first watched the crimson spill filling the bowl, then looked over at Yang Yang with heavy misgivings. *Shit,* he thought, *this snake chick is going to leech me dry tomorrow.*

CHAPTER 40

Malone

All the way home from Ma Cure's, Malone steeled his mind over what he had to do. The further away from Chinatown Park he got, the easier it seemed to him that making love with Yang Yang would be.

After a while he was smiling at the thought. *I should be flattered, really. If nothing else, it'll definitely be a once-in-a-lifetime experience.*

Grinning broadly at the image of Yang Yang's serpentine coils wrapped around him, Malone turned onto Charles Street.

His thoughts immediately cut out in abrupt dismay. He pulled up sharply.

From the junction, Malone could see the funeral home he and Posh now lived in. An orange glow flickered in a first floor window.

Malone groaned. That meant *dragon. Fuck!* His grin reversed itself into a grimace of disgust.

Posh has gotten high again and gone hunting.

The fire meant she was cooking someone.

Malone's grip on the steering wheel tightened like he'd break it.

Not now, not fucking today. Preferably not ever again. Can't Posh stay off the damn reich for even a month? Love isn't worth this shit.

He put the car in motion again.

Close to the house, he slowed the Mustang to a crawl, giving her no warning he was back. The orange flickering in their bedroom window brightened, in-creasing his apprehension.

A fire-breather's trick—yellow fire shot from the window.

***

191

Inside the house, Malone flung his coat down, then padded softly upstairs. On the landing, he silently got out the fire extinguisher and gas mask.

The corridor's darkness was temporarily defeated at the ajar bedroom door by the vertical slice of orange light escaping the crack. Malone held his breath, padded closer.

He smelt roast meat, heard the sickening whimpers that were really exhausted screams.

Malone had chosen this residence with great care: the crematorium was situated on a factory estate that abutted the Charles River. It being so far from The Grid meant he and Posh had no neighbors.

Whoever Posh had taken this time might have screamed for help for hours with no one hearing. And when no help came, they'd just scream, period. Till, like now, they were hollered out.

Malone reached the door-crack. He peered in and recoiled.

The victim lay on a charred patch of carpet. He was a young man in his twenties; what was left of his half-cooked face gave Malone that much information. That glance also told Malone he was too far gone for any help to do him any good.

Posh had roasted him *good*. Sputtering fat bubbled from his body onto the floor. The young man was so cooked it was unreal he was still alive.

"Please kill me," he moaned. "Please."

Posh's reply was a leonine roar. She was animal now, her thoughts instinctive feed patterns.

She walked into view then—a white porcelain dragon with pink roses painted all over her body, huge white wings folded on her back.

Malone marveled like he did each time he saw her. Except that she was made of ceramic and walked upright, she fitted the classic dragon description—the woven-scaled skin, the extended snout with its long teeth and piggy nose, the fierce yellow eyes, the muscular arms and legs with their scary-sharp talons, the clanking T-Rex gait when not airborne.

And the long, crocodile tail. That tail which could decapitate a man with a single swipe.

Even in dragon form, Posh had a female grace about her motions. Watching her move, Malone felt an ache in his heart.

Posh-dragon bent over the roasted man. She stabbed his chest with a talon and stirred his lungs awhile. Then she shook her head in dissatisfaction and played a burst of flame over him. He screamed inaudibly.

Malone clamped the gas mask over his face.

Fire extinguisher held before him like a shield, he burst into the room.

He waited till Posh turned to look at him before depressing the plunger.

Posh roared as the first burst of anesthetic foam hit her. She blew a huge jet of fire at Malone, but he was already past its focus. The flame was swallowed by the foam wave he left in his wake.

Circling her warily, keeping well out of range of her tail, Malone kept the extinguisher plunger depressed.

Their bedroom slowly filled up with foam.

Several more gouts of fire were eclipsed in extinguisher foam, while Posh sputtered her rage.

The space in the room reduced as Malone avoided being himself caught in the foam, lest it blur his vision. He was now forced to move closer to Posh than he'd have liked.

"Grrrrrrooaaarrrr!!" she roared.

Incensed at being thwarted in her meat lust, Posh lashed her tail out at Malone. Flexible as a whip, it cut the air towards him.

Malone was ready—he ducked. The ceramic tentacle blew out the glass of the window behind him.

His face set in a scowl, as, totally obscured in foam, Posh slowly sank to the floor, spitting black puffs of smoke.

A thunk—the sound of a heavy plate hitting a tabletop—and she was out cold.

Malone waited till the foam had all evaporated before going near her. He also ensured her tail wasn't flicking.

Posh-dragon lay on her side. She looked innocent; an oversized wall decoration fallen from its perch.

Printed on the underside of her tail, just where it became the smoothness of her groinital area, was the large red inscription: 'Porcelain Dragon, Genuine Chinese Chinaware. Made in China.' Below this was a spiral red and gold barcode.

As he always did, Malone got out the hammer. As he always did, he stood over Posh's body a long time, considering ending it now and here.

"Love's a fragile thing," his mother had always told him. "Relationships even more so. Once broken, they're almost impossible to repair." Looking down at his girlfriend—her body already turning back to its human form—Malone realized that in his case this was literal truth—all he had to do was smash Posh two or three times with the hammer while she was transformed and out cold, and she'd fragment into a million pieces.

Love . . . Posh . . . really was that fragile.

This nightmare would be over—for good.

He watched her ceramic snout shorten back into her human face; the transition from fired clay to twitching flesh; her painted-on roses dissolving into blush, smeared lipstick and the faintest marbling of veins; her reddish-brown hair reappear, her neck . . .

Hammer raised for the killer blow, Malone stood defeated. He couldn't do it—knew he'd never be able to, regardless of whatever protestations he might make to Jade Cure.

Posh was Malone's addiction—the one habit he couldn't shake. Like she couldn't shake her addiction to dragonreich.

***

Disgusted with himself, Malone turned to look at the young man Posh had been about eating.

Miraculously, considering the extent to which he'd been cooked, her victim was still alive. And awake—somehow transcending the anesthetic that had knocked Posh out. His blue eyes told a tale of utter disbelief. They stared out into space beyond Malone, seeing something outside the room. Maybe Heaven, maybe Hell.

Malone bent over him. "I'm sorry," he whispered. "I truly am."

The young man finally noticed Malone. "I know I'm dying," he gasped in a voice that sounded ripped from his shredded lungs, "but that's okay. I'm no longer in any pain—I feel like a head without a body now."

He grimaced; Malone realized he was smiling. "It'll be fine dying, but what is that thing? That's no normal dragon."

Malone winced under his fevered gaze. He shook his head. "No, it's some sort of mutant beast." *You've no fucking idea*, he thought. He felt helpless—what could he say? *Dude, that's my fucking girlfriend?*

The young man coughed, broth mixed with foam bubbled from the piercings Posh had made in his chest.

His blue eyes focused hard on Malone. "Man, I thought bad shit like this only happened in the movies."

"Life's a horror movie now," Malone said with feeling. This conversation was freaking him out horribly. "Today it's you, tomorrow it'll likely be me. Soon everyone in Boston will be dead."

"Yeah, man, I guess you're right," the young man said.

He coughed again and was dead.

***

Posh was now half-transformed back to herself. With her human top half and ceramic bottom parts, she looked like the white dinosaur version of a mermaid.

Malone left the room to conceal the hammer. He'd had it two months now. Posh had no idea how close to death she was each time Malone caught her strung-out on reich.

He returned with a plastic sheet and wrapped up the young man's corpse. Once done, he carried it downstairs to the funeral parlor and stuffed it into the crematorium furnace.

So far, he'd used the furnace four times. His familiarity with its perfection in disposing of the traces of murder disgusted him.

He watched through the furnace's glass windows, sighing deeply as the flames digested the body, finishing the job Posh had begun.

Malone felt like shit as he watched the corpse burn. He felt this young man's death was his fault.

He steeled his resolve to make love to Yang Yang the next day.

He realized now that he'd been immensely foolish to ever consider not doing so.

CHAPTER 41

Malone

Next morning.

There were dragons in the morning sky, but they were far off, embroiled in a territorial scrap out over Charles River.

Malone watched their distant fiberglass bodies glitter, transparent silhouettes against the pale sun. He heaved a heavy sigh of relief—getting to work would be easier today.

All I have to keep an eye out for now are the damned dinos. Driving this far every day is close to suicidal—I've really got to move my office under The Grid. Home too, once Posh is off the damn reich.

He smiled. That'll be later today. The prospect of the final fix for Posh's addiction had him feeling upbeat. First a quick drop-by the office to see if anyone wants me, then off to Chinatown Park to go find out what goddess pussy tastes like. . .

(Posh had been asleep when he'd left home, she always slept like the dead after her transformations. Malone was grateful—it prevented another awkward confrontation between them.)

He turned onto Revere Street, out of view of the dragons.

It began raining, a cornflake drizzle occasionally interspersed with nuts and fruit. He put a hand out the car window, caught a few, and ate them.

***

Malone drove fast through the morning.

He surveyed each approaching block of ruins carefully before navigating them. His eyes flickered perpetually left and right, anticipating danger.

There was so much weird shit happening now, Malone no longer trusted even himself. He'd heard of people accidentally driving into ODs that suddenly appeared in the middle of the street.

He caught a sudden movement above and ahead to his left. His right hand instinctively left the wheel and rested on his gun, lying ready in the passenger seat.

He swerved the Mustang up over cracked sidewalk and through the display window of a trashed department store.

Once inside, he looked around quickly, checking to ensure he was alone, wouldn't get jumped from behind by hungry lizards. He winced on sighting the claw rips in the tattered masonry, the telltale slashes in the long-abandoned displays and cashier counters. This was the problem with living this far out from The Grid. Out here, the dinos were practically a law to themselves.

The store seemed empty. Malone turned the car around in the cramped space, then switched off the engine.

From concealment, he watched the road.

Up ahead, smoke billowed from a huge hole in the side of a condo.

Malone listened hard. He heard screaming. He waited till the screaming stopped.

A huge quetzalcoatlus emerged from the hole in the building's side. Its shark-long head was coated in blood. Two headless human forms dangled between its jaws.

The dino-bird flapped its massive wings and took to the sky.

Malone waited till the quetzalcoatlus was a distant colored dot before setting the car in motion again.

He spat out the window into the raining cereal. Boston was becoming more and more dangerous by the day. No, he corrected himself, by the fucking hour.

***

Malone drove by a herd of skyscrapers. Most that he passed were half-transformed into beetles.

Their altering began at their penthouses, with their lightning rods and television antenna becoming insect antennae. Once those were fully developed, the changes proceeded downwards through the building, the concrete-to-flesh/chitin conversions occurring at a rate of about six stories a week.

The beetle became aware of its surroundings at about the time it was half-formed, by which time the upper-level portions of its elevators had split off from its body into its fore- and mid-legs. It was still however as helpless as a human infant, though its ability to squirt quick-setting cement projectiles from its mouth and thoracic spiracles kept away hungry dragons.

Malone passed a group of skyscraper residents loading their possessions into vans. They were either relocating to a more recently laid skyscraper or a condominium.

(Condos were unreliable dwellings, however. Firstly, one never knew when they'd develop wanderlust, uproot their foundation-feet and tramp off.

And, like Malone had witnessed shortly before, their not having any natural defenses made both they and their occupants easy prey for dinos.

Some pterodactyls even used Condos as nests. Heaven help anyone who moved into such a seemingly unoccupied building.)

All the working men had heavy-duty guns hung at their hips. Groups of children nervously watched the skies for dragons and pterodactyls. Others watched for terra-bound dinos.

Nearby several women raked fallen cornflakes into plastic boxes.

The residents hailed Malone as he drove by. He waved back.

He saw they'd shaved their relocation extremely close, the beetle's wings were already fully formed—the building's transformation near-complete.

Dangerous, Malone thought, wondering why they'd waited so long.

Some beetles prematurely attempted flight. Most toppled into nearby buildings. Others made it up into the air, but crashed; or their cement and steel underbodies broke off when they were airborne.

All three options meant certain death for any adamant inhabitants.

***

Malone stopped again at the intersection near his office. There were two sets of severed legs and a ripped-up torso scattered across the opposite sidewalk. Blood-filled dino footprints were crunched into the broken tarmac beside them. Tyrannosaurs from the size of them. The blood glittered wet—the predators would still be nearby.

Also, the dino footprints led in the direction of Malone's office.

Damn. He backed the car into the alley by the corner convenience store and settled to wait again.

A moving shadow on the alley's right wall caught his attention. Malone grabbed his gun off the seat and spun around, ready to shoot. He relaxed—a diplodocus was cropping tree leaves in the yard behind the alley.

Despite the dino's harmlessness, Malone kept a firm grip on the gun.

The rain had now changed from cornflakes to popping corn—a white, brown, and yellow snowfall almost totally hampering visibility.

Malone considered his options.

His office was two hundred yards away. He could drive on, chancing he wouldn't bust a tire or get his wheels stuck in a pothole. Or, he could park the car and walk, chancing he wouldn't run into the dinos, or that he'd be able to shoot his way out if he did.

He chose to walk. He knew this street like his face in the mirror, all its safe places. He'd make it.

Malone locked the car, then padded to the intersection.

He grimaced at the human remains strewn across the sidewalk.

Two people—likely potential clients of mine—just got fucked-up by dinos.

Gun in hand, he set off down Joy Street, picking a careful way through the dropping, popping corn.

He walked slowly to avoid triggering the dino's sensitivity to vibrations. He kept close to the curb, ready to leap through a doorway at the slightest hint of motion.

Malone felt queasy: the butchered torso he'd left upstreet had triggered unpleasant memories.

His attention shifted from navigating the falling popcorn. He relived his incarceration by Frank and Rachel Fischer. The intervening months hadn't made his memory of being eaten any less harrowing.

Each time Malone undressed, he saw the scar and remembered the cannibal pair. Beautiful sexless Rachel, obsessed with conquering the USA, and Frank, equally obsessed with loving her.

He wondered how Sara Fischer was doing now. True to her word, she'd brought him payment for his services the week after he'd returned Rachel's head to her.

She'd also tried to seduce him again. But for the fact that Malone was by then in love with Posh, she'd have succeeded.

Malone had decided fucking was how Sara grieved.

Which brought his mind back to later today. Will I actually be able to sex up the Snake Lady? It'll be a major disaster if I can't get it on with her. I'll have to ask Jade for some ginseng, or Ying-Yang potion...Chinese Viagra or whatever, just in case. But still...

CHAPTER 42

Malone

A snuffling sound jerked Malone back to the here and now.

He looked up. A T-Rex was peering down hungrily at him from a yawning gap in the second-story wall of the building he was passing.

Shit, he thought, *reminiscing has just killed me.*

The tyrannosaur launched itself at him. Malone ducked out of its way. It missed him by a hairsbreadth. The ground shook as the dino landed, its feet making sixteen-inch prints in the eroded tarmac.

Popcorn rained on them both.

The tyrannosaur spun round. Its yellow eyes glinted death at Malone. It was HUGE. It towered over him, an alligator-skinned juggernaut of destruction, the visible incarnation of the killing impulse.

Malone found himself rooted to the spot, as unable to flee as a headlight-entranced rabbit. He'd never been this close to a T-Rex before—the mere reek of the thing was overpowering.

A warped collage of scenes from his anticipated funeral zipped though his head.

What seemed to Malone an eternity lived in slow motion was in actuality two seconds.

The T-Rex roared; chunks of regurgitated meat splattered Malone. It retracted its head and looked sideways as if to locate his position.

Then, four-foot jaws yawning like the Grand Canyon, its head darted towards Malone with the unerring accuracy of a shark homing in on a blood drop two miles distant.

Adrenalin poured through Malone. Acting on pure instinct, he raised his gun and stuck it in the dino's mouth. He pulled the trigger at the exact instant that its teeth clamped down on his right shoulder, separating arm from body.

In a muffled explosion, the rear of the tyrannosaur's head blew outwards in a shower of white gore.

Malone staggered backward. Moments later, the dino crashed to the ground mere inches from him. Its exploded brains made it look like it was wearing a white crown.

Fuck the dino reign, Malone thought.

The popcorn rain slowly plugged the yawning hole in the dino's cranium as though it were itself a pothole.

Malone staggered back some more as the tyrannosaur's forelimb claws raked the earth towards him in its death spasms, excavating deep furrows.

Squeezing his right shoulder to staunch the flow of blood, with popcorn showering down on him like he was the floor of a movie theatre, Malone ran the remaining fifty yards to his office.

CHAPTER 43

Malone / Sara

Reeling dizzy with pain, Malone reached the bungalow. He staggered up his front steps. He somehow got the door open, then rushed across to the cabinet containing his first-aid kit.

***

A shot of 'Insta-Clot' into his shoulder stopped the bleeding; Supercetamol took care of the pain. Once certain he was no longer in danger of dying, Malone passed out.

Odd ominous voices awoke him.

"He's much tougher than I even imagined," one said.

Surfacing slowly from sopor, Malone fought to slot the voice into its socket of familiarity.

"I must admit to being impressed," another voice said. "Though he did lose an arm, I've never seen a human hold his ground so well against a dinosaur."

The metallic tones of this voice jerked Malone to full alertness. It was a Fork voice, which meant he was still in danger. *Shit.*

He warily opened his eyes, found himself staring into a familiar face.

"Mrs. Fischer . . . Sara? What are *you* doing here?"

The slutty sexagenarian visage leered down at him. The intervening three months had if anything only made Sara Fischer look more debauched.

She wore skintight raptor-skin pants and a low-cut silk top that left nothing to the imagination—her incongruously shapely large breasts adorned her chest like pawpaws, their brown nipples pricked the fabric like hypo-needles. Their rose-colored aureole were dual testaments to the pleasures of geriatric sex.

Malone had the feeling Sara was thinking of pulling down his pants right here and now and wrapping her silver-lacquered lips around his cock.

"I should ask you the same question," she replied, licking them at him. "Why are you still living *out here*?" She pointed to his arm. "You could get killed?"

Malone shrugged his remaining shoulder. "I planned on moving under The Grid; then I realized there was no way to let clients know where I'd moved to." He groaned. "How else would *you* have found me now?"

He levered himself upright in the stuffed-gorilla chair and looked around.

There *were* two Forks in the room, hovering either side of his front door.

Malone was struck by sudden certainty that his already messed-up existence was about becoming yet more so. First Posh getting stoned on reich and killing someone, then his losing his arm, and now Sara Fischer bringing Forks to his office.

All on the same morning. And he still had his tryst with Yang Yang today.

Sara laid a gnarled but perfectly manicured hand on his surviving elbow. "The Forks wish to hire you," she said with a cool smile.

Malone smiled insincerely at the cutlery pair. Hire me? Thank goodness I have the perfect excuse to escape whatever they want me to do for them.

(Like most other people, Malone felt the safest place to be around Forks was as far away from them as possible.)

"I'm glad at least that you don't want me to rescue Rachel from the Afterwife," he quipped weakly to Sara.

She giggled. "You're quite a man if you can still make cracks like that." She licked her lips at him again.

Malone grinned back. Maybe today wouldn't get any worse after all.

Then the Forks floated over and told him what they wanted.

***

Malone noted that both kitchen gods were golden. That meant this was serious business. Light shimmered off the female's Forks flawless breastensions.

"My name is Lord Tav and this is Lady Yaz," the male Fork said. "As Sara has just mentioned, we wish to hire you."

"We are very impressed with the display you put on against the dino outside," Lady Yaz added, "We never knew humans were that brave."

Malone wondered if the Forks were blind or just plain dumb; couldn't they see he'd just lost an arm? Who the hell in their right mind hired a one-armed private eye?

"I'd like to help you," he said politely (one was always polite to Forks), "But—"

"*Your injury?* Please hear us out first."

It was more a gentle command than a request. With Sara seated across from him, Malone settled himself back in the stuffed-ape chair and listened.

"We want you to retrieve the president's liver from Frank."

Malone stiffened. *Frank?*

Then he laughed, a humorless sound like sandpaper smoothing wood. "Let me understand this—Sara has a grudge against me over Rachel's death, and you two are here to help her kill me off. Why not just come out with it?"

The Forks laughed in unison, the sonority of tuning forks sounding in harmony. "No, nothing like that, Malone. Frank specifically demanded that *you* come get the president's liver."

Malone looked at Sara.

She nodded. "It's true; the asshole *did.*" Her expression turned angry. "He also stole Rachel's head."

Frank stealing Rachel's head made sense to Malone. Sara's first statement, however—confirming the Forks'—didn't.

"I'm confused," he said. "*What is* the 'president's liver?' And it's Frank, remember? If it's liver—he's probably already eaten it."

"He has not, Malone," Lady Yaz sang at him. She floated closer to Malone, till he could see his reflection in her breasts and sense her distinctly feminine aura. "He would not *dare* anger us to such an extent. He *could* damage it however, as could we, if we decide to forcefully retrieve it."

"Okay, un-confuse me. What's the Fork president doing with a liver? As far as we've been led to believe, you're not flesh-and-blood."

"It is not *our* president's liver. It is *your* president's."

Malone turned to gape at Sara.

"Jefferson Lincoln," Sara said miserably. She was unhappy whenever reminded of Jeff's death; though in the intervening months she'd come to derive pride from her actually fucking a US President into his grave. "After President Lincoln died three months ago, the Forks kept his liver. Then Frank stole it."

She burst into tears.

Malone wondered at her melodrama. "Why's this liver so important?"

"They're preserving it in Jeff's honor," Sara quickly replied, wiping her eyes. She knew Malone would reject the assignment if told the real reason the Forks wanted it back.

Malone was suddenly *very* tired. "Okay, so what does Frank want with me?"

Lord Tav spoke. "He speaks about unfinished business. He says you have a quarter of meat of his in your possession. Does this make sense to you?"

Malone nodded. "Yes—" Frank wanted him so he could eat the remaining quarter of his liver.

"—And . . . no," he finished. "I'm not doing it, nor do I wish to hear any more of this insanity."

He glared at Sara, who'd composed her emotions again and was busy repairing her makeup from a stegosaur-shell compact. "Go away *please*, all of you."

"They'll pay you very well," Sara said, with an encouraging smile.

"Yes we will," Lord Tav and Lady Yaz added in unison. "We'll pay you *very* well."

Malone smirked nastily from one to the other, all fear of the Forks temporarily forgotten. "What can you pay me that can possibly induce a one-armed man to set off on a suicide mission to hell knows where? And please remember I'm *right*-handed . . . sorry, I *used to be* right-handed—I can no longer either attack or defend myself from attack. There's absolutely nothing you can offer me to make it worth my while to tackle Frank again."

Convinced he'd made an irrefutable argument, he sat back, glaring at the glimmering cutlery-beings.

It was Lady Yaz who replied him, her words chilling him to his marrow.

"You have a girlfriend named Posh," she said, "a junkie pathetically hooked on dragonreich—what if we offer to cure her for you?"

CHAPTER 44

Malone

What *really* swayed Malone to accept the Fork's offer was his remembering the amount of blood he'd lost immediately after losing his arm.

That was guaranteed bad news with Yang Yang later. Okay so they could screw with her on top since he couldn't brace himself, but . . . *but* . . . the snake goddess had to drink his blood while they got it on. Malone was certain that if she leeched him in his current condition, she'd bleed him dry.

Out that option, he thought, *in the Fork-ing alternative. I'm really stuck between a rock and a hard place.*

"I'm still missing an arm," he pointed out to the Forks. "Is this a simple pickup? Even if it is, I'll need someone, Sara maybe, to drive my car."

Sara shook her head. "Not me, sweetheart. I'm not going anywhere near that sicko."

Malone couldn't fault her pragmatism. He stared questioningly at the Forks.

"It isn't simple," Lady Yaz replied. Frank says he has set up a number of riddles for you to solve; each one sequentially leading to the next. At the end of the trail you get the president's liver back for us."

"Uh-huh," Malone said slowly, "and my backup?"

"None. He requests you come alone."

Malone scowled at the Forks. "If you think I'm walking into—"

"We *will* however make you another arm."

"That's a relief." Malone replied. "How long will— Yeoooooowwww!"

It felt to Malone like the dino was eating his right shoulder all over again.

Eyes wide in disbelief, he watched.

Blood spurted from his wound, forming into a lengthening liquid tube that congealed into a duplicate of his dino-eaten arm. The agony continued till the red arm's fingertips—complete with fingernails—were completely formed.

The pain shut off as abruptly as it had begun. Malone gaped at the Forks in horror. "What have you done to me!?"

Lord Tav laughed. "That's your new arm—a *blood* arm—made *entirely* of your blood. Try it out—though liquid, it's stronger than the one you lost, with a few tricks that one did not possess."

"It's self-regenerating too," Lady Yaz added. "You cannot lose it again."

Malone touched the red arm. It felt solid enough. He applied finger pressure to it. The finger sank half an inch then encountered resistance. He flexed his fingers, noted he had full control.

"It *is* your arm," Lady Yaz insisted.

"Yes," Malone agreed numbly. "It is." He looked up at the Forks, "What else does it do?"

"Its fist packs quite a punch."

Sara Fischer giggled like great sex. She rummaged in her purse for a while, finally extracting a sheet of notepaper. She handed it to Malone. "Frank's first riddle or instructions for you."

Malone took the sheet from her.

It read:

'In the room above your office, lies a dead machine with a message for you.

Eat you soon,
Frank.'

Malone turned the note over to see if there was any additional writing. There wasn't.

"This is a dead end," he said. "This house is a bungalow. It doesn't have an upper floor."

"Are you certain of that?" Sara Fischer asked.

Malone rolled his eyes. "Of *course* I'm certain. I've worked here for—"

"We suggest you make certain before being so certain you are certain," both Forks said in unispeak.

Malone didn't reply. While turning the note over, he'd become aware of something strange about his blood hand—there was writing on its rear surface.

He raised it for closer examination.

There were three lines of black lettering each with a yellow-white button at its end.

From top to bottom they read:

Hetero Fist.
Gay Fist.
Lesbian Fist.

Their trio of companion buttons looked sickening, like large pus-filled zits begging to be popped.

"What is this?" Malone asked the Forks without looking up.

There was no reply.

"I said: what is this shit on my hand?"

Still no reply.

He looked up then, discovered he was alone. Sara Fischer and the Forks had vanished.

Malone stared at the odd inscriptions on his hand for a long time. Instinct warned him not to depress any of those studs just yet.

CHAPTER 45

Posh & Sookie

After leaving home distraught, Posh drove east to Kneeland Street, to Sookie Ling's brothel.

Sookie frowned on seeing how miserable Posh looked.

"Come, talk in office." She led the way, back.

Sookie's office was creepy—a small windowless room painted in garish contrasting colors.

"What wrong?" Sookie asked once they were seated. "Look unhappy, like cunt missing."

"I fucking need help," Posh replied. "I'm in so much of a mess I can't believe it."

Posh explained how she became a dragon whenever she used reich.

Sookie, eyelids painted black like shadows to her lime-colored eyes, listened, her thick lips set in a cool smile.

Sookie hid her shock when Posh mentioned how many people she'd eaten.

"No wonder always look well-fed now'days," she said nonchalantly when Posh finished. "Human meat tasty, yes?"

Posh glared at the Chinese woman's superior smile. "Stop joking, Sookie. I'm in serious shit here. I love Malone, but unless I find a cure for this addiction of mine, our relationship is worse than fucked."

Sookie grinned. "Ah, yes. Relationship always fucking. Fucking make wonderful relationship."

***

Posh was still horrified by yesterday evening's events. She'd held off snorting the drug for as long as she could—this time she'd lasted three whole weeks before succumbing to its lure.

It was clear sign of her weakness however, that she hadn't flushed the powder down the toilet. She'd pretended to, but instead stashed it in the toes of a pair of rolled up stockings.

Like all the previous times, she'd told herself she was strong enough to resist the craving, strong enough to know the dragonreich was there but never use it.

Yesterday—like she always did in the end—she'd succumbed again to the drug. She'd spilled a hill of the sparkling powder into her palm and snorted it up. Then she'd leaned back on the sofa with the living room spinning around her like the solar system.

The rush had been supremely sublime, like an endless orgasm. But then, with her looking surprised like she'd forgotten it would happen, her body altered to china, her mind dissolved into a primal flesh lust.

Everything after then was a collage of images that flashed across Posh's mind in place of coherent memory—a series of freeze-frames marking her as one of God's damned:

Perching motionless as a pterodactyl on a skyscraper ledge, swooping down, and then up again, with a screaming man in her claws; bringing him home; roasting him alive . . .

She blinked back tears. The most horrible image of all flashed through her head. Herself spurting fire at Malone . . .

***

Posh realized Sookie was addressing her.

"What did you say?"

Sookie indicated her own eyes with a silver dragon-lady fingernail. "Me addicted reich too. *Me* sell *you* drug. How get you off it?"

The uncontestable logic of her question flummoxed Posh. Sookie was right. She was both Posh's pusher and an addict herself. How in the world was she supposed to help?

Sookie smiled. "Ma Cure know how. Only she not herself at moment." Sookie burst out laughing. "She lose body! How very careless!"

Posh didn't like being reminded of *how* Ma had lost her body.

Sookie got a slim purple vial from her purse and spilled shimmering dust into her palm.

Posh watched her snort the reich up. Her horror over yesterday's experience was still sufficient in her to make her view the powder with repugnance, not longing.

Besides she still had her own stash at home. *And this time, oh fucking yes, this time I'm getting rid of it for good. But is that wise? Isn't it better to keep it there so I can know I'm stronger than it? Like I'm doing now?*

Sookie's eyes flashed like lighthouses. "Way view it, number one problem of reich—fucklessness desire." She raised a finger for emphasis. "Myself not fuck, two years now. No boyfriend, so no trouble."

She flipped her blue skirt off her thighs to reveal her naked crotch.

Posh's eyes widened. Like a lizard's crest, Sookie's pussy lips were red and scaly.

Sookie giggled at Posh's surprise. She lifted her left leg so Posh could see the green tentacles ringing her anus, some tinted fecal-brown.

"See, not you only reich fuck up." She smiled, dropped her leg. "Now what say? Ah, yes . . . Malone love you. Not screw him, he love someone else."

Posh nodded back glumly. For a fortnight after each dose of reich she had no libido whatever. She never turned down Malone's advances, but she hated faking the emotion she knew she should be feeling.

A knock on the door. The door opened.

Vicki Ho, Sookie's secretary, entered. Vicki was tall and fat. She always wore hot pants that showed off her humongous thighs.

She hurried over to Sookie and whispered to her. Sookie nodded. "Let come in."

Vicki looked pointedly at Posh.

"She fine," Sookie said. "Asshole tight friend."

Vicki Ho left. A moment later, she returned with Bulldog and Gorgeous Wong. The pair dragged a shivering man between them.

Posh froze on seeing them both. *Oh fucking no, not here!*

Gorgeous scowled at her. "Hi, Posh."

Damn, girl, you need to lighten up some, Posh thought. She'd heard Gorgeous and Bulldog were an item now, but romance clearly hadn't altered Gorgeous much. She still looked as severely secretarial as ever—hair drawn straight back and secured with a bronze pin, white kung fu suit.

The only difference about Gorgeous was her silver lipstick.

Well, that's an improvement, I guess.

Bulldog looked at Posh. "Haven't seen ya since that odd night," he grunted. "You keeping good?"

Posh nodded, relieved. Bulldog looked like he couldn't give a shit about her anymore.

"You found Herbie yet?" she stuttered.

Bulldog shook his head. "Nah, girl, he's vanished off the Earth."

"Not odd Herbie disappear," Sookie said. "Dragon eat up."

"We were all under the Grid that night, auntie," Gorgeous said. "A dragon didn't get him."

"She's telling the truth," Posh added. "I drove from them directly to Malone; never passed Herbie on the way."

Sookie shrugged. "Him miss good pussy business now anyways."

She turned a cold gaze to the captive shivering between Bulldog and Gorgeous. He was thirtyish, with rheumy blue-green eyes and long stringy light chestnut hair.

(Posh thought he looked like a wasted rock star. Either way, he was definitely a hardcore drug addict.)

"Business time," Sookie said. She stood up and walked over to the trio.

"Now, Emil, where hide Sookie dragonreich?"

The captive shivered some more. "I don't know where it—yeoooow!" his face contorted in pain.

Sookie had grabbed his testicles and was squeezing hard. Posh also thought her four-inch fingernails were sticking into his flesh.

"Talk, bastard," Sookie rasped. "Return big money shipment. Or biggest regret yours."

"What did he do?" Posh asked. She had the feeling she was about to witness something bad.

Sookie released her crippling grip on the man's testes.

"Idiot Emil steal dragonreich stock. Kill guards. Pretend triads commit crime."

Posh looked Emil over. He looked East-European. Russian, maybe.

"Sookie, this guy doesn't look like he could rob an open fridge."

Sookie snorted. "He do."

She glanced fiercely at Bulldog. "Tie robber down."

Bulldog secured Emil in a chair, roping him around the midriff and neck and binding his arms behind his back.

(Posh found this scenario doubly odd. *Bulldog's working for Sookie? Taking orders from her? Hell, Sookie used to be scared shitless of him.*)

Sookie tapped a little dragonreich powder into a glass and mixed it up with water.

Once again, revulsion filled Posh at the sight of the drug, but it was less than before. Thoughts of the high dragonreich gave assailed her will.

She broke out sweating. *Hell, no, I'm not taking that shit. I'll break this habit even if it kills me.*

Sookie fetched a hypo from a cabinet. Without bothering to sterilize the needle, she drew the reich mixture into it.

Damn, Posh thought, *she's going to OD him.* And she still didn't see how the hell this dweeb of a guy could take on Sookie's thugs, talk less of kill them.

(Sookie Ling was all cuteness and sleazy-sex as a madam, but drugs were another matter entirely. Sookie was a lioness where reich trading was concerned.

Posh had heard rumors that Sookie didn't mind murder. It looked like she was about to discover the truth first-hand.)

"I didn't do it," Emil moaned from the chair he was tied in. Snot dripped from his nose, over his lips, down his chin. He looked disgusting.

Bulldog, his ugly face fierce, yanked the man's head back. "Shut up! No one here believes ya, and the sooner ya get that straight—"

Gorgeous silenced Bulldog with a light touch to his hand. An almost invisible caress that told Posh their relationship was a strong bond.

"He did it," she told Posh. "He has a strange reaction to dragonreich." She nodded to Sookie. "Do it, aunty."

Sookie ripped the seated man's dirty shirt open and jabbed him in the chest with the syringe. He squealed as she depressed the plunger.

Sookie jerked out the syringe. Blood dribbled after it. She patted Emil on the cheek.

"Look, see how steal," she told Posh.

Posh looked.

Emil's mouth suddenly filled with huge jagged teeth. His aquamarine eyes turned red, his skin blue-grey and crawling with purple veins.

Posh was horrified by the transformation. Now she believed he'd killed those people. A horrible guilt flooded her. *Shit, is this what I'm like as a dragon? And Malone still loves me?*

The transformed Emil began thrashing to get free. Bulldog placed the muzzle of his blaster to his ear.

"Easy now, man. You don't wanna lose your head now, do you?"

Emil instantly stopped fighting.

"Interesting," Gorgeous said. "The monster remembers that guns are dangerous."

The erupted veins on Emil's blue face throbbed like red maggots. He foamed at the lips like a rabid dog.

Gorgeous peeped behind the chair. "His hands are just like his teeth," she said in mixed fear and admiration. "With him like this, none of our dealers would have stood a damn chance."

"Bastard ripped through them like they were sausage," Bulldog said, his finger twitching nervously on the gun trigger. "You should have seen the warehouse—looked like a dragon's den. Chunks everywhere."

Sookie gave Posh a cold smile. "Yes, like dragon house. Maybe eat sweet flesh too. Delicious long pig."

Posh got Sookie's point. She nodded. She didn't trust herself to speak. She was still seeing herself in the monster opposite.

She'd twice seen the results of her ravages at home—living room/bedroom awash with blood and strewn entrails. The other times, Malone had mercifully cleaned up before she awoke. She had no idea why she kept taking her victims back to their apartment. She just emerged from her meat lust to find herself there.

Sookie was talking to her:

"Not give asshole much reich," she said, putting the syringe away again. "Turn normal soon."

They waited. The room was packed with tension, with the fear that, unlikely as it was, the monster tied in the chair might get free and rip into all of them.

***

Five minutes later, Emil was human again. Same druggie drool, wasted look, shivers. In addition, he was visibly thinner.

It's because he didn't eat anyone, Posh realized.

Clearly relieved, Bulldog holstered his gun again.

"Welcome to living again," Sookie said. "Now tell, or go Hell."

Emil gaped at her. He looked sleepy.

Sleepy like me, Posh thought.

Gorgeous slapped him fully awake.

"Where is drugs!?" Sookie snapped. "No more joking!"

"I don't know!"

Sookie gave him a chilling smile. "Stupid wonderful idiot." She smiled all her teeth. "Untie foolish hands."

Gorgeous and Bulldog did so.

Sookie strutted back and forth in front of Emil.

"Now. Last time ask. Where keep reich?"

"I'm telling you—"

"Truly BIG fool. Great stupidness—massive like horse penis."

She nodded to her niece. Gorgeous pulled over a small table and arranged it in front of Emil. She placed his right hand on the tabletop.

"No, no," Sookie said. "Likely he right-handed, use left hand."

Gorgeous complied.

Sookie handed Bulldog a knife.

Watching the slim blade shimmer, Posh felt chilled, refrigerated. Yet she couldn't leave. Not that she didn't dare; she *had* to see this.

Emil tried to move his hand. Gorgeous stunned him with a hard punch. "I'm serious, Sookie," he mumbled. "I don't know—"

Sookie nodded at Bulldog. With infinite slowness, he cut off Emil's left thumb, slicing through its second joint. Emil screamed and gibbered as blood spurted from the wound.

Posh cringed. She felt like she was the one being cut.

Bulldog forced the knife all the way through the digit.

Emil sputtered in disbelief at the blood spurting from the stump. Sookie picked up his severed thumb and waved it in his face. "One finger less now. Still have nine. Toes too. Afterwards nose, then ears. Lips. She leant in close enough to kiss him. "Now tell—where fucking drugs!"

"Sookie, I don't—Yeoooooooowwww!"

Bulldog had sliced off his index finger.

Sookie smiled coldly. "Underestimate Sookie, yes? Think I bluffing. Ah." She looked angrily at Gorgeous. "Tie wrist, foolish girl, stop bleeding. Not let asshole die."

"Yes, auntie." Gorgeous made a tourniquet from a handkerchief.

Emil eyes were almost bugging out of his head now with pain and terror.

Posh felt incredibly conflicted. On one side she felt for the tortured man. But she also remembered the monster he'd just transformed into and what it had done. *Shit!*

But I'm a monster myself; one can't judge another.

"Talk now?" Sookie asked.

"I don't get what you're being so hardheaded about," Bulldog said. "Just tell us who the fuck sent you and we'll let you go."

Emil looked to Gorgeous, who nodded coolly.

Sookie retreated to her chair and crossed her legs. She looked like a movie director. She took a snort of reich and scrutinized Emil expectantly with green-flashing eyes.

"Okay," he gasped. "It was the Big Circle Triad. Yue Sheng ordered—Motherfuckerrrr!!!!!"

On a subtle nod from Sookie, Bulldog had sliced off Emil's middle finger. He gaped at Sookie in confusion, tears pouring from his eyes. "But I'm—"

"You fucking liar!" she yelled back, leaping to her feet and kicking her chair away. "Not triads! Triads not dare fuck Dragon Lady. All know dragon cunt poisonous cobra! Truth, asshole, or liar lips next!" She glared at Bulldog. "Whole mouth one time next!"

Emil was defeated. He visibly crumpled in his chair as all bluff left him. His expression one of utter agony, he stared at his ruined hand, his separated fingers in their pool of blood. He looked back up at Sookie, his eyes honest and pleading.

"Okay, I'll tell you the truth."

"Good asshole. Tell Aunty Sookie. Best Chinese doctor repair fingers."

"It was just me and Lucy Tang. We planned to—"

"Lucy Tang?" Sookie gaped incredulously at Emil, then at Gorgeous. "Lucy Tang?"

Gorgeous shrugged. "I told you she always had ideas above her status, auntie, but you always said she's your highest earning rent boy."

Posh knew Lucy Tang. A drop-dead-gorgeous drag queen smuggled in from Hong Kong on a North Korean food-produce submarine. Lucy wasn't just a prostitute, she was also an incredible actress and singer—she wowed every audience she performed for.

Posh looked at Emil's hand and winced. She didn't think Lucy Tang would remain as good-looking after this revelation.

Sookie calmed down. She smiled at Emil. "Tell loving Aunty Sookie more," she cooed.

Emil nodded. "Lucy found out how I transform and suggested we hit your warehouse for the dragonreich. She plans to corner your drug trade."

Sookie nodded. "See, truth easy. No lose more fingers. Okay, where drugs now?"

"Lucy has a place over in South Boston, on Summer Street. All the dragonreich is there."

Posh nodded. It made sense. South Boston was across the Fort Point Channel. Dragon-infested territory where only a Chinese would dare venture.

Unfortunately for Lucy Tang, those who'd be hunting her would be Chinese too.

Gorgeous smiled. "What's the house address?"

"Yeah, punk, you expecting us to go round knocking on every door so the dinos get us?"

Emil shook his head vigorously. "Four-ninety-five Summer Street—the Barnes Building at the D Street intersection. Sixth floor, apartment nine."

Posh had the clear sense that Emil was lying on this last. Or wasn't telling the whole truth. She kept quiet however—no one else seemed to think so.

"Okay," Sookie said. "I let go now. But last questions."

"Yes . . . anything."

Sookie retrieved her chair and sat in it. "Now, truth: you fucking Lucy?"

Emil looked embarrassed, then nodded.

Sookie giggled. "Ah, yes. Tell me: how Chinese asshole compare western? Tighter or slacker?"

Gorgeous, seated on a low stool, looked scandalized. "Auntie!"

Bulldog looked confused. Posh felt the day switch from the violent to the surreal.

"Shut up, always troublesome niece. I research anus. Maybe use more western men buttholes. Quality priority as madam."

She looked at Emil. "Talk, or fingers. Which anus tightest?"

Emil shuddered. "Chinese is much tighter. I can't explain it, but, Lucy's ass squeezes—"

"No need to explain," Gorgeous interrupted him. She licked her silvered lips, then smirked. "It's like I always tell you, auntie. "Male or female—Chinese pussy is the tightest in the world. Ask Bulldog."

Bulldog turned red with embarrassment. "Aw, Gorgeous, not *here*."

"Oh yes," Gorgeous enthused. "All women should learn kung fu. Such a tight vagina makes a man your slave for life."

"Too much tightness not good," her aunt retorted. "Man come too quick, woman not come at all. What use have slave, master unsatisfied?" She smiled, then added: "Kung fu not fuck technique anyhow. Ask Jackie Chan. Best for fight and blockbuster."

Posh was grateful when Emil, apparently as perplexed as she by this surreal interlude, said: "Can I go now? I need a doctor."

Sookie looked intently at him. "You not lie this? Lucy tighter than American boyfriends?"

Emil nodded.

Sookie smiled. "Okay, let go. But stay hour till find Lucy."

"Thanks, Sookie. It won't happ—"

Posh was as surprised as Emil when Bulldog slit the man's throat.

Emil gaped at Sookie as he died. "Bu . . . bu . . . but . . ." he gurgled piteously.

Sookie smiled. "Ah yes, forget tell. If let go, what stop become dragonreich monster, kill me, everyone here?"

Traumatized as she was by what she was witnessing, Posh couldn't argue with Sookie's logic.

But does it have to be so fucking gory? Shit, Emil's blood is pouring everywhere like Sookie intends painting her office floor with it.

CHAPTER 46

Posh

Posh drove away from Sookie's brothel. She was relieved that Bulldog hadn't asked for Herbie's pimpmobile back.

There were three cars ahead of her. Bulldog and Gorgeous led the convoy in Sookie's pink Porsche. They were followed by a red Corvette and white Lexus carrying six of Sookie's men.

The gangsters were headed for South Boston—the address Emil had given them.

Posh didn't want to be Lucy Tang when they found her.

She drove after the other cars for a while, along the Surface Road by Chinatown Park, then turned off at Lincoln. The gang cars sped on ahead, en route to Summer Street and the right/south turn towards Summer Street Bridge and South Boston.

Posh was also headed for Summer Street, from where a right turn led east to Beacon Hill. Her proposed route had originally been a no-driving zone, but since the fuck-up of everything, no one gave a shit about the traffic regulations that said no motoring through that part of the city. It was a straight way back home—that was all.

Approaching the intersection, Posh slowed.

She reached the spot where she'd picked up Malone on that cold, miserable night. Like on that night, the street was still deserted, two rows of burnt-out husks of building surviving over from before The Grid was built. The Grid's support pillars stood out in stark gleaming metal contrast to the general burning down.

Suddenly, everything overwhelmed Posh. She parked, bent over her steering wheel and broke down in tears.

Fuck, she thought, *I have to kick my habit. I don't do that, Malone will dump me, then I'll totally be screwed.*

It wasn't work/money, no. At worst shakes, if he kicked her out, she could start hooking again; Sookie would be overjoyed to employ her.

But Posh LOVED Malone now. She had to get clean for *his* sake, so as not to mess up the beautiful thing between them.

If I haven't already done so. Of recent, she'd been seeing the strain on his face.

Ironically, she suspected that the one person who *could* help her kick her habit was Jade Cure. But she'd not dared go see Jade since the 'incident' that lost Ma her body. Malone had told her it was okay, that Jade bore her no grudge, but Posh simply couldn't face the scorn she anticipated from the other girl.

Wow, I've a real problem here.

She wiped her eyes, started the car.

She turned left onto Summer Street, then instantly turned right again, heading up Devonshire.

Posh suddenly didn't feel up to going home just yet. Unreasoning dread filled her mind and breast, fear that the ghost of the young man she'd roasted—murdered—last night awaited her at the bungalow, his eyes full of accusation.

She decided to drive around Central Boston, go check out her and Herbie's old skyscraper on Water Street.

***

Posh parked on Water and got out.

Wow, she thought. Like she'd heard, her old residence was fully beetled now, about to take to the air.

She walked closer for a better view. Not too close though. Accidents happened.

A block ahead of her, the monster bug twitched in pain. Its humongous wings beat the air, creating their own wind. Its lowest legs kicked against the ground in its fight to sever the final concrete/steel tendons rooting it to Earth.

Posh stood entranced, glad to have something to take her mind off her worries.

She wasn't alone on the street. Others watched too, looking like bowling pins waiting to be knocked over.

Also watching were a detachment of military engineers on standby to instantly repair the hole in the Grid that the beetle would leave when it airlifted.

Posh didn't envy them. The soldiers were bedraggled, but they had no choice, it was either keep a twenty-four hour alert or let dragons into Central Boston.

The constant demands of repairing the existing areas of The Grid was one reason its expansion had been halted. There simply weren't enough resources—people and material—to cope with both.

Wow, Posh thought, as she watched her former home. *I really hope no one overslept in it and wound up—*

A familiar voice penetrated her thoughts. "Hello, Posh Lane."

Startled, she spun around. She winced when she saw who it was.

Beth Riggs—the crazy ex prison warden. The chicken-sex lady.

Beth's expression was a mixture of pleasure and anger, laminated with her usual borderline craziness.

Posh was instantly scared. *Oh, damn, I should have gone home.*

Beth read her fear and capitalized on it. She grabbed Posh's arm, spun her around, and womanhandled her away from the sentinels watching the Beetle, back toward Herbie's Lincoln.

Posh got some of her composure back. "Let go of me!"

In response, Beth licked her ear. Posh cringed as the woman's tongue filled her ear hole with saliva.

"We're going back to my place to make love first," Beth whispered. "After that you can leave." She scowled. "I really don't understand you prostitutes. I always paid you excellently for your services. I don't know why Herbie stopped you coming to me— I've not seen him for three months."

She saw Posh's determined look and smirked. "Don't be foolish, honey. I've a gun in my pocket. If you dare call attention to us, I'll shoot you. Remember there's no longer any police force—no one will arrest me."

She smiled seductively, pointing to the blue Lincoln's number plate. "Your car's right, Posh honey—let's go fuck. You're a prostitute, a little more sex today won't hurt you."

She nodded at the car door. "Open it and get in. Remember, any tricks and you'll wake up in Hell."

Disbelieving what was happening to her, Posh opened the car door and got in. She didn't doubt that Beth would carry out her threat to shoot her if she made a fuss.

Beth shut the passenger side door. "Now drive. Calmly and coolly. Do not attract any attention. My place, you know the way."

She stroked Posh's face, trailing fingers down her spittle-slobbered ear to her pale throat. "My chickens are waiting for you." She sighed with lust. "It's strange, honey, but in the months since I screwed you last, I've found no other cunnilinguist of your stellar quality."

Posh had no reply. She gripped the wheel tight and drove.

CHAPTER 47

Malone

Malone discovered the Forks had been telling the truth. The inner door to his office now opened into a previously non-existent ascending stairwell.

He stared in confusion at the spiraling stairway, then peered up at the landing.

He shut the door again, stood scratching his head in his office.

His bafflement passed. He accepted the stairwell's sudden intrusion on his reality with the same equanimity with which he was coming to terms with his blood-solid arm and hand. Just as he accepted that the rest of his bungalow—everywhere the inner office door had previously granted access to—had somehow gone missing.

Malone sat down in a gorilla-chair to collect/collate his thoughts.

There's no great rush to leave, he reasoned. Frank clearly wanted *his*—not the dead president's—liver.

And Frank, equally clearly, was in no hurry. *The psycho will wait however long it takes for me to reach him; else why would he set up this stupid obstacle course?*

Except . . . Malone smacked his forehead at the realization, *except of course, he's scared of me and is planning . . . no, counting . . . on me being killed by something else along the trail. Then he'll come eat up the pieces.*

Malone thought and thought. For all their power, the Forks don't know where Frank is. But they clearly know some things. They knew Posh was addicted, for instance.

But—the thought occurred to him suddenly—they could have read my mind to know that.

Malone had never considered the possibility of the kitchen gods being telepathic before. The thought scared him. He seriously hoped they weren't.

***

Malone tried plotting for eventualities un-fathomable. Finally, unable to form a plan, he gave up trying.

He was tense beyond relief. Too much didn't make sense here.

He decided to go investigate the new upper floor.

He swore on remembering that his gun was in the mouth of the dead T-Rex that had attacked him.

The only weapon in the office was a pocketknife. He stuck this in a trouser pocket and re-entered the stairwell.

***

Had Malone been in a less preoccupied state of mind, he'd have noticed something odd about the inner door he'd just walked through—it shimmered faintly all around its frame.

The opening was actually an Otherworld Door—an OD.

***

The stairway ascended to a solitary supervisor's kiosk standing in the middle of a large warehouse full of packing crates, machinery and forklifts.

There were no staff anywhere in sight.

Malone peered through the kiosk window out the warehouse door. Outside, a solitary Condo he knew wasn't resident on his street was busily uprooting itself, preparatory to walking off to trangels knew where.

Malone had no time to ponder the impossibility of this huge ground-level building existing *atop* his office.

Immediately as he stepped out the kiosk door he spied a motion of something white in the corner of his eye.

Next, he caught the glint of light on metal.

Malone immediately threw himself flat down onto the warehouse floor.

An arc of bullets fanned over him. The slugs slammed the kiosk door shut, cancelling any chance of retreat.

The firing stopped, then resumed. The bullet arc descended in jagged left to right swings, leaving a pocked tattoo of its trajectory in the kiosk wall.

Malone rolled sideways. Slugs kicked up stone fragments beside him. He leapt up and zig-zagged a path towards the closest stack of packing crates on his left.

He made it to safety.

Bullets peppered the crates hiding him for a few moments, then ceased.

Malone waited to ensure the shooting didn't resume, then peeped out to see who was attacking him.

Machine corpse, my ass, he thought, silently cursing Frank.

The shooter was a white human-shaped robot with a T-slot in its face in which two red dots blinked. Malone instantly recognized it as one of Rachel Fischer's upgraded machines.

The white robot dropped its automatic rifle and picked up a pump-action shotgun. It checked the weapon's cartridge clip, then strode purposefully across the warehouse towards the stacks of crates concealing Malone.

Malone's knife was useless now—he needed something heavy to attack the robot with.

The knife wasn't *that* useless, however. Malone began using it to force a crate's slats open.

"Give it up, Malone, you can't escape," the robot called to him. "Just hand your liver over, and we'll call it quits." Its voice was Frank's, but bleached of emotional coloration.

Malone got the side of the crate off. It was packed with cans of baked beans. He groaned.

He ran down the aisle between the crates, away from the approaching machine, looking for either a weapon or an exit.

The robot quickened its steps to match his. Gun raised and firing, it spun into the passageway as Malone reached its end.

Buckshot blew a crate apart beside Malone's head. He ducked as the air filled with splinters. Moments later, another crate exploded above him, showering him with rice.

He turned the corner, ducking sideways into another aisle.

This aisle was a duplicate of the one he'd just exited—two walls of stacked cartons with a three-feet-wide walkway between them. The cartons were 'MOM' sardine boxes, each sporting a pretty mermaid logo.

"Give up the liver, Malone," the robot said. For emphasis, it let off a shot.

Malone knew he couldn't keep running from it. In addition to being impossible to reason out of a pre-programmed course of action, robots were indefatigable.

This damn machine will keep after me for as long as it has ammo.

As long as it *has* ammo. The thought built the framework of a plan in his head. The plan fleshed out, became workable to Malone.

Acting with desperate speed, he ripped apart the nearest sardine carton. After stuffing his pockets with cans, he pulled the carton out of the stack. Its being dislodged set off a mini-avalanche of sardine cartons. With Malone assisting the carton-fall, soon the aisle was half-blocked with cardboard boxes.

He settled in the excavated hole in the box-wall and waited for the robot to turn the corner.

It did, to be immediately hit in the head by two sardine cans Malone threw at it.

Caught off-guard by the attack, it let off two blasts from its shotgun. While it stopped to figure out how to navigate the blocked aisle, Malone stepped into clear view.

"Hey, Tinhead! Catch!" He pelted three more cans at it. The robot fired at him as he ducked back into concealment. Carton fluff and sardine oil showered Malone.

He stepped out of hiding and performed the maneuver again, with the same response from the robot. The damage to the cartons flanking him was now so great that there were fish chunks in his hair.

He ducked out into the aisle again and hurled a further fusillade of cans at the robot. A single blast followed his leap back into hiding. This was followed by a series of resounding clicks.

"This won't take long, Malone."

Malone smiled grimly. The machine was out of ammo—it needed to reload.

He leapt out of concealment and charged the robot, scaling the sardine carton pile like he was a mountain goat; leaping off it like a leopard vacating a tree branch.

The robot was pulling cartridges from a plastic pouch attached to its waist when Malone came at it. It looked up in surprise, then attempted shifting its grip on the shotgun so it could wield it as a club.

Malone torpedoed into it before it completed the maneuver.

They went down in a heap.

Malone was up again in a flash. Ripping the gun from the startled machine's plastic hands, he proceeded to bash its head in as violently as he could.

He stopped only when there was so much smoke and sparks spurting from its shattered braincase that he feared setting the stacked cardboard boxes afire if he damaged it any more.

The robot kept jerking, however. Malone got out his knife and cut all the wires connecting its head and body. Its jerks subsided to intermittent twitches.

He sat down on a spilled crate to consider Frank's puzzle.

He now clearly had his 'dead machine upstairs.' All he had do was find the clue hidden in it.

***

After an hour of dismantling the robot—when its gears and circuit boards were strewn around like he was building it from scratch—he located Frank's message, secreted in the middle joint of the robot's right thumb.

It read:

'Overweight women need sex too.
Go to Club House and fuck Blubber.
Ensure she comes or you won't ever.
Eat you soon,
Frank.'

CHAPTER 48

Malone

Carrying the dead robot's shotgun, Malone stepped outside the warehouse.

He'd emerged into a main street outside The Grid. The area was a vista of wide open air spaces, burnt buildings, and lots of freshly-laid skyscrapers.

Close by, a family was moving their belongings into a skyscraper.

A house sign read 54 Newbury Street. That meant Back Bay, well west of Chinatown.

Malone was instantly on guard. But there were no dragons in sight, hopefully no dinos around either.

He needed transport. He decided to 'borrow' the moving family's truck when they were done unloading it.

***

"Malone?" the voice was soft and flutelike.

He spun round, shotgun at the ready. Then he froze, stood gaping at the speaker.

It was a horse. A very odd horse.

The horse was totally transparent. Like looking through water, Malone could see through it to the street on its other side. Its body had a slight blue tint.

Its saddle and bridle were transparent too, and seemed part of its body.

"Wh . . . what?" he sputtered at the see-thru beast.

"I am Glass Horse, Malone. Lord Tav and Lady Yaz sent me to help you on your quest."

Malone was still gaping at it. "Eh?"

The horse shook its head. Its glass mane fluttered like hair. It regarded him with clear eyes. "What is wrong?"

"I've never seen a transparent horse before."

"Few people have."

Malone decided one didn't look a gift horse in the mouth, even if it was made of glass. "Horse, do you know a place called Club House?"

"Certainly. That is Blubber's place."

"Take me there, I've an appointment with her."

"Climb on."

Malone mounted it and they set off.

***

Riding Glass Horse felt like riding a normal horse. The only difference was that Malone could look through it at the ground they galloped over.

Glass Horse suddenly ducked through a shattered doorway.

"What's the—"

"Ssshhh. A dragon is coming!"

The dragon walked into sight. It was twelve feet high at the shoulder, and moved with a lumbering tread on feet unfamiliar with the ground. Its body glimmered in the afternoon sun like a rock concert lightshow.

'Fiberglass jaws framing fiberglass maws, fiberglass claws making fiberglass laws,' so the folk song went.

The dragon was beautiful and deadly. It looked like a condensed rainbow, each of its transparent scales lit up with a different band of the visible spectrum.

Beneath them, its muscles and viscera also glittered their own rainbow pulses.

Malone had never seen anything so breathtaking.

The huge synthetic carnivore tramped past them, gazing from side to side and gnashing its teeth. Occasionally it scoured the side of a nearby building with a massive spurt of fire.

It passed so close by Malone that he could have reached out a hand and touched the metal screws holding its jaws together, run his fingers over its rainbow scales.

"That is a very terrible sight," Glass Horse whispered with admiration as the glittering behemoth trampled off towards a parked truck.

"Very terrible," Malone agreed.

"They say it comes from the Afterwife, that the trangels are its parents."

Malone snorted. "The Afterwife's nothing but a myth created by an unhappily married man with pseudo-gay tendencies. *Transsexual Heaven* . . . the Breast Milk Sea with the floating breast hills? Utter nonsense—someone watched too much anime porn . . . and now you're saying dragons originate there too? Wise up, horse."

"The Afterwife is real, Malone. I've been there."

"Yeah, fucking right. I'll believe in it when I see it."

"Don't mock the supernatural, Malone. It may be-come angry and haunt you."

"C'mon, horse, you don't honestly believe that nonsense."

The transparent horse's voice held quiet conviction: "No need to believe—I've see it."

Malone kept quiet, convinced that Glass Horse was bullshitting him. Together they watched the dragon savage the truck, ripping it apart and satisfying itself it was empty before lumbering off.

CHAPTER 49

Malone

They reached Club House five minutes later. The club was at the south end of Newbury Street, just before the Massachusetts Avenue intersection. It was a small blue building stuck between a condo and a dead skyscraper-bug that had toppled over while trying to take off too early.

"This is the place," Glass Horse said, its voice calm and serious. "I will wait out here until you are done."

Malone thanked it. After tucking the shotgun out of sight under his shirt, he walked over to the front door, besides which an asbestos-shielded Pontiac was parked.

***

The club interior was dusty. There were a few customers, a few waitresses, and an off-duty hooker.

Everyone stared at Malone when he entered. His bloody shirt with its missing right sleeve instantly caught their attention. Several people raised eyebrows at his exposed red arm.

Malone ignored their enquiring glances. He studied their faces to ensure Frank wasn't one of them.

(Malone wasn't taking Frank for granted. It wasn't just his recent clash with the white robot that had him cautious. He remembered Sara's angry words—the sheer audacity of Frank's stealing Rachel Fischer's head showed the man's resourcefulness.)

The drinkers lost interest in Malone and resumed drinking. He made his way over to the bar.

The barmaid, a once-pretty woman with a stressed-out look, smiled at him. "Are you Malone?"

He looked at her sharply. "You're expecting me?"

"Guy called up, said his name was Frank. He said you might come around, booked time for you with Blubber."

Malone relaxed a bit. He shed his apprehension that this too was a trap. He studied the drinkers again. No one was acting suspicious.

"What drink will you have, Malone?" the barmaid asked.

He read the labels off the shelved bottles. "What do you recommend?"

She winked. "Have some BBW, Malone, you'll need it."

He nodded, she poured, he drank.

The BBW tasted like he thought piss would taste if he ever decided to taste it. "What's in this shit?"

"Blubber's concentrated pee—it's proven to put you in the mood."

Malone spat what he hadn't already swallowed onto the barmaid. He glared knives at her, then exposed his concealed shotgun and rested it on the bar top.

"My reputation apparently didn't precede me here," he said. "You ever try nonsense like this with me again, and I'll feed you to a dragon. You dig?"

She flinched. "I didn't mean . . ."

"Just don't do it again. Where *is* Blubber? I need to get this over with *now*."

He realized the bar patrons were watching him again. He turned and glowered at them, tapping the shotgun barrel for emphasis. They resumed their previous activity of not watching him.

The barmaid stared at him, her spit-covered face twitching nervously, like she wanted to say something, but didn't dare.

Malone groaned. "What is it *now?*"

"Mr. Frank didn't pay, sir."

"For this stupid drink? You should be glad I'm not charging *you* for making me drink it."

"No, sir . . . for your time with Blubber. Mr. Frank said *you* would meet all expenses."

Malone first looked like he'd have a fit, then he burst out laughing.

"Mr. Frank is a degenerate cheapskate. How much is it?"

"Two thousand dollars for an hour, sir."

"That much?—I could rent *four* hookers for that long for that much!"

The barmaid's smile made a shy comeback. "Blubber is a *lot* of woman, Malone. Much more even than four prostitutes rolled into one."

CHAPTER 50

Malone

The upper-floor bedroom shut behind him, leaving him with . . . Blubber.

Malone looked on in major dismay.

There was an amorphous orange-flesh mass draped over a monster bed.

Wow, Posh darling, Malone thought. *You've no idea what I'm going through to get you detoxed.*

He walked over to the bed and peered at the 'woman' he was supposed to sexually gratify.

***

Blubber was the most obscenely obese person Malone had ever seen.

She looked like the mating of a duvet and a whale.

Malone had no idea where any one part of her began or ended—everything flowed together into one vast rolling expanse of womanity. She had hands and feet, but the rest of her was just rolls of fat that hid the bed from view. Her body hung over the bed's edges like a sheet.

"Hello," he said. "My name's Malone, I hear you're expecting me."

There was no reply.

Oddly, Malone found he wasn't disgusted, wasn't adverse to *the idea* of Blubber's incomprehensible grotesqueness. He recognized this mellowing of his emotions as the result of the 'BBW' the barmaid had tricked into him.

Am I really the same person who quibbled for so long over satisfying Yang Yang? he wondered, amazed. *And the Snake Lady even looks human.*

Blubber didn't look human, not by a long shot. She looked like a woman-pancake.

What needs be done, needs be done, he decided. *Now where is that pussy?*

Malone stripped off, dropped his clothes and weapons in a pile on the floor, and climbed onto Blubber.

He crawled over her body, looking for her face, her ears. She wobbled with his motion over her, a woman sea rippling with fat waves.

He found two eyes tucked in fatty clefts four feet apart. A nose. Thatches of long blonde hair planted at far-flung reaches of her.

Finally he located an ear.

He spoke into the ear. "I'm Malone, Frank sent me."

"I hear you're good in bed, Malone," Blubber replied dreamily. Her voice, a stretched moan as though she were drugged, seemed to come from her multitudes of folds. "Frank says you're *fantastic* in bed."

Malone rolled his eyes. "The absolute fucking best."

"Prove it and I'll give you a refund, Malone. Deal? All your money back if you're great in the sack?" Her voice had the slickness of oil. Her body rippled like a pond surface.

"Deal. Where is your vagina?" he asked. "You're so . . . much . . . woman, baby. It's a shame to keep you waiting."

"It's where it should be—between my legs. Fuck me good, Malone. Fuck me *real* good."

Malone did some calculations. Blubber's left foot projected from a fold draped over the bedside closest to him. Her right foot was ten feet away, right next to an ear.

That would place her vagina at about . . .

He searched midway between her legs, and after a few false stops mistaking skin folds for the real thing, located her sex beneath a thick thatch of blonde hair.

Circling it were two fat hillocks, which, from their darkened peaked crests and bottle cork tops, he suspected were her breasts.

Now this will take some doing, he thought.

Even without spreading her labia, Blubber's vagina yawned like a sleepy child.

Her vagina was so huge his penis would never fill it.

Out loud, he said: "I've found it baby, you're *so* beautiful. This was true—her sex had a nauseating loveliness to it.

Blubber's liquid voice bubbled out of her pussy at him like female ejaculate. "Fuck me good, Malone. Fuck me *real good*."

Malone looked down at his penis, already at half-mast and rising steadily. "Easy, boy," he whispered, "you're not the man for this job by a long shot."

He felt no inadequacy—it was simply a fact. Though he longed to plunge into Blubber's mass and take root like a tree in Mother Earth, it would never do. Frank's riddle said 'satisfy Blubber,' 'make *her* cum.'

Her clitoris looked normal enough. He suspected that if he gave her head, she'd orgasm. But she'd requested/demanded/commanded that he *fuck* her. But how? Her vagina looked like it would conveniently admit a fist.

Malone smiled then. He turned his blood hand over and studied the three zit-disgusting buttons, with their companion inscriptions: Hetero, Gay and Lesbian Fist.

Well, fisting was fucking too. Gay people had made it a socially acceptable form of sexual intercourse.

The question of which button to press was easy to answer. For all her distortions, Blubber was female, he, male.

Placing his right fingertips together, he inserted his blood hand between Blubber's labia and depressed the 'Hetero Fist' button with his left hand.

After that it was a gas.

***

Malone was impressed by the expertise with which his Hetero Fist serviced Blubber.

His blood arm, now swollen to twice-normal thickness, slid in and out of her of its own accord, pulling him after it and pushing him back again.

Occasionally it varied its rhythm, slowing down or speeding up, and once in a while it twisted left and right. Several times, like it was coming up for air, it jerked itself totally out of her body, only to plunge back in immediately, to the accompaniment of immense moans and groans from the fat landscape Malone knelt on.

"Frank was right, Malone. You're fantastic. You really fuck good. Hold on tight now—I'm gonna cum."

Blubber came. She came like she was the sea. She rolled in fat waves Malone was forced to surf.

Malone held on tight. He had to, as her rolls and folds became flesh dunes that threatened to buck him up to splat against the ceiling. He gripped the thatch of hair topping her sex with his left hand, while his right now pounded in and out of Blubber like it had a grudge against her cervix and wanted to annihilate it.

Her flesh rose so high above him that he feared it would squash him. Then, as a humongous fat-fold crest descended to smother him, he discovered he had another, larger, worry.

His body was painlessly liquefying—melting and being sucked into itself.

With lightning speed, Malone was liquefied up to his knees, his waist, his chest. Even faster, he worked out what was going on: he was being sucked up into his blood arm, and through it into Blubber.

"Blubber, stop it! Stop what you're doing!"

"Oh, you fuck real good, Malone. You fuck marvelously."

Her voice was a satiated dream painted in dripping oils.

Malone's head dissolved, and with that his consciousness. He flowed down into his chest and out into his red arm.

Once he was all gone, his blood arm rolled itself up like a condom before use, shortening down to itself disappear into Blubber's supersized super moist vagina.

Blubber moaned as the red appendage vanished from sight inside her. "You get *all* your money back, Malone, and a sixty-nine percent discount on all future visits. Oooooohhh . . . yeeeah!"

CHAPTER 51

Posh

Posh was naked on her hands and knees between Beth's legs, lapping cunt like a dog, with Beth's chopping board on her back.

On Posh's right, hapless fowls squawked piteously in their bucket. On her left, the remains of previous fowls lay scattered over the plastic sheet protecting the carpet.

Posh herself was covered with chicken blood.

Above her, Beth hacked a chicken into a million pieces. Her hand a blur, she squirmed in pleasure as Posh tongued her clitoris. Her muscular thighs quivered. Her back arched, thrusting her large breasts forward.

Beth groaned. She handed a skinned chicken drumstick down to Posh. "Love me with this immediately, darling!"

Gripping the bleeding chicken leg by its scaly talons, Posh fed it into the shaven vagina.

"Fuuccckkk!" Beth gushed as the drumstick entered her sex. A moment later, she handed down another bloody drumstick.

"And with this one also!" she gasped. "Double-fuck me quick, honey!"

Posh saw no need to lubricate Beth's anus. She positioned the drumstick at the little puckered entrance and pushed it in. Slickened with blood, the meat-stick slurped inside Beth.

"Yes!" Beth gasped at the pleasure of the penetration, slamming the cleaver through the chicken's breast bone with such force that Posh felt it in her own breasts.

Gripping both chicken legs in one fist, Posh double-dildoed Beth with them.

Beth almost went out of her mind from the sensation. She swept the chicken remains off the board with the cleaver, then yanked another live bird from the bucket. She hacked off its head, then raised it so its dying blood squirted on her chest.

Kneading the crimson gush into her breasts, she reached her first orgasm.

***

Posh squealed in pain when Beth's knees clamped tight on her ears as she came.

"Don't stop fucking me, bitch!" Beth growled. She spread her thighs again, wide as a gymnast.

"Here's some lube." She held the neck of yet another beheaded chicken over her crotch, squirting its blood down onto her cunt.

Posh obliged. She rammed both drumsticks in and out of Beth's sex holes.

The chicken leg in Beth's anus was now brown with shit, each re-emergence from her flesh assaulted Posh's nostrils with the smell.

Damn, Posh thought, *won't she ever finish?*

Posh wanted to be out of there—well away from there—as quick as possible. *And this fucking time it's for good. Under no fucking circumstances is anything bringing me to fucking Water Street ever again!*

Oh fuck!" Beth groaned, her thighs quivering as she spasmed again. Then she went limp.

Thank goodness, Posh thought. *Now to leave here. Beth can keep her fucking money. And on this sordid note, I hereby quit prostitution for good. Even if Malone dumps me, I'll rather panhandle.*

She pushed the chopping board off her back and made to get up.

Beth, however, forced her back down again with a foot on her waist. Posh flopped belly down onto the besmirched drop cloth, coating her breasts and belly in a mess of fowl guts.

"No!" Beth said, "I need a lot more today."

"I have to go," Posh pleaded. "I'm meeting my boy—"

"Not yet!" She glared down at Posh.

Posh shivered. Beth's eyes now had the same insane glint as when she'd forced Herbie to drink his cum out of that chicken.

Beth smiled. She removed her foot from Posh's back. "Today, we go the extra mile." She picked the second-to-last chicken out of the bucket. "Now kneel down again and lick my sex, like the good dog you are."

Posh nodded. She reached for the bloody cutting board.

"Leave it!" Beth said sharply. "This time your back is the board."

Disbelieving what she'd heard, Posh looked up at her. "What?" She froze, trembling.

Beth now held her gun. She licked her lips like the air tasted delicious. "Oh yes, honey. You heard me right. Your back is the board." She smiled lewdly at Posh's horror. "I've wanted to try this forever, but Herbie wouldn't let me. He said scars would make you less appealing to other customers."

"You're going to chop up a chicken on my bare back?"

Beth pointed the gun straight at Posh's face. "Either on *your* back or on your corpse's back. Choose one."

Seeing refusal meant instant death, Posh got into position—on hands and knees between Beth's super-toned legs.

God, please help me survive this.

She indicated the drumsticks in Beth's vagina and anus. "Should I keep on doing you with these?" she asked helplessly.

Beth shook her head. "Just eat me." She placed the shivering chicken down between Posh's shoulders and began chopping.

***

The cleaver rose. It fell again, cutting clean through the hen's neck and embedding itself into Posh's back.

Posh screamed. The pain belied description. Beth yanked the cleaver out of Posh's back and hacked again into the bird. This blow broke its spine, but didn't go all the way through its body, sparing Posh. The force of the blow however, smeared feathers into Posh's bubbling wound.

Posh's eyes gaped open in agony. She tried to scuttle away, but was stopped by Beth's gun muzzle prodding her eye.

"One more move back . . ."

Posh nodded mutely. She scuttled forward again.

"Lick me, bitch!"

Beth resumed hacking the chicken to bits. Posh licked her bloody cunt as the blows fell. She flinched each time the cleaver

243

ripped into her back. Even blunted by its passage through chicken meat before reaching her, the agony of each cut was indescribable. This had to be what being whipped with barbed wire felt like.

Shredded feather quills and fragments of chicken bone dug into the cuts, ripping her already torn skin and flesh apart further.

And the horrendous torment kept on coming, kept increasing.

***

In her ingenuity, her burning desire to cause Posh pain, Beth moved the uncut portions of fowl to undamaged parts of Posh's back before each new chop.

She regarded each fresh splitting of Posh's body—each division of her skin and underlying flesh and each new welling of blood—with studious interest, unsure what she expected to see in them other than confirmation of her own sexual superiority to this pathetic female trembling between her legs.

And all the while, she luxuriated in the feelings Posh's tongue provoked in her loins—cunt-ecstasy raging like a forest fire out of control.

***

Posh's tongue slid erratically over Beth's clitoris now, juddering as she surfed the waves of agony she floundered in. She felt she was in Hell. She couldn't stay where she was—the pain was too great. Yet also, she couldn't run to save herself—the image of her head blown to bits dangled before her eyes like a donkey's oversized scrotum.

Blood ran down over her sides, dripped to the floor. And now she knew this wasn't chicken blood, but hers.

Posh felt herself succumbing to shock. She fought against this culmination of her horror. If she collapsed, there was a good chance Beth might decide to treat her like an actual chicken—chop her up for the hell of it.

So she forced herself to keep licking Beth's vagina, inserting two fingers into her anus and fucking her with them.

***

The pain wasn't the worst of it. The more crushing blow was to Posh's spirit. Beth was making her feel utterly worthless—like she was less than garbage.

For Posh, this horrible experience was much worse than what she'd suffered with Oswald. She accepted that Oswald had been fucked-up in battle. But what was Beth's excuse—other than sheer nastiness? Posh pondered these questions between each slash of pain.

**

Beth's legs clenched around Posh's head again, announcing her orgasm. With a single blow, she chopped the last live chicken completely in two.

The blow buried the cleaver in Posh's back, deep between her right ribs.

The truncated fowl, separated into a mess of spilling entrails, squawked in piteous confusion as its blood spurted from it over its human chopping board.

Beth left the blade in Posh's back. She gripped Posh's head with both hands and ground it into her pussy.

"Fucking lick me, honey! I'm cumming! Oh, Gooooodddd, Yeeeeessssss!"

Beth had NEVER come like this before. It was a sexual explosion that blasted her out to space. It seemed to last forever and ever.

She felt she was dissolving, melting into Posh's tongue, blowing away on the wind like a dust mote. Her legs and arms felt like butter, like wax.

She came down from her come.

Posh looked up at her with pleading numbed eyes. The cleaver had fallen out of her back during Beth's orgasm.

Beth nodded at her. "Okay, honey. I'm fine now."

Posh collapsed onto the just truncated chicken. Its head poked from under her bloody body, its dead eyes as dull as hers.

Beth watched Posh tremble and twitch for a moment. Then, careful to take both gun and cleaver with her, she went to get money to pay her.

***

"Why?" Posh asked. "Why did you do this to me?"

She'd managed to stand up again, but had no strength to dress. Her back felt like a furnace she was carrying around. In addition, she was super-weak from blood loss. Blood was still dribbling from the web of cuts crisscrossing her back. Thin red trails streamed down over her ass and the backs of her legs.

Feathers, chicken meat, and bone fragments were plastered all over her; some imbedded deep in her wounds.

"Why?" Posh repeated.

Beth smiled. "Because I'm stronger than you, honey. What other reason do I need?" She held out the money. "Take it. I've included a huge bonus. Go see a doctor. When you're healed we'll do this again."

Posh gaped at her dully. "Again?"

"Yes, again. This bareback fuck was much better than I thought it would be." She licked her lips. "You're my bitch now, honey. You'll do what I tell you to, or I'll kill you."

Posh looked at her dully. "You'll *kill me* if I don't fuck you again?"

Beth smiled coldly. "I will." She held out the money. "Take it and go now. You can come back to visit later if you want. But now, honey, I need to take a nap. Great sex always wears me out."

She bent forward and kissed Posh full on the lips. Posh shrank back with revulsion.

Beth didn't notice. She leaned back smiling. "Your mouth stinks of me. Great. Think of it as a high class bitch scenting her territory."

Posh stared into Beth's face for a long moment.

Despite teetering on the brink of shock, she was chilled by the disregard for her feelings in the other's eyes.

She nodded dully. She took the money from Beth, then staggered naked to the door and let herself out.

***

Downstairs, Posh stumbled into her car.

She brushed away the feathers plastered all over her. *I look like I'm turning into a bird.*

Her back stuck to the seat once she settled into it.

Fuck, that hurts!

Every motion was agony—in several places Beth had chopped deep into her muscles. It was a miracle that she hadn't broken Posh's spine with the cleaver.

Posh groaned and leaned forward, leaving a crimson puddle on the seat back. She looked at it and winced. Her back was wet from re-opened cuts.

Fuck! I'm bleeding to death here.

Now Posh's ordeal was over, she was angry. An impotent rage, drained of force by the severity of her injuries.

She leaned painfully back again. I've got to get the hell out of here, before the fucking dinos smell the blood and have me for lunch.

She felt a flood of wetness on her back as a particularly deep incision opened up. A slow but certain dribble, the blood pooled under her buttocks.

Posh was suddenly very worried that Beth had sliced open a major blood vessel. *I could keep leaking till I'm empty.*

But where to go now? What to do?

She fast realized she had only one real choice.

Jade Cure. The one person she really didn't want to see, was likely the only one who could stop her bleeding to death.

At least the pain is keeping me awake, she thought as she drove off. *Preventing me from passing out. Hopefully I'll make it to Chinatown alive.*

CHAPTER 52

Malone

A fraction of a moment of pure hell—an interval when Malone was certain he'd died—and then he was alive and himself again.

And seated on a pink sofa in a purple parlor, still naked.

Malone looked around.

It was a nice comfy place, with flower-patterned curtains over the windows, thick pile rugs, a wall vision 3-D TV, a bookshelf, framed pictures on the wall . . .

Now what's going on? I've clearly satisfied Blubber sufficiently to get to the next stage of Frank's riddle. But where am I?

He got up and tried the front door. It was locked.

He nodded, pulled aside the window curtains, and looked out.

He was *very* high up, of that he was immediately assured. The clouds didn't seem that far overhead.

***

He returned his attention inside the room.

His attention was caught by a photo, a picture of a man and two winged women that occupied pride of place on the flower-strewn shelf above the television.

He walked over and examined it more closely. There was no doubt; the man was Herbie Stanton. Malone recognized Posh's ex-pimp from some snaps she'd shown him.

Malone was immediately tense. According to Sookie Ling, Herbie Stanton had been missing since the night he'd met Posh.

Malone backed away from the shelf till his progress was halted by an armchair. Absentminded, he sat down, trying to assemble this latest piece of an already insane puzzle.

Herbie Stanton is here? Where is this?

Malone got to his feet and looked at the picture again. Both Herbie's winged female companions were pretty. One, a redhead, looked to be about thirty, the other, a blonde, fifty-five.

The blonde seemed pleasant, though she had a no-nonsense air about her, the barest glint of steel in her eyes. The redhead looked like she was faking pleasance for the lens.

Malone reasoned: *I'm somewhere where Herbie Stanton can have two wives without anyone raising eyebrows. Where?*

He left the living room. *Herbie was a pimp, made his living off the flesh trade in women. If this is Heaven, he's been given two female angels for . . .*

Then realization hit Malone.

Hell, no, he thought in alarm, *not the Afterwife—the heaven for misogynists, sex offenders, wife beaters, philanderers. I'm not in fucking Traven—Transsexual Heaven—am I? It's a myth, for crying out loud! A delusion.*

Shit. Glass Horse's recent words about the supernatural haunting him for disrespect now haunted Malone.

Urgency gripped him, a sense of major crisis loom-ing.

First and foremost, he needed clothes, shoes.

He pushed a door open, entered a bedroom; a beautiful room such as one would expect to find in a nice apartment like this.

Only on the huge bed there was a HUGE worm.

***

The worm on the bed had to be at least twenty feet long. It was brown and segmented and coiled like an unbroken turd passed by someone squatting in grass. Additionally, its body was segmented, split into six-inch sections separated by rings of yellow muscle.

It smelt freshly bathed and perfumed.

The worm end facing Malone was an orifice wide enough to admit two fingers. Its muscular rim twitched as if it sensed Malone's presence. The entrance had two long limp feelers either side of it.

Then the worm shifted position, snoring gently, and Malone saw its pair of anal feelers for what they really were.

Human legs. Flexible like rubber.

Malone was hardened to horror, despite which it took all his willpower not to fill his underwear with excrement there and then.

He controlled himself, though his sanity ve-hemently rejected what he was seeing. It screamed at him to flee screaming from that bedroom.

Slowly, so as not to wake the sleeping worm, he walked round it silently to where he could see its head.

The worm's head was Herbie Stanton's.

Like his anus, Herbie's mouth had also been rounded into a smooth single-lipped taut 'O'-pening. All his teeth had been removed. But that wasn't the worst of it.

Malone realized with added horror that Herbie had no bones left anywhere in his body. *That* was why his legs flopped like tentacles, why his arms, visible six feet from his head, also flopped from non-existent shoulder-points.

He'd been deboned and *stretched*. Malone had no idea *how* you stretched a six-feet-tall man to twenty feet long. But he *had* been stretched, stretched till now his body was only four inches wide.

Malone leaned against the bedroom wall and shut his eyes.

The legends were true.

This was Traven.

But then: *What the hell then am I doing here?*
Am I dead?

***

Legend was, that when a *very* bad man died, he entered the Afterwife and was married as wife to a pair of transsexual angel husbands.

After the marriage ceremony, the 'husbands' had their new 'wife' 'altered' and the trio had uber-fantastic sex throughout the Afterwife.

The Afterwife was both a location and a fixed point in time—a single eternal moment that never ended.

***

Malone studied Herbie's peacefully snoring face, then moved his gaze to study his body. It did resemble an earthworm's—slickly moist muscle-stria—yet with that incongruous perfumed lilac smell.

Herbie gave off a strong impression of extreme pampering.

For the first time, Malone noted the oval bulges in the man-worm's body, like bumps in the body of a snake that had swallowed a nest of rats.

Legend said these were eggs—Herbie would continue laying regularly for his angel wives.

Malone's attention was caught by a farting sound. He padded back round to the man-worm's rear, saw a chalk-white oval pushing its way out of the ass-aperture.

He turned away in disgust, began searching the room for clothes. A closet yielded some—a shirt, trousers, and shoes; along with a pair of black gloves.

The clothes fit him perfectly. The shoes were a bit large, but he'd cope. He put the gloves on, pleased to no longer have to see his crimson arm and hand.

There was the creak of the front door opening.

Malone frantically looked around the bedroom for a weapon.

A plastic paperweight lay on the bedside dresser. A four-inch-high model of a lecherous male head, with metal eye-ovals framing pupil hollows.

Malone studied the sculpted face a moment. It was disturbingly true-to-life—looked almost possessed—with its 'love to fuck you, baby' expression, its flared nostrils, its leering pink tongue.

It had a red button in its forehead. He pointed the head so it was 'looking' at the wall and pressed the button. Nothing happened.

It was quite heavy, however, and could be used as a missile. He stuck it in his pocket and walked back to the living room.

CHAPTER 53

Malone

The new entrants were the two women in the photograph. Both carried shoeboxes and hatboxes galore.

Both wore pink tube tops and skintight white pants. Both their crotches bulged like they had ropes knotted in them.

Both had fluffy pink wings.

The middle-aged blonde smiled warmly on seeing Malone. "Well *hello,* handsome—when did you get in?" Her chest was extremely generous; looking at it, with her nipples threatening to puncture her top, Malone almost wanted to bed her.

He smiled back at her: "A better question would be—what am I doing here?"

"Well that's obvious," the second woman replied. "You didn't keep your cock in your pants when you should have." She snickered. "Now it's time to pay the price."

Malone looked her over with developing dislike. She was shorter than her companion, less pretty, and her thin lips were twisted like she'd swallowed something bitter.

"I'm sorry I caught you on a bad hair day," he told her. "I'll address myself to your friend from now on."

He smiled again at the blonde. The redhead glared angrily at him.

"My name's Malone. There's been a mix-up of some sort—I'm not even married."

The blonde stretched like she was just waking up. Her wings spread out to an impressive span—their pink feathers rustled like a brood of chickens at midnight. "I'm Blondie and my co-husband's Stacy. A mix-up? That's what *you all* say, *darling.* Would you like a drink?"

Her charm almost won him over. Then he glanced behind her, saw the ambiguous look on her framed picture face.

He laughed. "Nice try, *darling*. But I think if I drink anything in here, I'm sure to wind up like Herbie in there."

The redhead was irate. "You went into our *bedroom*!? You slut, you're even wearing Herbie's clothes!"

Malone shrugged. "He didn't look like he needed them anymore."

"You . . . You're a total asshole!"

"Calm yourself, Stacy darling. Malone didn't know it was our home. Did you, *darling*?"

"And he was ogling our worman!" she stared at Malone like she was about to attack him. Her pink wings pumped themselves up and down like shrugging shoulders.

"Calm down, Stacy, for fuck's sake!"

"But our worman's—"

"Your *what*?"

Blondie smiled. She stroked Malone's chin with a fingernail. "*Worman*, a combo of 'worm' and 'man.' It also sounds like 'woman,' which is nice, since we're the husbands and he the wife."

"Normally we're viewed by everyone as girls and girlish," Stacy spat. "Having a wife of our own does wonders for our self-esteem."

"Taking hormone shots, having plastic surgery, wearing frilly clothes and all—isn't *that* what you wanted?"

"Yeah, okay, but sometimes it gets too much. And don't you dare suggest that that's reasoning like a woman."

"What I want to know," Malone said, keeping the hysteria out of his voice with effort, "is why you had to stretch him that much? Couldn't you just . . . have sex with him as he was?"

"It's because of the *eggs*, darling. The longer a worman's body, the more womb length, which equals more incubation time."

Stacy seemed to get over her dislike of Malone. She sat opposite him, crumpling her wings behind her. She spread her legs wide so her penis was clearly outlined in the silken crotch of her pants. "The eggs are formed in the worman's throat, and travel down his body to his anus over a period of two weeks—it's like taking a shit. He has to be at least twenty feet long for the eggs to keep warm long enough to hatch."

Blondie also sat down. She poured herself some brandy from the snifter on the center table. "Anyway, Malone, you're stuck here. No one leaves Traven."

"You'll be our bitch and like it," Stacy mocked, tapping her cock for emphasis. "And you'll lay dragon eggs for us like a good worman."

Malone, in the process of working out which of the women he'd ever slept with had been married, was startled out of his reverie. "What was that you just said—about the eggs?"

Blondie began massaging her penis through her pants. She smiled at Malone, her face all sweetness: "You sure you don't want to suck on this, *darling?* It's an adult lollipop."

Malone waved her off. "About the eggs? What did you say?"

She grimaced. "They hatch into dragons. Duh, you know what dragons are, don't you—those fiberglass reptiles currently burning the USA to ashes?"

"Herbie was laying one when I went inside."

"Oh goodie!" Stacy yelped excitedly. "Was it white!? Was it white!?"

Malone nodded.

"I get a baby at last!" She leapt out of the chair, danced barefoot out of the living room.

Malone looked at Blondie. "What's that about?"

"We've always thought she's sterile. My eggs are brown and speckled. Hers should have been white, but till now Herbie hasn't laid her any. So she's been taking fertility shots. And she gets to fuck the mouth all the time now."

Malone said nothing. His eyes projected his bewilderment.

Blondie grinned, sipped some of her brandy. "Since you're joining our family, I'll explain, so you don't panic. We'll fix your ass and mouth so we can both screw you at once—threesomes are so romantic. We'll take out all your bones so you're really nice and stretchy—we're BIG girls—we don't want to rip you up, *darling.*"

She smiled sweetly. "Don't be scared, Malone, I promise you it's not torment or eternal damnation, or anything like that—the modifications make both your throat and rectum more sensitive than any clitoris any woman's ever had—you'll be cumming so much you'll be *shitting* eggs."

She burst into laughter.

"I see," Malone said dryly.

Stacy charged out of the bedroom at that moment.

"Blondie, where'd you put the Masher?"

Blondie looked up at her in alarm. "What are you talking about? It was on the dresser!"

"It's not on there now!"

"What's the Masher?" Malone asked innocently.

Stacy glared at him impatiently. "It's a weapon shaped like a lecher's head. In the right woman's hands, she can take over the world.

"We stole it from . . ." She looked at Malone closely. "You took it, didn't you?"

Malone pulled the head paperweight out of his pocket. "This?"

Both women looked at him in horror. "Be careful with that," Blondie said, extending a hand. "Don't push anything; just hand it over nice and slow."

"I'll make a deal with you two," Malone said, holding the 'Masher' pointing face-forward at the two transsexual angels. "You can have this thing back if you let me out of here."

"We've already told you no one EVER leaves either Traven or the Afterwife," Stacy snapped. "Now give me back that before I take it from you and fuck you with it!" She however made no attempt to come any closer.

Malone moved his finger over the red button in the Masher's forehead.

"Fucking don't press that!"

Blondie's voice was short and sharp. Her pretty face suddenly looked very worried, which made her look very old and not as pretty. Malone saw a thousand years of living in her face at that moment.

Her fear told him a lot about the potency of whatever the Masher was.

Stacy, however, scowled at Malone, her dislike of him overriding her fear. "Make this easy on yourself," she growled, "or I swear when you're our worman we'll have you fixed so you don't ever cum!"

Malone smirked. "Yeah, I thought there was eternal torment here as well. Anyway, I don't intend staying that long."

He smiled good-naturedly. "Look, girls, I'm going out the door and that's it." He raised the hand with the head-sculpture. "You two don't follow me and I promise to leave this thing where you can find it. It doesn't work anyway."

The slight smile that passed between the two women assured him it did.

***

Halfway out the door, Malone was jumped from behind by Stacy.

He'd expected this, and spun round to face her.

What he hadn't expected however was that she'd be turned on by danger. Her erection had burst her pants. It poked from her crotch—a stiff five-inch rod.

She slammed into him, a wing-propelled female torpedo. In the moment before she hit him, Malone's single thought was how glad he was to be leaving.

No way in fuck is that sliding up inside me either ever or forever.

Stacy knocked him into the door jamb. Malone staggered back into the room. Pain coursed through him, the impact with the jamb stacking on remembered aches from an hour spent bending over the white robot's corpse.

He ensured however that he kept his grip on the Masher.

Stacy fell back also, but immediately recovered her balance. Wings beating furiously, she leapt on Malone's back. She wrapped her arm around his neck, her feet around his hips. Dislodged pink feathers fluttered over them both.

Malone staggered about, fighting to shake her off.

Blondie slammed the door shut, then rushed to help Stacy overpower Malone.

She slapped Malone's face with a wing tip. The blow dazed him for an instant, but he quickly recovered. He got a hand up to cover his face and threw a punch at Blondie. She ducked. His red fist knocked a hole through her wing.

Blondie yelped in pain. She stood panting a while, examining the damage. Blood squirted from the rip and trickled down over her feathers.

"You fool," she said, "I'm going to make you sew me up again."

Malone was too preoccupied with Stacy to reply. She'd now replaced her chokehold around his throat with her fingers and was trying to throttle him into submission.

Letting go of his throat for a moment, Stacy jerked Malone's shirt out of his trousers. She inserted her erection beneath it and began dry-humping him. She ground her cock and balls against his back whilst resuming her chokehold.

Malone was disgusted beyond belief.

She's actually getting off on this shit, he thought.

This was more of a scrap than he'd bargained for. Stacy was disproportionately strong for her slight stature. He suspected the same to be the case with Blondie.

He realized that if both weren't so cautious of the Masher he was holding, he'd be in huge trouble.

Malone didn't want to hurt either woman if he could help it. He just wanted out of their lives.

Blondie jumped at him again, her fingers flexed into claws.

Malone raised his hand to protect his eyes. She slashed his arm instead, then growling, she gripped his wrist, chopping at it to make him drop the Masher.

Stacy ejaculated on Malone's back. She gave a little yelp, stiffened, went slightly limp, and then stiffened again, tightening her stranglehold on his throat.

Malone hardly felt her cum trickling down his back into his butt-crack. He was becoming groggy—Stacy's grip was cutting off the blood supply to his brain. Thankfully, she was no expert at strangulation—he doubted she'd ever attempted it before, she had no idea of how to compress his larynx—but she'd accidentally gotten her fingers positioned just right to incapacitate him if she maintained the pressure for too long.

He began staggering drunkenly around the room.

"I got your ass now," Stacy said.

"He's fading, he's fading!" Blondie said.

"Screw you both, I'm not," Malone gasped.

But it was true, he *was* fading. His thoughts were clouding and there were black spots in his vision.

In desperation he head-butted Blondie in the face. She let go of his wrist and reeled back.

She smiled evilly at him. Blood dribbled from her nostrils. It made her look like a demoness. She licked some of the red from her lips. "I think you just broke my nose, *darling*. So you want to fight dirty, uh? Well, let's get it on, you delicious prick!"

She pulled down her pants and pulled out her penis—a long thin organ. Malone groaned on seeing she was fully erect, having been aroused by the violence..

Leering at him, Blondie smeared blood from her nose over her 'womanhood' and masturbated herself a few strokes.

"Get ready, Malone," she said. "You're going to suck this cock afterwards, blood and all. You're gonna suck it till I fill your belly with my cum."

"Stop jerking off, Blondie! Get a fucking knife!"

Blondie stopped masturbating and nodded.

Oh no, you don't! Malone thought. This stops here and now.

He pointed the Masher at Blondie and pressed the red button. He'd held off doing so for as long as he reasonably could.

There was no sound. The weapon simply 'mashed' Blondie into the wall behind her.

Malone had the barest impression of Blondie 'separating' in a whoosh of invisible force that streaked across the room too fast for the eye to track. Then there was a human-shaped brown and pink splotch on the wall.

The wall now looked like someone had painted it with paint made from body parts. Bones, nerves, eyes, hair, penis, testicles, feathers, breast implants, nipples—all occupied their relative places in a human soup that while nauseating to view, had a disgusting naturalness to it.

The human paint dripped down the wall to pool on the rug. As it dripped, it spoke: "Ouch, Malone, that hurt," it said.

Malone felt close to losing his mind. He felt sickened by what he'd just done.

"Get off me or I'll shoot you too," he told Stacy coldly, "go be romantic with your worman or something."

Stacy let go of him and fled the living room, wings bobbing behind her like ducks on a pond.

Malone walked over to stare at the puddle Blondie had become. "Sorry, Blondie," he said. "I just want to leave." He paused. "I really think your tits and ass are terrific," he added lamely. "I'm just not into cocks—"

Blondie's mouth had now dripped to the floor. "Oh, cut the crap, Malone," it gurgled. "You're such a—" Her hair dripped over her mouth, pushing it into the body-part soup.

Malone turned to leave. Then he remembered Stacy. His instinct for self-preservation made him check on what she was doing. He padded silently to the bedroom, listened through the ajar door.

Stacy was on the phone, weeping and whispering harshly into the mouthpiece. "Listen, you cheap law-enforcement excuse for plastic surgery, I'm *not* joking. Some human loony perv just burst into my apartment, ogled our worman, and shot my co-husband with the Masher . . . what the fuck do you mean, *which* Masher? *How many Mashers are there?*

"Yeah I agree: IT IS AN EMERGENCY!!! *How* did he get hold of it? . . . Fuck this—you're supposed to be a police officer, protecting innocent civilians like myself. A *human* loony loose with the Trangel Masher and you're asking *how* he got it? HE OBVIOUSLY MUST HAVE STOLEN IT, YOU STOOOOPID BITCH!!!!! JUST GET YOUR RETARDED OVERFUCKED COP ANUSES OVER HERE. The address? Apartment three sev..."

Oops, just got framed. Malone turned and padded off.

He spent a long moment staring at the flesh puddle on the floor which had recently been Blondie, then walked over to the center table and dropped the Masher. Potent as it was, it wasn't the kind of weapon he ever wanted to handle again.

He left.

CHAPTER 54

Stacy

Stacy slammed the phone down.

The noise woke up Herbie Stanton.

The worman looked around the room, his face worried. "What's happening, Stacy?"

Stacy rushed over to the bed and cradled Herbie's head between her breasts.

"Oh, honey pie," she said. "An evil man just killed Blondie!"

Herbie's eyes widened. "Killed? I'm scared, Stacy."

"Stacy rocked Herbie's head like it was a baby, his neck dangling between her legs like a length of hose. "Don't be, darling. The cops will be here soon and they'll kill him too."

"I'm still scared, Stacy." Stacy felt the worman's extended body shivering in fear. She was instantly alarmed. This was bad, Herbie could break his eggs this way. And likely they'd be *her* eggs, not Blondie's.

Oh, Blondie, she thought suddenly, tears filling her eyes, her heart going out to her dead partner. *That son-of-a-bitch Malone deserves every bit of pain that's coming to him.*

She returned her attention to her shivering worman.

"It's alright, Herbie darling," she said softly. "I'm still here with you. I'll never leave you."

She freed her left nipple and pushed it into Herbie's mouth. "Have some milk, honey pie."

While her worman suckled on her nipple, Stacy cooed to him, muttering sweet nonsense till she felt Herbie's anaconda-long body relax. "Everything's going to be alright, darling," she said, faking confidence that she didn't feel.

Stacy was traumatized by what had just happened to Blondie, but she realized that she couldn't freak out. She had to be strong, strong for both herself and for Herbie.

She was also concerned. The cops would arrive soon. She needed a clear head, so she wouldn't trip herself up in the sequence of lies she planned on telling them about how Malone had broken in and threatened Blondie and herself with the Trangel Masher.

CHAPTER 55

Malone

While he navigated Traven's glossy black corridors, Malone's brain was navigated by blacker thoughts.

Okay, he thought, *this shit's gone much too far enough already. Frank, where the fuck are you so I can break your neck?*

He made a cautious passage down a brightly-lit stairway. He wished he could simply open a door and his quest be over. Better still, find himself back in his office with this day not even existing on the calendar.

He turned a corner and ran straight into a contingent of heavily-armed white robots stepping out of an elevator.

Shit.

The robots said nothing. They raised their guns and began firing, heading for Malone with purpose-filled strides.

Malone turned and ran. Gunshot noise filled the corridor.

Alerted by the noise, trangels began poking their heads out of their apartment doors.

All remained watching once they saw the fleeing Malone and his mechanical pursuers. Thinking he was fleeing a new arm of the Traven Police, several girls whistled as he sped past them.

One grabbed his buttocks as he passed her, digging her nails deep into the meat of his gluteal muscles.

She didn't let go; Malone found himself running on the spot.

He resisted the urge to knock her pretty face in. "Let the hell go of me, will you?"

She laughed at him, blue eyes twinkling "Trying to escape becoming a worman, cutie pie?"

Thankfully, the white robots weren't shooting any longer as they headed for Malone.

"Let go of me, dammit!"

The Trangel shook her head. "No, cutie pie. I'll petition the council for you. You can be *my* worman if you don't like who you're already with."

Malone was disgusted at how strong she was, with her skinny body and blue wings. Her finger grip on his buttocks was sheer agony, as painful as if she was ass-raping him, only doing it via a myriad of wrong apertures all at once.

Malone looked at the approaching robots. They were raising shotguns and taking aim at him.

He turned back to the angel holding onto him.

She giggled. "Ooh, cutie pie, you're going to *love* sucking my cock."

Malone hit her, a HARD sock to the jaw. She went down like he'd poleaxed her, to a chorus of admiring oohs and aahs from the other ladies watching. A number of their hands fell to grip swelling crotches.

Malone groaned. *What is it with trangels and violence?*

He ran on.

He turned the corridor corner and ran smack-dab into an oncoming contingent of four Forks. Four of them—two silver, two plastic.

Now this is odd, he thought. He understood the robot presence here—they were clearly after him. But the Forks? *What the hell are they doing in Traven?*

Malone put his concerns aside. He ran up to the cutlery contingent. Out of breath, he stopped in front of a silver female Fork with large lustrous breasts.

"My name's Bud Malone," he gasped. "I'm working for Lady Yaz and Lord Tav." He pointed over his shoulder. "Those machines are pains in my ass."

"We are dragon supervisors," the female Fork replied him. "The Lord Tav and Lady Yaz are our overlords. Therefore we will help you."

Like Malone, the robots had reached them now. The mechanicals pointed their weapons at the Forks.

A large model with black sergeant stripes stepped forward.

"Hand Malone over," it said. "Frank wants him."

"No," the female Fork replied. "Malone here is working for us. You machines will turn around and leave peacefully."

A plastic fork addressed Malone. "You may leave. We will handle this."

"He isn't going anywhere!" the robot sergeant yelled. "Attack, robots, attack!!!"

The robots fired on the Forks. The sound of gunfire reverberated in the corridor like Traven was a shooting range.

Two trangels opened their front doors to investigate the commotion. Both doors immediately slammed shut again, one occupant nursing a bullet-shredded wing. Malone could visualize her running to the phone and alerting the Traven cops to his whereabouts.

The gunfire continued. Malone realized none of it had hit either he or the Forks.

"We tire of this," the silver female Fork said. "Okay, machines, have it your way."

The Forks suddenly glowed a combination of silver streaked with plastic white. A beam of intertwined forces pulsed from them at the robots.

Malone watched while the force beam pulled the robots apart like they were children's toys. There was beauty to their deconstruction: it looked like a 3-D animation explaining their inner workings—a totally natural uncoupling of their parts.

Similarly their guns were also deconstructed.

Soon the robots were piles of neatly stacked arms, legs, heads, and torso shells, beside piles of spilt inner components and wires.

The white glow in the corridor subsided.

"You may proceed on your job for our lord and lady," the female Fork told Malone. "Inform them on our behalf that everything is going as planned here."

Malone nodded at the Forks. "Thanks. I'm lost. How do I leave here? The Trangel—" He stopped short of saying 'police.' He was wary of the Forks now the immediate danger was past.

"You will find a free elevator at the end of the corridor two turns to the left behind us."

The group of cutlery beings floated off, levitating over the demolished robots.

Malone nodded after them, then set off to find the described elevator.

CHAPTER 56

Malone

Malone entered the elevator. He was about to hit 'Basement,' when he remembered the cops. They'd likely be coming up from below.

He punched for six floors up instead; the first thing was to work out exactly where he was. To do that he needed a vantage point.

The elevator rose rapidly then stopped.

Malone opened the door, took a step forward, and fell downwards face first.

He sailed down past several metal railings, then lashed out with his blood hand and caught hold of one of them. His shoulder wrenched like it was being severed all over again, but his fall was broken.

Dangling like a length of string, he worked out where he was. He'd fallen through the door of a train carriage, and was currently hanging from the rear of an aisle seat.

(He was making the discovery that his blood arm both didn't feel pain and was surpassingly strong.)

He worked out what had happened.

This train was a beetle's forelimb. Its left uppermost. Far off, he could see its right companion. He was in the first carriage. Below this there would usually be six or seven more.

The train hung downwards, so he'd fallen from the elevator when it opened, rather than walked from it.

He thought it odd that he hadn't sensed the ninety degree change in orientation during transit.

He swore—this was a dead end. Had the damn Forks been trying to make him break his neck? And what the hell did they mean they were 'dragon supervisors?' In Traven? Were they postnatal doctors to the Trangel's wormen?

This got more fucked-up by the fucked-up minute.

Malone simmered down somewhat, finally realizing that despite being short of time, his fall into this train-limb was to his advantage.

First, he pulled himself up so his feet found firm purchase on the seat two below the one he was gripping, then, using the chair-arms like steps, he climbed down to the carriage exit. There, he let himself down into the next carriage, and repeated the process. He kept going through six more carriages till he was in the second-to-last one, then he lay down on a seat-back to rest and think.

CHAPTER 57

Malone

He was in probably the largest skyscraper-beetle in existence. From his vantage point, the creature extended forever, both downwards and sideways.

(The far-off 'right' limb he'd noticed earlier seemed rather to be embedded in the *middle* of the beetle's body. If even that distant place was its middle.)

The general belief that apartments on the converted floors of an insect building were uninhabitable was wrong, Malone discovered now.

The train-leg dangled twenty feet from Traven's walls, giving Malone a clear view into the closest apartment windows.

Lights blazed in bedrooms. He watched a pair of transsexual angel husbands servicing their worman wife. It was a strange type of sex: both husbands lay side by side on their backs and essentially masturbated themselves with the man-worm's mouth and anus. Occasionally the trangels kissed, occasionally they exchanged ends of their sextoyperson. Occasionally they masturbated each other with their worman's orifices.

In another bedroom, one Trangel fucked another doggy-style while their worman watched.

In the window to his left, a pair of trangels hovered over their bed, wings beating furiously. Even more furiously, they fucked the worman dangling between them like a live skipping rope with egg-lumps in it.

The trio's screams carried clearly to Malone through their window, through the night air. The worman sounded like it was in horrendous pain. Brown fluid dripped from both its ends over the legs of its lovers.

Memory of his recent encounter with Stacy and Blondie filled Malone. He was disgusted, both with what he was watching, and with himself for watching it. He felt like vomiting.

The transsexual angels climaxed simultaneously, then crumpled onto their bed like discarded tissue paper, opposing violent sexual armies tented in wings. Their worman lay between them—a used kitchen rag—slime dribbling from between its lips.

It had a blonde moustache. Its tiny eyes blinked in Malone's direction.

He saw it was smiling dreamily. It curled back and began fellating the penis closest to it.

***

Malone heard the scraping then.

It was coming from below him, seemingly from inside the train.

He peered downward, made out the fiberglass head of the dragon peering into the open door of the last carriage.

The dragon was equally inquisitively staring up at him.

It wasn't very large—about horse-sized. That meant it would be able to get through the train door if it was hungry.

It was.

The dragon reached one foreleg into the train, then another. Digging transparent claws into metal, it pulled itself inside.

Malone began climbing rapidly back up through the carriage.

He made it through the upper door just as the dragon got its shoulders fully inside the train and spouted fire up at him. He leapt aside; orange flames streamed past him. Once the blaze subsided, he quickly slammed the carriage door shut and resumed climbing.

Behind/below him, the dragon pushed the door up with its head. The heat in the carriage rose as it spewed flame around the opening, thinking Malone stood there. It levered the door fully open, began clambering up.

Now it was a race against time, with Malone just managing to make it through each successive upper doorway before the dragon entered the one below and attempted frying him again.

In the topmost carriage, Malone sealed and locked the lower door. The metal clearly wouldn't withstand a sustained burst of fire, but melting it away would buy him some time.

A rain of cement now began, as the beetle, sensing the dragon invading its body, attempted to neutralize it.

***

Heat bubbles began forming on the locked door below Malone. He imagined he could hear the dragon belching its frustration at the metal, impatient to be through to him.

Malone's only option now was to reenter Traven, take his chances with evading its police. He began climbing to the top of the carriage to access the elevator.

The cement rain shattered two carriage windows below him. He was getting out just in time—the cement was as much a danger to him as the dragon. If he got stuck in it . . .

He reached the top of the carriage. He was about pulling himself through, when a hand poked through the opening and gripped his wrist. The hand was followed a moment later by a hard lady-cop face.

"Just tell me you're Malone," she said coldly.

Her other hand appeared, waving a set of handcuffs.

***

Malone reacted immediately, letting go of the door jamb. His sudden increase in weight made her let go of him.

He dropped, caught a metal rail, sat on a seat back six seats down.

Now he wished he'd brought the Trangel Masher along.

"You're in big trouble, mister," the cop called down. "Real big trouble."

"You've *no idea* how big," Malone replied. He pointed at the bubbling door below. "There's a dragon on its way up."

The angel cop studied the indicated door, then looked at Malone. "So what are you waiting for? Let me help you up."

Malone shook his head. "Uh uh. I'd rather die than have sex with the likes of Blondie and Stacy for ever and ever and ever."

"Have it your way then." She ducked out of sight as the dragon poked its head through a hole melted in the door and let off a burst of fire at them.

Malone ducked back onto the seat, pressing himself close to the window.

Staring at the heat-rippled air as the tongues of flame subsided like a stove being turned down, he wondered what it was with him and dragons . . . reptiles in general: First Yang Yang, then porcelain Posh, then the T-rex that ate his arm, now *this*.

The cop's voice came to him. "Listen, Malone, it needs a few seconds to refill its hot-chambers between each burst. Try to make it out after the next one."

The dragon was now busy ripping the remaining metal off the door frame.

Shit, shit, shit, Malone thought, *I really don't want to die. I don't want to marry trangels and become a human worm, either, but I really, really, really, REALLY do not want to friggin' die.*

He decided to follow the policewoman's advice. He'd have to escape her somehow, most likely jump her before she cuffed him.

If you ladies think you're making a sex toy person out of me, you're raving mad!

Then there was a loud knock on the window behind him.

He turned around. He sagged in relief when he saw Glass Horse hovering there, tapping the glass with its hoof.

Malone opened the window as the dragon forced its rainbow-lighting shoulders through the carriage door.

"I've been looking all over the Afterwife for you," Glass Horse said. "I became worried when you didn't exit the club."

"Horse, I didn't know you could fly."

"Now you do."

"Remember, Malone—make a dash after its next flare," the policewoman called down. "I'll try to distract it."

Malone didn't hear her. He was already halfway out the train window, slipping onto Glass Horse's back.

"There's a dragon coming," he told it. "We need to get as FAR from here as possible, and *fast.*"

"Done." The transparent horse spun around and streaked away, galloping across the sky.

CHAPTER 58

Sara

Immediately on leaving Malone's office, Sara Fischer and the Forks translocated to his house to collect Posh.

They materialized in the couple's bedroom.

Wow, Sara thought, looking around the charred space. *Something really horrible happened here.*

The smell of burning was still thick in the air, along with a thin film of extinguisher foam on the floor. The odor of roast meat assaulted Sara. She fought not to gag from the stench.

Lady Yaz floated over to Sara's side. "Malone's girlfriend isn't in the house," she said.

Her words forced Sara's mind off how sick the smell in the room was making her. "She's not?"

"No."

"We need to find that young woman, and fast," Sara said. "Malone will be super-pissed if anything happens to Posh before he finishes your quest."

(Sara prayed fervently that Malone would evade Frank's traps. She hoped he'd also kill the son-of-a-bitch. The psychopathic bastard. She hated Frank with a passion for turning Rachel against her.)

"That cannot be allowed to occur," Lord Tav said. "We will ask the dragons to look out for her."

Sara nodded. It was after all how they'd discovered Posh was a dragon in the first place.

The trio vanished from Malone's torched bedroom and instantly reappeared out west, up in the air over the Charles River Basin, amidst a flock of dragons.

***

Floating in midair with transparent carnivorous reptiles all around her wasn't Sara's idea of fun. Below her blue water stretched like paint. Down to her left, Longfellow Bridge lay across the river. From this height it looked like a child's toy train bridge.

Sara knew she wasn't in any danger of falling. The air under her feet felt solid—a glass platform. The wind whipped around her, at this height cold and chilling despite the bright sun.

I don't get it, she thought, instinctive anxiety bubbling in her as the dragons noticed the kitchen gods in their midst and began milling around the trio, *why do they always have to bring me along on trips like this? Can't they just leave me at home?*

Protected as she was by the Forks' presence, Sara found it impossible to relax.

Reflected in the dragons' cold eyes now, she saw only Jeff Lincoln's face. She remembered his tales of how Washington had been destroyed. Remembered too how her beloved David had been eaten by one of these monsters.

She regarded the dragons, these streamlined fiber-glass creations from Heaven knew where, with their teeth as large as her body and their wings larger than those of jumbo jets, and shuddered.

And yet, floating in the air, surrounded by the reptiles, the humorous incongruity of her current situation wasn't lost on her.

These creatures, these fucking monsters are responsible for destroying the modern world, she thought. *And here I am in their midst, accompanying a pair of Forks to a conversation on the whereabouts of a single missing young woman.*

***

Contrary to Malone's fears, the Forks couldn't read minds. They *could* sense human presence in their immediate vicinity up to a fifty meter radius. Beyond that, however, there was no difference between people, animals, and trees to them.

So, by being in Malone's bedroom, the Forks could tell Posh wasn't in the house, but had no idea where she was.

It had been the dragons themselves—not the Forks—who'd found Posh.

During one of Lady Yaz and Lord Tav's regular conversations with the alpha female dragon, it had informed them of a 'strange creature' it had discovered, one that was both 'not-real-dragon' and human female.

The Fork pair had investigated the 'strange creature' and discovered it was Posh.

***

To Sara's relief, the throng of dragons dispersed, leaving just the massive alpha female, a huge beast with eyes the size of car windshields. The bolts holding its body together were the size of Sara's fists.

Wow! Sara thought, *this damn thing is bigger than my house.*

While Sara studied the ripples on the river surface half a mile below, Lord Tav conversed with the alpha female. The dragon replied to the Fork in roars like thunder claps.

Sara covered her ears to preserve her hearing, and wished the conversation quickly over.

There were undigested skeletons in the alpha female's transparent guts. Some were from massive fish, others dino skeletons. Sara winced on sighting several human skulls amongst them.

Damn, she thought, *what's the world come to?*

She turned and walked off across the sky, leaving the Forks and alpha-female alone.

The dragon herd was west, so she went east, towards the city.

It felt really odd to walk on nothing. The very concept was scary. Sara pondered the limits of the Forks' powers.

She stopped over the river bank, directly over the skeleton of a crashed tugboat.

Directly in front of her was Massachusetts General Hospital, now an expanse of roofless, windowless, fire-scoured buildings and collapsed walls.

Sara remembered what had happened to the patients. The dragons had eaten their way through the wards of the sick like the hospital was a reptile restaurant.

She shuddered and forced the horrid memory from her mind. She tore her gaze from the spifflicated hospital and looked farther inward—at Central Boston

At this distance The Grid seemed a liquid mirror flowing between the buildings. It reflected the sky, so those residents who lived above it occasionally imagined they were in the clouds.

The buildings themselves—both natural and artificial skyscrapers—looked like they stood in liquid metal.

The sight was so breathtaking, Sara suddenly felt exhilarated.

***

Finally, the Forks finished talking with the dragon matriarch. The glittering beast gave a last loud roar and flew off.

Sara turned around at the sound. Seeing the alpha-female departing, she set off to rejoin the Forks, only for them to materialize in front of her after just two steps.

"You startled me," Sara said.

"The dragons don't know where Posh is," Lady Yaz replied.

"They don't?"

"No. They can only sense her when she is in dragon form herself. We've ordered them to keep a lookout for her and alert us immediately if she transforms."

"That," Sara pointed out, "essentially means we have to wait till she's eating someone before collecting her."

"Unfortunately, yes."

The three faded from view en-route to the Fischer Mansion.

CHAPTER 59

Jade & Posh

With a final scowl out of the window, Jade concluded Malone had chickened out of romancing Yang Yang.

What a wimp, she thought.

She looked over at the white statue. *Wow, she's gonna be super pissed this time.*

Jade was herself pissed-off at Malone's no-show.

It had taken her an hour's persuasion to get Yang Yang to relent. The snake goddess had been adamant at first, insisting she wanted nothing more to do with 'dragon cunt licker,' then finally, delighted she'd get to have her way with Malone.

And now, where the hell is Malone? Ah yes, 'dragon cunt licking' again.

Jade winced. Malone had no idea what he was setting himself up for. *Dude, you'll be so high on Yang Yang's shit list—you'll be her toilet.*

She looked over at the Snake Lady statue, motionless and eerie beside the room's inner door, and shrugged. *I've done what I can.*

Jade couldn't wait any longer.

She had a date with her boyfriend, Mario—the Brazilian bartender at Tony Motta's place.

It was imperative that they talk heart-to-heart. Their relationship had been going good, but was now hitting a rough patch. Mario seemed to have commit-ment issues.

Jade sniggered at that. All men have commitment issues. They're utterly devoted to screwing us, but once we ask them to commit to the consequences of parting our legs and permitting access to our inner sanctum, they've always got baggage. She frowned. Mario had better listen to me this evening, or else . . .

Then Jade saw the blue Lincoln parked outside the ring of prostitutes promenading on the chessboard.

She groaned when Posh stumbled naked out of it, not even bothering to shut the car door behind her.

Oh, not fucking today. Even from a distance 'dragon cunt' was clearly covered in blood.

The jostle of hookers and prospective clients parted to let Posh through—an island of avoidance amidst their human sea.

Watching her stagger toward the pagoda, Jade knew her soul-searching discussion with Mario wasn't happening today.

She forgot her date—Posh looked close to death.

She rushed downstairs to help her.

***

"Your back looks like a chopping board," Jade said. "One made of meat."

"You don't fucking say . . . yeow!"

Jade removed bloodied fingers from over Posh's spine and probed sideways, spreading the edges of Beth's final slash between her ribs.

"Fuck! Stop it!" Posh howled.

"Sorry. Try to bear the pain. I need to find where you're bleeding so much from."

Ironically, Posh currently lay on exactly the same spot as she had when she'd lost her skin and transformed into a dragon; only on her belly this time.

"That's a weird statue," she said, noticing Yang Yang.

"Malone likes it too," Jade said, peering intently into the crevice between Posh's ribs. "He practically loves it." Then: "You don't remember the goddess from the last time you were here?"

Posh shook her head. "No. *Goddess?* What goddess?"

"Forget it. Where's Malone anyway?"

"Didn't see him this morning—he was gone when I woke up."

Jade nodded grimly. "Okay, I've found it. You've a cut vein in this slice between your ribs. It closes when you don't move, so you won't bleed then, but once—"

"I'm really, really sorry, Jade."

"What?"

Posh pointed weakly at Ma's head in the cabinet, beside what was clearly a jar of dragonreich. She'd recognize that iridescent, rainbow-shimmering powder anywhere. "I didn't mean to . . ." She began crying.

"It's okay," Jade said, stroking Posh's hair, "It just happened. Ma is still okay—she just needs another body."

She wiped Posh's tears away. "Have you been okay since then?"

Posh nodded. "I'm cured for good now."

Jade smiled back. "Hold on a moment, I'll get something to stop the bleeding. A paper-lock—like that keeping Ma alive—will suffice; then I'll clean you up."

***

Once Jade left, Posh's attention instantly riveted on the bottle of dragonreich shelved beside Ma's head. She'd never seen so much of the drug in one place before. From the way it sparkled, this was the pure uncut reich—possibly as much as Emil had murdered Sookie's dealers for.

The sparkling granules hypnotized Posh. Their glitter yanked her will out from under her like a carpet. She felt totally floored by their promise of the ultimate high.

The bottle of dragonreich whispered in Posh's head—*love me now. I will make you strong. Strong. Strong.*

No, Posh thought back weakly, *I won't. I don't need you anymore.*

The drug was insistent: *Strong enough to take on that bitch Beth, who reduced you to this bloodstained mess.*

No! Posh gasped.

Then: *Huh!?*

She snapped out of a daze to find herself standing at the cabinet, her hand reaching for the bottle of reich. She however didn't remembering picking herself off the floor and walking there.

She turned and stared dully at the bloody footprints linking her ankles to where she'd been lying down.

Oh, shit! I'd better get back over there fast, before Jade returns.

She turned away.

Don't, the drug moaned in her head.

Posh froze. She questioned her sanity. Was it really the powder speaking, or her own craving translating into its voice?

Look, I'm fucking dying here, okay, let me be.

I'll make you stronger than Beth, her craving retorted in a lover's whisper. *Much, MUCH stronger. Beth will be a gnat compared to you. She'll never be able to fuck you up again—never make chicken-love to you again. Instead you'll fuck Beth up good. REAL good.*

Posh smiled dreamily. *Now there's a plan.* During her drive to Chinatown, she'd pondered how to get Beth off her back. She'd ruled out telling Malone—secrets, secrets. Asking Sookie to send Bulldog and Gorgeous over to scare Beth had seemed workable, but now . . .

I'll handle my business myself, she thought. *Time I stand up for me.*

The memory flooded into her mind of how Beth had used her like she was nothing—trash.

Posh had finally been shit on one time too many.

She picked out the bottle of dragonreich from the cabinet and opened it.

She momentarily considered Ma's severed head. With a twinge of conscience she once again remembered exactly how Jade's mother had ended up shelved.

Do I really want to do this? she asked herself. *Do I really?*

Then images of Beth abusing her filled her mind and her anger returned magnified. She looked away from Ma. *Oh fucking yes, I do. I'm teaching that ex-prison cunt a lesson she'll never forget.*

She poured a huge heap of reich into her palm.

Whilst snorting it up, half her mind wondered: *What's keeping Jade?*

***

Jade sat on Ma's bed, heavily conflicted. She stared at the paper-lock she held, wondering which use to put it to.

She could either stop Posh's bleeding with it, or. . .

All she need do was wrap it around Posh's neck on some pretext to immobilize her, then saw off Posh's head, and bam!—

Ma had a new body. A great, sexy toned one too, so she could fuck all she wanted.

Jade scowled. It wouldn't be any loss either, all Posh would do once cured was begin eating people again. *Shit.*

The problem was . . . Well firstly, Posh was a friend of hers, and one didn't just kill one's friends.

She quashed that twinge of conscience. Oh, no, Posh was fucking dangerous. Worse than a rabid animal. The girl *needed* to be put down.

But, Malone . . . was the second problem.

Jade knew Malone would never forgive her if she killed Posh. He'd never forgive Ma even.

But Malone hasn't turned up today to screw the goddess, so possibly he doesn't mind Posh killing people anyway. No, Malone isn't that kind of person. Something's kept him . . .

Shit! This is damn hard!

Then she heard the loud crashing from the living room. Loud like a monster had gotten into the house.

Her eyes widened as she realized what had happened. *Oh, God, no! Posh has gotten into the dragonreich!*

***

Posh-dragon was no longer wounded. Her gleaming porcelain form was perfect and whole. Her wings beat with frustrated power. She was eager to be out of this confined space, this room that felt like a cage to her.

Her mind ravening like a wolf's, bloodlust and fire-rage pouring through her veins, Posh-dragon looked out of the pagoda window.

Her miniscule lizard mind focused on one point of hate.

North.

North was where the human Beth lived. Death, fire, roasting—

***

Jade peered carefully out of the bedroom.

Posh's tail was just disappearing through the window.

Jade's heart pounded furiously in her breast as she watched the last inch of flower-patterned tail clear the ledge and drift up into the sky after the porcelain dragon.

She slumped against the door jamb. Her thoughts were conflicted. On one hand, she was relieved not to have to choose between murdering Posh or not. On the other hand, she was worried at what damage the dragon would do. She could hear scared yelps from the prostitutes outside.

She rushed to the window and peered out.

No, the dragon wasn't attacking the prostitutes. It was headed north.

Relieved, Jade turned away from the window toward the cabinet.

Then she stared at the cabinet in shock.

She gaped at it in horror, her thoughts freezing in her mind like winter.

Ma's head was gone.

Fuck! Jade thought, running back to the window and gaping at Posh-dragon, now a mere distant speck. *The stupid bitch has eaten my mother's head!*

Jade calmed her alarm. *This is serious.* A dragon's digestive juices were stronger than a crocodile's, which could dissolve nails.

Jade considered: *The paper-lock will protect Ma—Posh wouldn't be able to bite through her head, she'd have to have swallowed it whole. But the lock won't keep Ma from being digested for long.*

She calculated that she had forty-five minutes at most to get Ma back.

With a grim frown, she got down the Dead God's Sword from the wall. *Sorry, Posh, darling. This time I'm butchering you good.*

But where was the fucking dragon headed?

Only one way to find out.

Jade pulled Yang Yang to the middle of the room.

She picked up the crystal lancet.

No time for fucking bowls now.

She slashed her palm, then cupped her pooling blood to the goddess's perfect white lips and began chanting.

She chanted a long time, building up sufficient magical charge so the goddess wouldn't shut down halfway through their conversation.

***

Yang Yang opened her eyes.

"Malone?" she said dreamily. "He here for me?" The snake goddess spoke an obscure hinterland dialect that Jade found as hard to understand as Ma's English.

"He'll be here later," Jade replied in Mandarin.

The goddess lifted her mouth from Jade's blood and frowned. "If stand me up, I curse—manhood break into four pieces."

Jade scowled. *Lady, I so do not have time for your pussy palaver now.*

"Malone will be here later," she lied. "Now though, his stupid 'dragon cunt' girlfriend has just eaten Ma's head and flown off somewhere. Where is she?"

Yang Yang's eyes widened. "Dragon Cunt here before? I check, see." She shut her eyes a moment, then opened them again. "Not far; she in Central Boston." She gripped Jade's hand with both of hers and took a deep slurp of blood.

Jade winced as the goddess's stone tongue chafed her palm cut. "Send me after her."

Yang Yang raised her head and smiled bloody lips. "I send you. You have Dead Sword, want kill too. Good. I teach how. Dragon Cunt strength greater weakness."

Jade gaped at her blankly. "Huh?"

The snake goddess nodded. "Sickness cure sickness." She giggled. "I teach. But only if promise not tell Malone hero until after fucking. Yes?"

Jade nodded. "Whatever you say. But I'm running out of time."

Yang Yang shook her head. "I goddess. Time not problem. I drink fill of hand blood first."

She pulled Jade's hand to her lips and began sucking voraciously.

CHAPTER 60

Malone

With sufficient distance between them and Traven, Malone and Glass Horse turned back to look at the beetle.

"That has to be the largest skyscraper that ever became an insect in existence," Malone said.

"Yes," the see-thru horse agreed. "It is monstrous."

Malone had greatly misjudged Traven's size whilst inside its train limb. The beetle was a mammoth intrusion on the heavens and the senses, a black mass extending right, left, and downwards.

A massive red neon sign lit up the beetle's thorax like it was a nightclub:

'Afterwife Traven Hilton.
Your Sissy Ass Is Forever Ours, Boy.'

There was a sudden bright burst of light in the train carriage Malone had recently vacated.

Like in a movie, the metal limb separated from the beetle. It began a slow end-over-end fall to earth.

"I think the dragon just angered the Traven Police," Malone said dryly. "Horse, let's get out of here."

"Which way?"

"I'm not sure. You seem to know your way around the Afterwife. How'd you get here anyway?"

"Through an OD."

"Can we leave by it?"

"It's no longer there."

Malone nodded. The horse's explanation made as much sense as himself being sucked here through Blubber's vagina. And he'd no idea how to reverse that transition, either.

"Get us well away from Traven for a start," he told Glass Horse. Just in case the trangels feel like pursuing. We'll find our way home later."

"The Traven border is nearby, I'll head for it." With that, Glass Horse spun around in midair and dashed off.

Malone sighed in relief as the Traven Hilton dwindled in the distance. If he didn't know where he was headed, he certainly knew where he didn't want to be.

***

An hour later they reached the border.
A cloud-suspended green neon sign proclaimed:

'You Are Now Exiting Traven Territory,
We Hope Your Asshole Enjoyed Your Stay Here, Asshole.
Please CUM Again Soonest.'

Malone muttered moodily.

***

They flew for a long stretch over Shitland, a desert of erotically quivering buttock dunes traversed by rivers of excrement in which swam moby dicks—mammoth penis-whales with vagina eyes and mouth blowholes.

The butt-dune clefts erupted shit like they all suffered acute dysentery.

"Fuck! Fuck!" the mobies shrieked to each other as they made their torpid progress through the shit rivers, aimlessly navigating the maze of butt-hillocks.

The smell made Malone retch. He leant sideways and let his stomach empty itself.

Afterwards, he felt much better—the stench had nothing to work on anymore.

He saw some puke had smeared on Glass Horse's flank. "Sorry, horse, I couldn't help it."

"Shit stinks," the horse replied.
Malone nodded.

His attention turned elsewhere. He'd just noticed that the 'Hetero Fist' inscription and button on the rear of his right hand had vanished.

***

The landscape changed shortly after this. The feces rivers were replaced by expanses of creamy white.

"See, Malone—I wasn't lying earlier. This is the Breast Milk Sea."

Malone gazed out over the seemingly endless white expanse. "No shit."

"None at all. Just Milk, and we'll soon reach the breast hills."

A few minutes later, the first breast hills came into view, bobbing in the white liquid like a rafted horizon.

They flew closer.

The breast hills were HUGE humanlike breasts of differing colors. Perfectly sculpted hemispherical expanses of female flesh with gorgeous rocket-sized nipples poking from areola the size of basketball courts. The black and dark brown breast hills were the largest, the smallest the mid-toned yellows. The hills were arranged both singly and in pairs like camel humps, with short flesh bridges forming the cleavage between those paired.

They reached the first breast hills. Milk squirted up from turgid nipples towards the fliers. Looping cream streams of immense force.

"Look out, horse!" Malone yelled.

"I'm looking!" Glass Horse swerved, keeping now to the portions of milk between neighboring breasts. "They can prove dangerous, knock us out of the air."

Malone found the breast hills incredibly erotic. He got an erection that subsided immediately once he noticed they were dropping lower in the sky.

"Horse, what's going on?"

"I'm tiring. I've flown too far and too fast. I'll land us and we'll walk. We're no longer in danger."

"There's nowhere to land except on one of the breast hills." The thought of being stranded next to a milk-squirting nipple didn't appeal to Malone in the least. All Afterwife legends agreed that breast hills were carnivorous. If you got too close to one, that was it. Its areole would split apart and eat you.

"Untrue, Malone. We've almost reached land. I'll make it there for sure, then . . . but stop talking—replying just tires me further."

***

They made it to land, a narrow peninsula that stabbed into the Milk Sea like a knife

By the time it landed them, Glass Horse was juddering in mid-air with its body dissolving and reconstituting itself at random. Malone seriously thought the horse wouldn't make it down in one piece, and they'd wind up adrift in milk.

Malone dismounted.

He patted Glass Horse on the back. "You did great, horse." He looked along the strip of land they stood on. "Where is this place?

"This is the Cleavage."

Malone mused this over. *The name makes sense—We're surrounded by humongous mammaries.*

"The Cleavage is home to the North Pole." Glass Horse paused to breathe. It wheezed, blinking colorless eyes at Malone. Then it pointed across the whiteness with a see-thru hoof: "Over the sea there is the North Pole. This land bridge curves to meet it."

"I'll take your word for it," Malone said.

Glass Horse dissolved into a transparent puddle that expanded and contracted rhythmically.

***

It was six hours before Glass Horse reconstituted itself again.

Malone dozed thrice during that period. Each time he jerked awake to the sound of milk spattering the white sea. Each time he fell asleep again wishing his mouth was big enough to suck on one of the huge nipples all around.

Finally, Glass Horse felt strong enough to walk. They set off, with Malone walking beside it.

***

While trudging, Malone thought about Posh.

He wondered what she was up to.

He was sure it could only be bad—very bad indeed.

Damn, I forgot to have the Forks restrain her. With me gone, nothing stops her going on a fresh dragonreich rampage. Oh, my girlfriend the carnivore.

He considered the flip side of the coin. If someone had the presence of mind to shoot Posh with a projectile weapon while she was a porcelain dragon, or hit her with something heavy, preferably metallic. . .

That would be it for Posh. For good. All that would be left behind would be a million fragments of romantic memory.

He pushed the thoughts from his mind.

I love Posh, he reminded himself. *That's why I'm here, running this madman's errand. Heaven help anyone who dares kill her.*

CHAPTER 61

Beth

Beth Riggs luxuriated in bed in afterglow relaxation.

Her vagina felt paved with soft downy feathers. She floated in and out of a doze, her mind full of images of barnyards filled with fluffy squawking birds.

Beth had grown up on her dad's poultry farm in Muscatine, Iowa. Her earliest memory was of crying when a rooster pecked her foot.

Her love of chickens had grown and grown, and become entangled with her sexual identity.

She LOVED chickens.

Beth grinned. The sex with Posh had been utterly fantastic.

Yeah, Posh is the absolutely best fuck in the world. Beth loved the terrified look in the little slut's eyes whenever she saw the chopping blade. Loved the way she trembled even with the board separating her from harm.

And today was . . . She shuddered deliciously with the memory *. . . aaaah!*

The problem with other people Beth had 'chickened' was that they weren't scared enough of her. Her orgasms suffered as a result. Sometimes she didn't cum at all, no matter how many fowls she chopped up. Beth needed fear, not just friction, to get her rocks off.

And yes, bareback was definitely *better*. A more direct connection between the chicken's death and the body of the cunnilingus provider.

But . . .

The sheer intensity of her passion on seeing each chicken spread in pieces on Posh's bloody skin had scared Beth. It had taken all her self-control not to hack much deeper into the woman's exposed back, smashing through her spine; opening her red meat to the air alongside the chicken's white.

Beth giggled. *Yes, it's bareback for me from now on. Sure it's messy, but it's supposed to be messy.* She shrugged. *I nicked Posh up quite a bit, but she'll be okay. It's necessary to be hard with these girls. A few cuts here and there never killed anyone—nothing a doctor can't fix.*

She trailed fingers over her clitoris. The sex bud tingled with her ministrations. Like flowing syrup, pleasure slowly drained into her thighs. Yes, she'd cum once more, it would knock her properly to sleep. She ran her free hand over her breasts, squeezing the vein-marbled flesh, teasing her nipples. She filled her mind with images of chickens.

Yes, she thought as her pleasure fluttered up again, *Posh is my fucking bitch now. When I say jump, she'd better jump or I'll kick her—*

She stiffened as the sound of beating wings reached her. *Shit. That sounds like outside my living room. Pterodactyl attack?*

***

Her body still afire with desire, Beth leapt out of bed and grabbed her gun off her dresser. Then she dashed into her living room.

With pterodactyls, the most important thing was to prevent them breaking in, a few gunshots would send this—

She stopped dead in her tracks and gaped at the white dragon forcing its way through her shattered window frame.

Beth was uncertain what surprised her more. That the creature's body was glazed like crockery, or that the seeming crockery was covered with painted-on roses.

Beth saw the dragon was inhaling. That meant only one thing.

Hell, no, she thought. She flung herself across the room, over the rear of her sofa, as the air filled with fire.

She landed hard. The impact jarred her gun from her palm. The weapon slewed away out of sight.

Beth peeked over the top of the sofa. The porcelain dragon was staring at her oddly. It growled like thunder, but didn't spit fire at her again. She was amazed at how big it was. *How the hell did it fit itself through my fucking window?*

The monster was between her and the bedroom. No way out there. Expecting to feel her back burning at any moment, Beth leapt off the sofa and ran for her front door.

She slipped and skidded on the strewn chunks of chicken from her and Posh's earlier lovemaking, but managed to keep her feet and keep going.

She reached the door and began fumbling with the key. *Fucking open up, damn you, fucking open up! Why won't you?*

Behind her, she heard the dragon bounding after her. Still not cooking her, thank God. But still the damn fucking key wouldn't unlock the door.

Then she realized that in her panic she was turning it the wrong way, anticlockwise instead of clockwise.

The dragon was right behind her now. She felt its breath hot on her back.

I don't get it! she shrieked in her mind, What does it fucking want with me!?

Beth got the door unlocked. She yanked it open, then found she couldn't open it fully. Panicking, she realized what the matter was.

The chain, the chain . . .

She shut the door again to unlatch the chain.

The dragon cuffed Beth on the side of the head.

Flying through the air as a result of the blow, Beth felt like the universe was exploding inside her mind. She crashed into the wall, stunned.

She watched the dragon approach her. Her amber eyes reflected its own. All she saw in their cold reptilian depths was her death.

The dragon picked Beth up and flung her across the room. She smashed into the opposite wall, crashing down beside the window.

A sharp pain greeted her landing. She looked down, dully registering that her right leg was broken. Six inches of white bone projected from her thigh. The pain was like she'd never experienced in her life.

In addition, her right breast had a huge cut in it from which blood was pouring.

The porcelain dragon stamped across to Beth. It hulked over her, exhaling hot air over her. Its claws clenched and unclenched like it would rip her to shreds with them.

Beth was utterly terrified.

And yet, most horrifying of all, she had the clear picture that this strange dragon wasn't ready to eat her just yet. It was playing with her, like a cat did with its mouse dinner. It was out to cause her as much pain as it could before it finally terminated her existence.

She dragged herself up on her good leg. Her only recourse now was to throw herself out of the broken window—to crash into The Grid ceiling nine floors down. *Fuck, it's better to fucking kill myself than be mauled and eaten.*

But suicide was denied her. The dragon sprayed a burst of fire over the window. Beth collapsed again, her left arm charred to burnt meat.

"Fucking kill me, you bastard!" she screamed at it, tears of agony and fear now streaming down her cheeks, "Why won't you fucking kill me!? Why won't you?"

In response, the dragon spat fire in her face.

Beth instinctively jerked her head aside. The flame melted the left side of her face. Her left eye cooked and burst, spilling boiling goo down her cheek. Blood and transparent serum bubbled through her charred flesh.

Beth screamed when she realized she'd been half-blinded. Then she screamed louder, horrified that she was still alive and there was more unpreventable suffering on her event horizon.

The dragon reared up to belch fire again.

Beth cringed in terror. "Pleeassseee!"

Then the unthinkable happened. The air to the dragon's left shimmered and a figure appeared in the room, materialized out of bare air.

Squinting through her single remaining eye, her mind wracked by her body's pain, Beth made out the figure clearly.

A tall Chinese girl. Grim-faced as death, with a sword slung at her waist. Her left hand dripped blood, her right hand was held clenched in a fist under her chin.

"Hey, dragon!" the Chinese girl yelled.

The porcelain dragon spun around to face her.

Without fear, the girl quickly raised the fist to her lips, straightened out her fingers, and blew the powder on her palm directly into the dragon's face.

Inhaling to spray fire on her, the dragon snorted up the iridescent cloud floating around its head.

"That's it for you, you stupid bitch," the girl said as it began sputtering like it was choking.

The dragon crashed to the floor. Twitching and kicking its feet, it transformed back into a human woman.

In her world of pain and grotesque disfigurement, Beth leaned back against the wall in total incomprehension. She'd recognized that the woman on the floor was Posh.

CHAPTER 62

Jade

Once Posh was immobilized, Jade Cure walked over to Beth.

She stared at the other woman's destroyed face and body in disbelief.

Her broken leg, charred arm, roasted face, the exposed bone of her burnt skull.

Damn, lady, Posh has totally fucked you up.

It hurt Jade to even look at her.

Beth sat stupefied. "P . . . Posh . . .?" she gibbered out of the remaining half of her mouth, jabbing a finger at Posh's naked body. "P . . . Posh?"

"It's her alright," Jade replied. "Don't worry—the shithead won't be cooking anyone ever again."

She rushed back over to Posh's side.

Posh was on her back, groaning in pain, her eyes open in agony. Her stomach was swollen, like she was pregnant outside her womb. Her naked body sparkled with the dragonreich powder Jade had blown over the dragon to revert it back to human form.

"Her strength also her weakness," Yang Yang had said. "Dragon sperm also cure monster it create."

Jade already knew it wasn't a workable solution. No way could Malone be expected to wait till Posh was a raging dragon each time before blowing reich over her.

Jade regarded Posh with disgust. *You stupid cow. You dared eat my mother?*

Posh gaped back at her. "Help me!" she whispered harshly, "My belly feels like it's tearing apart."

Jade smirked. "Oh, I'm fucking helping you all right." She pulled a paper-lock from her pocket and waved it in Posh's face. "Sorry, girlfriend, but you're about providing Ma with her new body."

The meaning of her words got through to Posh. Horror filled Posh's eyes.

"Please. Don't kill me."

Jade smirked. *"Please?"* She pointed to Beth. "Tell me, you fucking junkie: Do you have a divine right to eat people?"

Posh's expression turned from fear to utter rage. "Beth? She's crap! She's the—"

Posh froze into immobility as Jade wrapped the roll of paper around her neck. As frozen as the snake goddess was.

Jade pulled a knife from her belt. "Okay, now first, I need my Ma's head back."

She bent over Posh, prodding the protuberance with fingers, deciding where to cut.

Then, knife poised to begin, Jade froze herself.

She watched, confused, as the air in front of her shimmered, and an attractive elderly woman and two Forks materialized in the room.

***

"Not a second too soon," Sara Fischer said to her metal companions. She wagged an elegant bony finger at Jade. "Forget about doing that, kid. That young woman there is currently the most important person on the fucked-up planet."

"Yes," Lady Yaz said, floating forward. "She is important to Malone, who we have a deal with. That makes her important to us, and *we* run this planet."

Sara nodded at Jade. "They do, kid."

Jade stood up.

She pointed over to where Beth sat gibbering incoherencies and twitching in agony. "Posh is dangerous. In addition to almost killing that woman, she's eaten my mother's head. I want it back."

Sara looked over at Beth and grimaced. She looked down at Posh's frozen form, her eyes full of questions.

Jade dropped her knife and jerked the Dead God's Sword from its scabbard.

Sword raised in front of her, she stepped in front of Posh's body and stared pointedly at Sara. "I don't care if the Forks are

God Almighty himself; Posh doesn't leave here except I get my Ma's head out of her."

"Don't be silly, girl," Sara said. "You're way outclassed here. There's nothing you can do."

Jade's expression was adamant. "Oh, we'll see about that."

Sara admired Jade's pluckiness. *If only Rachel had been this dedicated to me. Oh, what am I thinking?*

"I mean it," Jade repeated, her oblique eyes thinning to dangerous slits. "Ma's head is in her, and I want it back."

"Okay," Lord Tav said, floating now alongside Lady Yaz. "Your mother's head is of no value to us. You can have it back."

On his words, Posh's belly bulged outward even more.

Then Jade saw it wasn't Posh's belly that was expanding, but Ma's head that was coming out through her skin, like a submerged swimmer breaking the water's surface.

When Ma's head was fully out, Jade picked it up. She examined it—it looked fine. Jade was relieved; the goddess *had* kept her word about time not being an issue.

"You okay now, kid?" Sara asked.

Jade nodded. She sheathed her sword, then looked down at Posh. Posh's stomach looked as normal as ever.

Jade remembered Beth. She pointed to the ruined woman. Can you help *her?*"

***

Beth was in torment. Horror was draped over her like folds of linen, along with pain like a cloak of many colors in its varied shades.

I'm in hell, she thought dully. *Dead and sucking Satan's cock. And without chickens.*

Sara Fischer and the Forks' sudden appearance reinforced her conviction. *Kitchen gods? In my apartment?*

Then she saw the Forks were floating toward her.

Beth was tired of pleading for her life or death. She hurt too badly. "Stop toying with me," she gasped. "Just fucking end this."

The pain ended. Like honey was being poured over her, like she was fluttering in orgasm, wellness pulsed through her.

She gaped dully at her charred and useless left arm as flesh once again built up over it.

"Thank you," she gasped as the same wellness dripped down the side of her face. Suddenly, she could see out of her left eye again.

Next her shattered leg was also fixed.

Now, Beth only felt so, so, so, so, so tired.

"She is okay now," she heard a far-off voice say right next to her. "She just needs to rest a little."

Then she fell asleep.

***

Jade warily regarded the forks. The ease with which they'd fixed Beth alarmed her.

She could now see that the loudly snoring woman on the ground by the wall was an attractive, tallish, muscular blonde.

Sara pointed to Posh. "Okay, let her up."

"Okay." Jade bent over Posh and unpeeled the paper coil from around her neck.

Posh sat up. She looked worriedly at the Forks. "It wasn't me."

Sara frowned at her. "What are you talking about?"

Posh pointed to Beth. "I didn't do—"

Then her face colored. "Who the hell fixed that bitch up? Shiiiiit!"

Posh looked around angrily. "I said: Who the hell repaired Beth's body?" Her anger at seeing her tormentor unharmed was so great that she lost all fear of the Forks.

She grabbed a jagged shard of glass from the shattered window off the floor and leapt to her feet. She ignored the glass cutting her own fingers.

Sara moved to restrain her. "Calm down, girl."

Posh glared at Sara. She waved the glass knife at her menacingly. "Get the hell out of my way, old lady. That bitch is suffering like she made me do!"

Sara got out of her way. She turned to the Forks. "Do something!"

"Calm down," Lady Yaz told Posh.

Slowed only by her caution not to cut her bare feet on the shattered glass, Posh continued advancing on Beth. "Not until I damage that slut in some way! She was chopping chickens on my back!"

"Let it go, Posh," Jade said wearily. "You're okay now."

"You stay out of this."

Jade rolled her eyes. She quickly stepped behind Posh and re-wrapped the paper-lock around her neck.

Posh's eyes widened in surprise. She froze, then crashed to the floor and again lay motionless as a statue. She still gripped her makeshift glass knife.

Jade shrugged at Sara. "She tends to get carried away."

Sara nodded. She was shaken by the intensity of the young woman's rage.

She looked back at Beth. Posh's accusation against *her* was even more shocking. *Chickens? What the hell is wrong with you kids nowadays?*

She turned her attention back to Jade, who now stood holding her mother's wizened head. Sara noted that a paper coil similar to that restraining Posh was wrapped around its severed end.

"Look, I've got to go," Jade said. "I'm late for a date with my boyfriend."

Sara nodded, "Thanks." She pointed to Posh's prone body. I take it that to reanimate her we simply unwrap the paper from her neck?"

Jade nodded. "Burn it afterwards, though, or it'll cause you major trouble later. It's very powerful Song Dynasty sorcery."

She turned to the Forks. "Can I ask you a favor?"

"We are thankful for your assistance," Lord Tav replied. "What do you desire?"

Despite looking like an ancient warrior princess with her sword and knife, Jade Cure somehow still managed to look embarrassed to boot. "I'm supposed to be meeting my boyfriend in a short while to discuss some heavy relationship issues. I can't go there direct from here, carrying Ma's head like this, and if I go home first to drop it off, I'll be late . . ."

Sara laughed. "You want them to teleport you back home? Is that it?"

Jade grinned. She nodded.

"No problem," Lady Yaz said. "Where do you live?"

"Chinatown Park. Upstairs in the old temple pagoda down where the hookers congregate."

"Done," Lady Yaz said.

Jade instantly disappeared.

Immediately afterwards, the Forks levitated Posh off the floor, and they, she, and Sara Fischer vanished also.

The apartment was silent except for Beth's snoring, a gentle nasal thunder that rumbled in waves from where she lay blissfully asleep.

CHAPTER 63

Malone

Malone and Glass Horse saw the approaching dust cloud and halted.

It rolled closer, splitting into smaller clouds that finally became pale-skinned women on motorbikes.

The biker women stopped a short distance from Malone and Glass Horse.

Malone immediately noted an oddity. The women all rode sidesaddle, like they only had one leg.

The leader climbed off her bike and *hopped* over to them.

Malone studied her as she drew near.

She was pretty, with a cute nose and glossy black hair that draped over her shoulders. Her skin was bone white; almost vampiric in its seeming bloodlessness. In contrast, her lips were roses of health.

She wore an army camo top and a long camo skirt, and carried a carbine.

Malone looked closer: the cut of her lower garment wasn't a skirt's cut—it looked more like a single-legged pair of pants.

Her footwear was a single foot-wide boot.

Malone glanced quickly at the other biker women. Each was as pallid-skinned as the next, with the same lustrous black hair, the same full lips. All were dressed similarly—the same one-legged pants, the same wide boot. All were armed with carbines.

He returned his attention to their leader, now noticing the 'MOM' embroidered patch on her left breast pocket.

She scowled at Malone. "Why are you two trespassing here?"

He smiled back. Her responding expression was dismissive, like she wouldn't really have cared to know him outside of the present circumstances.

"I asked you a question," she said. "What are you doing here on the peninsula?"

"I already told you they're tit-robbers, Gala!" a lusty voice called from behind her. Or maybe he's a pervert—come to rape us!"

"Is sex all you ever think about, Chloe?" another voice said. There was a burst of laughter from the other women.

Malone now saw that all the women had the MOM patches on their pockets.

Gala hopped closer to Malone. "So?"

"My name's Malone."

"And I am Glass Horse."

"Malone," Gala said, rolling his name off her tongue like it was rotting fruit. Her teeth were pointy and staggered so they interlocked when she shut her mouth. "If you've no business here—"

"Give her the note, Malone."

Malone turned to stare at Glass Horse in surprise. *"What note?"*

"The one in the Trangel Masher. Frank's next instructions to you."

Malone's stare widened further. "It had a *note* in it? Oh shit. I was in such a hurry to leave Traven that I didn't check."

The transparent horse stared at him deadpan. "Then, Malone, we're in trouble."

Malone looked back at Gala. She was smiling coldly. "So you like licking tranny lollipop, eh? You enjoy sucking—"

"No, I do not," he quickly interrupted.

"Stop lying, Malone, you handled the Trangel Masher, the tranny's most honored weapon. Only men favored and *loved* by them are permitted—"

"That is true," Glass Horse interrupted, "but Malone here is different. He is on a quest to—"

Gala silenced it with a 'talk-to-the-hand' gesture. She gazed steely-eyed at Malone. "I was saying: just your *handling* the Masher proves you're a spy. You're coming with us, we have special treatments for tranny lovers."

Malone weighed his chances of disarming her. He considered the distance between them and the fact that she had only one leg and could apparently only hop.

Gala read his intentions. She laughed mockingly.

"Surely you're not suicidal. Even if you take this weapon from me, it only has a clip of fifteen rounds. There are thirty of us, each armed with a carbine." She laughed again, her tongue wobbling in her mouth like a portable snake. "Or maybe you're bulletproof."

Malone was still undecided. He sized her up, looked at the row of motorcycle riders, gauging the distance separating her and the nearest. If he took Gala hostage . . .

Glass Horse also read the look in his eye.

"Don't resist," it said. "I'm not bulletproof."

"See," Gala said, "Your horse is smarter than you."

Her comment stung Malone.

"Look, we haven't got all day," Gala added. "You can either get pillion on my bike now or we'll riddle you both with holes and dump your bodies in the Milk Sea."

"You've a persuasive way with words," Malone replied to her dryly, "We'll go with you. Just let me ride my horse."

Gala nodded. "But no tricks."

Malone mounted Glass Horse. Surrounded by the pale biker women, they set off at a gallop, the motorcycles rolling at a speed the horse could match.

***

The peninsula extended for longer than Malone expected. Like a snake it coiled, winding its un-straight path through the Milk Sea, through a forest of breast hills that turned their nipples towards the passing procession and squirted milk at them.

Malone bent close to Glass Horse's ear. "How long before you can fly?" he whispered.

"Still a few hours. This long run is tiring me out again."

One of the women riders swung her bike in close to them. She was very attractive, her black hair cut short.

"Hi, I'm Chloe."

She yawned. Her neck sympathetically yawned into slits extending from ear to clavicle, pink vagina-like slashes that pulsed like they were breathing.

She peered through Glass Horse's body as it galloped. "Where'd you get this horse?" she asked. "It's pretty, like a big pearl on legs."

She said more, but Malone wasn't listening. He was shocked. He'd worked out that the slits in her neck were gills.

He thought a few moments, summing up the implications of this taken in concert with her wearing single-leg trousers and an extra-wide boot. He looked around. Like Gala, most of the other riders had *long* hair—their necks were hidden. The two who didn't also had gills.

He turned back to Chloe, pointed to her breast-pocket patch. "What does MOM stand for?"

She looked at him queerly. "Mermaids on Motor-bikes. What else?"

Malone smiled sweetly back.

Chloe thought he was hitting on her. She fussily swung her bike to join ranks with the others.

Malone spent the rest of the trip pondering the incongruity of armed biker mermaids in military uniforms.

***

The breast hills grew larger and sparser around them. Finally they reached a grouping of stone breasts so humongous they looked like divine sex toys.

Malone was struck speechless. His manhood was humbled in the presence of such massive mammary masterpieces.

Unlike their floating flesh counterparts, these mountainous breasts were an island amidst the Milk Sea, connected directly to the peninsula.

They rode up through the cleavage of the closest pair of breasts. Its 'walls' twitched either side of them.

A heady, musty scent filled the corridor—sex diffusing its way from meatstone into air mingled with the thick, sweaty, sticky smell of a long-unwashed body. Arousing and disgusting all at once.

301

Chloe rode in close to Malone again. "I'll see you tonight—if you're alive then," she whispered. She rode off again.

Then they topped the meatstone corridor and were staring down at the MOM camp.

CHAPTER 64

Malone

The camp was a series of green tents on one side of a mile-square enclosure. It was surrounded on three sides by the mountainous breasts. Its fourth side stared out over the Milk Sea.

From where Malone and Glass Horse entered the enclosure, however, they were unable to see the milky waves. The view directly ahead of them was dominated by the North Pole.

The North Pole was a gargantuan purple penis. It was fifty meters high and ten meters thick. It balanced on a tripod of HUGE testicles. It was covered with red metal veins that even at a distance could be noticed twitching.

Its glans spread atop it like a mushroom's cap, bathing its base in shade. Around its testicles were piles of white debris, as if the penis-head was shedding dandruff.

"Now *that's* impressive," Malone said.

They descended the cleavage to the valley. Closer to the North Pole they saw that the white piles at its base were bones.

Human bones.

A short distance from the monster penis was hung a tapestry woven in human hair, embroidered with depictions of mermaids dancing round it.

Malone and Glass Horse were led directly to the North Pole and shackled to its testicles.

"This is very gay," Malone grumbled. "Can't you chain us to a vagina instead? The South Hole or something?"

Gala sniggered. "Stop pretending you dislike lollipop. It doesn't wash."

He stared coldly back at her. "What do you intend doing with us?"

"Look around you. Study the bones. You'll work that out for yourself."

She left them. In formation, the MOMs hopped off towards the tents, splitting off into smaller groups upon arriving at each tent flap.

Malone sat down, eyeing the stacked bones.

"Well, horse," he said, "we seem about to be sacrificed to an erection. Talk about misplaced phallus worship."

***

The North Pole had metal rungs affixed into its side. These led up as far as Malone could make out.

It smelt too, like a million sweaty/unwashed groins.

The ground immediately around the meatstone phallus was speckled with faded maroon stains. Its base sported faint dark splatters.

Malone grimly noted the bloodstains—these mer-maids meant business.

The entire camp was clean and well kept. Like the North Pole, its floor was meatstone—purple marbled with red and black. Vegetation was sparse, a few fruit trees mingled with cacti.

Malone set his mind to figuring out their escape. The obvious plan was to wait till Glass Horse could fly again. That would work, as long as he could convince the MOMs not to kill them both.

He explained the plan to his see-thru companion.

"A sound plan," it agreed. "I'll keep quiet about it."

***

The MOMs returned an hour later. All were now changed into white T-shirts and short blue skirts that revealed their tails for what they were—orange-scaled appendages ending in foot-wide fins.

Now shoeless, the mermaids used their fins as feet. They wobbled like penguins, taking waddly steps on left and right fin divisions in turn.

Malone thought they looked like cute one-legged gymnasts.

There was nothing cute about their ever-present firearms though.

"Do you sleep with your guns on?"

"Shut up," Gala said. "Don't act cute—we've no time for your shit."

"Let me go and I won't keep stinking up your camp."

Chloe scowled. "Even the dumb aren't that dumb."

She stepped up close to him, ripped his jacket open, and placed a knife against his belly.

"This could go really badly for you," Chloe said in an icy voice. "It's best you tell us quickly what you know about those ass-fucked transsexual's plans to invade us."

What is your problem? Malone wondered. One moment you're acting like you want to get me into bed, the next like you want me dead.

He met her gaze evenly. "I already told you: I'm on a quest. I arrived here by mistake."

"Convince him," Gala commanded.

Chloe lifted the knife to Malone's chest. He brushed her off.

Gala shook her head at him. "Don't resist her. If you do, I'll shoot you."

Malone dropped his hands back to his side. He tensed in anticipation of what was coming.

Chloe dug the knife point into Malone's left breast. The other mermaids watched intently. Several licked their lips.

Malone yelled: "Yeeooowww! What the hell is wrong with you ladies!?"

Chloe pushed the knife in deeper. She twisted it. "Tell us the truth, cocksucker!"

Malone steeled himself against the pain. He grit his teeth, fought not to scream out again. He wasn't giving them the satisfaction.

"Stop!" Gala's voice was a harsh whisper.

Chloe stood back.

"Why aren't you bleeding?" Gala asked Malone.

He winced from the pain. "All my blood's in my right arm now. If that sounds confusing to you, I'm not yet used to the idea myself."

Gala cocked her head. An inquisitive look took over her face. "Show us."

He complied, removing gloves and jacket.

"OOOoooh." On seeing his blood arm, the mermaids all stared at him stunned. Chloe suddenly looked very contrite.

Malone groaned. "What is it now?

"I just told—"

He stopped. All the mermaids had thrown themselves prostrate on the ground in an attitude of worshipping him.

"First they hate you, now they love you," Glass Horse whispered. "You've a weird way with women, Malone."

***

The mermaids retreated to confer in loud awed whispers, then they dispersed.

Malone and Glass Horse shrugged at each other.

A short while later the pair were unshackled and led into one of the largest tents. Its middle was taken up by a tub sunken into the stone floor.

A naked Gala lolled in the water. Her milk-white breasts were as perfect as the meatstone giants enclosing the MOM camp.

She smiled at Malone.

"You need to unwind," she said smokily. "Join me."

Malone undressed. He joined her, still totally nonplussed by this about-face.

A mermaid brought them food and drink. White fish that tasted like cottage cheese, and lime-colored wine.

Glass Horse refused both food and drink, then promptly fell asleep.

Meal over, the server mermaids left, sealing the tent behind them.

Gala began fondling Malone's penis.

Glass Horse slept on, thankfully in Malone's opinion.

Once Malone was fully erect, Gala went down on him.

He groaned in disbelief at her perfect technique: Despite her interlocking dentition, she didn't teeth-scrape at all, padding their points with the inner side of her lips. Her wet cushiony mouth was a new kind of sexual heaven.

Writhing in submission to Gala's sexual expertise, Malone could practically see naked trangels singing hymns to anus worship.

He groaned some more, then spurted into her mouth.

He lay back, watching the movement of her throat as she swallowed his ejaculate, for the moment relieved of more than mere sexual tension.

Afterwards, Gala grinned at Malone like a piranha.

"I bet you're wondering why I'm treating you so nice now."

Malone nodded an afterglow nod.

"Selfish reasons: Our legend says a man with a red arm will come and make the North Pole cum."

Malone nodded patronizingly. Of course, it *had* to be something as stupid as this. "How am I supposed to do that, does it have a vagina somewhere?"

He stole a quick glance at Glass Horse. It was still asleep, the ground magnified through its body.

Sinuous as a snake, Gala fluttered around him in the pool, caressing him with her breasts.

"The legend says you'll jerk it off."

Malone burst out laughing. "How?"

She frowned, angry that he mocked her. "Don't be silly. How am *I* supposed to know that?"

"I'm sorry. It just sounds so ridiculous." Her white face was still adamant, so he bent and kissed her breasts, sucking both strawberry-tinged nipples long and hard.

Gala moaned. Her body shuddered against Malone's. Her tail flapped against his legs. She ran her fingers through his hair. She gripped him hard and shivered, then pushed him away sharply.

Malone looked at her. Gala's eyes were wide with lust.

"That's one way to say sorry," she gasped. "You're however not out of the hot water yet."

She lifted herself to sit on the pool's edge, then pushed aside a layer of golden crotch scales to reveal her vagina.

Malone regarded the mermaid's pussy—a pale pink pathway proclaiming penetrative pleasure, moist with creamy white secretion.

"Eat me," she moaned at him, tapping the pink slit. She looped her tail into a golden curve. "You can sit on my tail fin while doing so."

Malone made himself comfortable on the improvised stool and ate her, digging his tongue deep into the hollow of her cunt. She tasted clean and sweet.

Outside Gala's tent, her sentries giggled to her loud moans. Then to her louder breathless gasps and shrieks.

Glass Horse slept on.

CHAPTER 65

Malone

"The North Pole used to be much smaller," Gala said. "A long time ago, groups of MOMs like myself could lick and suck it to ejaculation. But then it became insensitive to our feelings, and our relationship deteriorated. We refused to have sex with it, and having no hands it couldn't masturbate.

"We let it become EXTREMELY sexually frustrated, to teach it to treat its worshippers better. That was our mistake.

"When we thought the North Pole had learnt its lesson, we patched up our differences with it. We became lovers again and resumed having sex with it. But now it could no longer cum. It had forgotten how to. We tried every trick we could think of to make it ejaculate, to no avail.

"Unable to exit it, the North Pole's semen converted into rockflesh, making it grow larger and larger still, till now you have what you—"

There was a sound like thunder. Shockwaves rippled the tent walls. Ground-transmitted vibrations rippled the pool water.

"That was a bomb," Malone said. "Are you ladies having weapons practice?"

Gala shook her head at him.

Moments later a MOM sentry burst into the tent. Her face an excited mask, she hopped quickly over to the bathtub.

"We're under attack! From both the Cleavage and the Milk Sea!"

Gala looked sharply at Malone, then back at the woman. "Trangel bitches?"

"No, these are robots!"

A bomb exploded outside the tent. The ground shook; the canvas wall ripped.

The mermaid sentry was knocked off her tail. She fell into the pool, floating limply face downward, blood gushing from her multi-punctured back.

***

With the ground rumbling beneath them like a truck engine, Malone and Gala hurriedly dressed, then rushed outside.

The air blast from a bomb fusillade capsized the tent behind them immediately after they emerged from it.

The camp was being attacked by white robots. Malone instantly recognized them as more of Rachel Fischer's New Korean imports.

The machines thronged the cleavage descent to the MOM camp. They looked like semen dripping between the mammoth breasts.

Ranks of armed mermaids were already on their bikes, streaming across the camp towards the breast-hill's access road.

"The robots want *me*," Malone told Gala. "Call your girls off. Give me a boat and I'll leave—draw them away from here."

"Like hell you will. We'll fight and defeat them. Afterwards you'll make the pole cum."

Malone had expected that answer. "Give me a gun then, so I don't get killed."

Gala nodded. She tossed him a pistol.

"The white robots are here for *you*, Malone."

Malone looked round. Glass Horse was pulling itself out from beneath the collapsed tent. Malone winced in embarrassment from having forgotten about it. "You okay, horse?

It got to its feet. "I am undamaged, thank you."

"Duck!" Malone yelled.

The three of them flung themselves to the ground.

A salvo of bullets flew over them

Malone shot the robot firing at them. It blew apart in a shower of scalding machine oil and melted plastic innards.

***

The white robots poured down the cleavage like spilt sugar.

Ranked behind this descending horde stood other, much larger white robots. These carried massive bazookas and rained rockets down on the camp.

This is bad, Malone thought, *really bad.*

Additional detachments of robots were disembarking from white sailboats at the quay formed by the quadrant of the island not bounded by the breasthills.

Like fleas deserting a drowning dog, like bees exiting a shaken hive, the beached robots rushed into the camp.

They instantly began firing on the riding MOMs. Bullets ripped across the camp. Mermaid bikes exploded, pitching their tail-legged riders skyward as though they were somersaulting on trampolines.

A number of mermaids swerved their bikes back to engage this new enemy in close-range fire. The remainder continued riding and shooting at the force descending through the breast hills.

***

The cleavage approach to the camp fast became a scene of major carnage, a vista of death and destruction, of bloodied white-and-gold-scaled flesh mingled with machine parts spurting oil. Piled mermaid and machine corpses formed an obstruction to the movement of both combatant forces.

The robot bazooka brigade stepped forward. They rained rockets down into the valley road, blowing the piled corpses out of the way. They bombed indiscriminately, killing large numbers of both theirs and the MOM forces.

Gala and Malone helplessly watched the slaughter. Along with Glass Horse, they were hiding behind a stack of sardine crates.

"I've got to get out there," Gala said miserably, almost weeping with frustration. "My girls are being blown to bits."

"So are the robots," Malone replied. He understood Gala's feelings. He'd kept firing till he was out of ammo. Then he'd dumped the gun. Now, forced to just watch the fighting, he was suffused with a feeling of impotence.

There had to be a way to repulse the attacking machines.

He looked back at the beach. No new robots were landing. Those already in camp had rushed past he and Gala's place of concealment and were attacking the mermaids.

A new group of mermaids arrived then from a far nook of the camp. They carried grenade launchers which they set up beside the North Pole, training them on isolated robots.

"Call your forces back," Malone told Gala. "Regroup yourselves behind the North Pole here. With most of the robots in the camp now, you can pick them off at your leisure."

"Except for the ones shelling us," she replied grimly.

Malone considered her words. She was right—something *had* to be done about the huge bombardier robots with their rocket launchers. The MOMs smaller grenade launchers hadn't the range to destroy them.

Gala flinched as several MOMs and their bikes were blown into sky-high fragments by a rocket.

She turned to Malone, anger and pain etched on her pallid face. In her anguish even her lips seemed drained of color. Her black hair was plastered to her cheeks and shoulders like a liquid shroud. "I can't keep watching this. I've got to get out there and direct the action."

Another fusillade of rockets hit the camp, filling the air with shrapnel.

A detachment of robots had meanwhile identified Malone and Gala's position. Moments later bullets peppered the North Pole above their heads. They ducked to avoid being punctured by the ricochets.

"Fuck this! I need a bike!" Gala growled. She shook off Malone's restraining hand and hopped off.

***

"Hey, wait!" Malone yelled, when Gala—now heavily laden with guns and ammo—zoomed past him a minute later.

"She didn't hear you," Glass Horse said.

Malone grunted. He knew that unless he did something fast Gala was riding to certain suicide.

He turned to Glass Horse. "Can you fly yet?"

"Yes. Time to leave?"

"Not yet, horse. Let's help the MOMs."

He climbed atop the horse. They rode over to the mermaids with the mortars. "Give me a case of grenades," Malone said.

They nodded. One lifted a case of tortoise-shelled metal balls up to him.

She frowned. "How do you intend getting up there? Even our best riders are being pushed back downhill."

Malone smiled coldly. "The horse has special talents."

"Hold on." Glass Horse galloped up into the air, to the amazed stares of the mermaids.

Unnoticed by either set of combatants, they flew over the breast hill to the right of that commandeered by the robot attackers. Malone was relieved to see that there were no robot reserves waiting behind the ring of breasts.

He wedged the grenade case between his thighs so it wouldn't slip.

"Okay, horse, let's hit 'em."

Grenades in hands, he poised himself while the horse dived-bombed the bombardier robot rearguard.

Malone flung the grenades amongst the robots, pulling their pins with his teeth and dispatching them in a blur of motion as Glass Horse flashed through their white metal ranks.

To a chorus of explosions and confused yells, Glass Horse swooped skyward again. It hung in mid-air while Malone surveyed the damage. Then it swooped again before the machines worked out what was going on.

Malone dropped more grenades. More of the giant robots exploded. Sparks and black smoke filled the air.

The robots began targeting them. "Take us up!" Malone yelled.

Glass Horse did so. From a safe distance overhead, Malone pelted grenades down on the robots.

Shortly, all the robot bombers lay as machine wreckage at the top of the pass. Several robots, having lost control of their limbs, rolled helplessly backward down the cleavage away from the MOM camp.

Malone had one grenade left. No matter, the job was done.

"Let's go help the girls clean house," he said. "Now they don't need fear bombing again, they can take their time and wipe out the remainder of the robots."

They flew out from behind the breast hills into the cleavage pass.

Malone was dismayed. The robots and MOMs had almost totally finished slaughtering themselves now. The pass was once again rendered impassable by piled mermaid corpses and mechanical wreckage.

***

Gala was still alive. She and a few other surviving MOMs were retreating down towards the camp, navigating the charnel piles like mountain bikers.

Several robots were climbing up over the corpse-piles to cut off the mermaids' escape.

"Make for Gala!" Malone yelled in Glass Horse's ear.

He glanced at the North Pole. Its base was now a makeshift fort. A group of mermaids had barricaded it with parts of the robots' sailboats dragged up from the quay.

A robot spotted Malone and Glass Horse approaching. It signaled to its companions. Two of them retrieved a rocket launcher from the body of one of their larger, demolished colleagues. They awaited the unsuspecting pair of fliers.

Malone and Glass Horse swooped over the robots.

With a whoosh of flame, a rocket spurted after them. It cleared the distance between machines and horse and rider with the speed of ejaculate aimed at a porn starlet's eye.

Suddenly sensing danger, Malone looked back. He sighted the rocket just before it hit them.

"Turn!" he yelled at Glass Horse, though knowing it was too late to do anything.

The rocket hit Glass Horse in the rump. Malone felt his mount blown out from beneath him.

His red right arm jerked upward by his side. He paid it no mind, too occupied by the strange sight of the transparent horse being borne skyward, a rocket stuck up its butt.

Then the rocket exploded and glass powder rained down on all and sundry.

Now Malone realized that he hadn't fallen. He looked up.

His red arm had transformed into a parachute above him. It separated into red strips at his shoulder which bloomed into a twenty-feet-wide umbrella ten feet above him.

Lamenting Glass Horse's death, Malone was borne by his parachute arm towards the North Pole.

***

The parachute draped itself over the North Pole like a condom. Dangling from the edge of its cap, Malone felt insignificant, like an un-wiped drop of ejaculate.

He looked around. This vantage point gave him an unparalleled view of the mermaid camp and its surroundings.

The Milk Sea extended in every direction except that from which he and Glass Horse had come. The peninsula was revealed as a penis-shaped land extension that could almost be the North Pole's solid shadow at mid-evening.

Malone felt a major depression set over him. Now that Glass Horse was blown to bits, he looked to be trapped here for the foreseeable future.

***

Malone's red arm shrunk to normal size again, leaving him clinging to a rung halfway up/down the North Pole.

He began climbing down, then stopped.

The carnage below him was unbelievable. Blown-apart mermaid bodies and busted metal humanoid shells lay everywhere. The flesh and metal corpses were so intertwined that it was impossible to tell which was which: The battleground seemed a single bleeding organism that was part woman, part fish, part human-appendaged machine.

Even at this height, the smell of fish-flesh frying in machine oil was sickening.

Below Malone, the robots and mermaids engaged in their last desperate confrontation. The battle was a massacre on both sides.

Malone was stunned by the doomed heroic violence with which the mermaids fought. The robots gave off the same air of manic purpose as the MOMs.

Malone felt oddly neglected. *He* was, after all, the bone of contention between them. But now, even the robots seemed to have forgotten all about him. Both sides in the conflict fought solely to see which could more thoroughly exterminate the other.

Using their larger, broken comrades as battering rams, the robots abandoned caution and charged the makeshift MOM defenses.

With Gala yelling orders, the MOMs resisted the first and second robot charges, but on the third, the barricade of boat metal crumpled like bread crust.

Metal ants overwhelming a sugar cube, the robots poured in amongst the mermaids.

Hand to hand fighting commenced.

Though slightly outnumbered, the mermaids gave as good as they got. Both their numbers and the robots' dwindled till there were a mere handful left on either side, and still they kept on fighting.

Malone got out his last grenade.

"Hey, up here, you metal louts!" he yelled.

There were four robots left. They had to exit the collapsed mermaid enclosure to see him, which was what Malone intended. Once the robots were in clear view, he pulled the grenade's pin and tossed it amongst them. Then he climbed as fast as he could.

He looked down after the explosion.

Two sets of robot legs remained where the machines had been standing.

After waiting a couple of minutes more to ensure there weren't any additional robots in hiding, Malone descended to the camp.

***

Malone's decisive action to end the conflict had been too late. All the previous survivors were now dead.

He sighted Gala. She lay twitching, holding her intestines in with her hands.

He rushed over to her side.

Gala was expiring fast. Blood seeped over her fingers. She smiled at him. "We fought well, didn't we? We taught those fucking machines a lesson in manners they won't forget in a hundred years."

She coughed. "You know, pain clears your mental ass of lots of unnecessary shit. I remember now how you're supposed to make the . . . the North Pole cum."

Malone sighed. "You can tell me that later. Where'd do you keep your medical supplies?"

"Shut up, Malone—I know I'm dying. Listen: Use your homosexual hand to jerk off the Pole—our lord and master. The legend says if you do that, you'll be able to leave here. If you don't . . ."

She coughed a huge gob of blood on him and was dead.

CHAPTER 66

Malone

Malone's 'homosexual hand' clearly meant his 'Gay Fist.'

After glumly considering his lack of options, Malone pressed the appropriate button on his red hand.

Both his hand and arm immediately began growing, expanding till they were the size of a two-story building. Despite their humongous size, however, Malone found he could still move both with ease. He reached out and gripped the North Pole.

Immediately his fingers closed around it—just as his 'Hetero Fist' had done with Blubber—his 'Gay Fist' took over control of his actions. It began jerking off the North Pole as though the monster meatstone phallus was Malone's penis and he was masturbating.

Twice Malone found himself feeling almost empathic sexual pleasure with the North Pole.

He let his hand get on with it. He braced himself to be sucked into his arm again as had happened previously, and hoped he wouldn't find himself back in Traven again. Or somewhere worse.

The North Pole's handjob took an inordinate amount of time. Malone's blood arm didn't tire, never paused in its pumping, but he soon tired of watching it.

Seeing as it was automatic and his arm appeared able to stretch indefinitely, he turned away and walked around the camp while it worked.

***

Malone traversed the MOM camp in increasing anger. The scale of devastation Frank had catalyzed here utterly revolted him.

Malone had witnessed the dragons destroy Boston. Nightmare scenes from those days were burnt permanently into his psyche—

318

unerasable strips of devastating mental celluloid. The carnage then had been total, inescapable, and unexplainable.

Barring that, this MOM camp massacre was the worst horror he'd ever witnessed.

***

The mass of carnage adorning the camp began moving, flowing together like it was rivers seeking an ocean. Malone jumped aside as Gala's liquefied body flowed toward, then past him, only her head still intact.

Liquid motorcycles, liquid leather, liquid meat and bone; all met in the camp center. They swirled dizzily skyward like they were a drunken DNA helix, then collapsed into an oblong mass. Then they repeated the procedure, spiraling and collapsing once again.

Slowly, the liquid solidified, took on recognizable form.

It all built up into a monster vagina, one proportionate in size with the North Pole. Neatly ranked on its labia were the heads of all the dead MOMs. Gala's head formed its clitoris.

The vagina had metal wheels like a train. Its plastic body—covered with placoid scales—looked like that of a decapitated monster shark. Furthering this impression was the massive dorsal fin along its top. Its body ended in a split caudal fin

Looking inside it, Malone saw metal gears whirl-ing.

Most odd, along its length was printed in six-foot-high white lettering: 'Vagina Fish—Made in Taiwan.'

Malone was very bothered by this new development. Here was his hand, busy giving a hand job to a monster penis not his own, and now he also had a monster metal/flesh/plastic vagina to cope with.

He hoped it was friendly.

Vagina Fish rolled close to him. Its clitoris Gala-head peered down at him from twelve feet up.

He smiled sheepishly, pointed to his hand pumping up and down on the North Pole. As he did so, it paused in mid-stroke, clenched hard behind the glans, and twisted left and right semicircles as if the North Pole was a bottle it found hard to open.

"Great work, Malone," Gala-clitoris said, in a languid voice reminiscent of Blubber's. "It's almost there now." The MOM heads studding the labia nodded. Chloe's head blew him a kiss.

The monster vagina yawned. "We're off for a swim now—see you later, masturbator."

Vagina Fish rolled off to the beach. Malone watched it disappear beneath the white waves, its dorsal and tail fins marking its passage out into the Milk Sea.

***

Malone felt the North Pole throbbing. He felt the rumbling in its testicle tripod. Feeling exalted, exhilarated, and disgusted with himself, suffused with gloriously delicious unwanted homosexual feelings, he brought the North Pole to its first climax for a thousand years.

CHAPTER 67

Malone

The North Pole came.

It was an ejaculation of nuclear proportions. Liquid translucence spurted from it in an endless vertical river, forming a burgeoning mushroom cloud above it. The sky darkened as the sun was obscured from giving light.

In the half-night, Malone's Gay Fist kept pumping the meatstone cock. The North Pole kept spurting, all the while shuddering like it would explode, monster throbs that vibrated Malone's teeth. He *knew* he'd need a dentist after this.

Then its violent throbbing subsided, its orgasm ended. Malone sighed with relief as his hand shrank back to normal size again. He watched the huge cum canopy in the sky with bemusement, with no idea what to expect next.

The semen mushroom broke up into fluffy white clouds. The sky lightened back into daylight. The majority of the cum clouds floated away, off across the Milk Sea. Some however, remained, hovering ominously over the now drooping glans.

It began raining.

"Shit!" Malone grumbled, dashing beneath the North Pole's glans canopy for cover.

No way am I getting soaked in cum, he thought. *And I'm still no closer to getting out of this place or/and finding Jefferson Lincoln's damn liver.*

It rained cum in torrents.

The semen transformed immediately it hit the ground, becoming polar bears, seals, and penguins. The animals milled restively as their numbers rose.

The density of animals began crowding Malone in his safe haven. The intensity of the cum rain was such that he didn't dare stand outside of the protective shadow of the glans, so he endured the furry press of their bodies, keeping a safe distance from the polar bears.

The penguins were annoying, pecking his legs.

Malone figured his best bet for departing the MOM camp was to climb the North Pole again and attempt a descent inside it, down through its pee hole. It certainly wouldn't be clogged after ejaculating such a copious amount. At any rate he'd investigate where it led.

Looking up,—about to grip a rung and begin his climb—he noticed that several of the semen-clouds circling the monster penis-head were metamorphosing into airboats—flying yachts.

A number of the forming airboats hovered close enough to the Pole's glans for Malone to leap onto if he was atop it. He gripped a rung, but let it go again when he saw that one of the airboats was descending.

It reached him and stopped.

The airboat was ten meters long, with two transparent sails and a large cabin amidships. It was solidly built of cum-wood planks, their translucent waxiness making it appear freshly polished.

A walrus poked its head over the side and looked around.

"Ye Malone, matey?" it addressed him. It voice was gruff, like its vocal cords had been cured with sea salt.

He nodded warily.

The walrus waved its flippers expansively. "I'se be Captain Gumdrop, matey. Ye is to come aboard. I've an order to pick ye up and drop ye off in Boston."

It tossed a rope ladder over the side. Malone caught it and climbed up.

The airboat lifted away from the teeming polar animals.

As they rose, there was a loud commotion from the direction of the beach.

Malone looked down at the mass of feverishly milling creatures.

Vagina Fish had returned from its swim.

The wheeled, fish-bodied vagina was now eating the polar bears and seals, scooping them up in droves into metal power-shovels extruded from its sex opening.

Even at this distance Malone could hear the sounds of breaking bone and crunching meat coming from inside it.

And polar animal screams.

"Yes!" Gala-clitoris yelled from atop Vagina Fish. "The North Pole has finally cum and there's food for everyone. Let's feast, sisters!"

The heads studding its labia nodded their affirmation.

They feasted messily, spraying chunks of bear and sealmeat everywhere like an uncapped blender. Vagina Fish grew more and more blood-splattered by the moment.

Those polar creatures closest to it tried fleeing, tried to force a way through the packed animal mass to temporary safety. To no avail.

Malone was too bemused to be horrified by the day's bizarro overload. He looked up, up, and away.

A belated look at his blood hand confirmed that its 'Gay Fist' button had now disappeared also. Only the 'Lesbian Fist' zit-button adorned its rear.

***

"Nothing like open skies, matey," Captain Gumdrop said. It patted Malone warmly on the shoulders with a flipper. Unlike the polar menagerie and boat, the walrus captain wasn't made of semen. It however stank like a soaked carpet.

Malone moved upwind from it.

The boat's sail filled with wind. It rose higher above the North Pole's glans. All around it cum clouds dissolved and rained on the erstwhile MOM camp, the semen-fall transforming into more bears, seals, and penguins on hitting the ground.

The walrus stood in the boat's prow, piloting it by an old-fashioned ship's wheel. It swung the boat starboard; they headed out over the Milk Sea.

"We go South now, matey."

"Who sent you?" Malone asked the walrus.

It laughed, stroked its left tusk, twiddled its whiskers. "What ye care, matey, s'long as I gets ye back to Boston?" It focused its sad black eyes on him, pointed to the ship's cabin with a flipper. "Ah, ye be wanting to go below deck, matey, grab ye'self fresh clothes from one ye lockers. Ye look like ye've been fighting pirates in ye Caribbean."

323

Malone nodded. He turned and headed for the cabin. Beyond it, the North Pole pierced the distant sky like a black lighthouse.

All else in sight was the whiteness of the Milk Sea and a myriad brown-skinned breast hills with dark chocolate nipples that spurted milk almost as high as the airboat. Far distant in the east, Malone thought he could make out Traven's beetle shape, but he wasn't certain—there was just a black blob distorting the unending whiteness of the milk horizon.

He sighed, went downstairs to change his clothes.

***

Malone was bothered as he descended the stairs. He'd now missed two of Frank's riddle notes, and still had no idea where the sicko was.

He considered: *The good thing is that I'm on my way out of the Afterwife, and still in one piece to boot.*

The air-yacht's under-deck was a short corridor flanked by two doors on each side. Malone opened the first door on his right, and stepped in.

Then something hit him on the back of the head and he was knocked out cold.

CHAPTER 68

Bulldog, Gorgeous, Lucy Tang.

South Boston. Mid-afternoon.

495 Summer Street—the Barnes building—was a monolithic nine-storey concrete and glass construct. Though heavily scorched, it remained relatively undamaged.

The three cars conveying Bulldog, Gorgeous, and Sookie's gang pulled up in front of the Barnes Building. They spilled out of their vehicles, keeping close to the sidewalk to evade observation.

Bulldog was nervous. He didn't like being over here in South Boston. His unease showed on his ugly face. His muscles felt like steel knots. Meat high tension wires.

Bulldog couldn't help his fear: Every so often groups of dragons flew hither and thither overhead, crossing the street like squadrons of USAF jets. The reptiles always looked down at the Chinese contingent, then ignored them.

"It ain't fair," he told Gorgeous. "Us whites getting eaten, and you lot don't."

Gorgeous, plain face severe as a mandarin's, scowled. "Stop being nervous, darling," she whispered so the other Chinese wouldn't hear. "I've told you there's no danger."

Bulldog still wasn't convinced. "Damn fuckin' reptile racists. I don't see why—"

Gorgeous squeezed his bicep painfully. "Stop worrying, Bully!" she hissed severely. "Let's get this over with!"

Bulldog relaxed. Gorgeous' strict voice always calmed him.

Just like Herbie's had.

***

Like he did from time to time, Bulldog tried thinking *hard* now. He gave up,—it hurt too much—his bashed-in skull refused to permit it. Thoughts clashed with each other in his head like warring armies, like his brain was playing concept pinball.

He relaxed back into comfortable moronity, raring like an animal—a jungle predator—for the conflict ahead.

Action was great, it came instinctively to Bulldog to fight, to hurt, to kill. But cogitating . . .

Bulldog was delighted that now Herbie was dead, he had Gorgeous to think for him. It was a relief to simply follow orders/instructions—to be pointed in the right directions.

***

Gorgeous, on her part, was smart. Once Herbie had gone missing, she'd quickly recognized the mental vacuum in Bulldog's head and slotted herself into it.

It was to her advantage: She needed a man, and tough woman that she was, she wanted the toughest man available to enhance her badass reputation in Chinatown.

Bulldog's cretinous ugliness made no difference to Gorgeous.

What did, was that he always got hard for her in bed and fucked her when and how she asked him to. Doggy-style was best, and once she'd spread her legs and labia and instructed him in the Ying-Yang arts, he'd become great at cunnilingus too.

Best of all, Bulldog did *whatever* Gorgeous told him to.

To date, she'd hid his inability to think for himself from everyone but her Aunt Sookie Ling.

Sookie, thinking fast, had used Bulldog's violent reputation to assemble her own gang.

Sookie's gang wasn't yet a triad, but it was getting damn close to being one.

***

Wang Hao, a thin hard-faced man, came over to talk to Gorgeous and Bulldog.

"We're ready," he said. "Do we attack now?"

Gorgeous looked at Bulldog. "We go in?"

"Yeah," he replied. "Dumb bitch ain't escapin' with Sookie's stash. But we gotta watch for traps."

Gorgeous looked the gangsters over. Six ruthless men, all armed with machine guns.

"You heard Bully," she said. "Watch your step. And don't shoot unless it's absolutely necessary—Aunt Sookie wants Lucy alive."

Wang Hao nodded. He waved his men toward the building's front entrance.

***

Staring through the five concrete floors beneath her, Lucy Tang grimly watched the armed men climbing the staircase to her sixth floor hideout.

Her gorgeous face was set cold as marble.

In addition to several other abilities, dragonreich allowed Lucy to see through solid objects. When, like now, she was high on the drug, the world around her became an architect's blueprint, sharp stark lines overlaid over other lines—reality in wireframe mode.

She looked through the six cautiously climbing men, down to where Gorgeous and Bulldog were discussing. After a while, the pair joined the climb to her apartment.

Come and die, all of you, Lucy thought.

Her emotions were distraught.

Sookie's thugs being here meant Emil had been captured. Her darling was surely dead now, killed by Bulldog.

Lucy's heart throbbed violently with the pain of her loss.

Hate filled her as she watched Bulldog's squat simian shape transpose itself up the steps.

I'll kill you all, she raged in her mind. *You murdering bastards. And I'm saving something extra special for you, Bulldog, for killing my love. And your ugly bitch Gorgeous gets to watch me do you, before I kill her too.*

She looked back up through the stairs. Wang Hao was now on the landing beneath her.

A bitter grin on her pink lips, she watched him wave his machine gun, signal the others to be quiet.

Lucy picked up Sookie's jar of pure reich from her center table.

"This is for you, Emil," she growled. She shook a pile of the iridescent powder into her palm and snorted it.

327

Nothing happened for the longest minute, then Lucy's body melted like candle wax.

The liquid meat flowed out of her dress and coated the floor and walls of her living room. It writhed as it went, like a flattened snake. It spread itself thin, then thickened, then thinned out again. It spread over the ceilings into a seamless blend. Only the doors and windows were untouched.

In under a minute, however, the room again looked normal. Instead of its original blue color, it was now a pale flesh tone, its texture smooth as a virgin's breasts, as a baby's backside.

The room waited impatiently.

***

Wang Hao kicked Lucy's door in. It crashed off its hinges onto the floor with a dull thud.

The men rushed into the apartment.

"This is a horrendous color to paint a room." Gorgeous said on entering. "I can't imagine anyone having such bad taste."

"Bulldog looked around. "Looks ordinary to me. Normal horrible girly pink."

Gorgeous' nose wrinkled in disgust. "That's the problem. It *isn't* pink, it's *flesh*—skin tone."

She scowled. "Typical drag queen bad taste—I guess anal sex makes you see garish colors when you cum. Sickening."

She winced. "Damn, she painted the floor and ceiling too?"

Bulldog noticed and frowned. "Yeah, now that's *real* odd."

Wang Hao had found Sookie's pilfered jar of dragonreich. He took it over to his bosses. "This is here, but Lucy isn't."

Gorgeous regarded the glittering powder with distaste. She had no use for narcotics— they dulled the fighting senses. A kung fu student has to keep her body pure at all times, her mind clear as a mountain stream. Only thus were you superior to your opponent.

Bulldog nodded at the jar of reich Wang Hao held. "Sookie will be pleased to have that back."

Gorgeous grunted a distracted reply. "Something isn't right about this room," she said. "I can sense it."

"Forget the friggin' color," Bulldog said. "Let's go."

Gorgeous nodded, eager to be free from the oppressive feeling the room gave her, the odd sense that it was watching and listening to them.

"We've no idea where Lucy's gone," she told Wang Hao. "Or when the thieving bitch will be back. Have four men wait here—"

"The door's gone," Bulldog said.

Her nerves already on edge, Gorgeous spun around to see what he meant.

There was no doorway. Behind the kicked-in door now lying on the floor, the entrance had sealed over.

Gorgeous looked down, caught a glimpse of joining edges of pink at the bottom of the missing entranceway.

"What the hell is going on?"

"The windows are covering over too, boss!" a young gangster yelled.

They looked around them. The pink wall paint was streaming down the windows, sealing them off also. The room's two other doors were also closing off.

Bulldog pulled out his gun. "It's a fucking trap!"

"This room," Gorgeous said, wide-eyed. "I think it's Lucy."

"Lucy," Wang Hao repeated.

The gangsters stared at each other in horror.

They all stood and waited, confused about what to do next, what to expect.

Then the flesh-colored walls and floor split apart into stacked rows of mouths lined with sword-long teeth.

The mouths began spitting teeth at the gangsters.

* * *

Wang Hao was the first hit. Punctured by two teeth, one through his head, the other through his heart, he toppled over into an impossible chasm in the floor that gobbled him up like a crocodile's mouth. The jar of dragonreich fell in with him.

"Shit!" Bulldog yelped.

The gangsters stood no chance. In under a minute, all except Gorgeous and Bulldog lay dead or dying on the floor, punctured through multiple times. Blood bubbled from their bodies onto the pink floor where the mouths drank it up like teens slurping sodas.

Gorgeous knocked flying teeth away from Bulldog and herself. She spun left and right, blocking, punching, and kicking the flying enamel spears out of the air. Her defensive motions were fluid and automatic; easier for her than defending against an assailant's punches.

"We need to do something!" she yelled to Bulldog. "It doesn't look about to run out of teeth!"

"You're right!" He grabbed a bloody machine gun off the floor, swung it at the huge mouth opposite them, and began firing.

The mouth's teeth fractured. Behind the shards, its throat was a dark tunnel penetrated by a tongue like an endless road. Bulldog spun from that mouth and fired at the mouths on the other walls.

Under them, the floor rippled with teeth.

Gorgeous ducked a tooth the length of an elephant tusk. At the same time, she skipped off the floor and kicked another tooth away.

As she landed, the floor slid sideways under her, a yawning mouth that had moments before been smooth skin.

Gorgeous dropped waist-deep into the midst of a circle of teeth.

She screamed as the meat floor bit into her.

Bulldog turned and saw Gorgeous was trapped. He rushed over to her and began firing into the mouth. Its teeth shattered, but as fast as they broke, the mouth grew fresh teeth that stabbed into Gorgeous again.

Gorgeous' face was pale with horror. *No,* she thought. *This isn't fucking happening.*

Her face wrenched with pain as she fought to climb out of the mouth. Each motion felt like hell, like she was being torn in two. Shards of bullet-shattered teeth hit her in the face, cutting her cheeks so blood streamed.

Bulldog's machine gun jammed. "Damn!" he yelled. He flung the weapon away, gripped Gorgeous' wrist, and tried to pull her out.

"Kick against it!" he yelled as he dragged her. "Kick against it!"

Gorgeous kicked into the mouth. Her shoes found no purchase, just slimy tongue surface that felt like she was endlessly slipping. Face twisted in agony, she hammered at the teeth.

Blood streamed over the enamel spears from the punctures they'd made in her.

Bulldog, his ugly face white with fear of losing Gorgeous like he'd lost Herbie, yanked hard on her arms. He braced himself on the rim of the mouth and stamped on the teeth, trying to break them.

Two flying teeth hit Bulldog in the back. One stabbed into his chest between his ribs, penetrating his left lung below his heart. The other tooth perforated him, exploding out through his belly.

Writhing in pain, blood spurting out of him, Bulldog continued fighting to free Gorgeous. Now they were both clearly dying, the realization penetrated his subnormal mind that he loved her.

Then, suddenly, the mouth in the floor clamped tight on Gorgeous' waist, and wrenched sideways, chomping her completely in two.

Gorgeous separated in the middle. Bulldog staggered back, dragging her upper body after him. Her entrails trailed down over his legs like ropes.

He stood staring at her in horror, while, not quite dead yet, Gorgeous' lips moved.

"I love you, Bully," she mouthed in a stream of blood that flooded down her chin and neck. Then her eyes shut and her head lolled sideways, properly dead.

"Shit, I love you too, babe," Bulldog groaned, holding her close as more teeth from the mouths on the walls speared into them both from all sides.

Even dying, Bulldog didn't really understand the nightmare they'd walked into that was killing them. To him, what was happening had all the illogic of a dream. *Lucy Tang is a room shooting teeth at us? What the fuck is wrong with today? First Emil, then this shit?*

He never figured it out. An arm-long tooth hit him in the head.

Like it had been intentionally aimed, the tooth entered Bulldog's head at the deep dent that had rendered him almost-imbecile. It punctured completely through his head from left to right, ripping off his ear at its exit.

Dead, Bulldog crashed to the floor, impaling himself further on the teeth already embedded in his body. He was still holding on tight to Gorgeous' remains.

In a wave, the floor rippled under Bulldog, opening a huge mouth that engulfed them both.

The floor chewed a while, then it was silent.

***

After a few moments, the meat surface dripped off the room's walls and floor, leaving them a normal blue again. The meat streamed across the room to the sofa and reformed Lucy Tang.

Lucy Tang lay on the sofa gasping. Her slight body was wracked with the pain of transformation. In addition, her left forearm was broken, both bones shattered when Bulldog had shot her as the wall.

Lucy felt her arm. It would heal. She was satisfied that she'd revenged Emil's passing. Good lovers were hard to come by. Few men had ever satisfied her like the Bulgarian had.

She looked around the once-again empty and ordinary room.

It's no longer safe staying here, she thought. *Sookie Ling is a persistent cunt. The bitch will send more thugs over once Bulldog and Gorgeous don't return.*

Lucy knew Sookie would be incensed when she found out her niece was dead. She'd start a vendetta of her own. Sookie was old school Chinese—blood was always revenged.

Mingled with her anguish at losing Emil, Lucy felt some comfort. Sookie too, would now feel the hurt of losing a dearly loved one.

Lucy was leaving, but she wasn't running scared. No tail between the legs like a scared fox for her. She frowned, her slanted eyes thinning. *We'll definitely meet again, Sookie Ling. One day very soon, and then it will be a reckoning of blood and fire between us. Fire like a rain of dragons.*

Lucy Tang intended staking her own claim in Chinatown's drug trade. *No one, not you Sookie, not even the fucking triads, is standing in my way. This showdown has only firmed my resolve.*

But first . . . first Lucy needed to heal and, after that . . . she needed to build her own army to take on Chinatown's other armies.

Carefully nursing her broken arm, she got off the sofa and went into her bedroom.

***

Biting her lips from the pain, Lucy Tang dressed in a green silk cheongsam patterned with yellow flowers.

Then she fixed her broken arm up in a sling.

That done, she packed her essential possessions into a small suitcase. She filled a dino-leather handbag with her cosmetics, money and, most important, Sookie's filched dragonreich.

The reich was the financial muscle to kick-start Lucy's empire.

Finally, Lucy sat before her dressing mirror and did her makeup. It took a long time, but she persevered. Even when not performing onstage, Lucy Tang liked looking perfect, like a drag queen fuck machine. It didn't matter if a roomful of dinos were after her, she wasn't leaving here without looking absolutely flawless.

Watching the beautiful Lucy Tang girlishly apply her cosmetics, no one would believe that she'd just killed and eaten eight people.

Eight very dangerous people.

CHAPTER 69

Malone

Malone awoke. His head felt broken in two. He opened his eyes. He tried moving his hands but couldn't.

He realized he was trapped.

He was seated, shackled firmly in a chair. From the numbness all over his body, he determined that he'd been anaesthetized while out cold.

His eyes slowly focused on the individual sitting three feet across from him.

A nerdy, handsome face with cold blue eyes frowned back at him.

Malone groaned. "Frank?"

"Bout time you woke up," Frank spat, his expression manic with hatred. "It's time for payback."

"Look, Frank . . ."

Tears filled Frank's eyes. "You killed Rachel, you asshole. You murdered the only woman I ever loved."

Malone's face reflected his disgust. "She didn't love you. She was just using you for—"

Frank slapped him hard. "Don't you dare say that, you murderer! She loved me! She was just bad at expressing her emotions."

The blow cleared the remaining wooliness from Malone's head. He glared angrily at Frank.

Tears were streaming down Frank's cheeks. "But don't worry, Malone. Don't you worry at all. I'll avenge my love." He began laughing through his tears. "Oh, yes. I'll avenge Rachel. She'll be so proud."

Malone abandoned his anger. What was important now was getting free and out of here live. Frank was acting more insane by the moment.

Frank started giggling. "Thankfully, you're just in time to join me for dinner."

Dinner? Oh no, Malone thought.

Following Frank's pointing finger, Malone looked down.

He gaped in horror at his belly.

It was slit open. The remaining quarter of his liver was out of his body and encased in . . . *fuck* . . . in Rachel Fischer's sectional microwave.

The chair Malone sat in had a fold-over table flap like a toddler's. The machine rested on this.

Frank bent forward and clicked on the microwave.

He smiled nastily at Malone. "Any questions, shithead?"

Malone didn't reply. Spite was useless now, counterproductive even. Instead he looked around the cabin, seeking a means of escape.

The door was behind him. He twisted his head and confirmed that it was locked. *No point yelling to Captain Gumdrop for help then. The walrus might be dead anyway.* He winced as a thought struck him. *Damn, the walrus is likely in Frank's employ.*

He peered out through the cabin's single port. The late afternoon sky offered no solution to his dilemma.

***

Frank watched the shifting play of expressions on Malone's face. They pleased him immensely. Yes, let this prick suffer.

He wiped the tears from his eyes. Amused, he watched Malone's gaze float around the room.

"Forget it, asshole," he said. "There's no escape. You're dead meat."

As though affirming this truth, the microwave timer sounded then. Frank opened it up. The smell of roast Malone filled the room.

Frank's eyes glittered with psychotic pleasure. "Aah, medium rare; just how I like you."

He pulled his chair up to Malone—who seemed still lost in thought—and tucked a napkin into his collar.

***

"Hold on a minute," Malone said as Frank bent to start eating him.

Frank peered at him narrowly. "Can't this wait till later? I don't like cold food."

"Put the damn fork down and listen," Malone said. "Or I'll friggin' spew all over your damn dinner. It is my liver after all."

"What is it?" Frank said testily. "Make it snappy, will you?"

"I want to know where the president's liver is," Malone replied.

Frank scowled, then calmed.

He pointed. "The fucking liver is over there."

Malone followed Frank's finger. On a table by the wall on his left rested a sickly yellow lump flanked by several empty beer bottles. He flinched when it twitched.

"That thing? It looks like moldy loaf of corn bread."

Frank grinned.

"Don't look so confused, Malone. That *is* the president's liver. Did anyone tell you Jefferson Lincoln was an alcoholic? Oh, yes, he was. No doubt about it. His liver is so riddled through with sixteen sorts of cirrhosis that it's worse than inedible—tastes like leather."

Malone winced. "That fucking horror looks *alive*."

Frank shrugged. "It is. Some magic crap the Forks did to it. Even worse—it's still an alcoholic—it drank all that beer you see over there. I expect it to awaken shortly, when it'll be hungover again and begging me for change so it can buy itself some Jack Daniels."

"It can *talk?*"

Frank nodded. "More Fork bullshit magic."

Malone regarded the unhealthy looking lump of flesh with new respect.

Frank giggled. "Stealing it is my biggest regret ever. I'd have thrown it away—but then I'd have the kitchen gods after me for sure." He smiled. "So they can have it back—good riddance."

Then like a veil had dropped over Frank's face, his expression altered. His face once again became a mask of hatred.

"Payback, Malone," he growled. "That's what we're here for. You killed Rachel remember? The smartest woman I ever met in my life, and you came along and beheaded her. You psychotic asshole!"

"Look in the mirror."

Frank resumed crying instead. Tears streamed down his cheeks. "You . . . you . . . bastard, you murderer! How do you sleep at night?"

"How are the Forks going to get their treasure back if you kill me?" Malone asked.

Frank grinned through his tears. "Don't worry your corpse about that. I'll take it back and drop it off myself. Apologize nicely is all."

"What?"

Frank laughed. "Why not?"

"Okay," Malone said. "You can resume having dinner. Just cut the liver totally out of me first."

Frank shook his head. "No."

"Fuck you, Frank. Cut it out now or I'll start puking on it. Just looking at you fills me with sufficient nausea."

Frank glared at him. With a violent swipe of his knife, he severed Malone's liver from his body. "I'll really enjoy killing you, Malone. "I swore on Rachel's grave when I buried her that I'd avenge her murder, and I will. I wanted her machines to do it, for irony's sake. But you just kept getting away."

"I'm so sad I caused you two a national nutrient shortage," Malone said coldly. He nodded at the plate of liver. "Take that somewhere else. I'm not watching you."

Frank carried both plate and microwave oven a distance away and sat down again.

***

Malone thought fast. I've found the president's liver. I've also lost my own liver, and look about dying into the bargain. I can't even press my 'Lesbian Fist' button—whatever good that will do.

Malone had read somewhere that lesbians hated men. He doubted the depths of their abhorrence for men could ever match the emotional black hole Frank's existence registered inside him.

He wanted to kill this psycho son-of-a-bitch with every straining fiber of his violated being, but how?

"I can do it," a tough female voice said inside his head.

Startled, he looked over at Frank. Oblivious to Malone, Frank was just removing Malone's reheated liver from the microwave. He clearly hadn't heard anything.

"Just think your replies to me. He can't hear us," the voice said.

"Who are you?"

"Lesbian Fist—who else were you expecting?"

Malone decided that made sense. Just then Frank looked his way, mouth full of meat.

"Why don't you bleed anymore, Malone? And why'd you dye your arm red?"

"I donated my red blood cells to charity. Fuck off, Frank, haven't you heard it's bad manners to talk with your mouth full?"

Frank scowled. He swallowed, took another bite of Malone's liver and chewed it savagely.

"I want to fucking kill this bastard," Malone thought.

"Lesbian Fist is the person for you then. Don't worry about starting me up—I'm now thought-activated. So do I fist this asshole?"

Malone liked the poetic irony of the question. "Yes, fist the asshole."

***

Malone's blood arm thinned and flailed across the room to where Frank, his back to Malone, was eating. At the arm's far end, Malone's hand was so small now that he doubted it could harm Frank. It looked about the size of his penis glans.

"Size isn't important," Lesbian Fist said. "Technique is what matters."

Malone's blood arm had now landed behind Frank. Like a snake, it slithered beneath his chair, and coiled itself like a spring.

It struck.

There was the sound of plastic shattering as Lesbian Fist punctured up through the chair, then Frank's gasps of perplexed disbelief as the hand penetrated his pants and anus, and started fucking him.

"No!" he screamed. He tried to jump up only to find himself bound to the chair by three loops of Malone's arm that dropped over him like a trio of hangmen's nooses.

He turned to look at Malone, gaped when he saw it was Malone's red arm violating him.

Then he screamed as Lesbian Fist burst through the upper wall of his rectum, and pumping like a pneumatic drill, fucked a meat-ripping path up through his guts.

***

Malone's arm soaked up Frank's blood faster than it poured from him. The blood invigorated Malone like he was a vampire.

In a sudden burst of strength, he burst the shackles holding him in place.

He remained seated, savoring the horrified look on Frank's face as the man realized what was happening to him. *Stupid cannibal asshole.*

He enjoyed also the feeling of power transmitted to him through his arm.

***

Lesbian Fist burst its way up into Frank's chest, up into his neck, mashing his organs into slush with the force of its passage. Absorbing Frank's blood, it swelled inside him till it was the size of Malone's thigh.

Frank's torso bulged like he'd swallowed a barrel. He no longer screamed. Now he just twitched and jerked convulsively as if he were a human-shaped glove Lesbian Fist was wearing.

Then, in a final burst of force, Lesbian Fist exploded out through Frank's neck, blowing his head off his shoulders.

Malone grinned as it gave him the 'okay' sign. "Real tight asshole this, but I got the job done," it said.

He walked over and high-fived it.

They laughed. Malone waited while it shrunk its way out of Frank's corpse and back to normal size.

With a sizzle, the 'Lesbian Fist' button also disappeared off the back of Malone's hand.

CHAPTER 70

Malone

The president's liver *reeked* of booze with a capital 'R'.

Malone prodded it.

"My name's P-Liver and I'm an alcoholic," it said. "Every day and in every way, I'm getter better and better; the booze however keeps getting the better of me." It punctuated its comment with a loud burp.

"This isn't Alcoholic's Anonymous," Malone said. "My name's Malone. I'm here to take you back home."

"Damn, Malone, I'm so hungover. Can you spare some change? I need to buy a bottle."

"We're currently too far from any shops for you to bother."

Looking at P-Liver made Malone super-queasy. The organ was utterly disgusting; like a monster tumor. Its gall bladder looked like a turd. And the way it twitched . . .

Fear of the Forks, respect for their powers, renewed in him.

I just hope they're this good when it comes to fixing people, he thought, remembering Posh.

"I really need a drink."

Malone searched the room for alcohol. He found a bottle of whiskey and carried it over to P-Liver.

"My name is P-Liver, buddy, and don't you dare forget it. I need a damn drink, Malone. I'm hungover like a mule kicked me to death last night."

It punctuated its words with a yellow burp-bubble. The bubble popped. It stank worse than the breath of any wino Malone had ever encountered.

He held his breath. P-Liver was speaking to him through its truncated portal vein, so he upended the bottle of whiskey into that opening, screwing it well in. The bottle stood upright on P-liver's bulk like a glass tree it was growing.

340

Loud glugging sounds came from the liver.

Malone left it to its booze.

He examined his own liver. What remained of it was too cooked to be of any use to him ever again. *The Forks need to fix me too,* he thought, *else I'm so, so dead.*

In anger, he spat on Frank's corpse, then kicked his head across the room like it was a football. He realized he was being childish, and grimacing, stopped.

A loud burp came from P-Liver. Malone turned around in time to see the whiskey bottle pop off its 'mouth.' The bottle rolled off it, off the table, and onto the floor.

P-Liver started snoring. Malone walked back over to it.

He looked around for a bag to carry it in. He found none, then decided to use Frank's bloody shirt.

Before he could cross the cabin to undress the corpse, however, the boat gave a violent shudder.

Next—concurrent with a bloodcurdling scream from the deck—a semi-circular row of transparent columns pierced both the cabin ceiling and floor to Malone's right, dividing the room in two. On the other side of the see-thru pillars, Frank's corpse disappeared from view.

Malone stared at the almost interlocking see-through stalactites and stalagmites for a long instant before recognition struck him.

Teeth. *Dragon* Teeth.

At that moment, in another violent shaking of the boat, the dragon's upper and lower jaws came together and wrenched away, leaving Malone gaping out at the monster through the hole they left in their wake.

The distant outskirts of Boston registered on his mind for the briefest of instants before he turned and dashed outside, up the stairs to the deck.

He reached the deck before realizing he'd forgotten P-Liver. He rushed back down again, grabbed it off its table, and rushed back up again.

Captain Gumdrop was dead. The walrus's headless corpse lay on the airboat deck. It had clearly expired in the same closing of jaws that sliced away half the boat's larboard side.

The airboat now bobbed unstably in the breeze. The dragon hovered round it, dwarfing it by ten orders of magnitude. Its wings, see-thru as ghosts, glittered like lightning.

Below lay the north-east Atlantic.

The portion of the airboat the dragon had eaten had gotten stuck in its throat.

Or maybe, Malone reasoned, *seeing as the boat is made of solidified cum, this dragon is female and simply having a problem swallowing it.*

He understood the behemoth's plight. His last girlfriend before Posh had had a similar difficulty. She'd always brushed her teeth for ten minutes after he came in her mouth.

Realizing the dragon hadn't noticed him, Malone dropped flat to the deck and crawled over to the boat's edge. He peered down at the rippling water.

His dilemma was simple: how to get to Boston—its skyscrapers and beetles, the beckoning horizon—alive and in one piece.

***

The dragon finally got the chunks of spermwood down its throat. It returned its attention to the airboat.

It spread its jaws wide, ready to take another bite.

Malone realized his only chance of survival now was to dive into the Atlantic and swim. He did some quick calculation, figuring how to carry P-Liver into the operation.

Then there was no longer any time to think. The dragon's teeth came close enough for him to reach out and touch. They momentarily hovered over him like a kaleidoscope of misshapen transparent birds.

Malone stuffed the president's liver into his slit belly and jumped over the airboat's side.

The dragon devoured the entire airboat in one bite.

Malone plummeted like a rock under gravity. Below him the Atlantic looked like a blue mirror.

No way am I surviving this in one piece.

He flailed his right hand upward, instinctively trying to grip something no longer there.

His red arm began unraveling as if he'd com-manded it to.

The crimson blood-cord jerked taut. Malone stopped falling.

He looked up. His blood arm had wrapped itself around one of the dragon's talons.

Malone swung in space beneath the beast. He patiently waited for it to finish eating the airboat to decide what it intended doing next.

The boat disappeared into the dragon. The transparent monster beat the air a few times with its wings, then spun and headed toward Boston.

Dragons couldn't see through themselves.

Hidden below it, Malone heaved several sighs of relief.

CHAPTER 71

Malone/Lucy Tang

They were coming in from the north.

Makes sense, Malone thought. *That cock was the North Pole, wasn't it?*

Logan International Airport floated by under them.

Malone pondered the metal puddles below on the runways and outside the hangars and terminals. *Damn, those used to be aircraft—the acme of human aeronautical engineering now reduced to mirror smears on tarmac.*

During the short flight over the Atlantic, Malone had developed some control over his extended blood arm.

Now, spotting the dragon's siblings watching from shattered airport lounge windows, he reeled himself up closer to its underbody.

Several dinos also peered inquisitively from the windows of the air traffic controllers' tower.

On Malone's right, a flock of pterodactyls flew through a shimmering midair Otherworld Door and vanished from sight.

He peered through the OD after them. The world it revealed looked like the Martian surface—an endless red expanse of dunes lit by two orange oblongs like demon eyes.

Malone shuddered.

***

Past the airport and off the coast, the dragon dipped once towards the water, then rose again. It headed for South Boston, a nacreous mass streaking across the harbor with the wharfs and piers as distant shoreline indentations to its right.

Thunder lizards tramped through the new coastal marshes that had arrived alongside the dinosaurs, feeding on rushes the size of bamboos. Their graceful curved necks looked like question marks asking the New Past why it existed.

The thunder lizards' name—the literal meaning of 'brontosaurus'—was an irony. People called them that for lack of a better term. The forty-meter-long sauropods *weren't* apatosauruses, that was clear—their heads looked odd and they were *much* larger, but what the fuck were they? The only viable reference was to a creature once proven not to exist.

Malone lengthened his blood arm till he was skiing along the ocean surface. His heels made a furrow of spray behind him.

The dragon flew between two thunder lizards. Malone stared at the humongous twin expanses of brown dino body, muscle and bone as solid as a house wall.

The Boston City Council had begun harvesting some of the smaller dinos for their meat, but no one was yet ready to tackle the thunder lizards. Not because of their size, but because of the difficulty butchering the kill would entail. Malone had heard of a project to fit old whalers with repulsors to keep the dragons at bay during thunder lizard hunts. So far, apparently, no vessels were yet ready.

The dragon swooped in toward the Boston Fish Pier.

"Time to leave," Malone said aloud. "I get off here."

He unraveled his arm and dropped into an empty patch of water to the left of the platform.

He remained submerged for a while, till the dragon was gone. Then he swam the short distance to shore, and tramped up the beach amidst thatches of bamboo rushes.

Iridescent reptiles like overgrown chameleons peered at him from their perches on the oversized rushes, wondering if he was good to eat.

A large transparent catfish swished between his legs.

Malone quickened his pace. He'd not so far heard of transparent gators, but didn't want to find out firsthand if they existed.

***

The buildings to the right of the Fish Pier were all collapsed, totally blocking off Seaport Boulevard.

Malone swore and trudged inward.

Congress Street—which also led west across the Fort Point Channel—was also obstructed, this time by a massive ancient vehicle pileup. The heap of melted cars and trucks—several with burnt skeletons inside them—formed an insurmountable barrier to any westward progress.

He shrugged, walked straight ahead, down D Street, crossing an acreage of concrete rubble towards Summer Street.

This is the second time I'm headed for the city with my stomach ripped open, he thought grimly.

The anesthetic Frank had pumped him full of was wearing off now, and pain was returning to his body.

Damn, he remembered. *I've no fucking liver anymore.*

On cue, P-Liver burped inside him.

Malone ignored the organ. He kept his focus on the piles of charred rubble everywhere that once been South Boston.

My quest is over; no way I'm getting eaten by a fucking dinosaur at this stage.

***

At the D Street/Summer Street intersection, Malone paused and looked around for a working car. Most lining the road were wrecks. The few that weren't had deflated tires.

He grimaced. *I can't believe I'm gonna have to walk all the way.*

Then he saw the three repulsor-studded cars parked outside the Barnes Building. A red Corvette, a Lexus and a pink Porsche GT.

Malone recognized the Porsche as Sookie's.

He heaved a massive sigh of relief and stumbled towards it.

Then the Barnes Building front door opened, and Lucy Tang walked out pulling a white suitcase after her, her beautiful face set grim as death.

Malone knew Lucy as one of Sookie's girls.

He waved to her. "Hi Lucy, is Sookie here?"

Lucy noticed Malone. "Hi, baby," she said coquettishly. Then she winced in pain. Malone now noticed that her left arm was bloody and in a sling.

She shook her head. "No, Sookie ain't here, baby." She let go of her suitcase and reached into her purse with her good hand.

Malone grimaced on seeing her pull out a gun and point it at him.

Lucy smiled coldly, her flirtatiousness all gone. "I no longer work for Sookie Ling."

Malone nodded back. "Okay. But why are you pointing your gun at me? I don't work for her either."

"You're a friend of hers, she might have sent you to kill me."

Malone winced. "Lucy, your arm looks broken, but you aren't blind, are you?" He indicated his wet clothes, pointed to the hole in his belly. "Do I look like I'm out hunting anyone?"

She frowned. "I don't know who to trust at the moment, Malone. Best to be safe." Her brown eyes appraised him. "You're not Chinese—have no dragon protection, so how did you get out here? You must have come along with Gorgeous and Bulldog."

Oops, Malone thought. *This is bad. Where are Gorgeous and Bulldog?*

Outwardly, he forced a smile. "Lucy, you wouldn't believe me if I told you where I've been today, trust me."

"I'm sorry, Malone," the beautiful transvestite replied. "I can't trust anyone at the moment. I'm in too much danger."

Malone nodded. "Okay, that's fine. Just don't get trigger-happy. I'm not here after you. I'm looking to go home, that's all."

Malone looked up at a familiar noise.

A dragon was swooping down low over Summer Street toward them.

The monstrous firebreather studied the pair—who from overhead looked like pawns on a charred chessboard—for a moment, then lost interest in them. It floated away in a clash of iridescent wings.

Malone repressed an instinctive shudder.

He looked back at Lucy Tang.

She gestured to the Porsche with her gun. "Get in. You're driving."

Malone dallied.

"I'll shoot you if you don't comply."

"Lucy, I'm fucking injured."

A beautiful replying smile. "So am I. Must be the day for it. Get in, Malone."

Already on the driver's side, Malone opened the door and got into the Porsche. He dully noted that the key was in the ignition.

Lucy Tang lugged her stuff onto the car's back seat, then climbed in beside Malone.

He started the car. "Where are we headed?" he asked. *Wow,* he thought momentarily, *she looks so perfectly female, its hard to believe she's a guy.*

Lucy grimaced as a stab of pain sheared through her arm. "Where are *you* headed, Malone?"

"North End. I've a delivery to make."

"Not my way. Drop me off on South Street. I need to get my arm fixed."

Malone nodded. He spun the Porsche around and headed for Summer Street Bridge.

***

Lucy had Malone park the Porsche in front of an old apartment building.

Her arm was hurting her so bad now that he helped her carry her suitcase up the steps to the front door.

Lucy rang the buzzer. The door was opened by an elderly Chinese woman.

Lucy turned to Malone. "You can keep Sookie's car—for me, it's an instant giveaway."

She frowned. "It's pointless telling her you dropped me off here. I'll be gone before anyone arrives." She indicated the old woman, who'd retreated into the house, laden with Lucy's baggage. "You'll only get old Jiang Quing here into trouble."

Malone nodded. "I wasn't thinking of telling Sookie anything. I'll just drop off her car for her, say I found it down in South Boston."

Lucy turned to follow the old woman into the house.

"Hold on a minute," Malone said.

She turned back. "Yes?"

"What happened to Bulldog and Gorgeous? I'm assuming *they* drove Sookie's car over to your place."

Lucy Tang smiled coldly. "They're both dead, Malone. A room ate them. You can tell Sookie that for me. Tell her also that I'll be seeing her again . . . soon."

She entered the house. Malone walked back to Sookie's Porsche.

He fired it up, turned it around, headed north.

***

While driving, Malone did some thinking. Now his quest was over, he pondered how it had been coordinated, worked from riddle to riddle.

He suspected that Frank—bloodthirsty for revenge—had coerced the Forks into setting up his obstacle course, under threat of destroying Jefferson Lincoln's liver if they refused. That would also explain how the blasted white robots had kept turning up everywhere he did like they were adhering to a schedule.

He also suspected that the Forks had tried to give him an edge by sending Glass Horse to help him.

He figured Sara would be able to confirm/fault his hypothesis.

CHAPTER 72

Malone, Sara, Posh

The Fischer Mansion was the same as Malone remembered it: Rich HQ.

Malone agreed that Sara's repulsor-studded home was fortuitously situated: Skyscraper beetles didn't breed up in North End.

He scowled, *Maybe the fucking bugs are allergic to the rich.*

Inside him P-Liver was grumbling again.

"Shut up, you're almost home."

"I need a drink."

Malone ignored it. He parked the car some distance from the mansion house and stared wide-eyed at its new addition—four raptors chained by its front entrance, two on each side.

Malone shook his head at the audacity of the gesture.

Security dinosaurs? You've got to be shitting me!

The quartet of raptors were restrained by thick metal collars around their necks and shackles on their rear legs. Thirty foot chains ran from each of these into six holes on either side of the entranceway.

The dinos eyed Malone hungrily. He smiled, waved nicely at them. In response they began growling like tigers.

He pressed the car horn and kept it pressed.

"Stop making that damn racket," Jefferson Lincoln's liver grumbled inside him. "My hangover's bad enough as it is—I don't need your stingy teetotal ass aggravating it. I need a really stiff scotch to chase it away now. Hey, economize on the ice, bartender, you son-of-a-bitch."

In response, Malone reached inside his belly and pulled P-Liver out. He hung it out of the car window and pointed to the raptors, which had begun salivating on sighting it.

"You don't fucking shut up and I'll toss you to those dinos. Your owner was a crap president, you're a crap liver—shut your yap!"

He dropped it on the passenger seat. P-Liver burped in horror and quit moaning.

They waited.

Shortly after, the front door opened, concurrent with the chains restraining the raptors being winched into the wall.

The dinos growled their frustration as they were pulled away from the mansion entrance.

Sara Fischer appeared in the doorway. She smiled granny-sexily at Malone and waved him over.

Malone waited till her dinosaur sentries were each fifteen feet from her front door before getting out of the car and walking over to her, P-Liver tucked beneath his arm like a sheaf of office work he was in a hurry to dispose of.

***

Sara hugged Malone.

"I'm delighted you made it back alive," she said, rubbing her cheek against his.

Then she pushed him away and looked him over—his damp clothes, his harried expression. She winced at the rip in his belly. "Frank again?"

He nodded. "Bastard ate the rest of my liver. He won't be eating anyone else's though."

Sara's eyes widened. "You killed him?"

He nodded. "He won't be missed."

"And Rachel's head? Were you able to . . ." The words failed her.

Malone shook his head. "Frank says he buried her—I believe him." He smiled sadly. "The son-of-a-bitch really did love her, Sara. Too bad he was such a shithead. He'd have made a fantastic son-in-law."

He looked away as tears welled in Sara's eyes.

Sara dried her eyes. She pointed to P-Liver. "It looks worse than last time I saw it."

Malone wrinkled his nose in disgust. "It drinks like a fish."

"I need some booze," P-Liver said. "If I don't get it, I'm going to—"

Sara gaped at the talking organ.

"I told you to fucking shut up," Malone growled. "Those raptors are still hungry."

P-Liver shut up.

Sara overcame her surprise. She laughed. "Now there's a way to keep it quiet."

She indicated the raptors, all of which were straining at their chains in an effort to reach Malone and herself.

"How'd you like my new security staff?"

"I don't. Is it a new rich trend?"

Sara giggled. Nah. It's just to keep away other creeps like that Frank. I've got them on all the other doors as well."

Malone nodded. "Is Posh okay?" His expression turned concerned. "She's here, right?"

Sara nodded back. "Yes, she is."

An odd expression came over her face. "She's fine, but there's a slight . . ." She smiled. "Best you see for yourself."

Bemused, Malone followed Sara inside.

***

Lord Tav and Lady Yaz were in the living room.

"He's back," Sara announced.

Both Forks rotated to face them.

"Thank you, Malone," they said in unispeak, floating P-Liver out of his hands. "We're greatly in your debt."

They levitated the grumbling organ over a center table, then caused a tray to appear beneath it.

"I need a fucking dri—"

A bottle of brandy appeared in P-liver's vein-mouth, stoppering it. The sound of loud glugging filled the room.

"Where's Posh," Malone asked impatiently. Sara's choice of words, her odd reticence to say more than 'there's a slight . . .' had him worried.

"Ah, yes," Lord Tav said. "She's upstairs. We'll fetch her for you."

Posh materialized in the doorway.

"Baby!" she shrieked in delight on sighting Malone. "You're back!"

Damn, I've been screwed. Malone gaped in shock-horror as Posh flew across the room at him.

Posh was still a dragon. White Porcelain painted with roses; clearly strung out on dragonreich like . . .

But then he saw the incongruity: Posh on reich never recognized him; all she had on her mind then was roasting and eating him.

This Posh-dragon however was *smiling* at him. She reached him, landed, and massive wings fluttering behind her, gripped him like she intended breaking him in half. She slobbered him with kisses, occasionally pulling back and regarding Malone with love-filled reptilian eyes.

He held her, not understanding. Her body was cold kitchen chinaware. She *was* Posh; dragon transformed, only *different*.

He turned to Lord Tav. "I asked you to *cure* her ass, not mess her up worse. What went wrong?"

The Fork vibrated a tuning fork laugh. "Nothing, she *is* cured. She's no longer addicted to dragonreich."

"We asked her what she'd like to be," Lady Yaz added. "She said she wanted to be a porcelain dragon. So we got her high on dragonreich, and cured her addiction while she was in that form."

Malone grimaced. *Oh yes, that sounds like Posh all right.* "Can she change back?"

"No, she's fixed like this for good."

Posh stopped snuggling up to him for a moment. She stepped back. "It's okay, baby, I'm still your woman." She lifted her left leg Karate style, so its shin touched her forehead. Malone saw what she meant: at the split of her thighs, she had a very pretty vagina. Flesh and blood and with a cute clitoris. Moist-looking too.

She dropped her leg, snuggled in close again. "We can make love all day long. I'm so happy."

Malone shrugged mentally. At least she *was* cured, wouldn't go cannibal behind his back anymore. Also, this was a million times better than his being an eternally double-fucked worman in Traven.

He turned back to the pair of shimmering forks. He pointed to the room's center table, to P-Liver, who'd now half-drained the brandy bottle upended in its 'mouth.'

"That reminds me. You owe me one liver. I'd take that one, but it's wino crap, can't even think except its drunk—I doubt it remembers how to process food anymore. What the hell do you need it for anyway?"

The Forks hovered over to the middle of the room. "Come and sit down," they called.

Malone and Posh did so.

"Among us Forks," Lord Tav said. "P-Liver is the symbol of authority. It belonged to the last human ruler, ergo, it symbolizes the continuation of his rulership."

"It's just a drunk organ," Malone said. "It doesn't mean shi—"

"Actuality doesn't matter anymore in this world we've created. What does is symbolism, interpretation, perception. We, ferramenta sapiens, don't think like you humans do.

"All you need understand is this: as long as the president's liver is here, we're King and Queen of the world."

Malone nodded. "Okay, but you soon won't have anything left to rule if the dragons keep roasting and eating everyone."

He remembered then the dragon supervisor Forks who'd helped him. "Hey, you've always known that they come from Traven, haven't you?—I mean the dragons."

Both Forks laughed; the room lighting shimmered off their prongs.

They kept laughing. Sara nodded to Malone. "They do. They also *like* the current state of the world. Are very pleased with it, in fact."

The cutlery king and queen's laughter melted into an all-suffusing melody, a visible sepia liquidity that dripped down the room's curtains, a sheet of molten gold that flowed over the room's surfaces.

Both Forks now altered their positions. Prongs interlocking with hers, Lord Tav lay atop Lady Yaz on a sofa.

His slid his body over hers, his prongs through hers.

"They're having sex," Sara whispered lasciviously to Malone. "The urge comes on them occasionally, and is irresistible. We're expected to politely not notice, that's all."

Malone smiled tightly.

The humming in the room grew louder and louder. Lady Yaz's breasts now glowed like monster rubies in the light.

"I hear major orgasm coming on," Sara Fischer said. She slipped a hand between her thighs, began rubbing herself.

Malone looked from the copulating Forks to the masturbating sexagenarian. "What's this about the Forks liking the current state of everything?"

Sara's reply was anecstatic gasp, then a crescendo of moans as she reached orgasm, dipping wet fingers deep into her splayed sex to milk her sensations to the fullest.

Posh—looking like a decaying photograph in the mahogany light—whispered into Malone's right ear. "The Forks are responsible for the New Past: the dragons and dinos, Traven, the trangels, the wormen, the ODs . . . *everything*."

"But *why*?"

Posh sighed. "They say humanity's *forked* everybody long enough, and now it's their time to *fork* us in return."

Malone nodded. It was as good/stupid an explanation as any he'd yet heard. The horrible revelation didn't shock him. He'd been through too much insanity—had become inured to further oddity.

He looked at his blood arm, then at the hole in his belly, then at the fucking Forks. "And my new liver?"

On the table P-Liver burped its empty bottle off itself. The bottle crashed and shattered on the floor. P-Liver began snoring.

"My liver," Malone repeated, louder.

"Lady Yaz gasped beneath Lord Tav. "Oh, damn you, human!"

"I'm not being a pain in the butt."

"You are, you are!"

Malone caught Sara's warning glance. He leaned in close to her, and whispered. "Remember we're supposed to *not notice* them having sex? That's all I'm doing—not noticing."

"We're having a young girl for dinner tonight," Lord Tav said in a tiger-striped voice. "You can have *her* liver as a replacement for yours."

Sara Fischer saw the look of disgust on Malone's face. "They didn't kill her. She was a terrorist—anti-wealth fundamentalist fanatic—blew herself up in an attempt to destroy my house."

"We however sensed her presence in time and controlled the blast so it only destroyed her head," Lord Tav added. "Her body's still . . ." the Fork gasped from the effort of maintaining a conversation while his sensory prongs were violently atingle.

"Okay," Malone said. "I'll take it. I just hope she wasn't a drunk like P—"

"Oh fucking shut up, Malone!!!" Lady Yaz shrieked, dropping all pretense of unnoticed lady-Fork modesty. "I'm trying to fucking cum here!"

She gasped louder, much louder, as did her partner. Her metal breasts lit up like light bulbs.

The room's sepia tint blew out into a shit-colored crescendo, an explosion in an extinct photographer's darkroom.

For a brief moment, both interlocked Forks were illuminated transparencies—odd-shaped bones and organs visible within them—then they were normal superhuman creatures again.

Beside them, Jefferson Lincoln's liver burped an alcoholic bubble.

The End

ABOUT THE AUTHOR

Wol-vriey is Nigerian, and quite tall.

He currently resides in a state of uneasy stalemate with his threatening-to-thin-beyond-redemption hair, and believes there actually are things that go bump in the night.

Wol-vriey recycles the ridiculous into reasonable reality for the reader.

His WEIRRRD philosophy?

WEIRRRD = Warp/Write Everything into Real-istic Ridiculous Readable Distorted Dream Dimension Descriptions.

Wol-vriey blogs at:

http://oddityfarm.wordpress.com

OTHER GREAT TITLES FROM

Burning Bulb
PUBLISHING

WWW.BURNINGBULBPUBLISHING.COM

WOL-VRIEY
BIZARRO AND TRANSGRESSIVE FICTION

BOSTON POSH (BUD MALONE #1)

In 2028 AD, the USA is a nation ravaged by hungry dragons and dinosaurs. In Boston, Massachusetts, private eye Bud Malone is hired to rescue a kidnapped heiress. But nothing is as it seems.

Malone works to unravel a tangled web involving Boston Chinatown, a 200-year-old woman with a 9-year-old body, white robots, a human-liver-eating psychopath, a golem, a porcelain dragon, and a snake goddess with a crush on him. There's also a woman obsessed with chicken sex. Then Malone meets Posh Lane, a gorgeous call girl who's desperate to quit her pimp.

Romantic sparks ignite between Posh and Malone, but Posh's past suddenly catches up with her in a BIG way. To save Posh, Malone agrees to run a quest for Earth's new rulers, the Forks. But, Malone has no idea that agreeing to the Fork's odd request will send him on the weirdest trip he's ever been on in his life.

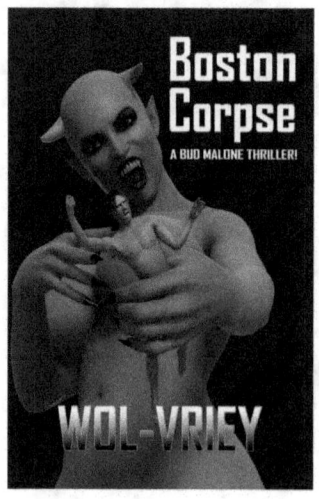

BOSTON CORPSE (BUD MALONE #2)

MAGIC CAN BE MURDER! - Drag queen Lucy Tang is back in Boston, and is hell-bent on settling her vindetta against casino owner Sookie Ling. And suddenly, Bud Malone, PI, has the case of his life to resolve.

When Boston's robot police force are baffled by a mind transfer case, they come to Malone for help. The one person who can likely help Malone out here is the witch Soledad Bathory. But Soledad seems to know a lot more than she's telling him. It's a case not made easier when Malone meets Soledad's beautiful cousin, Josephine 'Slave' Bailey. Slave has her own plans for Malone, most of which involve teaching him BDSM and making him her new Master.

Oh, and Rick Rogers owes Sookie Ling a whole lot of money, a gambling debt that's going to be literally Hell to pay!

BOSTON CORPSE - Not your average detective novel!

Burning Bulb
PUBLISHING

WOL-VRIEY
BIZARRO AND TRANSGRESSIVE FICTION

VAGINA MUNDI

Rachel Risk is a professional thief with super-strong hair that can stretch like tentacles to manipulate objects. Ashley Status has both a digitally augmented brain, and 'muscle-purses' in her arms and legs in which she stores inflatable objects—cars, guns, rocket launchers, etc.

When Raye is framed as the fall girl in a jewel robbery, the pair flee Chicago's vengeful robot gangsters and take refuge in the Hotel Bizarre, where the gorgeous 'vagina singer,' Femina, is performing for a week.

But the Hotel Bizarre is even stranger than its name suggests, and very soon Raye and Ash are involved in an deadly adventure, a struggle for survival the likes of which they'd never imagined possible—with loads of deviant sex, drugs, music, and violence at every turn. And just what is the old woman in the skin desert really doing with all those cats glued to her walls?

VAGINA MUNDI—a Bizarro Hymn in praise of WOMAN!

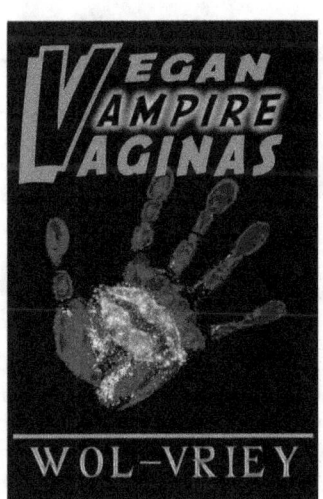

VEGAN VAMPIRE VAGINAS

The biggest bank heist in US history. And Tom Palmer can't remember pulling it off. And no, this isn't your standard case of amnesia. After a one-night-stand gone horribly wrong, Boston salesman Tom Palmer wakes up with a vagina implanted in his left hand. Then his day gets worse.

Tom is transported across space-time to a nightmare version of Boston, one where the Bizarro virus has transformed half the population into cannibals. Worst of all, Tom discovers that in this new Boston, he's the infamous gangster Pussypalm, wanted for robbing the Federal Reserve Bank of Boston a year ago. He also learns that the vagina in his hand is prophetic, i.e. it talks . . . after sex.

With 130 people left dead during his bank heist and six billion dollars missing, Tom knows he's living on borrowed time. It is in his best interests not to remember anything. Because once he does . . .

Burning Bulb
PUBLISHING

WOL-VRIEY
BIZARRO AND TRANSGRESSIVE FICTION

VEGAN ZOMBIE APOCALYPSE

In the post-apocalypse worlderness, zombies rule the earth. They're allergic to meat, and brains literally make them explode. Zombies now eat blood potatoes, parasitic tubers grown in the flesh of humancows corralled in maximum security farms. Two fugitives meet in the ancient ruins of Texas. The first is Soil 15-f, a womancow who's escaped her farm a week before she's due to be killed and her blood potato crop harvested. The second fugitive is Able Kane, former head necros food technician, now sentenced to death for heresy. But Soil is no ordinary humancow.

Unknown to herself, she's the vegan zombie agricultural revolution, and the zombies desperately want her back. And the necros equally desperately want Able Kane dead. He's fled with a forbidden discovery which will reshape the world for the worse if used. And Able is just hardheaded/misguided enough to use it.

MELANIE NEMESIS CATCHPOLE

In Springfield, Massachusetts, Melanie Catchpole is hired to fetch back a magic teddy bear worth millions of dollars from a warehouse across town. Problem is, the warehouse is down in Springfield's O-Zone-that totally weird sector of the city where Bizarro fell to Earth. The 'O' is a fairytale land, a place where dreams and nightmares literally live and breathe.

Worse still, the gingers—mutant cannibals—prowl the O. The gingers have already eaten everyone else Melanie's employers sent to get back the magic teddy bear.

Accompanied by the handsome but ruthless Doug Fisher (who she finds sexy but doesn't dare entrust her heart to), Melanie enters the O-Zone. Melanie and Doug are instantly caught up in an adventure they'd never have believed credible even if written as fiction . . . and Melanie's used to experiencing the very weird as the norm.

And now, additionally, there's a mystery to unravel: What does the dark, freezing-cold being called The Fixer want with Mary, the barkeep's daughter?

Burning Bulb
PUBLISHING

WOL-VRIEY
BIZARRO AND TRANSGRESSIVE FICTION

BIG TROUBLE IN LITTLE ASS

From Bizarro master storyteller Wol-vriey comes a truly weird western tale that will leave you awe-struck and on the edge of your seat...

In the town named Little Ass, tight-assed prostitute Rosa overhears a gunslinger's plans to assassinate rancher Edison Bennett. Once the badass Bennett learns of the plot, he ensures there'll be hell to pay for any attempt on his life!

Yes, it's going to take all of gunslinger Jude's shooting prowess, his eclectic collection of strange firearms, a trusty horse that requires an owners' manual, and the help of the lovely and invigorating Nell (who's EXTREMELY odd when the going gets weird), to survive the Bizarro hell that Edison Bennett unleashes in order to hold onto the land that he'd stolen from Madam Zizi.

BIZARRO 101 (A BASIC PRIMER)

Welcome to the strange place:

A collection of 37 flash fiction stories designed to introduce one to the Bizarro/New Weird Genre.

Weird, dreamy, nightmarish, absurd, sad, surreal, humorous . . . this collection of tales is all this and more.

***

"This primer is the very essence of any and all styles and types of Bizarro writing. Wol-vriey collects, distills, and bottles up these 37 tiny stories for your sensory enjoyment. This is an absolute must-read for anyone new to the genre, because it demonstrates the scope of what Bizarro is, and what it can be."
　　　　　　　　　　　—Teresa Pollack, Bizarro commentator and blogger

Burning Bulb
PUBLISHING

ANTHOLOGIES
BIZARRO AND TRANSGRESSIVE FICTION

THE BIG BOOK OF BIZARRO

The Big Book of Bizarro brings together the peculiar prose of an international cast of the most grotesquely-gonzo, genre-grinding modern writers who ever put pen to paper (or mouse to pad), including:

NIGHT OF THE LIVING DEAD horror writers John Russo & George Kosana; HUSTLER MAGAZINE erotica contributors Eva Hore, Andrée Lachapelle, & J. Troy Seate and established Bizarro genre authors D. Harlan Wilson, William Pauley III, Wol-vriey, Laird Long, Richard Godwin and so many more!

From Alien abductions to Zombie sex, The Big Book of Bizarro contains OVER FIFTY STORIES of the most outrélandish transgressive fiction that you'll ever lay your capricious and curious hands upon!

WARNING: This book may be one of the most controversial and dangerous books you'll ever read.

WESTWARD HOES

Nine outlaw writers rode into town from obscurity to pen nine tantalizing tales of horror and fantasy, and leaving once they branded their own personal marks on the weird western genre and became living legends of the American Frontier experience.

Like drunken Indian scouts, the writers fervidly tracked down and captured the Western genre, tore off its fashionable veneer and ravished its exposed essence.

So belly up to the bar with your favorite soiled dove and enjoy perusing these thrilling tales of Old West debauchery, danger and desire; compiled by the publisher of The Big Book of Bizarro and featuring the bizarro novella *Big Trouble in Little Ass* by Wol-vriey.

Burning Bulb
PUBLISHING

ANTHOLOGIES
BIZARRO AND TRANSGRESSIVE FICTION

THE BIG BOOK OF BIZARRO SPECIAL KINDLE EDITIONS

OTHER AWESOME COLLECTIONS

Burning Bulb
PUBLISHING

GARY LEE VINCENT'S
DARKENED
THE WEST VIRGINIA VAMPIRE SERIES

DARKENED HILLS

When evil descends on a small West Virginia town, who will survive?

Jonathan did not start out his life to become a rambler, it just worked out that way. William was a troubled youth with something to hide. Both were from Melas, a small town tucked away in the West Virginia hills... a town where disappearances are happening more and more frequently.

After the suicide of a wanted serial killer, the townsfolk thought the nightmare was over. But when a centuries-old vampire is discovered they find out the hard way it's just getting started. Dark secrets can only stay hidden for so long and when the devil comes to collect, there will be hell to pay. Can Jonathan and William find a way to stop the vampire before it's too late? Find out in *Darkened Hills!*

DARKENED HOLLOWS

In the heart-stopping sequel to the award-winning *Darkened Hills*, Jonathan and William must return to West Virginia to face possible criminal charges stemming from their last visit to the damned town of Melas, where both had narrowly escaped the clutches of a vampire seethe.

And as livestock start mysteriously getting murdered with all of their blood drained, worried farmers are searching for answers - leaving the local Sheriff and his deputy racing against time to learn the cause before a more violent crime is committed.

Burning Bulb
PUBLISHING

WWW.DARKENEDHILLS.COM

GARY LEE VINCENT'S
DARKENED
THE WEST VIRGINIA VAMPIRE SERIES

DARKENED WATERS

When the world goes to hell, the chosen must arise!

As Talman Cane orchestrates a flood of epic proportions in this third installment of the *Darkened* series the towns of Melas and Tarklin are caught completely off guard by the deluge. Hell-bent on finishing what they started, the evil brothers return to the lunatic asylum to take care of the witnesses and add to the ever-growing army of the undead.

Aided by Lucifer himself and the insane vampire demon Legion, the stage is set to channel all of the forces of hell to come forth. In an all-out race to survive, Jonathan, William, and Amanda soon discover they are up against impossible odds as Lucifer opens the Gateway to Hell, ushering in the zombie apocalypse and the End Times.

DARKENED SOULS

Melas and the Madison House are about to be rebuilt.
True evil is about to be reborne!

Young ex-priest and vampire-killer William is drawn back to the West Virginian town that almost killed him, where his vampire arch-enemy Victor Rothenstein still stalks the earth.

The town of Melas lies destroyed after the battle of the End of Days. But why is wealthy Jackie Nixon so eager to rebuild it using the bone dust of murdered souls?

Terrible evil has visited before, but the Gateway to Hell is about to be reopened in a horrific climax. And this time – it's personal.

WWW.DARKENEDHILLS.COM

Burning Bulb
PUBLISHING

RISE OF THE DEAD

AN EARTH-SHATTERING ANTHOLOGY OF ZOMBIE TERROR

Featuring Stories By:

John A. Russo   Tyson Blue   E.L. Stice   Nelson W. Pyles
Andy Rausch   Stephen Spignesi   R.D. Riley   Zakary McGaha
David J. Fairhead   Gary Lee Vincent   David C. Hayes   Rachel Montgomery
Paul Victor Wargelin   David F. Walker   William Vitka
Rich Bottles Jr.   Douglas Brode

RISE OF THE DEAD - a collection of seventeen
tales of unspeakable zombie terror. Featuring a foreword and
short story by John A. Russo!

www.TheJohnRusso.com

Burning Bulb
PUBLISHING

THE BOOBY HATCH

With NIGHT OF THE LIVING DEAD, John Russo helped blaze a path in the horror genre that has never been equalled. In this hillarious erotic novel, he blazes a path through the wild, zany Sex Revolution of the 1970s.

Sweet, innocent Cherry Jankowski works for Joyful Novelties, where she tests sex toys ranging from the ridiculous to the sublime. But she can't find love or peace of mind and her efforts are hampered by a Peeping Tom, an exhibitionist, a cross-dressing boyfriend, a quack psychiatrist, and even her own product-testing partner, Marcello Fettucini, who can't get it up anymore and is scared of losing his job!

www.TheJohnRusso.com

WEST VIRGINIA-THEMED HUMORROROTICA

BY RICH BOTTLES JR.

HELLHOLE WEST VIRGINIA

From the heights of Mothman's perch high atop the Silver Bridge in Point Pleasant to the depths of Hellhole Cavern in Pendleton County, evil lurks within the shadows as the sun sets upon the haunted hills and hollows of West Virginia.

Bizarro author Rich Bottles Jr. blows the coffin lid off horror genre clichés with this tour de force cast of Eco-friendly vampires, beach-yearning zombies and sex-starved she-devils.

LUMBERJACKED

If you are easily offended or do not possess a truly depraved sense of humor, this story may not be the light summer reading fare you desire. As for the four feisty female freshmen stranded on top of West Virginia's third highest mountain, they have no choice but to experience the sick, twisted debauchery and perverted mayhem described deep inside the tight unbroken bindings of this horrific missive.

Lumberjacked takes the reader to a nightmarish world where character development and aesthetic integrity are prematurely cut short by the swinging axes of maniacal lumberjacks, who are hell bent on death and destruction in the remote forests of Appalachia. And at the climax, when paranoia crosses over to the paranormal, Lumberjacked makes Deliverance look like a family raft trip down the Lower Gauley.

THE MANACLED

What happens when twin brothers lease out the former West Virginia State Penitentiary with the false purpose of filming a documentary on supernatural phenomena, but their true intention is to make a pornographic movie?

Chaos ensues as the disturbed spirits of murdered convicts, along with the reanimated dead from the neighboring Indian Burial Mound, take their vengeance on the unwary and undressed trespassers.

Zombies, ghosts, mobsters and porn collide in this bizarro tale from horror author Rich Bottles Jr.

Burning Bulb
PUBLISHING

NIGHT OF THE LIVING DEAD

Why does **Night of the Living Dead** hit with such chilling impact?
Is it because everyday people in a commonplace house are suddenly the
victims of a monstrous invasion? Or is it because the ghouls who surround
the house with grasping claws were once ordinary people, too?

Decide for yourself as you read, and the horror grips you. All the
cannibalism, suspense and frenzy of the smash-hit move are here in the
novel.

www.TheJohnRusso.com

Burning Bulb
PUBLISHING

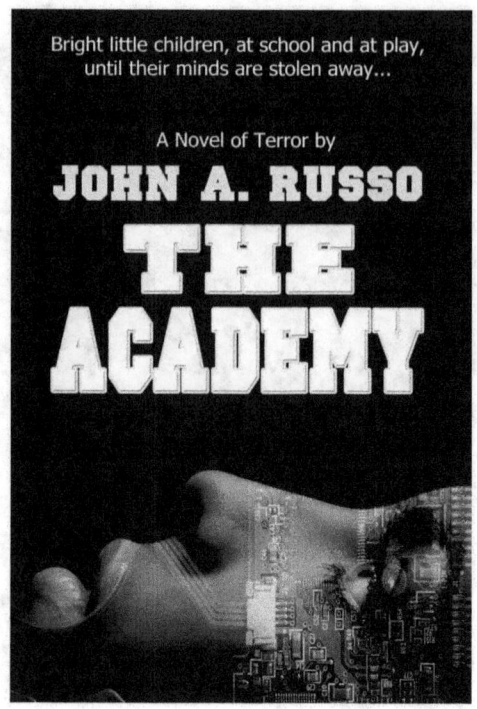

Bright little children, at school and at play,
until their minds are stolen away...

A Novel of Terror by

JOHN A. RUSSO
THE ACADEMY

THE ACADEMY

The Academy. It's every parent's dream, turning their little darlings into geniuses, superachievers, perfect little children.

And if there's a problem, the Academy fixes that too. It's a simple operation. Just a little device. Then a teeny pink scar on a tender little skull . . .

One boy knows the secret. Now he wants his mind back. But it's much, much too late. Too late for anything but the ugly feelings. The bad feelings. The messy sexy feelings. The knife-cold hatred, the murderous rage, for total, screaming, blood-drenching revenge . . .

www.TheJohnRusso.com

Burning Bulb
PUBLISHING

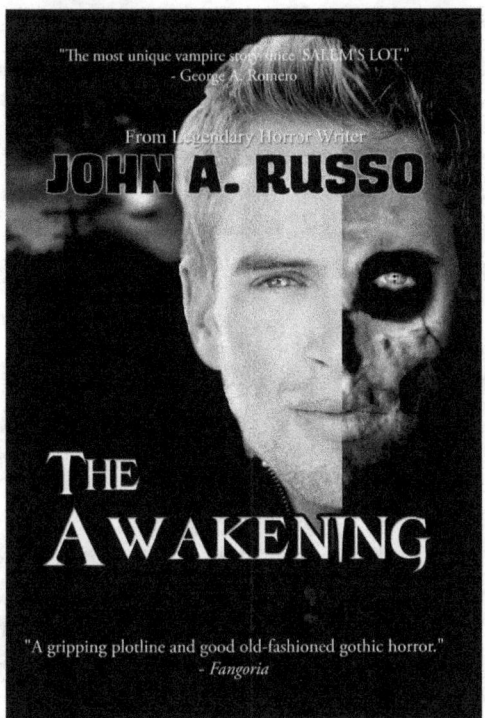

THE AWAKENING

For two hundred years, he has rested. Now he rises. Now he will be satisfied. Nothing can stop him. No one can resist him.

Benjamin Latham is young and handsome, his eighteenth-century mind wakened to a bizarre twentieth-century world. And there is the need deep within . . . an animal need, frightening, murderous, unholy . . . a vital need that must be fed.

And with his need comes a power over men and women to do his bidding, to quiet his dark craving . . .

Until the murders begin. And the inquiries. All suggesting the same hideous truth.

Now Benjamin must find a sanctuary: a lover, a partner, a friend. Someone who can share his darkness. Someone he can lead to . . . The Awakening.

www.TheJohnRusso.com

Burning Bulb
PUBLISHING

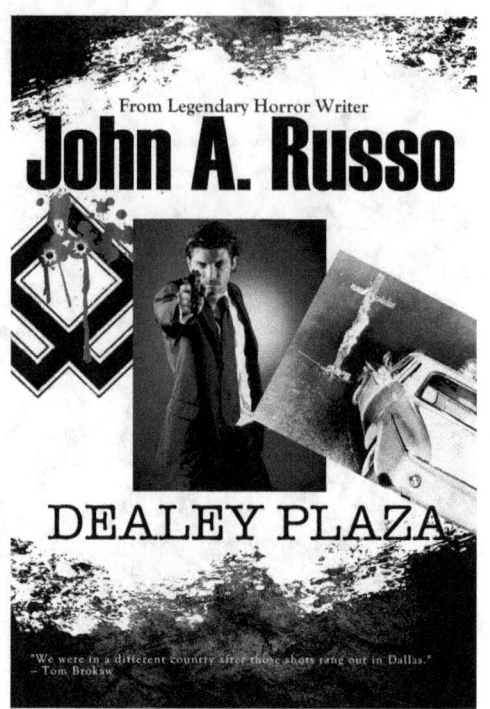

DEALEY PLAZA

From legendary horror and suspense writer JOHN RUSSO comes a harrowing tale where no one is safe!

Dealey Plaza is one of the most notorious places in America, and when youthful conspiracy buffs go there in 1964 to stage their own reenactment of the Kennedy Assassination, four of them are brutally murdered ~ the first victims of a hate-filled legacy that continues for four more decades.

The survivors of that long-ago Dallas trip, each of them now icons of the American way of life, are about to be honored ~ or killed.

Who will live and who will die? Will it be country-western star Lori McCoy? Her loving husband? Her scheming ex-husband? Or the case-hardened FBI agent and longtime friend who risks his life trying to protect them?

www.DealeyPlazaBook.com

Burning Bulb
PUBLISHING

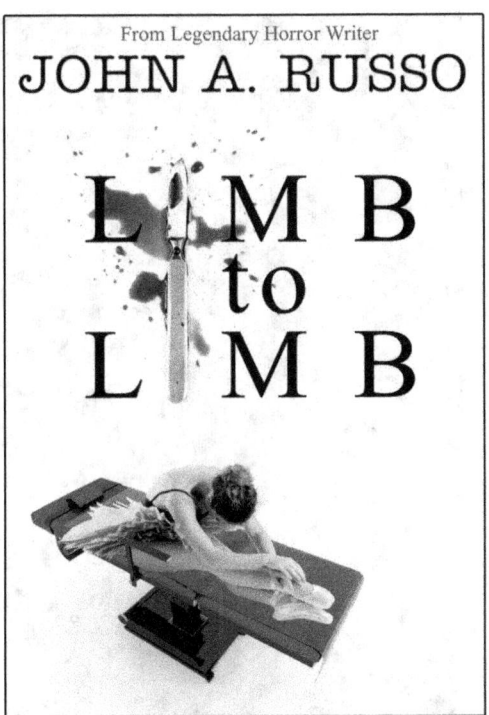

From Legendary Horror Writer

JOHN A. RUSSO

LIMB to LIMB

LIMB TO LIMB

SUCH A PRETTY GIRL . . .
Tiffany Blake was a beautiful long-limbed dancer with a glorious future and
the backing of a rich benefactor. Then a monstrous accident severed her leg
at the hip.

SUCH A COLD, CRUEL KNIFE . . .
And now her fellow dancers are disappearing without a trace. One by one
they fall victim to a dark and deadly pattern of evil – caught by the bloody,
brutal logic that would have them pay with their lovely bodies for the cruel
fate of another . . .victims of the sadistic madman whose flashing knife will
make them writhe a gruesome new dance.

www.TheJohnRusso.com

Burning Bulb
PUBLISHING

"A sense of infectious fun, straight from the author's pen."
– Nightmare Library

From Legendary Horror Writer
JOHN A. RUSSO

LIVING THINGS

"Russo carries his talent for the horrific neatly over into the novel form."
– West Coast Review of Books

LIVING THINGS

Beneath the shimmering Miami sun sprawls one of the Mafia's biggest empires, a glittering world of lavish beachfront mansions, neon-painted nightclubs, beautiful women, expensive cars—and absolute control over the state's billion-dollar drug trade. But, one by one, its ganglords and henchmen are falling prey to a new rival. His powers are fueled by monstrous ancient rituals; his hellish undead legions slaughter mobsters and innocent citizens alike, his unholy lust for power is virtually unstoppable.

Now a burned-out ex-detective and a brilliant anthropologist must enter a gruesome, nightmare world to fight this master of malevolence and illusion. Their time is short, their weapons few, and they face an ultimate, terrifying choice - annihilation or the loss of their souls to the eternal torment of those who never die. . .

www.TheJohnRusso.com

Burning Bulb
PUBLISHING

MAD WORLD BY ANDY RAUSCH

"*Mad World* is dark, twisted, no-holds-barred fun."
—Jason Starr, author of *Bust*, *Slide*, and *The Max*

EVERYONE'S PLAYING AN ANGLE IN THE CITY OF ANGELS

Mad World tells the stories of a black hitman who doubles as a university professor, a Catholic priest who longs to be a gangster, a would-be author from Kansas, a gay phone sex operator who claims he's straight, a group of rich twentysomethings playing a deadly game of life and death, a vicious Mafia boss, and a sleazy Hollywood movie director. As each of their stories intersect, the body count piles up and the action comes nonstop in this tense, white-knuckle thriller by first-time author Andy Rausch.

"A wild ride. If you like it gangster, *Mad World* delivers."
—Daniel Birch, author of *Get Some*

Burning Bulb
PUBLISHING

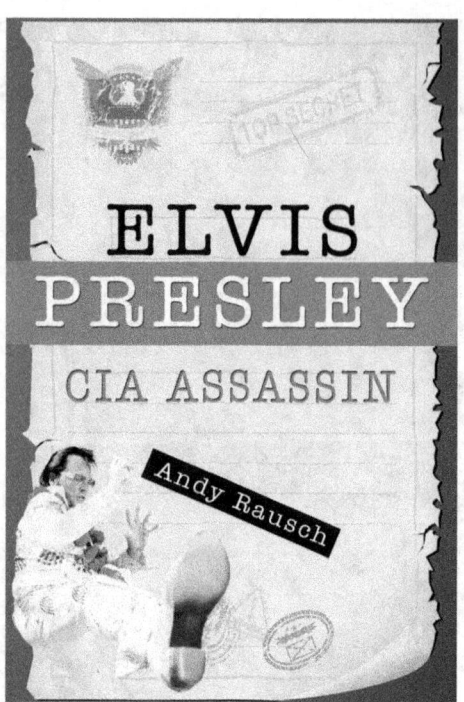

ELVIS PRESLEY, CIA ASSASSIN

"I can guarantee you. Read this book and you'll never look at Elvis the same way again!"
~ Douglas Brode, author of ELVIS CINEMA AND POPULAR CULTURE

SOON TO BE A MAJOR MOTION PICTURE

In 1970, singer Elvis Presley secretly met with President Richard Nixon. This new comedic novel imagines that Presley became a Central Intelligence Agency operative, eventually moving up through the ranks to become a skilled assassin.

Presented in an oral history fashion, the book tells us about Presley's secret transformation by the people who knew him best.

Did he fake his death in 1977? Was Presley involved with the Watergate scandal? The Iran hostage crisis? Communicating with aliens?

Read this book to find out the answers to these and many more questions.

Burning Bulb
PUBLISHING

THE TAILSMAN

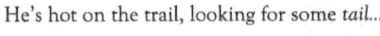

BURNING BULB COMICS

From the creators of *The Big Book of Bizarro* and *Westward Hoes* comes a new comic unlike anything you have ever seen!

He's hot on the trail, looking for some *tail...*

Sly Franko was a man of the West, a forger of the wild frontier. Like the Country Western song that would be written years after he died, the words, "Faster horses, younger women, and more money," seemed to be the anthem of this horn dog cowboy.

Franko would ride into town on a blazing saddle, find the closest saloon to wet the whistle, belly up to a good card game, and find him a hot-loving hussy to get his cowpoke on with.

However, Sly might have met his match when a visit to bathroom leads to terror and death. Can Sly and his poker buddies solve the mystery before more of the townsfolk are murdered? Find out in this exciting premier issue of *The Tailsman!*

WWW.BURNINGBULBCOMICS.COM

THE HAGS OF BLACK COUNTY

by Michelle Bowser

Ruled by a committee of Hags, and fueled by toothless rivalries, Black County lurks just far enough out of the way to be completely unnoticed by the rest of civilization. Its inhabitants have been mentally warped for generations and the land itself seems to have the power to drive anyone unlucky enough to visit into ridiculous hillbilly madness. When a construction Company needs to bury a pipeline through its ludicrous hills and valleys, a twisted charm goes to work and every aspect of already bizarre Black County life takes a gory turn for the hysterical. Take a preposterous trip along with its citizens, both native and new, through escapades such as the Hag parade, the grand opening of Madame Skunk's House of Ill Repute, the demolition derby riot and the rabid, zombie clown apocalypse.

THE ABANDONED SOUL

by Daniel Sellers

After spending most of his 20s in a drug and alcohol fueled daze, a young man finally hits rock bottom. Having used up his friends and their good graces, he ends up squatting in an abandoned house. Forcibly sobering he begins to realize that he is not alone in this abandoned house. Left with one last friend and a mountain of regrets, he must decide if this presence is a guilty conscience, or a malicious hunter.

WE WISH YOU A HAPPY KILLDAY

by Jason Heroux

"We Wish You a Happy Killday" is the story of an international b eloved holiday called "Killday" where one day a year everyone over the age of fifteen is permitted to register for a license allowing them to kill one other person. But this year Chad Ovenstock doesn't feel like killing anyone. His friends and family urge him to participate in the festivities, but he can't seem to get into the holiday spirit. On the day before Killday Chad comes in contact with Ambrose, an old friend who suffered a nervous breakdown and is now part of The One Ant Army, a mysterious cult dedicated to making the future disappear. When the holiday finally arrives Chad refuses to participate and tries to survive on his own, surrounded by constant gunfire, countless corpses, and the nagging suspicion that Ambrose may have secretly brainwashed him into becoming a member of The One Ant Army cult.

Burning Bulb
PUBLISHING